Praise for *Celtika* and Robert Holdstock

"Dazzling . . . Holdstock more than lives up to his billing as one of the finest living crafters of myth."
—*Publishers Weekly* (starred review)

"Strong and striking . . . Holdstock masterfully conflates two great myths of two disparate cultures. The personalities of Jason and Medea are consistent with their legends, but their motivations are revealed with a sure, contemporary astuteness."
—*San Francisco Chronicle*

"It astonishes."
—*Kirkus Reviews*

"Holdstock is the finest writer of metamorphic fantasy now working."
—*The Washington Post*

"Our finest living mythmaker."
—Stephen Baxter

"Marvelous . . . Highly recommended."
—*Interzone*

"No other author has so successfully captured the magic of the wildwood."
—Michael Moorcock

CELTIKA

Book One of the Merlin Codex

ROBERT HOLDSTOCK

TOR®
fantasy

A TOM DOHERTY ASSOCIATES BOOK
NEW YORK

To my brother Celts from Kent: Pete, Chris and James

CELTIKA: BOOK ONE OF THE MERLIN CODEX

First published in Great Britain by Earthlight, 2001
An Imprint of Simon & Schuster UK Ltd
A Viacom Company

A Tor Book
Published by Tom Doherty Associates, LLC
175 Fifth Avenue
New York, NY 10010

www.tor.com

Tor® is a registered trademark of Tom Doherty Associates, LLC.

ISBN: 0-765-34904-3

First Edition: March 2003
First mass market edition: January 2004

Printed in the United States of America

0 9 8 7 6 5 4 3 2 1

Acknowledgements

My thanks to Yvonne Aburrow and my Finnish translator, Leena Peltonen, for their conversations on matters of the *Northsong*. Parts of R. Andrew Heidel's *A Flower*, from his poetry collection *Beyond the Wall of Sleep* (Mortco), and Philip Kane's *Invocation 1*, from *The Wildwood King* (Capall Bann) are incorporated into the text with their kind permission.

My special thanks to Sarah, Howard, John Jarrold and Mary Bruton for their patience and encouragement.

It was so old a ship—who knows, who knows?
—And yet so beautiful, I watched in vain
To see the mast burst open with a rose
And the whole deck put on its leaves again.

from *The Old Ships* by James Elroy Flecker

Tho' much is taken, much abides; and tho'
We are not now that strength which in old days
Moved earth and heaven; that which we are, we are;
One equal temper of heroic hearts,
Made weak by time and fate, but strong in will
To strive, to seek, to find, and not to yield.

from *Ulysses*, by Alfred Lord Tennyson

Contents

	Prologue	1
PART ONE	Resurrection	7
PART TWO	The Spirit of the Ship	73
PART THREE	In Ghostland	115
PART FOUR	Hawk Watching	203
PART FIVE	The Hot Gates	283
	Afterword	371

Prologue

Iolkos, in Greek Land, 978 Old Era.

Though I wasn't there to see it at the time, this is what I heard:

Only one of the old crew had stayed in Iolkos, living at the edge of the city, close to the docks at Pagasae. Each day at dusk, Tisaminas walked along the crumbling harbour wall, passing the lines of black-sailed war galleys, bobbing fishing boats and colourful trading vessels to reach a backwater of the port where a rotting ship was moored. An ageing, angry man sat huddled in its stern, wrapped against the evening cool in a heavy sheepskin cloak.

'Goodnight, old friend!' Tisaminas called down to the deck. 'Is there anything I can get for you?'

The gaze that met his own was bright with fury, the voice a growl. 'My sons! Help me find the bodies of my sons, Tisaminas!'

'I can't. It's the one thing that none of us can do. Antiokus, perhaps, the young enchanter; but he's long gone. We could never do it. You know that well enough. But is there anything else you want? Ask for anything. I'll try to walk around the moon for you, if you like.'

The man below huddled deeper in his cloak, staring at the prow, gazing into time. 'My two sons on the funeral bier, Tisaminas. And a torch in my hand. The chance to say goodbye to them. Nothing more. Save for the head of that witch, their mother, stuck on the end of my spear! That's all I want.'

The ritual never changed, a ritual of anger and despair; the same words, the same desperation, the same hopelessness, week after week across the years.

Tisaminas answered as he always answered. 'They're dead. They're gone. Medea killed them twenty years ago and we were all helpless to stop her. She has fled to her own country, to an underworld that can only be dreamed about by the likes of you and me. What you ask can *only* be dreamed, my friend. I'll still walk around the moon for you. Or I can bring you food and drink . . . a slightly easier task.'

The man on the deck sighed. After a while he said, 'I don't want you to walk around the moon. Too far away. And I will eat and drink only what falls from the sky.'

'Then goodnight, Jason.'

'Goodnight. Thank you for watching me.'

'I'll watch you to the end. You know that.'

'And I want that end so much, Tisaminas,' Jason cried. 'Truly I do. And so does *Argo*. She talks to me in my dreams.' Again, his eyes were blazing. 'But not before that witch is feast for crows!'

Tisaminas unpacked bread, cheese and olives from his pack, and tossed this simple food down to the deck of the once great ship where Jason swept it into his cloak, before huddling again in *Argo*'s bosom, in the protecting oak, to brood and dream of his murdered boys.

Why did Tisaminas stay close that night? Some inkling of our old friend's fate, perhaps, whispered by the goddess whose watchful eyes peered from *Argo*'s prow. He lingered, out of sight of the raging, weeping hero on the cracked, warped planks, intensely sad himself.

'It's coming to an end. I shouldn't have said the words. I've willed them true! What will I do without you, Jason? What will any of us do?'

The moon sat full and low between the headlands. It had been there for hours, unmoving, as if caught in time. The only sign of change in the silent harbour was the restless ebb and flow of the dark sea against the harbour wall and the lines of tethered galleys. Tisaminas didn't understand what was happening.

'If only Antiokus was here,' he murmured to the night. 'He could explain this. Time has slowed . . .'

He noticed, then, that torches were burning on each headland, men standing on the cliffs, staring back towards the port.

'This *is* the moment,' Tisaminas breathed, and tears filled his eyes as he searched the darkness for Jason, below him.

As if his words had broken a charm, a rotten spar cracked away from *Argo*'s mast, crashed down to the deck of the ageing ship, striking the hero who sat there in a dream. The wound was mortal, by the sounds of the cracking bones and the sudden flow of blood and pain from Jason's mouth.

Tisaminas turned to run, to raise the call, but a voice whispered to him, 'Stay here. Remember what you see.'

He glanced behind him. A dark-eyed girl stood there, wrapped in a green cloak. She smiled at him, then drew his attention back to *Argo*.

The old ship began to shift on the water. It slipped its moorings and turned towards the open sea. It drifted quietly between the dark war galleys of Iolkos, compelled by neither oars nor sail. On each headland more torches burned, twin lines of fire on the very edges of the cliffs, marking the passing of Jason towards the embracing moon.

'They all knew,' the man on the harbour wall said aloud. 'The old crew—and their sons and their daughters—they all knew. She called us all!'

He found his own torch and waved it. The fires on the headlands looped and signalled back. 'She told us all,' Tisaminas shouted as the ship passed between the cliffs. 'She called to us all!'

And he added quietly, 'Thank you for that at least, *Argo*. Goodbye, old friend!'

From the distant heights the torches were tossed into the sea, falling streams of flame marking the departure of a great man as the proud ship sailed below them. The moon rose suddenly and swiftly into the vault of stars, catching up with time, dropping below the hills of Iolkos in the west. Suddenly, everything was dark again, the funeral ship swallowed by the night and by the ocean.

Tisaminas turned to the girl. He was apprehensive. He knew he was in the presence not of a mortal but of the goddess who had protected Jason for the better part of his life.

'It's over, then. Over at last. After all these years of agony.'

'Yes. It's over at last. Jason is in safe hands.'

Tisaminas said, '*Argo* is frail. But will she take him to a safe place of burial? Out of sight and out of mind?'

'Yes,' said the girl, 'she'll take him to a safe place of burial.'

Then she laughed, turning away, her cloak swirling. 'But one among you will always know where to find him!'

The northern country of Pohjola, 700 years later.

Only half remembering this frozen land, he had struggled through the snow for a lifetime, it seemed, sometimes dragging his packhorses by their bridles, always reluctant to charm them and make his life easier. His bones 'itched', as if to say, 'The power is here, you can use magic to stop this misery!'

But he wanted his strength in full for when he reached the ice-bound and mysterious Screaming Lake. So he suffered the winter and the endless night. And the horses suffered with him. And where the snow lay shallow he ran, and where animals had ploughed their own deep tracks through the drifts he followed in their prints, and in this way, moon by moon, he crossed the night-pale snow waste, coming closer to the land of the Pohjola, and the strange place he sought.

Knowing where he was, he was already wearing wolfbone and beartooth around his neck, and had tied the skins of mink and fox to the ragged, stinking furs in which he'd wrapped himself, half a year ago, when he had first left the plains and marshes of Karelia and crossed the ice-bridge to the mountains of the north.

There was no dawn or dusk in the winter in this odd land,

only moonlit clouds, patches of stars and the spirit-glow of lights to the north. His body alone, and the brief visits of the moon, suggested when sleep was needed. The horses didn't like it.

'My bones itch,' the young man said through his frosted beard, as he brushed the ice from the flaring nostrils of his two proud companions, holding his torch closer to inspect their eyes and necks for damage. 'They itch because they are carved and inscribed with all the magic that I have ever needed, and will continue to need in my long life to come. I was born this way, hundreds and hundreds of good horses like you ago! And yes, I suppose I could use a little of that magic to make life more tolerable. And of all the horses I have known, you two are certainly the best. Which is why I haven't named you. I will grieve for you too much as it is, when you're gone. Horses improve as the centuries drift by! So I *could* charm up a little warmth . . . but I *won't*. I prefer to save it for when we'll truly need it. Come on, horses . . . this is not so bad. We'll soon be at the lake. For the moment, just one more hour of travel? And then we'll stop for food. I promise!'

Cold, frosting breath in his face, and a bleak look from the two animals, was all he received by way of reply to this lengthy pleading. It was as if they knew that the lightness of their packs meant that their food was almost finished. Already their bones showed stark against the skin, below their blankets, where the rationing was beginning to bite.

No day, only endless night. The last time he had been here—five generations ago, now—it had been endless day, and he had thought he would never see the stars again. Now he longed for the sun. And dawn *was* coming. The many-coloured lights to the north were dancing higher, the fiery breath of the waking goddess, streaming into the starry, Stygian heavens.

'Day is coming, horses. And though I'm glad of that, I must be at the Screaming Lake before it arrives. Too many things wake with the dawn in this chill-boned land. So come on . . . one last try? One last hour? For me? For your young-old master, Merlin?'

Cold-eyed silence, save for the freezing breath.

'I will not waste my precious bones on getting there,' the young man said. He was impatient, now, and angry. 'I *must* save my magic!'

He dropped the tethers, turned and walked through the thick snow, following the shallow path made by a pack of wolves. He howled and growled as he picked up their scent, rattled the wolf's-bone talisman on his chest. Teasing.

After a moment, the horses followed quickly.

But then, I've always had a way with animals!

PART ONE

Resurrection

CHAPTER ONE

—

Niiv

I was neither a stranger in this territory, nor familiar with it. The last time I had passed this way, the route into the wilderness of forest and snow that was the northern land of Pohjola had been an open gorge, guarded by nothing more sinister than white foxes, chattering mink and dark-winged carrion birds. But in five generations or more, things had changed.

As I came out of the birch forest into the gathering mouth of the gorge I faced a barrier of grim-faced wooden statues, five times a man's height, each ringed with torches that illuminated the leering features.

I counted ten such grotesques. They spanned the gorge. Between them, a thick thorn fence barred anything but a snow-rat from passing, and if there was a gate through this sinister wall, I couldn't see it.

I used the thorns as hooks and erected a crude shelter from the tent-skins in my baggage. I fed the horses then studied each tree-face in turn. One leaf-haired, grim-eyed mask held my gaze for several moments before I realised what it was. The knowledge shocked me. It was an image of Skogen, an old trickster friend of mine; his name meant 'shadow of unseen forests'. That is exactly what he had been. In the remote past, when he had still been in human form, we had adventured together. Now he was here, in eternal night, a god in wood, face cracked by ice. He had no business being here. When I called out his name the torches that girdled his neck seemed to flicker with amusement. I was not amused, and nervous memory was returning.

Now a second face suddenly became familiar to me, once I had seen through the rough-hew of its carving. Another old 'friend' from the early years, this one gentler.

'Well, well. Sinisalo. You used to climb trees. Now you *are* one. You used to play tricks on me then run away like the wind. Now you're rooted.'

Sinisalo was the 'eternal child in the land'. I myself had once been *sinisalo*. All of life's creatures are *sinisalo* for a brief moment. The child's power is usually left behind in the process of growth. But for some of us, that funny, frisky fawn always remains at the edge of our vision, to be summoned at will. The eternal child. Here she was, five thousand years on, a memory in carved birch.

'Sinisalo,' I whispered again, with affection, and blew a kiss.

The face on the towering trunk didn't change its expression, but large, dark birds began to rise from their winter nests and perch upon the craggy ledges of all the statues.

It had been a long time since I had last encountered these entities, and I had forgotten most of them. What I remembered was that every time I encountered them, in stone, or wood, or bone or as masks or colourful patterns on the walls of caves, whenever our paths crossed, my life changed. For the worse. It had always seemed to me that these ten old faces in my world were watching me, appearing to me as unwelcome portents of a shift in my life of travel, security and pleasure on the path I walked. Not that these frozen wastelands of rock, ice and forest were a pleasure to cross, but I was here on personal business, and had been anticipating a change for the *better*.

No, these gruesome, grinning totems were not at all a welcome sight. My bones itched. Their names—all but Skogen and Sinisalo—continued to elude me. That there was life in the wood, that they had tracked me down for their own purpose, did not escape me. I wondered if they could read my confusion and my reluctance to remember more clearly.

'Listen!' I shouted. 'I know two of you. I'd probably know all of you if I could recognise you. I'm a friend. I walk the Path. This is my hundredth time of walking. At least! Who's counting? I've been here a hundred times before. And now I need to go on. Please call the people who erected you. I would like to talk to them. I need the gate opened!

A long sleep later—I was exhausted; the crows woke me to the ever-present northern darkness—I stood before the wall, staring at the torches of reindeer riders, one of whom had dismounted and was standing, gazing down at me from some structure in the centre of the thorn barrier. I could see that there were five riders in all, each so heavily draped in dyed and decorated fur cloaks and hats that they seemed enormous as they straddled their beasts. The creatures were amply decked out with winter colours on their antlers, and draped in colourful blankets and cowls, through which their freezing breath emerged like elemental life-forms.

The man who stared down at me asked me who I was. I could see only his eyes. I replied in a dialect of his language that I was the young warrior who had last come this way five generations ago and fought with their ancestor hero Lemkainon, against the bearskin-shrouded Kullaavo, the dark spirit of the land.

'You fought with Lemkainon? Against that monster?'

'Yes.'

'Didn't do much good. Kullaavo is still in the forest.'

'We tried.'

I told him the name I had used during that encounter. I reminded him that my return had been predicted, exactly on or around this time. The man breathed frost at me, then said,

'If that's true, then you're an enchanter. Some of them live until the flesh abandons their bones. Even then the bones sometimes keep on rattling. *Are* you an enchanter?'

'Yes. Let me through.'

He peered harder at me. He probably couldn't see me very clearly in the dark. 'How many birds do you fly?'

I was certain he was asking how old I was; the Pohjoli measured the age of shamans by the number of spirit-birds they could inhabit when they entered the dream-trance, usually one bird for every ten years of life.

'Two,' I answered.

'Only two? But you were here five generations ago, you said.'

'I keep to two because I travel faster that way.' *The younger, the better.*

'More birds, more skills, surely.' *The older, the wiser.*

'Well, yes. But fewer birds, more appetites.' *And more energy. Self-evident!*

I had been alive since before the land of the Pohjoli had grown from the great ice. But I still only flew two birds—a hawk and a raven, by the way, though I hadn't seen them for a while; they weren't my favourite companions—because it was more important to keep youth on my side. At least for the moment.

My inquisitor thought about my reply for a moment, then asked me my business in Pohjola.

'I'm going to swim in the Screaming Lake,' I replied.

He seemed astonished. 'A terrible place. There are more dead men in the waters there than are living in the whole of the land of Kalevala. Why would you want to bother with a place like that?'

'I'm looking for a sunken ship.'

'There are a hundred ships at the bottom of that lake,' the guardian said. 'The old man of the water has built his palace from their timbers and the bones of the drowned. It's a dreadful place to go.'

'No water man will have touched the ship *I'm* looking for.'

The man on the wall squeezed his nose as he thought about

my words. 'It seems unlikely. Enaaki is voracious. Anyway, the ice is a man's height thick. Not even the *voytazi* can get through it.'

The *voytazi*, I knew, were the water demons who snared men on the shore and dragged them down to a terrible death. The Pohjoli lived in terror of them.

'I have a way of getting through it.'

The reindeer rider laughed. 'Anyone can get through it *downwards*. Digging down isn't the problem. The lake is full of the song-chanters, bead-rattlers and drum-whackers who've done that. But the ice will close over your head. How will you get out?'

'I may have a way of doing it,' I bragged.

'Then you have a secret,' my host retorted, 'which you must reveal before we can let you through.'

I thought he was making a joke and laughed, then realised that he was quite serious. People in the Northland were hungry for 'charms', I remembered, and they were traded as easily as the Greeks traded olives and milk-white cheeses.

I was getting irritated with this man. It was clear he wasn't going to give way to just any young-looking grease-haired, long-bearded, crow-savaged, mule-packing, stinking stranger; not without trade. And though I suspected he had little time for enchanters themselves—the song-chanting, bead-rattling drum-whackers as he had dismissed them—I hazarded that he was greedy for those little devices of enchantment that in this country they called *sedjas*.

'I'll reveal nothing of such a secret, and you know it. But I have talismans to trade, and a cure for the Winter Bleak which I'll show you later. Let me through. I *must* get to the lake.'

'You have a cure for the Winter Bleak?'

Every man, woman, child and wolf in this long-night wasteland dreamed of a cure for the misery that affected them as frost crept from tree branch to their own hearts. I had long ago discovered that the best cure for it was to believe there *was* a cure for it.

Reindeer man squeezed the ice from his nose again. 'What's your business with the ship?'

Exasperated, impatient, I said more than I wanted to. 'I believe I know her name. I once sailed with her captain. He's still with her. I hope to throw flowers on his grave.'

Reindeer man grunted, then looked about him at the totem trunks.

'I don't understand. But it looks to me as if the *rajathuks* have accepted you.' He thought hard for a moment, then shrugged. 'So you may pass through.'

I took time to look in turn at each guardian tree—each *rajathuk*—and thank it.

The gate had been dragged back. I quickly crossed into the territory of Pohjola, tugging on the tethers of my reluctant horses, then watched as the tangled mass of thorn and wicker was returned to its place between the towering wooden idols.

I was introduced to each of the riders who were waiting for me, though only a hulking man called Jouhkan showed the slightest interest in me.

Lutapio, the leader of the riders and my interrogator at the wall, was inspecting my horses. He offered to trade them for reindeer, but I refused. I liked my animals. Good horses, even packhorses, were hard to come by and I'd had this pair for five years. They had become good friends. Losing horses to Time, to Death, and losing hounds or wild cats, other good friends, is one of the most difficult things about walking the long path. My path is rich with the graves of old friends, or memorials to their memory.

I had supposed Lutapio was looking for some payment for the hospitality he was about to offer me, but he waved my suggestion away. I was welcome to travel with them to the lake, just as soon as their business in this forested wasteland was concluded, which would not be for a while.

Their business was at the spirit hill of Louhi, Mistress of the Northlands, a very sacred place, a narrow cave leading into the sheer, icy wall of a mountain, guarded by crowded and tangled winter trees. Blue-red flames flickered in two stone basins on either side of the entrance, and the gleaming white of bears' skulls picked up the eerie light as they dangled from branches.

The reindeer riders had set up two low tents close by, and two bigger fires burned, kept roaring by the rest of the group, who restlessly scoured the woods for forage. Reindeer snuffled and snorted at the tethers.

Curious, I approached the cave, but Lutapio insisted that I stay outside. I could hear song, the sound of three women's voices, I felt, one of them almost chanting, the others harmonising. The song turned into a scream of pain, then there was silence, followed by the sound of weeping and wood being angrily snapped.

The cycle was repeated. Lutapio tugged me back to the warmth and offered me a drink.

'Her name is Niiv. She may or may not speak to you, it all depends.' He didn't specify on what her conversation might depend. 'Her father died in the lake, not long ago. He was the greatest of the dream travellers, and several different animals would take his spirit, though he was strongest in the bear. Niiv is his eldest daughter. His eldest son was killed by a moon-mad wolf. Jouhkan, his youngest son, has no desire to dream travel. So Niiv is here, with her sisters, to ask Louhi if it is right for her to take over her father's dreams. To do this she must become her father for a while, and live through his pain and his life and then at last his death. This is almost the end, as you can hear. She must be terrified.'

'And if Northland's Mistress says no?'

'She won't go back,' Lutapio said matter-of-factly, pointing to a ditch that had been dug through the snow into the frozen ground below. It was marked with a post from which an amber necklace hung.

'I hope the Mistress approves of her,' I volunteered.

Several of the men laughed, including Lutapio, who said, 'Knowing Niiv, Louhi will be eating out of her hand.'

'How far is it to the lake?' I asked later.

'Five rests, perhaps six if you're slow. Jouhkan and Niiv will take you. The lake shore is crowded with strangers, many of them enchanters. The place stinks of potions, spells and shit. You'd be wise to keep your wits about you. Though somehow, I believe you will.'

I thanked Lutapio and assured him that I was prepared for the circus that I would find. Six rests he had said, and I supposed he meant periods of sleep, approximating to a night. When night lasts nearly half a year, days cease to be meaningful, but I had a fair idea of how far I had to go, now, and the journey was to be shorter than I'd expected.

An icy wind began to blow from the mouth of the mountain sanctuary of Northland's Mistress. Our warming fires guttered, sparks flying on to the taut hides of the tents, but quickly dying on the layer of stinking grease that covered the skins. A little while later the three women emerged, running, bent almost double; I heard laughter from below the brightly coloured mufflers that encased their faces, all but their eyes, which flashed brightly in the light of the fires. They scampered to their own tent and ducked through the low flap, pulling it shut. The laughter became louder, and then they sang again, but this time with true, pure joy, three voices that bubbled, shrieked and chattered tunefully.

Whoever she was, Niiv now had a little magic, her father's magic, and she was delighted.

Lutapio and the others crawled into the tent to sleep. I crouched by the fire for a while, wondering whether to probe a little into the Lady of the North; I had heard of Louhi, of course; her effect and influence were everywhere. But I had never encountered her. My idle thoughts were interrupted when one of the women came out of her tent, glanced at me, then came over to me, kneeling down in the snow so that her voluminous skirts spread around her. She wore a red woollen cap pulled down to her eyes, and a scarf that covered her face. Pale blue eyes searched me from that slit in her winter mask. I was disturbed by the intensity of that gaze, almost charmed by it, caught by it as a fish is caught on a bone hook. I couldn't help thinking: *this woman knows me*.

We sat in this way for what seemed an age. I fiddled with burning sticks and she mimed the slow slapping of her hands together as she watched me unflinchingly.

She suddenly spoke. 'You're one of those who walks the Path around the world. Aren't you?'

Taken by surprise at this sudden insight, I answered, 'Yes. I am. How did you know?'

'Frost-haired Louhi showed me how to look. She seems disturbed by you. I can't see your face for all that beard. I wonder who you are? I'll find out. You're going to the lake.'

It was a statement, but I still answered. 'Yes. Looking for a ship.'

'I'll find out who you are,' she repeated almost menacingly, then clambered to her feet, brushed the snow from her skirts and swirled back to her tent.

'I'd have told you if you'd asked,' I muttered to her rump as it vanished into the skins.

After the sleep, a fresh reindeer was harnessed for me and I was helped up by Jouhkan. I found the saddling awkward, my thighs spread too wide for total comfort, and the reins, slung between the antlers, clumsy and hard to control.

The three sisters laughed behind their woollen masks, then called to me in a slightly mocking way—I was being teased rather than insulted—before turning their own reindeer away from the sanctuary and trotting off along a holloway through the snow. My own mount bucked and was off in pursuit. Since I was holding the tethers of my pack animals I was almost hauled from the saddle blanket, but kept my grip and bounced uncomfortably behind the amused young women.

Jouhkan tickled my horses with his spear and helped them forward. And in this way we made our first progress south-wards, turning away from the northern lights into bleak forest again and following proven tracks and trails. The travel was tiring, but I could have happily kept going. I could almost *smell* the coming dawn. My guides liked to stop regularly, however, crouching in a huddle and exchanging small talk and scraps of food, delays that I found irritating.

'You won't get there any faster by wishing it,' Niiv teased me.

She was eating the last of the salted fish. She was forbidden to eat the meat, she had told me, since she was the daughter of a shaman who had died during her coming of age. She was not properly 'born' yet, but whispered to me that she was already pregnant. It was none of my business. She would soon make an offering at the tomb of the Lady of Pohjola, who could make the appropriate adjustments, if she saw fit. Everything was working out well, she believed. Jouhkan was her older brother, and guardian, but he was well aware that Niiv was a rule unto herself.

'I'm here to protect her from bears and wolves,' he said with a smile. 'She'd rather dance with them . . . and probably would.'

Denied the fish, Jouhkan and I chewed our way through strips of reindeer meat so putrid I almost asked my host whether in fact I was eating a drowned man's dried bowels. But there was nothing else to eat, so I kept quiet. To take away the taste I watched the beautiful young woman. Crystals of snow and salt lined her mouth as she chewed noisily and greedily. She was watching me with such curiosity that I felt my brow furrow, a sign of nervousness that she clearly noticed instantly. There was always a knowing smile on her face.

'Where you're going is the most dangerous of all the lakes in Pohjola; in any land. Except for Tuonela, the black lake. Did you know that?'

I agreed that it was dangerous, but I hadn't heard more about it than that it was a lake where a screaming ship lay in its depths. Feeling so strongly that it was my old galley that had sunk itself and my good friend there, I had stayed at a distance. I knew of the old man of the lake, but something in Niiv's tone gave me pause for thought. I'd have to be prepared to unloose a little of my talent, I suspected.

She went on, 'The song-chanters spend a week on the shore during the long summer, singing to the waters, persuading Enaaki, the old man of the water, to let them swim down. Sometimes he snatches them from the bank and dismembers them. But usually he'll agree to a visit when winter comes. He eats entrails and you'll need to supply him with at least one full reindeer's worth—a horse's might do—if you're going to persuade him to let you swim down to his lair. Did you know that?'

I hadn't. If I found that this offering was essential—I

doubted that it would be—I'd have to find some way to trade for a reindeer. My horses were not available.

Niiv was relishing her task of enlightenment.

'There are more than a hundred *voytazi*, pike-toothed spirits, guarding the sunken ships. Enaaki's palace is like a labyrinth, walls of wood tied together with weed, and a roof of human bones. It stretches down for miles into the gloom. The lake has no true bottom, only the roof of Enaaki's palace, full of spy holes and traps. If he comes up to take you, you'll be dragged down so fast, and so deep, that your ghost will still be in the water above, swimming on, unaware.'

'I'll make sure I give him a good meal of entrails.'

'You *must*.' She watched me for a moment, then frowned. 'Enaaki will have eaten your friend a long time ago. It's only his ghost that screams.'

'If that's true, then I've wasted my time.'

Then her words came home to me. She had guessed so easily that I had come here not to honour the dead, but in the hope that my friend was still alive, and that I believed it was *his* tormented presence in the depths that uttered the terrible scream for which the lake was named.

'But I don't believe it is true,' I went on, cautious now.

'Why not?'

'Because of the ship that protects him. Not even Enaaki can eat this particular ship.'

'If it *is* the ship,' she taunted.

'Yes.'

'If it *is* your friend.'

'Yes.'

'How old are you, Merlin? Tell me that.'

She had leaned forward, almost hungrily. Her breath was astonishingly sweet, despite her meal of fish. Before I could stop myself, I had leaned towards her as well, almost nose to nose, drawn to her without thinking, as lover is to lover.

I came close to telling her the truth. All that stopped me, as she radiated almost irresistible charm and beauty, was that I couldn't summon the right words to explain the thousands of years I had been walking the circular path that surrounded both the world of reality and the underworlds that opened into it.

'Older than I look,' I muttered lamely.

'Well, yes. I know that. Every so often a skull appears on your face. You should be long dead. A thousand times dead. Tell me how you've managed to keep the youth in you alive!'

'You'd do better to ask the youth. And he's long, long gone.'

She thought about that, then tapped my nose, not with an elegant finger but with the last morsel of salted perch. 'I don't think he is,' she whispered.

She cocked her head, smiled through the snow and salt as she popped the fish into her mouth, then pulled up her muffler, ready to return to her tent, to sleep, though she stayed for a while by the fire. Jouhkan stared at me, his jaw working slowly as he softened dried meat in his bark-stained teeth. He had not understood much of the conversation.

'If you find your friend intact, and not in pieces in Enaaki's kitchen, how *will* you get him back to dry land? As Lutapio told you, the ice is a man's height thick. It can close over you in seconds.'

Again, that careful curiosity. The question seemed so innocent, but even Jouhkan was probing for the secrets I might hold.

All I said was, 'Ask me in a few rests' time. I have to get there first. I have to learn some rules.' I was still ravenous. 'May I have some more reindeer meat?'

Jouhkan looked puzzled at that. 'Reindeer meat?'

I pointed to the brown sinew that he held in his gloved hand. He laughed, shaking his head. 'This isn't reindeer . . . Did you think it was reindeer? I wish it were!' He snarled at his meal. 'It makes my stomach churn to think where this came from . . .'

'My mistake!' I said hurriedly. 'Please don't elaborate.'

He passed me a strip of the disgusting flesh. I noticed that Niiv was laughing silently behind her muffler.

CHAPTER TWO

—

Urtha of Alba

'Will you answer a question for me?' I called to Niiv during the third period of our journey to the lake. She had been in a sullen mood for two 'days', and sick twice. Her sisters were riding apart from her, though there had been no arguments between the three of them. We hadn't talked very much, there had been very little opportunity. A biting wind had been cutting through the forest. It cut to the bone. It cut all thoughts except those to do with keeping warm and getting home. It was quieter now, just the sound of hooves on fresh snow and the grunting of the animals. Niiv was riding ahead of me.

'Yes. If you will answer one of mine.'

My curiosity about the woman was deepening, though I was anxious to hide the fact. She was familiar in a way that disturbed me, not because I could feel the kindling of powers of enchantment in her muffled head, but oddly because of the way she laughed. 'Who's the father of the child you carry?'

She glanced at me over her shoulder, then rode on in silence for a while before saying, 'I don't know.'

'You don't know the father? Were you asleep at the time?'

'It hasn't been decided!' she amended angrily, adding, 'Yet!'

I felt a thrill of comprehension. And a chill at the same time. Familiar words echoed across the generations. I watched her body swaying on the back of her steed. She was vibrancy incarnate. She was staring slightly to the left, aware of my gaze on her. She waited. She remained silent. She knew I was more than curious.

'I see,' I said. 'There's no child as such, just a hope in your head. Just a dream. Nothing inside you yet.'

'There *is* a child,' she said sharply, and after a moment added: 'It's simply that the child, as yet, has not got its father. The child so far is Niiv, and Niiv alone. It's waiting for its father. I keep telling it to be patient, but children are such demanding things.' She glanced back at me again as she said this, and I saw that she was amused, teasing me. 'This one wants to be born. But without a father, how can it grow properly?'

'How indeed?'

We rode on in silence for a long, long time. I spent a lot of that time trying to decide whether Niiv frightened me or fascinated me. As she had spoken I had felt my flesh crawl. My bones were almost singing! All my life I had believed that my skills in charm—some call it enchantment—were carved on my bones, and though I wasn't using charm at this time (it's costly), the bones themselves were very effective amulets, always signalling to me to be careful.

Indeed, warning signals were everywhere, most particularly in the flash and swirl of fire in the night sky behind us, silent and sinister. That northern horizon was alive with cascading light, a shimmering fall of burning colour that was constantly reflected in the polished bead and bone of Niiv's elaborate headdress.

My concerns were twofold. It was clear to me that Niiv was *playing* with the skills in charm she had been given by the Lady of the North. She was dabbling in sorcery in the most obvious way. She had started a child in her womb, sensing that this earthly vessel would be useful in absorbing other life and other skills. I had known of this trick from the moment I had started on the Path, and knew how to take avoiding action. It was a dangerous strategy, and Niiv was still too young to control it; and so she, too, was dangerous. She had certainly learned some small magic from her father, though I doubted that he had intended to teach her. Everything suggested to me that she had stolen her small skills from him. And now her father was dead, horribly drowned. And she had used that death to claim his right in enchantment. Her brother seemed to exist in an airy world of his own, riding well behind us. Niiv had no one advising her, no one counselling her, no one ready to control her excesses. And I was aware that not even Niiv knew how dangerous she was.

Dangerous! And though I had admitted my own nature to her, as I would admit it to anyone—that I was a simple shaman, all of whom lied about their age and skills—she had somehow seen behind the lie. She knew I was no ordinary shaman. She had seen a skull peering through my face. She had recognised me as 'one of those who walks the Path'. She had raw talent. I would need to be careful in speech and behaviour from now on.

My second consideration was the simple familiarity of the woman, and I suspected that this, too, would be the subject of her own question to me.

After a while I asked her, 'What was your mother's name?'

'My mother? She was named for the blue of the lake in high summer. Why do you ask?'

'What was your grandmother's name?'

'My grandmother was named for the frost that glitters on the branches in the dead of winter. Why do you ask?'

'And your great-grandmother?'

Niiv hesitated before answering, not looking at me. The beasts struggled and snorted as they ploughed through the snow.

'The same as my mother. Why do you ask?'

'And your great-grandmother's . . . grandmother?'

'My great-grandmother's grandmother? How curious you are, Merlin. How strangely curious. My great-grandmother's grandmother was named for the mist that hangs in the trees in autumn.'

'Little Meerga,' I whispered, but said aloud, 'You have a long memory.'

'We don't forget,' Niiv agreed. 'All my grandmothers watch me from the bosom of the Northland Mistress. Why are you asking me all this?'

'You remind me of someone.'

Niiv laughed. 'Not little Meerga. She died two hundred winters ago.'

'I know.'

Little Meerga. Mist Lady. I watched Niiv ride and remembered her ancestor; it was so obvious to me now, now that I had placed the connection. The eyes were the same, the laugh was the same, the provocative way of riding was the same. The spark of outrage was the same.

I was sad for a while, though I couldn't help laughing when I remembered my first encounter with the woman whose descendant—my own descendant, my own great-something-grand-daughter—now rode ahead of me . . .

Meerga was fragrant and knowing as she slipped into my tent, accompanied by her sister. I was excited at the prospect of the encounter—though not the look in her eyes when she first glimpsed me. Her sister, who was even more appalled at the sight of me, asked her several times if she was sure about what she was doing. Meerga reassured and dismissed her sister, then again looked doubtful herself.

We took a drink and ate some pieces of fish, sitting on opposite sides of the small fire whose flame cast a pleasant glow on her pale face. Something must have warmed her, though probably not my conversation, because suddenly she stood, invited me to stand, then began to undress.

Below her woollen cloak she was wearing a red and blue patterned dress of fine linen; the aroma of bluebells drifted from the fabric. She slipped the shoulder knots and let the dress fall away, to reveal an undergarment of white, gauzy material that was heady with the scent of spring flowers. The dried petals had been sewn into the seams, to make a pattern of circles around her body. She was very beautiful and she watched me through wide, blue eyes as she deftly untied the bows at the shoulder. The undertunic fell to reveal a garment of gossamer thinness, from which came the scent of rosewater mixed with the fragrance that excites, the aroma that has nothing to do with flowers.

She started to lift this final garment above her thighs, then teased me: 'Aren't you going to shed some of that fur?'

'Well, if you're sure.'

I slipped my wolfskin cloak from my shoulders, kicked it away, revealing my deerskin shirt and trousers. Though the trousers were loose around the groin, for obvious reasons, the shirt had congealed to the undergarment I wore, whose nature at that moment I couldn't remember. I dropped the trousers and noticed Meerga's shocked glance, then looked down and shared her shock.

I had washed all my clothes in the sacred river of the Aeduii, a tributary of the great river Daan. Thoroughly washed them! Then again, that had been in summer—I wasn't sure which summer precisely—and in a much warmer country. I'd simply not noticed the decay.

I apologised, then used my flattened palm like a blade to separate shirt from vest; the pungent aroma of fungal spores and sweat mingled with Meerga's roses. It was a quite pleasant combination, I thought. But she had put her hand over her mouth, speaking through her fingers. 'Do you have any skin under there?'

'I'm sure I do . . .'

The vest came away eventually, though it tore at areas where insects had burrowed. I'd not noticed them until now, and now they hurt as they bled. Naked, I stared down at a body that had been conquered and ransacked by a world that had nothing to do with the kings, armies and the greed of my own kind.

'I'm sure I can do something about this . . .' I started to

say, but a gust of cold air announced Meerga's appalled departure, overcoat flung carelessly round her shoulders.

But she came back an hour or so later, with various ointments and mosses, and set about cleaning me up. And at some time during the night, her daughter was conceived, though I had long since left the lakeside when the girl came into the world, and the line that led to Niiv had been commenced.

The laugh and the look; it had remained over two hundred winters . . .

I decided not to reveal this insight to the girl, so I simply said, 'But you wanted to ask me a personal question in return? Ask away.'

'Thank you,' Niiv said as we rode on slowly through the forest of birch. She seemed disappointed that the previous exchange had ended. 'But now isn't the time. I'll ask you later. When we've reached the lake. I hope you're prepared for the question.'

'All my life I've felt prepared for everything except riding reindeers. So if your question is do I like reindeers, the answer is no. And if your question is do I like what I'm eating, certainly not. Do I like watching you ride? Yes. I like watching you ride.'

She laughed quietly at that, I noticed.

'Do I wish I was back in the warm climate by the blue seas that lie to the south of here? Most definitely. Would I like to become the father of your unborn child? Now *there's* a question.'

'But not the question I want to ask you,' Niiv said instantly, with not a flinch or twitch or hint of anger at my presumption as she guided her buck through the snow.

'But would I, though . . .' I mused.

'But would you, though,' she teased.

'I don't know the answer.'

'Nor do I. As I said: it wasn't the question.'

She glanced back with what I imagined was an impish smile, though the night and her woollen mask exposed nothing but a torchlit twinkle in her eyes. The rest was imagination.

And the itching on my bones made me long to scratch below my filthy cloak.

Because I had been anxious to get on, and because my companions were also young, we came to the lake after only five periods of sleep. I was starving, as was Niiv whose excitement and boldness had grown as we had neared her home, and the wind was from the south and the smells of cooking were almost irresistible.

Nevertheless, the woman instructed Jouhkan and me to stay where we were, among the sparse trees, while she ran quickly towards the glow of the fires we could see ahead of us.

Jouhkan was scratching his strong, yellow beard. 'There's something up,' he muttered. 'Probably a new arrival. She has a nose for these things. Even before the Northland's Mistress gave her a new set of nostrils!'

If that was true, then she had a better nose than I. All I could smell on the breeze was food, piss, sweat and reindeers. And the tangy aroma of a fruit, a yellow berry that grew all through the long Pohjolan night, a fragrant if tiny piece of magic in the dark. Jouhkan's comment added to my conviction that Niiv herself had been born talented in sorcery. Although at first at a very simple level, she was now like a briar rose, growing out of control. I was very much on my guard with her.

Niiv came scampering back, her head exposed, fair hair flowing, her skirts caked with snow. She was breathless and unhappy and the moment she reached me she touched ungloved hands to my face, staring at me.

'They're Galliks,' she said. 'Apparently very dangerous. I don't know them, but there are other visitors who do. They are nicknamed "quill-heads" because of what they do to their hair. Do you know them?'

Galliks? Quill-heads? I knew them well enough. Lime-streaked hair, stiffened in battle like frosted wood or stripped feathers, bodies painted with the faces, eyes and members of their ancestors, voices trained to shout above the sound of falling water, arms strengthened to allow them to hold their full body weight by one hand as they flung themselves out from their chariots, clinging to the knotted mane of their galloping horse. Yes, I knew them well enough. The Greeklanders called them *keltoi.*

Galliks, *keltoi, bolgae,* Celts, they were known by so many names, and all had names for their tribes and great clans based on deeds, or creatures, or ancestors, or visions. They were a widespread and confusing people, usually hospitable, highly honourable. How dangerous they would turn out to be depended from where, in the western lands they dominated, this particular group had come.

'When did they arrive?'

'Some time ago, while I was singing with Louhi. They seem to be very unhappy.'

'What are they looking for?'

'What are *you* looking for? What is anybody looking for? The same thing in different guise. This place attracts madness and hope as warm skin attracts a mosquito. Please be careful of them. They've already made threats against a neighbouring camp. They've set up their own tents close to my village.'

And then she gave me that look again, the look that said *I know you!* And she knew that I was older than my face, and she smiled, adding, 'I think you should ask for lodgings with those brutes. If you could persuade the *rajathuks* to let you pass into Pohjola, you might be able to persuade the Galliks to keep their iron dry.'

Certainly I would seek lodgings with them—they might well be useful to me, and I was familiar with most of their dialects. First, though, I had to pay a call on an old friend.

The frozen lake was far wider than I'd remembered. Its forested shore was alive with fire, fifty camps or more, hundreds of fires burning and cooking and warming the black of night, away into the distance. The ice stretched out before me, marked and patterned through the long winter by shamans trying to fathom its secrets. Even now, out in the midnight gloom above the frost, I could see naked figures moving and dancing, skating and crawling, some of them beating at the great lid of frozen water that separated them from the world of ghosts, ships and ancient offerings at the bottom of the wide mere. Several tall, grey, indistinct figures stood motionless in a circle at the centre of the lake.

The surrounding woods were eerie ghosts in the starlight, their shapes silvering when the moon rose, sometimes shimmering when the falling veils of light in the north streamed at their most brilliant. The roots of these woods sucked the spirits from the lake. They bristled with the past, whispered with lost voices. This lake was one of several places that touched into distant Time itself. What I sought might as easily be in one of these massive birches, or in a copse of thorn, as in the old ship in the lake mud, far below the ice.

I listened for hours, listened for the scream of desperation, the howling voice calling for what it had lost. But the lake, for now at least, was silent.

Time would tell, though time was in short supply. With spring would come danger.

Later, I approached the two squat tents erected by the *keltoi*. A single man crouched in his furs, guarding the entrance to the crude enclosure. He eyed me suspiciously, asking my name and my business, and from his dialect I placed him as coming from the edge of the world itself, the Island of the Dead which I knew as Ghostland, though Alba was its more familiar name.

This island was close to the land of my birth. Its high places were marked with the same stones and spirals. Its caves stank of the same earth, the same dreams. For reasons I hadn't begun to understand, the dead accumulated there, hiding in its forests and at the sources of its rivers, the vast domain of Ghostland, at the island's heart. Many tribes lived on the border of this domain, protected by old and powerful defences against the spirits which walked, rode and fought there. Alba was a strange island, a place in which I did not feel comfortable, which is why I visited it rarely.

A stretch of water separated the white chalk cliffs of the island from the white cliffs at the edge of the huge land where I walked my path, but the men who prowled those sea-carved edges often signalled to each other using sunlight on their shields. In good weather and calm seas, small ships crossed the straits, and some of them managed to return.

I was allowed access to the fire inside the tent and found a chieftain, four of his retinue of warriors, and two *druidi*, the priests or sorcerers of the *keltoi*.

These island men were gruff in their speech, very crude in tongue, welcoming in their hospitality—I was invited immediately to share the tent and the food, payment to be discussed later—but each carried a severed head in a leather bag, and each took pleasure in showing me his trophy. The smell of the cedar oil was stimulating. The chieftain claimed that the grim skull he himself carried would sometimes sing to him of triumphs to come.

The men addressed these heads as if they were friends, asking forgiveness for closing them up again in their sacks at the end of a conversation, but food had to be taken.

I had seen this many times before, and not just with the strange Alba islanders.

The *druidi* were in disgrace, I was soon told. They had tried several times to penetrate the ice to find some lost and significant object from their chieftain's land, and failed. Now they sat, sullen and thoughtful, away from the warlord. They were trim-bearded and crop-haired, though each had a single, long plait hanging from the left temple. They wore new deerskin trousers and thick fleece jackets. The older man had a splendid gold half-moon breastplate, a *lunula*, slung around his neck. They were both better dressed than the warriors, who sat huddled in brightly patterned cloaks, woollen trousers and long, beaten leather boots that were now quite rank in odour.

The chieftain's name was Urtha. He was a bright and irascible man, still youthful though combat-scarred, given to both great laughter and flights of fury. Like many men I had met in my long journey, his language often sounded insulting and was peppered with obscenities. I sensed that no offence was ever intended; it was simply the way of talking.

He introduced his companions. Two were conscripts from a neighbouring tribe from among the Coritani, with whom Urtha's clan of the Cornovidi were currently at peace. They were called Borovos, a hot-tempered, flame-haired youngster—who alone was responsible for the aggressive reputation of this group, I discovered—and his cousin Cucallos, who huddled inside a hooded black cloak and dreamed of other days and wild-riding raids. The other two were members of Urtha's elite band of horse-warriors, which he called his *uthiin*. Most chieftains encouraged such bands to ride with them, and they took a name that reflected their leader. They were bound to the warlord by codes of honour and taboo, and had a status far higher than ordinary horsemen. These two, hard-faced, war-scarred, hard-drinking but pleasant, were called Manandoun and Cathabach.

The rest of his *uthiin* were guarding his fortress and his family, back on the island, under the temporary leadership of his greatest friend, and foster brother, Cunomaglos.

'Dog Lord!' Urtha laughed. 'A fine name for that battlefield hound. The place, my fine fort, will be safe in his hands.'

'What are you searching for?' I asked him.

He scowled at me. 'If I tell you that you'll search for it too.'

'I have enough on my mind,' I replied. 'My only interest is in a ship that lies at the bottom of the lake.'

'The ship that screams like a man dying?'

'Yes. Are you after the same ship?'

'No. Not at all. No ships involved.'

'Then why not give me a hint of what it is? We may be able to help each other.'

'No,' Urtha said emphatically. 'But I *will* tell you that it's an old treasure. One of five lost treasures. The others are scattered in the south somewhere. This one is important to me, though. Very important. Because of a dream I had about my sons, and the fate of my land. I need to know a little more. That's why I'm here. I can't tell you any more than that, except that these one-braids,' he gestured at the huddled druids, 'used an oracle—dead blackbirds, if I remember . . .' his warriors, who had been listening, sniggered to a man, '. . . and the oracle said to sail north. To *this* piss-hole place! We've been trying to get here for nearly a season. At least, I think that's true. How can I tell? Nobody told me that there was only *night* in the north.' He lowered his voice irritably. 'I'm going to make sure I get some new oracles when I get home. But don't let them know.

'And I'm missing my wife. Aylamunda. *And* I'm missing my daughter, little Munda—little terror!—she's nearly four, now. And I like her very much. Even at four, she teases me . . . and I fall for it! She already knows more about hunting than I do. She's got the goddess in her creases, if you know what I mean. She'll be strong, one of these days. I pity the poor bugger who'll have to marry her. But she's great fun. She can run with my three favourite hounds, Maglerd, Gelard and Ulgerd. Wonderful creatures! I miss them too. I should have brought them with me.'

'And your sons? Do you have sons?'

'I'm sorry you mentioned them,' he grumbled. 'Demons. Twin demons. Five years old. It took charm of heroic proportion to persuade their foster father, a chief of the Coritani, to keep them for as long as he did. Borovos and Cucallos, here, are among his knights, and they know what I mean. I didn't want the little horrors back, but he sent them back when they were five, with a fine black bull and heifer as an apology. When I go home, I'll have to start the proper fathering myself. I imagine they've driven poor, noble Cunomaglos, their new guardian, to distraction by now. If not to combat! Yes, I'd hoped to have two more years of peace. Little grim-faces,' he went on, more to himself than to me. 'Not idle. Not stupid. But too quick to get angry with everything, according to their foster father. There'll be trouble when I'm dead. Those two will fight each other, through greed I expect, tear the land apart, unless I can find a way to change things . . .'

He continued to mutter inaudibly for a moment or two.

All the male children of the chiefs of the *keltoi* were fostered for up to seven years, I remembered, before being returned to their natural parents. It was called 'the separation', and was usually a painful time, though not, it seemed, in Urtha's case. The return was called 'the greeting', and was a time of testing and bonding, which could be equally painful because of its hostility. One in three of all returning princes would end up as a marsh sacrifice in his early adulthood, pegged down in shallow water, strangled, throat opened with a knife.

But I wanted to make friends with Urtha, at least for the moment. 'Do I understand your priests told you this? That there will be trouble in your land?'

'Yes . . . They're the ones who read the signs, after I told them my dream.'

'Then I suppose it must be true.'

Urtha glanced at me sharply, then looked at the gloomy enchanters. 'I see what you mean,' he agreed in a whisper. 'They're useless now, maybe they were useless then. Maybe things *will* turn out better.'

'I'm tired,' I said. 'And I have a task of my own.'

'The screaming ship, you said.'

'The screaming ship.'

'Don't know much about it, but good luck. You'll need it if you're going to freeze your balls trying to raise her from below that ice.'

'Thank you. But in a few days, by way of thanks for your courtesy, I'll see what I can *see*, if you know what I mean . . . if you'd like that.'

He scratched his thick, black beard, thinking about what I'd said. 'You're an enchanter?'

Why hide it, I thought. Anyway, he would find out in a while, either when he realised I was going *down* to the ship, not raising her, or from Niiv, who I suspected did not hold the notion of discretion high among her virtues. 'Yes.' And I added, with a smile, 'I'm the best.'

He laughed. 'They all say that. Anyway, you're too young. You're no older than me.'

I cannot remember, now, why I said what I said next, why I trusted Urtha with an answer which, though vague, I had kept from Niiv. 'I'm very *much* older than you. But I'm an old man who stays young.' He looked at me blankly. 'When I was born,' I went on, 'your land was still empty of anything but forest. The oldest animals still stalked the river edges . . .'

'How long ago was that?'

'A long time ago. Hundreds of good horses ago.'

'You're a moonstruck liar,' Urtha said after a moment, a canny smile on his lips. 'That's not a complaint, you understand. Not at all a complaint. You may be a liar, and moonstruck, but I suspect you lie well, and since all we see is stars and moon . . . I'll look forward to a few of your stories.' He glanced gloomily around. 'Nothing else to do but drink and piss in *this* gods-forsaken place.'

'I'm not a liar,' I said evenly. 'But I'm not insulted by your doubts.'

'Nothing more to be said, then,' he grinned. 'Only something to be *drunk*!' He reached for a leather flask and waved it towards me.

'I agree.'

A discomforting event occurred soon after, which put me on my guard. The next 'evening', which is to say after the formal meal before sleeping, one of Urtha's retinue—Cathabach, I think—led me into the snowbound forest. Urtha and the rest of his men were there, staring up at the dangling clothing of his two enchanters, stretched over crude wooden, human frames. As I'd approached I'd noticed that a certain amount of humorous commentary had been abruptly stopped. Only frost-breathed reverence greeted me as I came up beside the chief.

'This is what happens if you don't get it right,' Urtha said. 'What a shame. For all their faults, they had talents.'

'What happened to them?' I asked, sensing mischief had been done.

But Urtha simply pointed to tracks in the snow, leading

into the wilderness. 'They went "wolf",' he said. 'It's something such men do when they need to escape.'

'Are they dead?'

Urtha laughed. 'Not yet. Just going home the hard way.'

Such men as Urtha's druids were held in high esteem by many *keltoi* tribes, I knew, occupying high stature. But not, it seemed, in Urtha's land. Make a mistake: run naked through midnight snow.

He stepped forward and stripped the deerskin trousers from one of the mannikins. He pulled the fleece jacket from the shoulders, and untied the gold *lunula* from around the other stick-man's neck. To my surprise he offered me the trousers.

'Any good to you? They're shit-stained I expect, but you can clean them up, and they're well stitched. Better than the stinking rags you're wearing at the moment.'

'Thank you.'

'Do you want the jacket as well? Good for this climate.'

'I won't say no. Thank you again.'

'Don't thank me,' he said with a searching look at me. 'I'm not giving them to you. We'll trade, in time.' He passed me the thick fleece, then held the half-moon golden *lunula* in his hands, stroking it with his thumbs. 'I'm glad to have this back for the moment. It's very old. Very old indeed. It has . . . memories.'

I sensed that Urtha wanted a response from me but I said nothing. After a while he looked at me, his eyes sad. 'It belongs to my family. That man had the right to wear it. Now I can keep it for a while, until I find a *better* man to wear it. I'm glad you came out of the night, Merlin.'

He clutched the *lunula* in his folded arms, his gaze in the distance. A few moments passed and he sighed. 'So it's done. They've gone. Ah well . . .'

Again he glanced at me, then walked away.

I clutched my new clothes and stared after him, wondering how many years I would have to add to my flesh and bones in order to heighten my powers of insight.

Urtha was curious about me, and that made me curious

about him. The disappearance of the druids, and the reclaiming of the tribal 'moon', suggested that change was in the wind for the warlord.

All because I had 'come out of the night'.

CHAPTER THREE

—

Argo

Niiv was like a brightly coloured bird in her furs and shawl, racing around me as we walked through the snow, chattering constantly. 'How are you going to do it? How are you going to do it? Tell me, Merlin. Tell me!'

In the days that we'd been back at the ice-covered lake, the shaman's daughter had dispensed with the formalities and ritual that she had inherited after her visit to the Mistress of the North. Instead of taking up a position of meditation and learning inside the skin and bone but where her father had spent so much of his life sending his spirit out on the wing, or on the fin, or by forest running, she had declared: 'There is so much more to be learned from the strangers! The *sedjas* will guard me, but if I shut myself off and breathe smoke and beat the skin drums, out of sight of all these others, then what could I hope to understand of the world to the south?'

Her spirited and forceful denial of tradition was not welcomed behind the high wall and heavy gates of her village, but was allowed, and the stinking skin lodge, with its potions, poisons, fungi, bark extracts, fish oils and eye-opening, if dizzying, fermentations remained closed, the flaps of the door pinned together by the narrow bones of some wading bird or other.

The child skipped and laughed and teased through these last days of the long winter night, sniffing at me, questioning me, ignoring her uncle, Lemanku, who counselled against her overt curiosity; breaking all the rules; using her newly granted talents in charm to try to turn me inside out, unaware that after so many thousands of years on the Path I could hear every unspoken question in her mind (if I'd wanted to) and could keep her at a distance quite easily.

It was not Niiv who represented the problem for me. It was overcoming mindless, ancient Enaaki in his lake. Older powers take more understanding. We grow too wise to comprehend the bleakness from the beginning of Time.

'How *are* you going to do it?' the harpy insisted yet again.

'I've told you. I'm going to gouge a hole through the ice and swim down to the bottom of the lake.'

'You'll die at once. There are a thousand corpses in the water, all of them fools like you who thought they could simply smear grease on their bodies, dive in and find out the secrets of the lake. No, I'm sure you must have a trick. You have a special charm to protect you. A *sedja*.'

I spoke the truth when I told her, 'No special charm at all. If what I hope is down there *is* down there—then I'll be protected from below.'

Well . . . possibly.

I gathered up snow into a ball and threw it at her, striking her squarely on the nose, stopping her in her tracks. She was outraged. I apologised.

'I thought you'd duck.'

She shook her head furiously, snow crystals spraying. 'I thought only children played like that with snow,' she admonished.

'Still a child at heart. Sorry.'

'You're not a child, you're a madman,' she went on. 'And a liar. You *must* know so much more than you're telling me.'

If only that were true, I thought. I could smell her frosting breath. From below her clothes came the aroma of musk and I kept remembering her ancestor, Meerga, whose musky odour still haunted me. Her pale eyes were like jewels. Despite the cold I was aroused and charmed by this dancing bird in her blue, white and red-dyed furs.

She knew I liked her. I could see the sparkle in the way she watched me. But she was so inquisitive, quite certain that I was in command of a hidden sorcery.

'Very well. If you must know, I've eaten a whole reindeer antler, which I first carved with the Seven Cries and Chants that open the gates to the Frozen Deep, and under these new clothes my body is wrapped in fish guts and liver, so that Enaaki won't smell the human inside.'

'That's ridiculous,' she muttered irritably. 'Enaaki will smell you at once. You're making fun of me now.'

I had no special skills in frozen lakes; it was a matter of small magic to survive drowning and the cold for an hour or so—enough time, I hoped, to make the contact with the deep. My problem was one of time—I had to get through the lid of ice before these brief glowing dawns became stronger, every instinct in me told me this. The ship only screamed in winter, never in summer. Bright dawn was very near and everything I needed to accomplish had to be accomplished before the sun melted the white whiskers of ice on the trees.

'I wasn't making fun of you.'

'It doesn't matter. If you don't prepare, you'll drown. One more white-belly to be hooked out and fed back in pieces to Enaaki. Make a joke of it if you want, but you need a guide. I can help you to find one. But only if you want to.'

And she turned and stalked away, leaving me wondering where, among the camps that ringed the lake, I would find a full beast's-worth of entrails to feed to the sinister lake guardian.

The best way to move across the lake, I discovered over the next few days, was on bone-blades shaped from the shoulders of reindeer. These had been carefully carved by a local man, who earned a good living at it, and he skilfully attached them to whatever footwear might be needed. A push and a shove and even the most ungainly of ageing shamans could begin to move across the frozen surface. By bending forward and holding hands behind the back, the movement was swifter and more control could be maintained. I practised for a while, turning in elaborate circles and speeding around the edge of the lake, staying clear of the territorial markings of the various encampments, weaving between other visitors who seemed to be using this astonishing means of movement more for entertainment than serious business.

Niiv floated out towards me. She was *Pohjolan* and skilled in ice dancing. She led me deeper, to where several shamans, all of them greased and naked except for their bone-bladed shoes, danced in a complex pattern around one part of the surface, trying to summon the power to carve a huge hole in the ice, she said. They skidded and slipped, bony white bodies in the torchlit night, cascading streams of ice marking each abrupt end to an elaborate dance of enchantment.

Even the dogs wore blades on their paws, huge white hounds howling wildly as their masters threw antlers for them to chase.

All of this was happening at the edge of the lake. The centre was guarded by ice statues, ten in all, a circle of gigantic, frosted figures ('cold-night' *sedja*, Niiv whispered, winter talismans) that stared towards the encircling forest through melting features. Inside this wide and protected circle was where the real activity was occurring. Here, holes to the water below had been carved, scraped, boiled and burned, but they closed up as fast as they could be used and it was easy enough to see that below the lid of ice the lake was fish-belly white with the naked dead, mostly visitors to the area, drawn by legend rather than applying local magic. Pohjolan men used long poles to reach through narrow holes and haul the corpses to the surface. Below the dead, though, were those who had managed to control their bodies. They floated as if suspended in the lake, arms crossed on chests, turning slowly, hovering in the cold waters as they tried to summon the spirits of the deep for whatever purposes preoccupied them.

I would have to go down among them.

And after three 'days' of education and preparation, I finally felt ready to do just that. With Jouhkan's help, I made a passage through the ice, then stripped naked, swallowed the small *sedja* I had fashioned from a fish bone, and slid feet-first down the tunnel.

Prepared for the spirits that inhabited the water, I was not prepared for the water itself, and the cold was not just shocking it was almost predatory. I screamed as I plunged downwards, wasting breath for a moment, convinced that a thousand teeth were ripping my flesh. I watched as my body grew extensions of ice. It was all I could do to remember my purpose here as I hung, suspended in the lake, among the slowly turning shapes of shamans and priests, their bodies eerily illuminated from above, where the ice was alive with torchlight. Below, there was a stranger glow, but even my young man's body was being defeated by the pure, hellish *chill*.

So I summoned a little magic, ageing a little, but warmed myself and swam as deep as I could, below the level of the shamans. I summoned what sight I could and scanned the depths. There were ruins below me, or what looked like ruins, probably Enaaki's hiding place, and faces that watched me, pulling back into the shadows as they caught my gaze. I saw the glitter of gold, the gleam of bronze and the sheen of iron, a wasteland of trophies, offerings and secrets cast into the lake over the ages. And the masts and prows of ships that had sunk here and lay at all angles, weed-covered and broken, ransacked for their timbers.

A sudden swirling around me and lean, translucent faces peered hard at me, elemental water guardians rising from where they prowled over the sunken dead. They seemed distressed by my presence so deep, but didn't try to fight me. I had prepared for this descent for three days, offering more than just a meal of entrails to the entities below. I had sung and chanted in the groves, and I followed carefully the instructions of the young shaman who had taken pity on me, and made a personal drum, whittled birch bark, and scratched my name on stones, which I had dropped through the ice into the deeps.

Now I felt a certain confidence, and at last I put a name to my quest.

Air bubbling from my lungs, I called to the old ship, the grave ship, the ship that screamed . . .

'Argo!' I called, and the sound spread down into the lake, booming through the swirls and eddies of the deeps.

'Argo! Answer me!'

I looked hard for the signs of her below. I called again, swimming deeper, then called twice more. I began to lose track of time. The *voytazi* kept track of me, I noticed, a vortex of eyes, mouths and bony fingers, keeping at a distance.

Too cold to feel panic, I began to entertain the grim thought that perhaps I had been wrong. Perhaps she had not come here after all but lay elsewhere in the deeps, in another lake or a hidden sea, guarding her captain's remains.

But then: that whispering voice with which I had become so familiar in my time with Jason, during the long journey through the heart of the world, before we had returned to Iolkos, the voice of sentience that was the ship herself:

'Leave us in peace. Go up. Leave us to sleep.'

'Argo?'

The water below me *pulsed*. The lake seemed angry. I could see a shattered vessel, dark and indistinct, its hull fringed by twisted branches that reached out like tendrils. The branches of the sacred oak that formed her keel, I realised— she had kept on growing!

'Argo! Is Jason alive?'

Before I could speak further, invisible hands caught me. I was dragged up towards the ice, flung vigorously against the roof, a dizzying blow. I heard laughter. My tormentors sank down, swimming quickly like eels. For a while I stayed where I was, bobbing gently among the bloated dead, then my lungs began to burst. My control had gone and I was on the verge of drowning. I tried to summon warmth, but failed. I scrabbled along the underside of the ice, increasingly desperate, then saw a hook probing down, fishing close to a corpse. I pushed the dead man aside and clung on to that welcome curve of bone. The upwards passage was almost too narrow for my shoulders, but someone above knew I was a living being, and hauled and hauled until at last my head gasped above the surface. Niiv came running to me with a heavy cloak. In the glimmering dawn, and by the light of torches, I saw tears in her eyes.

'I thought I'd lost you,' she said angrily. 'I *told* you to prepare better!'

I had no response to that. My talents had failed me in the realm of Enaaki—or perhaps because of the power of Argo herself—and the lesson was a sobering one.

A while later, warmed and revived from my lazy, arrogantly ill-prepared excursion downwards, I lay on the ice, close to a hook hole, and again called to Argo, begging her to respond.

'It's Antiokus. You *must* remember me. I was with you when you sailed on the quest for the fleece of gold. Jason, please hear me. Your sons are not dead! Listen to me. Your sons are alive! Argo, tell him what I've said.'

I kept trying. I have no idea how long I lay there, staring down through the hole, which was already beginning to melt at its edges as the sluggish sun crept, worm-like, above the southern horizon. Pike-faced *voytazi* taunted me, flashing their toothy grins then disappearing, teasing me with the threat to drag me down.

'Argo!' I persevered. 'You must believe me! The world has changed in a very strange way. But the news is good for Jason. Argo! Answer me!'

And then at last the voice, again, whispering to me from the icy depths.

'He does not wish to return. His life ended when Medea killed his boys.'

'I know,' I said to her. 'I was there. I saw what she did. But it was only a pretence. What she did was an illusion. The blood on their bodies was just illusion.'

I felt the ice shake beneath me, as if the whole lake below had pulsed with shock.

There was only silence from Argo, but I intuited that she was puzzled, and that my words were seeping through the wood of her hull and into Jason.

I said it again: 'Jason: Your sons are still alive. They have grown into men. You can find them. Come back to us!'

A moment later, the ice below me bucked. Then cracked open with a sound like a whiplash, a great split exposing the pure water below.

I stood, slithered and crawled my way back to the margin of the lake where the circle of torches blazed in the hands of the visitors.

She was coming up. In that second when the ice had opened, before I had fled for safety, I had seen Argo's shadow start to rise, branches like craggy fronds reaching from the shattered hull.

To the north, the lights in the heavens streamed almost as far as the zenith. The winter night was passing faster now. The frost-white trees were beginning to show colour. The rising of Argo was coinciding with the first true passage into dawn. Even as we stood, the brightness grew stronger over the bleak forest to the south, dawn fire rising in a steady arc.

And then she struck the ice. The surface of the lake exploded upwards, a fountain of glittering shards falling around the dark hull as the old ship, mast-shattered and weed-wracked, nosed up from the deeps, the tall prow draining water, rising with solemnity, almost dignity, branches snapping off like oars, until it had half stretched out from the lake . . . then falling back, the stern coming up, the crouching figure of the goddess draped in long-fronded weed, the whole boat shuddering like a waking beast on the cold water, then settling and becoming still.

Hanging from the mast in a web of ropes and weeds was the shape of a man, his head stretched back as if he had died screaming to the heavens. Water came out of his open mouth. Dawn light caught the living glitter of his eyes. Even from the edge of the lake I sensed that he was watching me.

'I knew you would survive...' I whispered to him. He wouldn't have heard, of course. He wasn't dead, but he was in deep cold.

But something was wrong with Argo. She was too still, now, too quiet for the vibrant, urgent ship. When she had been launched she had strained at the ropes. More than sixty men had been needed to hold her on the slipway. She had writhed and wrestled to get free, to find the ocean, and when she had finally been released she had struck the water of the harbour with such speed and energy that she had sunk for a moment before surfacing and turning to open water. The argonauts had been hard-pressed to get aboard her, swimming out and crawling up the ropes to find their benches and their oars, to slow the impatient ship and turn her back to the docks.

She had been such a strong ship. So alive! But now...

I walked out across the ice again, Niiv and Urtha with me carrying torches. The oak ship creaked as she warmed. Jason's body gently swung where he was suspended. I touched the slippery planks, walked round to the prow and stared at the blue-painted eyes.

'What is it?' Niiv asked quietly.

'She's dead. The ship is dead.'

Poor Argo. She had sailed so far with her precious cargo. She had taken Jason to the deepest grave she could find, a place of memory and magic. She had not expected to rise again, but my voice, my message, had set the heart in the oak at work once more and she had striven to return to the surface. The effort, it seemed, had been too much, and she had perished even as she passed life back to the captain.

'I'm sorry,' I whispered. 'I didn't know how hard it would be for you.'

Urtha called, 'The dead man is moaning. He's not a dead man at all. I've seen this happen before...'

Jason's head had dropped and he was beginning to thrash in the web of ropes. Urtha was fascinated. 'When a man drowns in a winter lake he stops breathing, but sometimes the spirit stays with him. It happened to an enemy of mine. A remarkable thing. He was drowned for a night and a day after our fight at the edge of a mere, but suddenly floated to the surface and opened his eyes.'

'Did you become friends after that?' Niiv asked him.

Urtha looked at her, confused. 'Friends?'

'It was an omen. An omen of friendship.'

'Was it? I had no idea. I took his head. I've still got it.'

'Help me with him,' I said sharply, cutting across Urtha's reminiscences. We hauled ourselves on to the deck, slipping on the slimy surface, clinging to the net that held my old friend. Urtha used his bronze knife to slash the weeds and hemp and Jason slipped into my arms with a further rush of water from his lungs and the howl of the new born.

A sled had been hauled across to Argo, and Urtha and I gently lowered Jason down to the waiting Pohjoli, who wrapped him in skins and hauled him back to the shore, to the reviving warmth of a tent and a furiously burning birch-wood fire.

CHAPTER FOUR

—

Jason

The ice was melting. Dawn had struck and torches were only needed for journeys into the deeper forest. Around the lake the scenes of activity were becoming more animated. As the world began to wake so, it seemed, did the passions and humour of the visitors to this northern place. Argo remained silent and alone in her basin in the ice.

Jason came in and out of consciousness for several days, his words rambling and incoherent, his mood occasionally violent. The crushing wound on his chest had started to bleed again and was bathed and tended by the Pohjoli, who had lichens and plant and bark extracts for every sort of wound, it seemed.

I waited patiently, and after five rests was told that Jason wanted to see me.

He had trimmed his beard but his hair hung long, the grey and black combed out straight. The scars on his face looked pale, but he was otherwise as burnished as when I'd last seen him alive, in Iolkos. And those dark eyes, those quizzical, canny eyes, were as sharp as ever. His hands shook as he

grasped mine, the fingers still weak. His smile was as beguiling and ambiguous as ever, but he seemed genuinely glad
that I was there.

'Antiokus. Young Antiokus . . .'

'I'm known as Merlin now.'

'Antiokus, Merlin . . . what does it matter? It's *you*. And
how is it that you haven't aged in the twenty years since you
deserted me?'

'I have. I wear it well.'

'You certainly do. Not me, alas. Why did you leave me? Why
did you desert me? I was so angry! I needed you so badly.'

'I always told you,' I said to him, still holding his hands
in an embrace, 'that I am destined to move on a path that
circles the world.'

'Yes, yes. I know,' he said impatiently. 'And every cavern
and valley that leads down into the underworld . . .'

'I spent longer with you than I should have. But when the
company is good, and the adventure is good, and the food is
good, and . . . ' I glanced across the tent. A young woman sat
there, wrapped in black furs, watching us quietly and sleepily.
'When everything is good, and everything was always very
good with you, Jason . . .'

'It was, wasn't it?'

'Yes. And when it's that good . . . I allow myself a little
leeway. But eventually, I am always called back.'

He grinned again, his breath still cold, as if there were still
ice in his lungs, but his eyes blazed with new life as he
watched me. 'That was a great voyage, that river voyage after
we had stolen the Golden Fleece. Wasn't it?'

'Yes. A great voyage.'

'What strange and wonderful encounters we had. What
strange kingdoms we found. Did you ever see Heracles again?'

'No, though I've heard a great deal about him since. He's
never out of trouble.'

'I wish you had stayed longer with us. You should have
stayed! I truly missed you after that witch killed my sons—'

He broke off abruptly, frowning, repeated the words, 'My

sons . . .' then turned and sat down heavily on the wooden bench.

'I've been dreaming something strange,' he said.

'Tell me about the dream.'

Face in hands, head shaking, he whispered, 'Just a dream. A waking dream. A dream through the Ivory Gate, Antiokus . . . false and unwelcome.'

'Describe it to me.'

'Why? It was just a voice . . . a voice whispering to me that my sons are still alive. Such madness!'

'What madness is that?'

He glanced up at me, then smiled wanly. 'The madness of an old man desperate to hold on to his past, I suppose.'

'You're not old,' I said. 'You don't know what age is. When Argo took you from the harbour at Iolkos, and brought you here to die, you had seen less than fifty summers.'

'It felt like ten thousand.'

'That *is* a lot,' I agreed with a smile. Probably more than my own, I thought.

I'd lost count of my years, though there was a way to find out, should I choose to waste my time seeking out the deep gorge in the forests to the west, where I had been born and where the record of my life was stored.

'And by the way,' I added. 'It was no dream.'

'What was no dream?'

'The voice. It was my voice. I called to you. Argo revived you . . .' I thought sadly of the ship, still out on the lake. 'Argo died bringing you back. And her body is in bad shape. But we can rebuild her; we can find a new spirit for her.'

Jason was staring at me, his face almost blank, a child struggling with a new idea. All wisdom, all connivance was gone from his rugged features as his dream and my reality began to rattle at his mental bars.

'My sons are dead. Medea cut off their heads before my eyes . . .'

'I know. I was there, remember? It was my last day with you. I was thinking about my next journey, and my talent for insight had somehow been stolen from me once I'd entered the palace. I wasn't watching closely . . .'

'What are you saying?' the warrior asked quietly. 'Antiokus, what are you saying?'

'It might be best if I showed you, Jason.'

'Showed me what?'

'How we were all deceived.'

I hoped I could summon the vision. I had spent a long time preparing for it. It would cost me—I would age a little—but this was a man who had been my friend, and who had once saved my life when my own talents had failed me. What he and Medea had done to each other was unforgivable, and perhaps that is why I had finally left him to his fate, all that time ago. But now that I knew the truth, I felt strongly that I owed it to Jason to tell him what I'd discovered. It would be worth a few days on my flesh to convince Jason that he had mourned in vain. Or so I thought.

I was too young, at this time, to think through the consequences of such an action, of what the knowledge might do to the man.

'Where are we going?' he asked.

'Get dressed. Warm clothes. Wipe your eyes. And follow me to the groves!'

Niiv was intrigued by what I was doing and insisted on accompanying us on the long journey through the heavy forest. Jouhkan came with us, and the youthful shaman who had helped me in my earlier preparations, and would now supervise my offering and ritual when we returned to the appropriate clearing. He wasn't at all sure that I could achieve what I wanted, but if I did, then he too would have increased his skills.

In the time I had been by the lake I had learned a great deal about the *rajathuks*, the wooden totems of this land. At one time or another I had met them all, though only four had been friends with me. My difficulty was that those friendships were so very long in my past! I had maintained my appearance and mind as a young man, and my memory was powerful. But

Time is a terrible enemy of detail and accuracy.

Those friends, now these idols, were very powerful sources of enchantment and vision, each specialised in a different way. The one who could help now was Skogen, the shadow of forgotten forests. It might be persuaded to draw out the memory of the tragedy in Iolkos from behind our eyes and present it in all its gory trickery again.

A winding archway of hazel marked the final approach to the sanctuary of the *Skogen*. At its end we faced a wall of crude stone, covered with niches in which carved bones and animal skulls had been placed over the years. Our guide added something in a pouch to one of the niches on our behalf. We passed round the wall and into the grove where four circles of wooden pillars surrounded the stone effigy. Four torches cast a net of flickering shadows. Acrid smoke billowed from small fires around the grove.

The stone was twice my height, a grey slab deeply and intricately carved with scenes from the past. The face that watched us was leafy and gnarled, the eyes at a curious slant. These were eyes that could see the shadows of the past and already I sensed its curiosity about Jason.

We were kept in the outer circle for a long while, repeating a short charm as instructed and inhaling the fumes from one of the fires. The priest performed one of the sing-chant rituals that are so common in northern lands, and scarified his skin. After a while he came back to us, grinning through broken teeth and dark beard. He picked up his skin drum and began to beat it rapidly with a piece of bone.

'He's very curious about you. Ask to see whatever it is you want.'

Jason and I stepped forward into the second circle, looked up at the watching face. Around us, the beat of the drum became a frantic, rhythmic tattoo, exaggeratedly loud, that seemed to make the whole grove shake. I was dizzy with the smoke. The trees seem to revolve around us, only Skogen staying still. This was the dream-trance, the crude magic of the shamans. At my prompting, Jason called out in a slurred and anxious voice,

'The death of my sons. Show me the death of my sons.' The request etched his face with pain, I saw.

For a moment the grove continued to thunder. Then abruptly it was still and silent.

I stared at Skogen, at the wide, stone eyes.

I heard the sound of men running, the stink of burning wood, the screaming of children and the clash of metal blades . . .

Jason cried out, 'Oh gods! I remember that stink of blood and burning leaves! The witch is here!'

The grove seemed to draw in on itself and a strange fire dazzled my eyes . . .

We had fought our way through the palace grounds and seven of us survived to enter the building, storming its halls and corridors, finally facing the unnatural flames at its heart. I recognised their supernatural nature and hesitated, but before I could say a word Jason had leapt through the fire. Close on his heels, I followed him, slipping and sliding on the polished marble floor that stretched to Medea's private chambers. The other argonauts, those who had survived the earlier fighting, burst through the flames behind me, round shields held at arm's length before their faces, swords extended.

After that, things happened so fast I had retained only a fragment of memory of the moments before the dreadful deed we would witness.

'Antiokus!' Jason shouted in warning. 'Look to your left!'

I turned in time to parry the javelin thrust from one of Medea's guards. The wide blade struck my arm a glancing blow and the man slipped forward on to my sword. As he fell, his ram's-skull helmet grazed my cheek, which was not a good omen. Jason and the others were already running along the narrowing, blue-walled corridor in pursuit of the fleeing woman and the boys she dragged with her. I fled after them, watched by the sinister dark eyes of golden rams, painted along the length of the passage. The boys were shouting, alarmed and confused by what was happening.

A rank of warriors, lightly armoured, helmeted and with

wide shields, barred our way and Jason flung himself into the fray, fighting with a frenzy that I would more normally have associated with the tribes of the *keltoi* in the west. We broke through, scattering the grim-faced men, leaving Tisaminas and Castor to finish the slaughter.

Medea had fled to the Bull Sanctuary, and as Jason led us towards the bronze-barred gate, now closed and locked by the desperate woman, so we realised our mistake.

Behind us, across the narrow passage, a stone slab fell and trapped us. Ahead of us, the towering bull effigy, before which Medea stood triumphant, split in two, revealing itself as a doorway. There, outside, was the road to the north. A chariot and six horsemen were waiting, the animals impatient and frightened as their riders struggled to control them. I recognised the armoured charioteer as Cretantes, Medea's confidant and adviser from her homeland.

The poor little boys struggled in her grasp, suddenly aware that their fate was destined to be a greater terror in their mother's arms than the one she had told them to expect from their father.

Jason flung himself against the bars of the sanctuary, begging the black-shrouded woman to release the boys.

'Too late. Too late!' she cried from behind her black veil. '*My* blood can't save them from the ravages of *your* blood. You betrayed the ones you love, Jason. You betrayed us brutally with that woman!'

'You burned her alive!'

'Yes. And now you will burn in Hell! Nothing will change in you, Jason. Nothing can! If I could cut you out of the boys, and still let them live, then that is what I'd do. But I can't. So say goodbye to your sons!'

Jason's howl was vulpine. 'Antiokus! Use your magic!'

'I can't!' I cried. 'It isn't there!'

He flung his sword at the woman but the throw went wide. And at that moment, Medea did the terrible deed, moving so fast I saw only the merest glint of light on the blade with which she cut the throats of the twins. She turned away from us, covering their bodies with her robes, stooping to her work as Jason screamed. She wrapped and tied the heads in strips of her veil, tossing them to Cretantes, who put them in pouches at his waist. Then Medea dragged the bodies to the horses where they were flung over the blankets and tied into place.

A moment later, the troop had gone, leaving dust swirling into the sanctuary, and the smell and sight of innocent blood, and two cruel Furies taunting the argonauts, trapped in Medea's lair.

Jason slumped, fingers still gripping the gate. He had battered himself unconscious against the bars of the temple; his eyes and face were bruised, his mouth raw. Orgominos was pushing against the stone door behind us, trying to find the lever that would release us from the trap. I felt helpless: all power in magic had drained from me from the moment I entered the palace, an impotence which astonished and confused me, and I assumed had occurred because Medea had used her own sorcery to 'numb' me for the moment of the deaths. Now I felt that familiar tingle below the flesh again, ability returning, saw at once how to open the door and persuaded it to do so. We dragged Jason's body outside, through the fires, and into the fresh air.

Medea's surviving Colchean guards were nowhere to be seen. They had certainly slipped away to join her in her flight.

'Find horses,' I said to Orgominos. 'Get the others, wounded or not.'

Tisaminas crouched down beside me, lifted Jason's battered head. Jason opened his eyes, then reached out to grab me by the shoulder. 'Why didn't you stop her?' he whispered.

'I'm sorry,' I said. 'I warned you she was more powerful than me. I tried, Jason. With all my heart, I tried.'

Jason's look was grim, tearful, but he acknowledged my words. 'I know you did. I'm sure you did. You've been a good friend. I know you would have tried.' He groaned as he attempted to move. 'Come on, help me up! Tisaminas, help me up. And fetch horses! We have to follow . . .'

'The horses are on their way,' I told him.

'She will run to the north, Antiokus. I know the way she

thinks. She'll run to the shore, to the hidden harbour. We can catch her!'

'We can certainly try,' I said, though in my heart I knew that Medea had slipped away for ever. She had always out-witted Jason.

As I watched the man struggle to regain his composure and organise his thoughts, I suddenly felt very sad. The sadness quickly became overwhelming. I might even have murmured aloud, 'Oh no . . .'

Jason sensed that something was wrong. Dark, moist eyes watched me through their pain.

'Antiokus . . .' he said softly. 'If you think it's vengeance that directs me, you're wrong. It isn't Medea I'm after. Not yet, at least. It's my boys.' He was shaking violently as he reached to embrace me. 'I will need to grieve for them before anything. But she has *taken their bodies*! Antiokus—stranger to this land that you are, you are not so much a stranger here that you don't understand this: how can I grieve over just their memory? I *must* have my sons back. In my arms! They belong to *me*, not to *her*.' His grip on my shoulders was crushing my flesh, his face close to my own. 'My good friend . . . Antiokus. Don't be sad. Help me!'

I couldn't speak. I couldn't tell him what I was thinking. How could I tell him that it was time for me to move on, that I would soon have to leave him? He knew that something was upsetting me, and being Jason he was trying to instil courage in me. But he had misunderstood the cause of my sorrow, thinking I was angry that he would pursue Medea so soon after his loved ones had died.

Orgominos rode up, with five horses on tethers.

Bruised and battered, bewildered and clinging to his reason by the narrowest of grips, Jason drew away from me, flung himself on to one of them, called for us all, called for me in particular with a long, hard look, then led the pursuit of his fleeing wife, through the open gates of the palace.

I rode with him, but for a few hours only.

*   *   *

At that time, in Iolkos, we could hardly believe what we had seen. Such an abominable murder! And yet we had had to believe. It had happened before our eyes.

But now, in the grove of the *skogen*, Medea's actions became transparent, and at last I saw the way we had been deceived. As the scenario unfurled I could not bear to watch Jason as he witnessed Medea's conjuration, but I heard the thunder of his heart and the quickness of his breath as the truth at last came home to him.

One nick to the throat on each boy, drawing blood as a powerful drug was passed into the flesh. The boys collapsed in seconds. Pig's blood shocked our senses as it seemed to spurt from their necks. Medea stooped over their bodies and from beneath her skirts pulled heads made of wax and horsehair, wrapping them in strips of her veil. She threw them to Cretantes, then summoned her strength and dragged her sleeping sons to the horses, letting us see only their trailing legs.

So fast, so clever, so persuasive!

Jason's heartbeat, as he relived the truth, was like the drumming of a war galley in full attack.

All day we had pursued Medea. Her chariot of oak and wicker sped across the hills, its wheels turned more by her will than by her horses. At some point she escaped the pursuit. We found ourselves chasing only her guards and her chariot, the charioteer a man in woman's clothing. Medea had slipped away, with Cretantes and the boys, and run to a cove on the shore, where a small ship had taken her to the eastern ocean and into a territory that was at war with Iolkos.

Oddly, I must have glimpsed this event from the hills above the sea, though I had not realised what I was seeing. But the *skogen* picked it out of my confusion and amplified the scene in its singing grove.

The galley had eight oars, worked vigorously. The furled sail was black and gold, Medea's colours, arrogantly displayed as if she knew, now, she was safe. Narrow-hulled, sitting low in the water, it slipped quickly towards the open sea, to the east, towards Rhodes, perhaps, or the ruined city of Troy. Medea sat, crying bitterly, her arms around her sons, who were now awake. They were squabbling, rubbing at the sore cuts on their necks, unaware that their mother was watching the headland and saying goodbye to a life she had come to love—until Jason's betrayal of that love. She was a widow in heart, leaving behind a man dying of despair because of her fateful conjuration. Jason had paid the price of his treachery; Medea had condemned herself and her sons to a life in exile.

The grove was filled with the sound of a man crying with rage.

'Is this true?' Jason demanded of me. 'Is this true? Or just a trick?'

'Everything you saw is true,' I whispered and the man threw back his head and howled at the fading stars.

'All those wasted years! All that time in mourning! And I should have been hunting her down. I gave up the chase too quickly—I should have been hunting her down!'

His tears were of anger and frustration. His glance at me was bitter, as if somehow I was to blame.

'All those wasted years, Antiokus! I could have had my sons by my side! May the goddess be damned for not telling me!' he shouted.

And with that last furious curse, Jason left the forest sanctuary.

I stayed in the grove until the song-chant ritual of leaving was complete, then rode back to the lake with Jouhkan and an uncharacteristically silent Niiv.

'Where is he?' I asked Urtha when we came to the camp. He pointed out across the lake and I saw Jason standing on the broken ice at the prow of dead Argo, his arms raised to the ship as if trying to call her back. The ice was melting fast. It gleamed in the dawn. The frozen silence was giving way to the sound of running water. The ice itself creaked and cracked as it 'gave up the ghost'.

Later, Jason came to Urtha's tent. I was eating, Niiv sitting silently and thoughtfully beside me, watching the fire. He asked permission to enter and Urtha waved him in. Jason had cut his ragged beard down to a stubble and had tied his long hair into a single plait that reached down his back almost to the waist. He had found a pair of red, Roman trousers, tight around the thigh and cut above the knees, and a pair of grey fur boots. He still wore the black sheepskin cloak in which he had spent the last years of his life in Iolkos.

His eyes were sad as he stared at me. He dropped to a crouch and warmed his hands at the wood fire.

'The ship is dead. Argo is dead. The goddess has left her.'

'I know. The effort of resurrection was too much.'

'I take back what I said in the grove, Antiokus. Everything! Perhaps Medea had blinded the goddess as much as she had blinded us.'

'Most likely.'

'But the ship is still useful. When the ice melts, we'll tow Argo to the shore and rebuild her. And if we can find a decent trunk of oak in this wretched land, and lay a new keel, perhaps we can call the goddess back.'

'That's a good thought,' I offered.

'Yes. But if not, we'll have to sail without her.'

It had already occurred to me that Argo could be rebuilt under the protection of one of the local goddesses, unrefined and unpredictable though they were. I kept the thought to myself for the moment because Jason was still watching me, the furrow between his eyes deepening.

'How did you know?' he asked at last. 'How did you find out about Kinos and Thesokorus?'

I told him that I had found only Thesokorus, the 'little bull leaper', as Jason had called him for his adventurous spirit. Of the 'little dreamer', Kinos, I'd heard only a riddle.

'Thesokorus. He'll be so grown, now,' Jason mused.

'He's known by another name.'

'Names don't matter. Did you see him? Does he take after me?'

I had been anticipating this moment with some apprehension. Not so much because of the truth of what had happened to his beloved boys, but because of what Jason would now have to learn about himself.

I knew about Thesokorus because I had passed by an oracle and heard a series of questions from a son about his father.

CHAPTER FIVE

—

In Makedonia

From where I sat, in the shade of an oak at the edge of the town square, I could see the hazy hills and the sparkle of sunlight on the marble gates that marked the entrance to the sanctuary of the oracle.

I had been here for eight days, waiting for the sounding of the bronze horn from the high slopes above this white-walled Makedonian town. The oracle was under the protection of the god Poseidon; the oracle herself was capricious and unreliable and it was rumoured she was a shade of Persephone, who walked the dark corridors of Hades. No human medium was used to express the voice of this goddess; the voice came directly from the cave where, when it suited her, she rose from the gloom. She was nameless, never addresssed directly, known only as the 'caught breath of Time'; and she came and vanished from her caverns like a breeze on a still summer's day.

I had heard stories of visitors waiting a year or more until they were called to consult her, and I had already decided to move on along my path in a day or so, since my main purpose here was curiosity rather than consultation. I had time enough on my hands to visit the strangest of places in the world, should I hear of them.

The town was small and was already crowded with groups of Romans, Makedonians, Etruscans, Carthaginians, Scythians and Illyrians, most of whom had pitched their camps outside the walls and now idly wandered its narrow streets in search of wine, olives and the succulent mutton that was produced in the clay ovens throughout the day. The visitors were bored, listless, irritable and offensive to each other, but at least they seemed at ease with the local population.

Unlike the small group who sat edgily in the shade of three twisted olive trees, across the square from where I spent my hours in thought.

There were six of them. They were nervous, suspicious and defensive. I had recognised them at once as what the Greeklanders called *keltoi*, a warrior band from the northern countries, Hercynia, Hyperborea, Gaul Land and the like. To the locals, to the Romans especially, they were barbarians. I knew better. I had encountered many of their tribes on my journeys and I knew of their reputation for fairness, chivalry, single combat and complete adherence to a set of laws and codes that at once made them the most welcoming of hosts, and the most uncompromising of enemies.

Watching them, I couldn't tell from which part of the wilderness of forest, marsh and mountain to the north they came. Not from among the clans of Alba or Gaul in the west, I was sure of that. Their kilts, trousers and short cloaks were dyed blue and red, their hair tied in topknots with colourfully beaded string, since they were not at war. Their moustaches were long, covering their mouths, the drooping tips stiffened into points with animal fat and reaching below their chins. They walked with an arrogant bearing, staring menacingly and lingeringly at any passer-by.

At all times one of them stood guard, holding his patterned oval shield in front of him, his spear resting lightly against his shoulder. The others sat in the shade of the olive trees, drinking wine from clay flagons and eating copious quantities of fruit, meat and olives. This was having a devastating effect on their digestions. Their horses were tethered close by, much to the annoyance of the townspeople, who felt these northerners should have camped outside the walls like all the other visitors.

I was deeply curious. The men were all fair-haired except for the leader. His own skin, by contrast, had an olive complexion, his hair grey-blue with limewater, but his eyes, unlike the blue eyes of his companions, were dark and brooding, his moustache quite black. He was certainly not clan-born. When it was his turn to stand watch on the group, leaning on a shield bearing the image of Medusa, he seemed particularly aware of the young but wild-looking man who surveyed him from across the square.

I was uncomfortable with that appraisal.

The temple to Athena, a crude white-washed stone building with two smoking censers on its rough steps, overlooked the activities in the square and was occasionally visited by priests, asking the goddess if the oracle was on her way. Each day at dusk they came out on to the steps and proclaimed, 'She is still in the underworld, walking to us through the caverns.'

This resulted in a groan of disappointment from Roman and Greek, but the *keltoi* simply laughed cynically and spat olive stones in unison across the square.

They seemed very relaxed, despite their posturing, probably because they were enjoying this fine weather.

On the eighth day, shortly before dawn, the hills at last reverberated with the low note of the bronze horn. Five times the horn was sounded and the town erupted into life. Each party broke camp, saddled their horses, gathered their dogs and struck off at the trot for the foothills. The temple of Athena resonated with chanting, welcoming the rising of the oracle. Chickens ran, pigs squealed and dogs barked. There was a great deal of angry shouting from the locals as their Roman lodgers departed for the hills without paying.

The *keltoi* watched all of this carefully, and when the square was quiet they calmly saddled their horses, drained the last of the wine from the flagons, belched, laughed, made rude gestures and comments, and rode out of the small town. As they left the square, they looked back at me, watching me with steady, sinister gazes until they had disappeared from sight.

I bided my time, then fetched one of my own horses and followed along the steep track to the oracle.

I'd been here before, on more than one occasion, though several generations ago, and I knew where to go and hide, to listen while the oracle engaged with her devotees.

A series of gullies, each with a marble arch at its mouth, led deeply into the foothills, winding through craggy rock and clinging bushes until the land opened at the gleaming temple of Poseidon. This single building stood before a dense woodland of oak and tall, fragrant cedars, growing over massive piles of grey rock, which barred the way to the deep gully and cave system where the oracle resided. A giant, ram-headed bronze horn hung from two poles, the mouth opened towards the lowland. It swung gently on its rope harnessing.

Here, a number of shelters had been constructed for the visitors and there was much activity as horses were rubbed down, fed and watered, and cooking fires started. I tethered my own horse in the shade, left feed and water in clay dishes, and slipped away, skirting through the edge of the woods. Soon I came to the rock recesses that bordered the chasm where the voice of the oracle would speak. Sound, here, echoed hugely. The slightest whisper seemed as intimate at this distance as it would have been to the questioner by the cleft.

There was a smell of sulphur in the air, and of burned flesh. I could hear the shuffling and organising of the oracle's attendants. A low, moaning wind spoke from the bowels of the earth. The edge of the woodland was alive with silent, perching crows.

The visitors came and asked their questions. The voice of the oracle was gentle, that of an older woman, kindly, sometimes amusing. Wherever she was sitting, she was hidden from view. It was a hot day and the air was heavy. I drifted into slumber in the overhang, the scent of sulphur and thyme in my nostrils.

It was hours before I woke. Already the day was slipping towards evening, though still the crows sat in their thousands, silent and motionless on the canopy of the wood. The oracle was being consulted in the language of the Greeklanders, but with the accent of a northerner. I glanced round the rock. As I'd thought, this was the strange-looking *keltoi*.

'I have heard of an army gathering in the north,' he was saying. 'The talk is of a Great Quest, led by a man called Brennos. Am I wise to think of joining this army?'

The oracle was silent for a long time and the young man became restless. Only the gusting wind from the cave, with its suggestion of breathing, implied that the question was being considered.

Then the answer came.

'No harm, Orgetorix, but the harm of sword and spear will come to you if you join the Quest. But it will take you to the place where you were born, and you will have to make a dire decision.'

'What decision?'

'Unclear. Unclear. The torment of your dreams a hundred-fold.'

Now the silence was the *keltoi*'s. I could see him, standing in the circle of rocks before the narrow entrance to the world below. His arms were folded, his head down; he was deep in thought.

Orgetorix? A strong name. King of Killers!

He suddenly came to life again. 'I have more questions.'

'Ask them,' the oracle whispered, and I was surprised. This oracle was indulgent—or was indulging this particular visitor.

The question came: 'I know what my father did. A ghost showed me when I was a boy. I am aware of his betrayal. But I never knew his name. So I ask you: what was my father's name?'

'Rottenbones!'

Orgetorix hesitated. The word had been coldly, harshly whispered fom the oracle. His own breathing sounded angry, but he controlled the emotion, saying only, 'A terrible name. That is a terrible name. Now answer me truthfully.'

'Your father was a terrible man. Ask no more about him.'

'I demand to know his name.'

'Your demand is no more than smoke in a storm.'

'Then tell me: what was my mother's name?'

'Your mother was Medea. Daughter of Aeëtes, King of Colchis. She hid you from your father, very far away. The effort was very great. The loss was very great. She died in great pain.'

For a moment the words hung in my head like a strange dialect, familiar yet unfamiliar, almost recognisable, but elusive; not quite focused. Then they hit me with the power of a spear butt to the front of the head. The words rang.

Medea? Of Colchis?

How I managed to control my surprise I cannot answer. I'm sure I gasped out loud. The name resonated like a scream of anguish. Medea? Not possible!

There was something stranger than I could comprehend at work here. Whether game or coincidence I couldn't tell; but I was suddenly afraid, and that fear had no foundation, except that it came from my recognition that nothing occurring below me was *right*.

But . . . *Medea*? Now I recognised something in the young *keltoi*'s voice—that softness of tone that could so quickly turn commanding. Indeed, he sounded very like his father. Jason! Son of Aeson and the wise Alcimede.

Was it possible that this was one of Jason's sons?

He should have long since been in his grave.

Loose stones rolled from the ledge as I drew back to try to consider what I was witnessing. I thought I must have been discovered. The conversation by the speaking pit was interrupted for a moment, but then continued.

The *keltoi* asked, 'How far am I . . . how far from home?'

'Very far. You can never go back. There is no going back. You have lost your world.'

If son this was, which son? And where was the other?

'Is my father dead?' the young man asked quietly, and

there was an element of menace in the question.

'Long ago. You can never go back, Orgetorix. Only forward. And that is the end of your questioning.'

There was angry movement by the oracle, the sound of metal rattling. 'No. One more question.'

'No more questions. Your time here is finished.'

'One more! I offer my shield hand for one more question!' He sounded defiant.

I heard the sound of a sword being drawn. Glancing round the rock, I saw Orgetorix about to cut through his wrist.

'What in your life is worth a hand?' the oracle asked pointedly.

'A *brother* is worth a hand.'

Softly: 'Well, then. Save your hand.'

He sheathed the weapon. 'I remember my brother, but only as if in a dream. That was his nickname: "Little Dreamer". We were taken away together, from our home, with blood on our bodies. We were fostered. We grew up in a wild land in a fine fortress. We trained in arms together. And then I lost him. He disappeared like a shadow in the night. Where is my brother?'

The oracle was silent for a long time. Then the voice said quietly, 'He lives, now, between sea-swept walls. His name can be heard where the serpent lives. He rules in his world, though he doesn't know it. And that is all . . .'

'That's all? That's nothing!'

Frustrated now, the oracle hissed: 'Because you are lost, I have given you more than I should. Because you showed enterprise in finding this place, I have stayed with you longer than I should. But my time here is finished. And there is someone listening to us. And I am afraid for you.'

The young warrior backed away from the chasm, looking around the sanctuary, his hand on the hilt of his sword. But he failed to see the watcher in the cave. He left the oracle, reluctantly but now alert for attack. He entered the wood again, to return to his companions.

* * *

Medea!

That woman had been powerful to an extent I had never imagined. I had no doubt that what I had just witnessed was true. Displaced in time, this *was* Jason's eldest son, Thesokorus, calling himself Orgetorix, brother of 'Little Dreamer'. Her trickery, her sorcery, had bordered on the magnificent! It must certainly have killed her to have hidden her sons in so distant a world.

I had hardly known her, yet she had been at the centre of my life for those few years I had spent with Jason. A black veil, that glittering coat of bronze and gold, the rattling beads, the scurrying walk, the unearthly incantations, the smell of sacrificial blood and burning herbs . . . I had preferred to stay away from it. I had not interfered in the relationship between my lusty, adventurous friend and his stolen love.

My heart had broken for him, though, when she had killed his boys.

After the encounter at the oracle, I stayed in that Makedonian town for several days, thinking hard. Orgetorix and his horsemen had slipped away. I was surprised they had disappeared so completely, but despite my small effort, using a little charm, I could not find them. That was strange, but no matter. They were heading north, to join an army and participate in a great adventure.

By morning I had decided on a quest of my own: to also go north, but to the place I had long believed Argo had taken Jason for mutual burial. I had journeyed past that lake so many times. I had heard the local legends of the ship from the 'hot south', and the man aboard who screamed for his sons. But I had never looked any closer. I'd had no reason to. Now I would go there to see if the ship, who had so loved the man that she had chosen to stay with him, might have kept him warm.

And I found him! And now I had a frightening truth to convey to him.

'No amount of searching, no years of hunting,' I said to him, 'would have been sufficient to find your sons. Medea didn't hide them in the world as you knew it. Not on any island, however remote; or in the mountains, however far; or in caverns below the ground, however deep. She didn't take them to her home in Colchis, or to the barbarian north . . .'

Jason's gaze was gloomy but interested. 'Where, then?'

'She hid them in Time. In the future. She hid them *now*.'

'She summoned Cronos?'

'I don't know what she summoned. I hardly dare think about it.'

Jason stared at me. 'And when . . . when is now? *More* than twenty years?'

How would he react? It took me so long to find the words. Should I try to prepare him for the news, or just blurt it out? I thought it unlikely that he would believe me at first, so perhaps a quick answer and leave him to think about it.

'Seven hundred years!'

He stared at me as if the words meant nothing, only the slightest frown dimpling his forehead. Then just the merest shake of his head.

I went on, 'She couldn't have known how Argo would protect you through time as well. You've been at the bottom of this lake for so long that the world you know has changed beyond recognition. Perhaps I should have left you there . . . I'm suddenly frightened . . .' *that I've done the wrong thing,* I added to myself.

Still the silent stare.

'I'm sorry, Jason.'

Everything he had ever known, every town, every city, was either dust and ruin or lay buried beneath new walls. I'd watched them crumble. I'd seen the world change. Everything Jason had once depended on had been wiped away by the years and by invasion.

I told him what I could; answered his questions as best I could. If he was curious as to the circumstances of Medea's death, he kept the question close to his heart. When I had finished my account of his lost years, I murmured, 'Everything you loved is in its grave . . .'

His frown deepened. He leaned towards me and whispered, 'Except for my sons.'

'Yes. If the oracle is to be believed. Except for your sons.'

'And you,' he added hoarsely. 'Don't forget you.' His tired gaze was searching. 'You came to find me. You crossed half a world to find me. Why?'

I shook my head, alarmed by the question. Why indeed? All I could think to say was, 'Because I was happy then. On Argo. In Iolkos. And I knew where to find you. I know this lake. I've heard the man crying. I couldn't be sure, but I felt certain it was you. And after all, I had the time to find out, right or wrong.'

He thought about this answer, then turned away and stared at the fire, sinking slowly forward where he sat, his face in his hands, burying himself from the concerned gaze of the world around him.

After a while he got up and left the tent. I had been so pre-occupied with Jason that I'd failed to notice that both Niiv and Urtha had been listening to me, though neither would have understood our conversation. Niiv, nevertheless, was transparently curious, and quite delighted. Had I revealed something to her, not in words, but in a more silent language? I would have to be careful.

Urtha watched me curiously. 'He seems upset, your friend.'

'I've just told him how far he is from home.'

'That's enough to upset anybody,' Urtha grumbled. 'How far from home is he, exactly?'

'Put it this way, he can never go back.'

'You weren't very tactful, I think.'

'No. I don't suppose I was. He's been in that lake a long time, Urtha. He was once a great friend of mine. He got me out of a difficult situation, once. You wouldn't believe it, even if I told it to you as a story—'

'I've heard that before,' Urtha said with a smirk. 'It usually means there's not much of a story.'

'Well, maybe not. I know how *grotesque* you *keltoi* like your stories to be. But he did help me. Jason and I are tied by the sort of bond that you would understand well. He behaved like a monster to his family; his wife punished him horribly.'

Urtha visibly winced at the thought of that.

'All of which is in the past. The point is, for the last year I've dragged my poor horses across half the world to find Jason again, to bring him strange news—'

Urtha laughed quietly as he watched me. 'Yes. Strange friends you have: drowned at the bottom of lakes . . .'

'Just the one friend at the bottom of a lake. And now that I've found him, I'm beginning to wonder where that urge came from.'

'To raise him from the dead?'

'To raise him from the dead.'

'A debt of honour. A bond, you said.'

'Or someone using it to use me . . .'

Urtha laughed and drank from his flask. 'You've lost me there. I hope your stories are more coherent. Grotesque is fine. But we certainly approve of coherence. I'll ask again: how far is he from home?'

Niiv was annoyed that she couldn't understand, but I kept talking in Urtha's language. And I came to a decision and told him what I had told Jason, swearing him to silence, even if he didn't believe a word of what I'd said.

He listened impassively, then drank more liquor as he thought about my words.

'Seven hundred years? I know a valley where there's a tree that old. Covered with carvings. Very sacred place. The tree's falling apart, though. You've got a better bark, if you're telling the truth.'

'I told you, I don't lie.'

'And I'm starting to believe you. So my advice to you is, don't advertise your age too widely. Nor your skills. Enaaki and his water demons may be at the bottom of the lake in his palace of wood and bones, interested in nothing but entrails, but there are people in the camps around the edge, here, who would know only too well what to do with a clever man like you.'

'I'll take that advice as a gesture of friendship.'

'Yes, you must. Friendship is important. Because I'm keen to find out what to do with you myself!' He grinned broadly.

Freezing air gusted from the entrance to the tent as Jason ducked back into the warmth. He came over to the fire and dropped to a crouch, staring at Urtha, Niiv, then at me. 'Do they know?'

'I've told Urtha. I may tell Niiv, but she's dabbling in sorcery. I want to talk to her first.'

'Tell her,' Jason said. 'It makes no difference. We might well need her. We'll certainly need our friend here.'

'Be careful, Jason,' I counselled. 'You are so far out of your time. So far away from your world.'

He rose from his crouch, towering over me, his eyes ablaze, but with challenge and hope, not anger. All he said was, 'I don't care about that! Why should I? When we ventured for the fleece in our youth, when we stole the treasures and the oracle from Colchis, when we fled from our pursuers across the sea and into the marshes, and along unknown rivers, through gorges and dark forests, through lands haunted by the worst of *nightmares*, didn't we then live in worlds that meant nothing to us? Well, didn't we? Answer me!'

'Yes.'

He had referred to Medea as 'the oracle'. I wondered if he was burning to know her fate, or blocking all thought of her from his mind.

'Yes!' he went on. 'We lived by our wits, Antiokus, remember? And by our swords, and by our ship . . . and by the whim of the goddess!'

He was *alive* again! He paced around the tent, vibrant and quick in movement and thought.

'We had no idea where we were, or where we were going in. We just rowed Argo against the flow of dark water, carried her over land when we had to, hoping we were heading for home.'

'I remember.'

'I'm glad you remember. So believe me when I say this!' He leaned down close to me, speaking like a man reborn in faith. 'All my life I have accepted that my world is the world I *live* in! I don't care about time. I don't care about place. I'm here! *This* is my world, now, Antiokus. New, strange, all to be discovered. And, I hope, in daylight! And if what you say is true, at least one of my sons is living in this world as well! I can find him again. It is this sort of challenge I was born for. What better reason, my enchanter friend, for shaking off the ice, rebuilding our ship, and sailing south to the sun? Eh?'

'I can think of no better reason, Jason.'

'Good. Good!' I stood and he embraced me, grinning. 'And we can recruit oarsmen from around this lake, and as we journey. Go to sleep and dream. *Merlin*. Dream well. I'll do the same. When we wake, we'll haul Argo to dry land. And bring her back to life as well!'

PART TWO

—

The Spirit of the Ship

CHAPTER SIX

—

The Spirit of the Ship

I had never forgotten Argo's beauty. Even now, as she lay listless on the lakeside, rotting, weed-wracked, her slender hull streaked with bright colour and images of the gods and elementals of Jason's Greek Land, she was wonderful to witness. There was a sleekness about her despite the broken stubs of the branches that had sprung from her, a flowing shape to the hull from the sharp prow to the elegant curve of her stern, rising to the split and quiet-eyed wooden image of Hera. She almost shuddered when touched, a memory of life, and seemed to whisper as she lay on the hard ground, propped up and tethered.

And she was whispering: build me back. Build me better. Build me for the quest. I've been dying too long.

I had thought the ship had died on surfacing from Enaaki's swift-toothed realm, but walking round her, torch held high, I felt the final spark of life still glowing, the last guardian holding on as she had held on for nearly a thousand years.

*   *   *

Now that the sun was showing herself, however fleetingly, I could measure days again. And for two short days and their still-long nights Jason knelt before the prow of Argo and spoke to her in the silence of his soul. On the third day he dug a deep pit, filled it with kindling and logs, then called for Niiv's uncle, Lemanku, a carpenter and boat-builder. He had offered his skills to Jason; Jouhkan, too, had offered to help. Lemanku cut through the faded effigy of Hera and brought the sightless goddess to the pit. Jason stood the head above the logs then killed a reindeer calf with his bare hands, strangling the creature in front of the gathered red-cloaked Pohjoli, who watched with great interest. They waved their torches and sang short bursts of warbling, high-pitched song to show their approval as the sacrifice progressed.

Hacking off the head of the beast, Jason tossed it on to the logs, then set light to the kindling.

Soon a great fire roared from the pit.

Working with a strange frenzy, Jason jointed the dead animal and skewered the pieces on stakes across the fire. Niiv helped him keep the fire burning.

When the head was charred to the bone, he poured a flask of the heady, blinding local drink on top of it. The flames rose and turned blue, flickering eerily for several minutes.

When everything was done, and the embers smouldered, the roasted flesh sweet on the air, Jason stood before Argo.

'Goodbye, Old Ship. Goodbye, Old Swan. But now I will see you put on flower again. I will see leaf spring from your deck. New life to this great old ship. I loved you once, Argo, when you were guided by Hera, great-hearted Hera. I will love you again with a new guardian spirit. I promise this with my life!'

Then he turned to Lemanku and Jouhkan and said, 'Now for your part in this. Break her down to the inner ribs and inner ship. But stop there. We start again from there. Don't touch anything of the old ship inside.'

His words surprised me. This was the first time Jason had ever referred to the 'old ship inside'. I had sailed with him on an adventure that had lasted years, had cost lives and taken us to the strangest lands, had caused the death of his sons (or so he'd thought) and condemned him to twenty years of misery. He had never once mentioned that he also knew what I had intuited when I had first come aboard his Argo, in Iolkos, lifetimes ago, shortly before she was launched for Colchis and the fleece . . .

I had seen nothing of the construction of Argo, those centuries ago in Greek Land, when Jason had first ordered it and the boat-builder Argos had emerged from the night and nowhere and offered his services. By the time my journey round the Path brought me to Pagasae, north of Iolkos, the ship was already on the slipway and ready for launching. The silent boat-builder had finished his work; the rotten and ancient hulk that always lay at Argo's heart had been encased in fine new wood and bright paint, decorated with symbols of sea and sky and the protecting gods. Jason himself had gone to Zeus's oracle at Dodona and cut a branch from the sacred oak for Argo's new keel.

I followed the crowd—most of whom had gathered to see the band of heroes that Jason had summoned as his sailors—and on impulse asked the bright-eyed young man who was making the dedication to Hera (Jason himself) if he had need of an enchanter on the vessel.

'No need at all,' he replied, not moving his open hands from the smoke that drifted from the offering. He didn't even look my way.

'I've come from the Orkades, through Hyperborea and western Illyria. It's blighted country. Day has turned into night, the wind has turned into fire and the ancestral dead are walking from their tombs. I could do with some new friends. I also tell a good story.'

Though not on this occasion; the land to the north and west *was* blighted, and I had fled the terror, not wanting to stay and try to understand its cause.

'A storyteller?' Now he glanced at me, thought for a moment, then grinned. 'Why not? It would compensate for Heracles talking about himself all the time. Can you use an oar?'

'For rowing and fighting, yes. Any other uses I can learn. I can also hold on to ropes, rudders and men retching in a storm . . .'

'There'll be a few of those!'

'And I know enough to piss downwind in a gale—'

'An educated man! Try to teach Heracles the habit, would you?'

'—and how to navigate in thick cloud. I also speak more languages than most men have ever heard of, and can understand new ones within half a day.'

'We're not short of babble-speakers.' Did he mean translators? 'And we'll need no more than three languages on this voyage: my commands, your responses and songs in any tongue you like. But as long as you can row, and if you really can navigate in cloud . . . you can navigate in *cloud*?'

'There's a trick to it.'

'I have a wave-reader and a wind-reader, but a cloud-reader? That trick I'll allow. And as long as you keep all other sorcery to yourself, you're welcome. And I mean what I say. *All* other tricks. I don't want them on board. Is that clear?'

'Very clear,' I agreed, though his refusal to countenance the use of charm and enchantment puzzled me; most sailors would have sacrificed dearly for such talents on their decks. Jason, of course, was no mere sailor, and he had a fussy and fractious guardian watching him from high Olympus.

'We sail with the next tide,' he added. 'Come aboard when you're ready. No horses, though. Not live ones, at least. And then only their haunches.'

So I sold my two horses—at least I wouldn't know their fate—and joined the rank of argonauts, their only greeting being to present me with a long pole of ash and instruct me on how to fashion my oar.

A wan and nervy, though very pleasant young man called Hylas helped me. Working with wood was not one of my strengths. Hylas was Heracles' servant and long-suffering lover. A young man of good humour and intellectual finesse, he was clearly exasperated with the relationship. Heracles was faithful to a fault to the youth, which by other accounts was a courtesy he did not extend to his female consorts; but Hylas, whilst acknowledging the big man's kindnesses, was at breaking point, not just with the demands upon his body, but with his master's monstrous self-centredness.

'He'll do anything, go anywhere, for fame. He'll accept any challenge for self-aggrandisement. He ignores the gods at his whim, and argues with them all the time. He calls himself the "sower of seed and future song". Can you believe that? He has forty sons, as many daughters, all of them bastards, and left each of them with an account of his deeds and heroisms to date, with instructions that they should spread the stories to the four quarters of the world just as soon as they can walk and talk! He's only here to help Jason find this sacred golden fleece because some god or other whispered that this particular quest might be the best remembered beyond his days. It would be unthinkable not to be a part of it, therefore. After all, who will remember the rest of the crew?'

He fell silent. Brooding.

'Ego . . . ergo, Argo, eh?' I suggested with a smile.

Hylas laughed, the mood of desperation broken. I was surprised, indeed impressed, that he had understood the western dialect of the simple joke.

'Something like that,' he agreed. 'Something like that. But I tell you, Antiokus, on my life: at the first opportunity, the first landfall, I'm making good my escape. If I seem to have deserted Jason, it will not have been through any lack of courage for the quest. Will you remember that? I feel I can trust you. This is no life I'm leading . . . my dreams are filled with wonders, visions, and strange speech—and I come close to understanding them all! I need to find them for myself. I am being directed. But how can I explore the world the gods have granted me when I'm roped to an ox-balled man-boar who wears nothing but a cloak made from the pelts of wildcats, and shits as he walks along because he says it saves time on his journeys?'

'A very good question,' I reassured Hylas. 'A good question several times over, in fact.'

Hylas's dreams were his gate to a broader, deeper world than that of the mountains and valleys of his own home. He had the inbuilt talent to digest strangeness and turn it into the familiar. He was a natural interpreter. And though he was by no means alone in this ability—Jason's earlier point to me— he was unusual in being tied by the heart to a man, an adventurer, a 'gods-favoured'—Heracles—whose deeds were beginning to be known even as far as Hyperborea.

'I'll assist you,' I added. 'Just ask me for help when you need it. But you must promise never to reveal to anyone what I do for you, or how I did it. Should I do it.'

'On my shield!' the youth whispered with earnest gratitude, and a little curiosity which soon faded behind a smile of relief. 'You've given me some hope, Antiokus. A little courage too. Something to nurture. Good for the heart. Thank you! You're shaving the wood too shallow, by the way. At this rate it'll take until winter. Here, give the oar to me. I'll do it for you.'

He ran from the ship when we moored on the Cianian coast, near Mount Arganthon, a full month later when the voyage was well under way, and I tricked Heracles into thinking his young companion had been taken and drowned by nymphs from a pool in the woods. The pool was small and sweet and the nymphs enticing, but they were wholly innocent of any murder.

They fled down to the mud when Heracles stabbed the pool with his spear a thousand times, screaming abuse. He drank a flagon of vinegar and pissed and puked into the savaged waters. He left the Argo immediately after that, to wander aimlessly for a while, ignoring the gods as usual, his heart broken.

When he had gone, Hylas crept back on board from his hiding place and we put him ashore some days later at the mouth of the river Acheron, at his own request. After that, I don't know what happened to him. But I missed his bright spirit and good humour.

That was later, after Argo had begun her quest. But at the dockside in Pagasae, with my own oar now finished by the same skilful youth, marked with my name and added to the wood pile ready to be loaded, I ascended the ramp to inspect the ship itself. And quickly realised that this was no ordinary vessel. There was nothing that I could identify, and I was not prepared to open my soul to a deeper understanding, but below the deck, somewhere to the fore, there was an older heart than the massive oak beam that had been shaped to form her keel.

I ducked down into the bilges, started to move forward, and was *warned away*! I could think of it in no other terms than that. Not a voice, not a vision, just the most intense feeling that I was entering a place that was not just private or out of bounds, but was *forbidden*.

Mystified, thrilled, I decided to go back on to land, intending to find Argos, the shipwright who had constructed this galley, and ask him about his creation. But as if she sensed my curiosity, and had been made angry by my presence, Argo began to strain at the rope tethers. Her hull groaned, the wooden tenons holding her fast above the slipway began to pull from the hard earth, the ropes singing with the strain. The ship twisted and slid about on the mud ramp, like a throat-cut pig thrashing in its own blood. I clutched the housing for the mast with all my strength, expecting at any moment to be pitched over the side. Argo bucked and protested below my feet.

Launch me, she seemed to be saying. *Test me in the water. Hurry!*

The air was filled with a sound like Furies screaming.

Jason grabbed a double-bladed axe from one of his colleagues, called to Heracles to do the same, stepped swiftly forward and shouted: 'The rest of you, into the water. You! Cloud navigator! Throw down the scaling nets!'

As the argonauts stripped to the skin and raced for the sea, Heracles and Jason each hacked at the retaining ropes, cutting through in unison.

Released, Argo streaked down the ramp, stern-first into the harbour water, plunging deep below the surface, almost drowning me. When she came up she shuddered, an animal refreshing itself after a cold swim. I flung down the coiled net ladders, two to a side, then went to the prow, staring down at the shouting men who swam vigorously towards us. Who they were, where they had come from, what skills they possessed, all of this was alien to me at this time, but they circled Argo, laughing, as if capturing a bull, and though the ship turned under her own control, facing each cheering hero in turn, she stayed in the circle, calmed herself, then allowed the men to haul themselves aboard.

Heracles followed them, dragging a dozen oars through the harbour waters, lifting them two at a time to the waiting hands of the crew. Six oars each side—she would be rowed by twenty on the open sea—we took the galley gently back to the harbour side, where we tethered her again and started to load supplies.

'What a ship!' a delighted and muddy Jason cried as he came aboard by jumping from the quay. 'With vigour like this in her keel, we'll make the haven at Colchis in one night's dream! Never mind three months! The fleece is closer than we think.'

Events were to prove otherwise, of course, as I have written elsewhere.

Argo was not one ship, but many, and a fragment of each, even the oldest, was locked in the prow, the ship's heart, hidden in the slender double hull. Hera had been only the latest in a long line of guardians of this Otherworldly vessel. To crouch in her prow was to feel the flow of rivers and seas that had persisted through time, to smell old wood, old leather, old ropes, shaped and stretched into vessels that had drifted, sailed, rowed and ploughed beyond the known worlds of their builders.

So much life in one cold hulk.

Now, lifetimes later, the skin was ripped from the rotting remnant of that proud and vigorous ship. In the frost-sheened, rosy dawn, and under Jason's supervision, Lemanku tore away the planks of the hull to expose part of the hidden heart of Argo. I watched in fascination as the ship-shaped cage of branches was revealed, a tangled network of growth from the old oak that had been laid by Argos, filling the hull like veins. The growth had *split* the planking, but held it together too, in a protecting embrace.

Lemanku was stunned by what his work was uncovering. He showed me how the wood was not just of oak, but of several types of tree: elm and birch and beech, though these elements were confined towards the prow.

Jason's instructions were clear:

'Cut her back to within a man's length of the block of wood that rises into the prow.'

He was pruning the Argo!

'Lay the new keel, then build out from there; enclose the prow area at the end.'

Lemanku said, 'This ship was constructed in a way I've never seen. Very primitive.'

Jason asked him what he meant, and Lemanku showed how each plank had been placed edge to edge along the hull, crudely lashed with rope, then sealed with black tar, or something similar.

'I'm surprised this ship didn't break up in the first storm.'

'But she *didn't* break up in the first storm. Nor any other storm. I sailed her along forty rivers, through water that was foaming white, sometimes so close to freezing solid that blocks of ice struck her left and right. I sailed Argo in the shadow of moving mountains, at the edge of thrashing forests, and she never failed me. How can you can build her stronger?'

'I didn't say I could build her stronger,' Lemanku said evenly. 'Just better. I can build her to carry more, and sail faster.'

Without pause, without thanks, Jason said, 'I like the sound of that. How many men do you need?'

'Experienced ship builders: ten. Iron workers: twenty. Charcoal burners: five . . .' The list went on. 'I can raise most of them.'

'I'll get the rest for you,' Jason said, glancing at me. 'You and I together, Antiokus? A little recruiting?'

'We'd better get started. As dawn grows brighter by the day, this lake will be left alone for half a year. Everybody leaves.'

Lemanku demonstrated how the planks could be *overlapped* then nailed together with iron to create a stronger, more flexible hull. This was Jason's first encounter with the hard metal. He watched the process of forging and tempering with fascination. The nails were made long, thick and crude, ready to be battened off, flattened out on the inner side of the hull.

Even so, he wanted rope lashing. Lemanku was puzzled, but Jason was insistent.

'I was taught that to be secure at sea the rope that holds a ship together should weigh more than the men who sail her.'

'Then you'll need more ballast,' Lemanku countered. 'The rope will soak up water and make the ship top-heavy.'

'Are your ropes made of sponges, then? I'll have to trust you. The ballast will be in skin bags. We can throw it out and recruit it whenever we pass a rocky beach! But we need the ropes. They'll hold Argo together not just in a storm, but when we *overland* her. To haul a ship like this uphill, through forest, you have to hold her in a cradle. A cradle of rope. Haul her from the front and you'll strip the keel!'

'I know that,' Lemanku retorted proudly. 'I've built boats all my life. I've hauled them over ice and over rock. I know how to brace the keel, and broaden it, and grease the log rollers with fish gut, fat and liver. It's been my business all my life. You intend to *haul* the ship? Where?'

'I don't know where. But every river has its shallows, and every sea gets blocked by land. It's a precaution. Fish guts on the rollers?'

'Eases the passage.'

'I believe you. Between us we'll build a wonderful vessel. Just give me my ropes!'

Lemanku laughed out loud. The two men set out their plan for building new flesh on Argo's bones, then Jason left the shipwright to his work.

*   *   *

While Lemanku continued to prune the wreck, Jason, Jouhkan and myself borrowed his shallow skiff and sailed steadily around the edge of the lake, in search of a new crew to row new Argo when she was complete. We had already recruited Urtha and his four companions, though there was a small price to pay: first we would row to Urtha's homeland so that he could see his family once again, and Borovos and Cucallos could visit their own clan. This was only a short detour from the route back to Greek Land. In exchange, Urtha would lend Jason five of his *uthiin* warriors, all of whom, he was sure, would be eager for the adventure, the search for Orgetorix. Fighters, marksmen and experts in everything—like all *keltoi*, Urtha added—they would be invaluable.

Jason agreed. For the moment, though, we were short of hands.

Most of the occupants of the winter settlements had constructed crude jetties, mooring places among the reeds or stretching from the muddy shore that were now exposed as the ice melted. High fences or earth banks protected the tents and rough shelters from unwelcome visitors. Torches burned everywhere. Hounds of several breeds strained and howled at the leash.

Jason had borrowed a bronze horn from Urtha and used it to announce not just our arrival, but the fact that we wished to trade. Twice we were greeted with such hostility and distrust that we made a circumspect retreat, but five times we landed and shared the food and drink of the motley visitors to the lake of the Screaming Ship.

Our task was to recruit at least twenty men or women capable of using, or learning to use, an oar. Twenty argonauts willing to abandon their business in the north and sail blindly south again.

Jason now demonstrated his tactful way with words, his teasing way with story. He drank, joked, flattered and mocked. He was far older than most of the men around whose fires he sat, but he was so quick, so deft with a wooden blade, that in the mock challenges he often called for himself, he either won by a ruse, or lost in a flurry of limbs and a burst of laughter.

His account of Argo's first voyage to Colchis and back was unrecognisable to someone who had been there. Rocks had crashed together a hand's width from our stern; the fleece, once plucked from its heavily guarded sanctuary, had been pursued by warriors who grew in seconds from the scattered teeth of snakes; whole forests had pursued us on flailing roots along a great river that flowed from snow-capped mountains in a land populated by cannibal women and tree-wielding apes clad in the skins and bones of their wives' victims.

I think he was referring to the river Daan, and the people at its headwaters had been hospitable and friendly, helping us drag Argo across the land bridge between two rivers, so that we could sail south again, to the warm seas off Liguria and its haunted islands.

But he whetted their appetites for adventure. And he read his audience better than I could ever have done; he knew instinctively, it seemed, when to win approval by insult and when by challenge.

'One in every two of the bravest aboard Argo will die. Hold that in your heads as you decide whether to join me. Don't come easily to me. If you do that, I'll kill you myself!

'I'll say it again: one in every two of the strongest will fail at some point. One in every two of the swiftest will be run down by creatures out of our nightmares. One in every two of the wisest will be tangled in a knot of deceit and seduction that will trap them for ever. The risk is that great! I know this! I've taken the risk before, and on that occasion survived . . .

'As then, so now! Believe me! But the reward will be greater for those of us who survive.'

And when asked what we would be seeking, he said, 'My eldest son.'

'And how will searching for your eldest son reward us?'

'Because of the opportunities along the way. Until you see bright-hulled Argo you won't understand, and she is being built at this moment, over there, where you see the glow of the forge in the night. Argo is like you or me, always looking for trouble; she has a nose—if a ship may have a nose—for the mysteries that lie concealed in the world that seems so familiar and ordinary to us. She has been to the Otherworld and back . . . and so have I . . .'

He was asked, 'When did you lose your sons?'

'A lifetime ago. They were taken from me by a woman who had been vomited from the mouth of Hel herself. No woman would recognise that creature as one of her own kind. No man could touch her skin and not realise she was long dead, kept alive only by hate and malice. *Medea.* Say the name and shudder. *Medea.* Killer of brothers. Killer of kings. Queen of Tricksters. But long in her tomb, now, and you should be grateful for that.'

CHAPTER SEVEN

—

Recruitment

Torchlight flickering on the black lake signalled the arrival of the first new argonauts. Two small boats were rowed towards us through the broken ice, the moan of a horn announcing our first recruits as from the settlement of the Germanii, stocky men with flaxen hair and beards, who wore heavy cloaks of bear and wolf fur against the cold. They had been cautious of Jason, when he had told them of the adventure to come. They had not seemed impressed by his story; indeed, they had seemed indifferent to the idea of the spoils and hoards that might be taken along the way.

What intrigued them, it seemed, was that they had heard of 'speaking caves' which could tell men's fates. They would journey in search of such an oracle, then (and would have no difficulty finding one: 'speaking caves' scattered the parched, scrubby hills of the land of Jason's birth).

They were strong. Our three recruits were Gutthas, Erdzwulf and Gebrinagoth.

Over the nights, other new argonauts drifted in, most by boat, some by foot, one by horse.

A young pair of adventurers, Conan and Gwyrion of the Cymbrii, crossed the dangerous lake in a shallow skiff. They were subdued, thin and hungry, poorly dressed for the climate. Indeed, their clothing of colourful check-patterned trousers and cloak, and woollen shirts, was more suitable for a summer raid in the Southlands. Each had a golden-handled knife and a small round shield with the bearded, wild-haired features of Llew beaten in gold upon it.

Jason welcomed them, urged them to fatten up, to get some strength (even their beards were wispy!), and asked them why they had ventured this far north.

They hadn't intended to, they explained. For pure devilry, set a challenge during a feast in their father's hall, they had stolen Llew's famous bronze and wicker chariot, pulled by its two fine black mares, and equipped with throwing spears that always returned to the hand that had thrown them. Having stolen the chariot from its garage, they whipped the horses into a gallop and rode by moonlight round Llew's famous, high-walled *dun*.

But the horses never tired. They galloped on and nothing the boys could do could stop the wild ride. Over hill, through forest, over misting sea and frozen river, the chariot had been drawn north, finally throwing the young thieves out and plunging through the ice and into the lake. For a long time they had been left to their own devices. That they had survived, and even stolen a skiff, suggested that they could make their devices work.

They had learned a lesson. Now they wanted to go south. And home. Jason accepted them willingly.

The Cymbrii had learned of Jason and his new Argo from their neighbours by the lake, Volkas, dark-haired warriors who wore thin plates of iron over their chests and thighs, and rattled bone knives against them to signal pleasure or irritation. The Volkas, too, had been intrigued by Jason's quest. They were led by a man called Michovar. They came by foot, running, packs on backs, spears held in brawny hands, iron protection glinting. The Volkas agreed to row with us as far as their homeland, by whatever route we took. That was their reason for coming with us; they had been too long away from home, and those among them who knew about boats had died during the winter.

Our numbers, recruited, it seemed, from the lost and lonely, were increasing. With Cathabach and Manandoun from Urtha's *uthiin* horsemen, and his neighbours Borovos and Cucallos, we now numbered at least twelve, and possibly thirteen, since Lemanku was keen to join us. His age worried Jason. I pointed out that Jason was older than the boat-builder. Jason suggested that some men aged better than others, and Lemanku's taste for cloudberry wine had not helped him. But a boat-builder aboard a boat on a long and potentially shattering journey would be a useful addition.

Lemanku's oar was almost certainly guaranteed.

Soon after this, the wailing and whining of three dying wildcats announced the arrival of Elkavar from Hibernia. He had come through the woods and stood silently as the droning from below his arms died away. Urtha was delighted to see him.

'Music at last! You'll be a guest at my table. Or at least, what passes for a table in this snowball on a cow's backside of a country . . . '

Urtha had long since become impatient with the Pohjolan vocal wails and whines that constituted song. The young man's leather air-pouch and three pipes, a musical instrument played by pumping his elbows, sounded much the same to me, but clearly not to Urtha and the other *keltoi*.

'I'm sorry to startle you,' the new arrival said in a soft and awkward dialect of Urtha's language, 'but in the country where I come from you quickly learn to mind your Ps and Qs. When I see men from Ghostland, and remember my part in the raid at Dun Eimros not so long ago, where I won in combat against the champion of the king Keinodunos—a hard match that was, a hard head to steal—well, when I see such as yourselves, I can't be sure of my welcome.'

Ghostland was close to Urtha's territory, and to Hibernians such as Elkavar would have seemed to encompass the whole of the land, though in fact it was inaccessible except to the dead. Neither Urtha's group, nor I, knew of the skirmish or the king referred to, but none of us were strangers to raiding and this man was clearly remembering a coastal attack, and its prompt and bloody settlement.

'If that bag of pipes can raise our spirits when you play them,' Jason said through Urtha, 'then you're more than welcome.' I suppose he was thinking of Orpheus and his exquisite harpsong.

'The way I play them will more likely raise the dead,' the young man retorted with a grin. 'But it looks as if you could use them anyway. The dead, I mean. That's a big ship for so few pairs of hands.'

'You're welcome to add yours,' Jason replied.

'Then add them I shall. I'm Elkavar. I know how to use an oar and I can throw a spear from one hilltop to another using only my right foot. For some reason, we're trained to do that sort of thing in my country, though I'm glad to say I've never had to resort to it.'

He was not tall and not heavy in build and he looked hungry, his face quite drawn. His russet hair was cut short. He had a ready smile, but a quick and careful look in his eyes, both hunted and curious.

When he had settled by the fire, and eaten a little meat, he asked a strange question. 'Is there anybody here who can tell me where I am? I know that I'm north—I recognise the bright patterns of some stars—the Elk, there, and Deirdre's breasts. But some have vanished. I've travelled further under the sky than I knew was possible. And besides, this cold land can only be north. When we raid to the north it's always cold and wet. I don't know why we bother, really. South is warm and misty, and there's always good wine and good cheese. But this endless night!' He looked at Jason. 'So I'll ask again. Where am I?'

Jason laughed, 'I'm not the best qualified to answer that question. You'd better ask Merlin. He can work enchantment, but is too lazy to do so. As a matter of interest, though, how did you get here?'

'Well, I'm not the best qualified to answer *that*,' Elkavar replied with a weary laugh. But he gave us an account of what he knew.

He had been fleeing from a failed raid in his own land. Running south towards his own tribal territory, pursued by five fleet-footed men, he had managed to stay ahead of them, keeping to rough woodland and shallow rivers. Five days after the running had begun he had passed his clan-marked boundary and rested among the tree-covered hills of the dead, the mounds of earth that concealed the roads and tracks that led *under* the world.

Cheered by his escape he had indulged himself in a song.

'Just the one, and not even a song of triumph! Just of joy to be home. Sometimes I wonder if I have the sense in my head of a goose at winter's start, still honking as the knives are sharpened.'

The wailing and whining of dying wildcats had given away his place of hiding.

'All the silent hills have small entrances to the hidden roads,' he went on. 'When the bastards came out of the night at me, I had little choice but to dive in and crawl for my life. I crawled for ages before I was able to stand. Then I stood and walked, and kept on walking, and I was thinking: this has to come out *somewhere* in the country! But I kept walking, always in twilight, no stars, no sign of life, nothing but the tunnel and the dangling roots of the forest above—and then I came out by this freezing lake. When I tried to go back into the cave—somewhere over there—it was just a cave. And I recognise some of the stars, but I'm north! Some of my stars are missing.'

'We're sailing south,' Jason said. 'We'll get your stars back for you.'

'Well, I thank you for that. And I've heard you're sailing in search of your son. I'll stay with you until you do. Anything, just so long as I'm south again.'

Jason took me aside.

'Could this cave of his be useful? Should we explore it?'

'We can't take the ship through. And if Elkavar himself couldn't return, then I doubt any of the rest of us could.'

'You, perhaps.'

I told him that I knew of several such underways along the path I walked, dark roads that connected lands that were far apart. But like so much else in my world and his, those silent roads frightened me and I avoided them deliberately.

Our pairs of hands increased as the finishing flourishes of paint and shield were put on Argo.

By foot came Tairon of Crete, frozen and miserable, his travelling companions long since in their icy graves. He shared Elkavar's enthusiasm for returning to the warm south. He could offer weak rowing but strong bowing; his bow was small and shaped from horn, but when he demonstrated its use I was reminded of Odysseus, who had shot an arrow through a line of axe-rings before slaying his wife's oppressors.

Tairon was the eldest son of one of his island's oldest families. He had come north in search of the clay tablets carved by Daedalus, which showed the true pattern and keys to the labyrinth built to imprison the Minotaur. The world to which Tairon belonged was older, even, than Jason's.

If Tairon was immortal, however, he gave no sign of it, and when I used a little of my charm to see into his heart there was only youthfulness and that clumsy curiosity that condemns all men to quest beyond their abilities.

Tairon would be a man to watch; confusing and intriguing in equal measure, but for the moment simply eager to sail south.

The last to arrive at this time was a youthful Scythian, by all the signs younger than he was pretending, from his soft voice to his small hands. His name was Ullan. I couldn't remember Ullan from our recruiting circuit of the lake, and something was defying my wits at that moment. His face was painted black because of the loss of his companion, he advised us, during the foul, freezing winter, and he was robed and cowled in a heavy cape, also black. He declined, for the moment, to say why he had come to the Screaming Lake.

Jason was unsure about him.

'An ancestor of mine sailed with you to Colchis in search of the fleece, many hundreds of years ago,' the youth said.

'Which one?'

'You knew her as Atalanta. She hid her true nature from you, at the time, her true homeland. It would have been dangerous for her, otherwise. You were at war with her country.'

'I remember her,' Jason said. 'She went ashore with Hylas at the mouth of the Acheron, soon after Heracles deserted us, looking for the boy. She didn't return. She didn't see the fleece. She didn't take part in the fight at the end.'

'She was going home. She was hitching a ride. As many of your new argonauts will do, she simply stepped into your life, then out of it. But she never stopped talking about the time she'd spent aboard this Argo. I would like to step aboard for a while.'

'And your family has remembered this for more generations than I can imagine?' Jason was sceptical.

'Where I come from,' Ullan said pointedly, 'there's not a great deal to talk about. A good story lasts. Am I to sail with you?'

'You look skinny.'

'We can't all be as strong as Heracles, and slim Hylas helped pull his weight, didn't he? And Tisaminas wasn't exactly the best at getting the blade *into* the water, rather than just slapping its surface. So the story goes.'

'Yes,' Jason said, clearly impressed at the remembered detail. 'Yes, it's true. He was a good friend but a hopeless oarsman. Do you have any specialities?'

Ullan smiled. 'I can move unseen and unheard through the wildest wood: and bring you supper.'

'A hunter.'

'Am I to come aboard?'

'You are.'

'Are you sure?'

'I'm sure.'

'Then it's "huntress". My name's Ullanna.' She pulled

back her hood and blew Jason a cheeky kiss. 'Just get me south.'

Jason laughed. 'With pleasure. There's nowhere else to go!'

The only arrival by horse was a Dacian of great stature, a man as old as Jason, his beard a nest of grey, edged with black. He dismounted, leading his horse to where Argo was propped, torchlit and half built. He slapped the unfinished hull.

'Is there room on this ship for a horse?' he demanded in Jason's language.

'What can the horse do?' Jason asked.

The Dacian laughed dismissively. 'What can he do? He can gallop, turn on the spot, show fearlessness in battle. He's faithful to his master, can carry a great weight . . . without complaint. He eats from the land, minds his own business, makes dung, makes a *lot* of dung . . . which is useful. Isn't it? Some think so, at least. In short, I love this horse.' He slapped the animal's broad flank. 'I certainly won't go without him.'

'What else can he do?'

The Dacian glanced at Jason, then looked at his steed again, stroking the dark mane. 'What else can he do? That's not enough? Well, he's warm at night. I can vouch for that. Yes. Very warm. Even in the worst snow, lost on a mountainside, you won't be cold curled up against his back. And there's room for a lot of men against my proud horse. A very warm beast!'

More affectionate stroking.

'What else can he do?' Jason persisted.

The Dacian looked irritated. After a long pause he asked quietly, 'What else did you have in mind?'

'Can he cook? Can he row? Can he sing to keep up our spirits as he gallops? Can he perform magic?'

The horseman stared impassively at Jason for a moment, then said dryly, 'I have no idea. It never occurred to me to ask him. I'd hoped strength, warmth and copious dung-making would be enough.'

'Can he placate Poseidon?'

'Poseidon? What's Poseidon?'

'Sea-god. Bad news when he's in a temper. Big waves. Broken ships.'

'Now that you mention it,' the tall man said thoughtfully, 'he's a strong swimmer.'

'We don't need swimmers, we need oarsmen.'

The Dacian's stare was withering. 'He's a horse. He has no fingers. But is that a coil of rope I see? May I use it?'

Without waiting for an answer he went to where bales of rope were stacked, ready for lashing the new Argo's timbers. He tied two lengths around a thick-trunked and deep-rooted tree at the edgewood, then ran it back to his horse, twining the cord crudely around the beast's shoulders. Turning the horse to face the lake he slapped its haunches.

'Go for a swim.'

The animal cantered to the lake's edge, then stepped carefully through the icy shallows, soon reaching its depth and beginning to strike at the water. It took the full tension of the rope and at that moment I expected to see the animal stop and struggle back to the bank, but it kept on swimming, and behind us the tall tree creaked, bent, complained, groaned, then uprooted, crashed down, was dragged over the ground, its branches scattering us and whipping the side of Argo as it went.

The Dacian called to his horse, which turned for the shore.

Jason stared at the fallen tree, then nodded to the other man.

'We'll make room for the horse.'

'Good. He's called Ruvio. My name's Rubobostes. I'm pretty useful too.'

Blush, Spark and Gleam were in the past; with Tree Fire the lake had cracked and begun its melt. Now the Opening Eye watched us mistily, the sun rising, half visible, semi-cyclopean and seemingly sleepy, for a prolonged period of every day.

'Kainohooki has kicked away the door of his winter tomb,'

the mothers told their children. 'He has slept for so long, digesting his last meal, now he's lighting his farts to brighten the day. He has bear to hunt, reindeer to tame, fish to catch, and *enniki voytazi* to spear, hang up and dry out for the witches to use. Kainohooki is a friend.'

I'd heard it all before. True, the shores of the lake, and the melting ponds, began to smell rank, the first outsurge of trapped stink from the long winter.

I'd seen such marsh odour catch fire and burn with shocking, tragic results—boats burned to cinders as they were being constructed on muddy slipways, heron-hunters roasted alive as they lurked in the rushes, waiting for their prey, though this tended to occur more during the high summer on the river plains—so I felt a slight relief that only Kainohooki, and not the Pohjoli themselves, indulged in sparking their winter emissions.

Life came back to Argo suddenly and unexpectedly, when the spark of the new sun was at its brightest.

Lemanku and two others were working inside the hull. The new keel had been laid, a fine piece of Pohjolan birch, beautifully carved and trimmed, part of it hollowed to contain the stub of the old Dodonian oak whose strength had taken Jason on his earlier voyage. Lemanku had gone to the spirit grove of Mielikki herself, the Lady of the Forest, and after a long ceremony, and the involvement of much drumming and singing, had cut down one of the tall ancestor birches. Mielikki would be our new protectress.

Jason was somewhere at a distance, still recruiting, and I was helping the Dacian shape an oar. Fire burned around us, four dogs were playing noisy chase with each other, and the ringing of metal being forged was a steady, ruthless aggravation to the ears.

Everything stopped, all movement, all sound, when Lemanku's howl of pain and fear split the cold air. Startled, I stared at the half-hull of the ship. Lemanku came tumbling over the side, still howling. His eyes were raw, bloody pits. He crawled down the ramp, then stumbled towards the lake.

Behind him, one of the Pohjolan workmen shouted, 'He was in the prow. Something ripped him!'

Lemanku, in his eagerness to finish fitting the keel, had disobeyed Jason's strict instruction: that only he would work in this old and dangerous part of the vessel.

I ran towards the wounded man. Lemanku fell into the lake, splashing his face with his hands. The water around him *boiled*! Still crying out in terror, he forced himself to kneel. A pattern radiated out from him, like snakes arrowing across the lake surface into the distance, streams of movement that vanished from him, flowing towards the far woods.

Something else made the water bubble, the rising of the broad flat head of a *voytazi*. I ran quickly to Lemanku, just as the cold fish mouth was opening to strike. I was ready to sacrifice a little age to protect the shipwright, but the demon withdrew, perhaps remembering me from my dive, many days in the past.

As best I could I helped the heavy man to his feet. He was sick as he stood, but was quiet, now, water and blood streaming from his punctured eyes. Lemanku's days of seeing were over.

'Come to the fire,' I urged him, and he let me lead him back to warmth and relative safety.

'The spark has gone,' he whispered, shuddering, as he sipped a bowl of broth. 'She was so fast. She came out of nowhere. Such shimmering, brilliant woods. She came out of nowhere and took the spark away. Only night. Only dark. She'll kill me if I go back aboard . . .'

She? Did he mean Argo? Gentle, protecting Argo had done this terrible thing? I couldn't believe it, but Lemanku added, 'I must go to her grove. I must beg for my life . . .'

'Whose grove?'

'Mielikki. Mielikki is in the ship, now. Jason wanted such good wood, and birch from that grove is the finest. I thought she would spare just the one tree. Such good birch. I thought I'd done everything right. I'll pay for that mistake with my life as well as the dark. You all will. You'll need gentle gods to help you if you sail in that ship now.'

Lemanku's wife and two daughters arrived, the youngest weeping uncontrollably as she saw her father's ruined face. His wife attended with quick and methodical efficiency to the wounds, but her eyes, on me, were cold. 'You should have known. You could have stopped him, your friend, that *ghost*.'

She meant Jason.

'Stopped him?'

'He wanted the tree too badly. He tricked this man with charming words. But you . . . you see further than the rest of us. I can smell it in you. You could have stopped him. That ship will kill you all, now.'

How quickly she had intuited the situation. Perhaps, unknown to Jason or me, there had been argument after argument in the lodge of this unhappy ship-builder, desperate attempts to persuade him not to take wood from the sacred grove of Mielikki, Lemanku answering that the Lady of the Forest *always* offered her boughs and trunks for boats. It was the way it was done.

Boats, yes. Boats for her people. Boats for those who hunted her forests and sailed the lakes and rivers of her own kind. But not ships that had sailed from beyond the Watching Eye. Ships of strangers, with alien spirits in her keel.

Mielikki was capricious. And she was in Argo, now, and she was not happy.

I had expected that Jason would respond in a typically Jason manner on hearing what had happened, which is to say with blistering fury and angry recrimination; in fact, he responded in another typically Jason way: with great concern for Lemanku, tempered with the practical observation that: 'He still knows what he's doing when it comes to ships, doesn't he? He can feel his way around the hull, can't he? If he tells me where to hammer a nail, I'll hammer the damned nail! Get him better and get him back to work.'

And he was typically dismissive when it came to the danger posed by the new guardian of Argo. 'Capricious? They're all capricious! Tell me something I don't know. Do you think we couldn't have sailed to Colchis, stolen the fleece and returned to Iolkos in less than a season *and* without loss? We could have done it easily if the *goddess* had been so inclined to let us. She wanted her fun. She was playing an elaborate game with other gods, other spectres, other shadows on the mountain! I learned about such games before I even had my beard. It's a risk we take on any voyage, and the reason why so few among us are born suited to the challenge. How old did you say you were, Antiokus?'

'Very old.'

'So don't pretend you don't know what I'm talking about.'

I knew very well what he was talking about. I murmured, 'Odysseus shared your view.'

'Odysseus was arrogant,' he said quickly, a hard look in his eyes as he took the jibe and turned it back. 'Odysseus challenged Poseidon's power and was punished. I'm not challenging ... I just say that I know. I know and I accept. I challenged nothing in my life but Medea's right to my sons. And Medea was a witch, not a goddess. And she's dead, now, rotten: food for gorse and thistle! I don't pretend to be better than the gods, Antiokus. You can't compare me to that fool Odysseus.'

'He was no fool.'

'He was cunning, I accept. But he shouted his mouth off. That makes him ... foolish. He deserved his fate.'

'He invited his fate.'

'Deserved, invited, what's the difference? His strategy—that upturned ship, with its hollow hull, dragged by horses along the beach—yes, it was a trick, and a good one, and it broke the walls of Troy when it was captured and taken inside. He was a clever man. I have no doubt that he worked it out on his own—how to hide men in a ruined ship—in that bright world inside his *clever* head. I give him his due. But instead of sacrificing to the gods, instead of giving them their *undue* due, he ignored them. And that is *not* the behaviour of a clever man ... I will never make that same mistake. Are you listening, Mielikki? Help us in our voyage and I'll cut any throat you want over a fire in a brazen dish! My life on it.'

Reckless man. I watched him watching me, his face full of

strength and determination and challenge. He had been young, when he had quested for the fleece; and Odysseus had been older and wiser and more arrogant. Now Jason was older still, and angry. He had aged, but like wine in a wreck on the sea bed, without sampling life, or being sampled by it. He was a man in two parts: still young for the fight, yet old with thought and cunning. His middle years were hollow, like that broken but cunningly hollowed ship, tethered to horses, which the Trojans had dragged through their walls, only to have it spill out murderous Greeklanders from between its double hull; hollow, perhaps, like Argo herself, with her secret space that so far was denied to us, yet which contained a ghost in a ghostly world of brilliant forest, that could strike and blind any man or woman who came too close.

CHAPTER EIGHT

—

Departure

The rebuilding of Argo was finished, though she had not yet been dedicated to her new, protecting goddess. And as if aware of this moment of transition from dead wood to new ship, the first flights of swans came, emerging from the glow of the slowly rising sun itself, silent but for the murmur of their wings. They passed over us, wave after wave of them, black-throated, red-billed, circling out over the frost-speckled forest then gliding in formations back towards the lake. Hundreds of them, aerial spirits signalling the coming of spring. They continued to come down on the water for an hour or more, fighting, squabbling, noisy, waiting for fish and spirit-fish to rise, so that they might feed.

I stood on the lakeside with Urtha and Jason, in awe of the spectacle. Niiv darted here and there, a child about to burst with some inner delight. The argonauts staggered unkempt and weary from their beds around the shipyard, peering at the swans as they circled and settled to the lake, discussing the likely taste of these big and angry birds.

The Pohjolis danced and sang; they danced with Niiv's delight, and the swans' movements; they sang like the dead arisen, a babbling, ululating celebration, mostly women's voices, that was so infectious it even had our surly Volkas making tentative and half-humoured dancing motions with each other, a mock in part, but also a signal that they too felt the rising of the new season and the completion of something that ranged beyond the years: our ship! Our Argo.

She was leaner than the old ship, but she still had the same Greekland grace about her, steep-prowed, single-masted, decorated from prow to stern with shield-shaped patterns, in glorious colours, that represented the new argonauts who would take her oars. Her eyes, on each side of the hull, were canny; she would watch both river and sea with care.

Niiv brought her uncle, empty-eyed Lemanku, to complete the ship. His sons dragged the oaken image of Mielikki, Lady of the Forest, to the stern of Argo, to the slot for the carved head. Lemanku had worked feverishly at the figure, his fingers feeling their way across the rough wood. He had insisted that the task should be his and his alone.

The face that regarded us, when the image was raised, was sinister, the eyes narrowed, the nose slender, the mouth half twisted in a smile that might have signified contempt or pity. Hair had been carved, tumbling to the small breasts; bear's teeth had been fixed around the neck in a protecting band; the skulls of small birds were tied with leather twine, a grim necklace. But feathers and dried flowers ringed the crown, softening the malevolent aspect of the face.

Gutthas of the Germanii and Urtha of Alba lifted the wooden figurehead into position, and Jason hammered home the wooden pegs to hold her firm. Because of his need for ropes, ropes were tied about the statue, knotted firmly, then coated with pitch.

The moment Mielikki was in position, Argo shuddered on the ramp, but unlike at Iolkos, she remained calm, not straining at the hawsers. The Dacian's horse was harnessed and ready to take the strain if the ship struggled before Jason was ready.

While several of the argonauts hollowed out the bank for a slipway, laying birch rollers to the edge of the lake, Jason and Lemanku prepared an altar for the dedicatory sacrifice, a simple affair of dry wood piled to make a platform at waist height, wide enough to take the offering. Lemanku scratched an image of Enaaki on birch and laid it down; Jason whittled a crude effigy of Apollo and painted it black. He tied swan feathers into a bundle for Athene, last protectress. A bigger offering would be needed for Mielikki.

To get this, Urtha rowed him out on to the lake in a shallow boat, moving cautiously among the swans. Jason used a rope loop to snare and draw a great bird to the boat, then broke its wings with a paddle. Pursued by angry birds, Urtha struck for the bank, the broken swan dragging in the water, dragged alive to the altar, tied, and prepared for the fire.

Lemanku and his niece, Niiv, now clothed in a white fur cloak and colourful cap, came to officiate at the ceremony.

'Hold on! This won't do! This won't do!'

Rubobostes the Dacian had barged through the circle and now laid his sword, compliantly and defencelessly, on the altar. 'Swans feathers? Bark carvings? Swans? Jason, this won't do at all. If I'm to sail with my horse, I need to know that Istarta has been propitiated. You must sacrifice to Istarta, otherwise the rivers will run against us, and two-legged wolves will dog our tracks through the forest. We will have no chance at all. Swans feathers? Not good enough.'

Rubobostes' claim was translated for the rest of the crew.

Gebrinagoth of the Germanii stepped forward and laid his sword on the altar. 'I agree. Though Istarta doesn't worry *me*. But we need the protection of Belinus and Belinus is an angry god. Without the dedicating fire receiving the heart of a hare, still beating, this trip will be unsafe.'

One of the sallow Cymbrii started to raise his voice, and Michovar of the Volkas also tried to be heard. Jason stood, arms folded, watching the assembly.

I moved away from the gathering as the discussions became more heated. After a while Jason came over to me and sat down on a rock. 'This will take for ever,' he said. 'I need these men, I need their strength and their wiles, but I have no idea how to satisfy their gods.'

'Chop something up and burn the best bits. It happens everywhere.'

'They all want different animals.'

I sympathised with him. 'Since there's no question that you're leader and captain, why not pull rank and just sacrifice to Apollo and the Lady of the Forest? She'll be our protecting goddess, after all.'

'Each of them needs his charmed guardian,' Jason sighed. 'Rubobostes wants to sacrifice to someone who is bringer of fire, guardian of travellers, and healer of wounds taken in battle. He needs a living bat and the front paws of a wolf! The Cymbrii want to sacrifice to Indirabus, warlike watcher over the traveller and bringer of eloquence. They won't sail unless we can find a piglet. The Germanii want a snow hare for their fire-god and protector. The Cretan, Tairon, is proposing we sacrifice an infant by roasting it alive inside a metal urn! What madness!'

'Quite commonplace in your time, Jason,' I reminded him, 'and for many years after your time. It was gruesome, yes, but hardly madness.'

'Really? And where do you imagine they will find an urn of suitable size in this gods-forsaken place? Madness!'

I let him take a breath. He leaned forward on his knees, staring at the fires around Argo and the gathering of sailors. 'I'll have to sail without them. Perhaps the Lady of the Forest will take pity on me and let Argo move at speed with just six of us at the oars.'

'They're too keen to go south to argue for long,' I counselled. 'Besides, I've travelled many times around the world, and I've seen loss and death, change and innovation. What strikes me most about your argonauts is that they all want much the same protection, and they all have a Lord or Lady who will supply it. But the *same* protection. All their gods are the same gods under different names. So raise a new symbol, one for all of you, one who will absorb the protection of

Belinus and Istarta and all the rest, and convey it to the argonauts.'

'That's a good idea,' Jason said, scratching his greying beard. He smiled and slapped my knee. 'Argo herself, of course. She has fragments in her that are so timeless I can hardly bring myself to think of those long gone days. If the world began in fire, there is still a spark in her prow. If it began in flood, there is mud and moisture down below the deck. If it began in winter, we'll find a shard of ice deep in her heart! She has been there all the time and I hadn't seen it. You have a true far sight, my friend. But what image shall I raise to represent her? Whatever I carve, it must have the attributes of fire, healing, navigation, eloquence . . . and hares, pigs, wolves . . . *bats!* . . .'

'An oar,' I suggested.

He frowned. 'An oar? Why?'

'The oar whispers *eloquently* through the water . . .'

'Hah! Not with this bunch of hare-brained wolfpaws . . .'

'But in *practised* hands, it whispers. Doesn't it?'

'I suppose so.'

'And it can be used as a weapon?'

'Cumbersome in the hands of anyone but Heracles—maybe Rubobostes—but yes. It can.'

'And it can keep a man alive if he's drowning and finds the floating wood? Yes, an oar. It must be an oar!'

Suddenly, Jason was excited. 'An oar carved by every man and woman who will sail with us! Yes. This is good, this is right! An oar whose forming has involved the sweat and toil and thoughts and heart and hopes, and a little blood, of every argonaut. Which goes for you too, Antiokus.'

'Merlin,' I reminded him.

'Merlin. Whatever. You carve it too. This is wonderful! My eyes have been opened to the subtleties of the overworld. The gods come to us in many forms; but every tribe must make its own image of the protector. This is an education!'

'I'm pleased to have been of service.'

'Shall I carve a face on it? On the blade?'

'Whose face will you carve?' I asked pointedly. 'Will you

make the eyes open or closed? Will it smile or frown? Will you carve a woman's face, or a man's? Both? Neither? Painted or unpainted?'

Jason silenced me with a raised hand. 'I understand the point. Advise me, Merlin . . . friend, wise counsel.'

'It's not necessary to carve a face.'

Jason was unsure, tugging at his beard again. 'But we should carve something. All statues have *something* carved on them. I don't feel comfortable without a carving.'

'It really isn't necessary. The idea and your incantation will be enough . . .'

'What about symbols? We'll need the sun when we sail, and we'll need the winds to be fair, and calm seas, and we'll need to placate rivers, and to avoid landing at strange sanctuaries, which often leads to misunderstanding. I could carve the signs for all of those. I still remember how to do it from my education in Iolkos.'

'We'll find all those charms along the way, and from the men who row. You have some talented oarsmen among the argonauts.'

He hesitated. 'So . . . nothing carved at all. Just an oar. A plain oar, shaped from oak. Each argonaut to do his or her part. Cut the branch; scrape the bark; chisel the shaft; shape the blade; polish the blade. That's it. Nothing else.'

'And each argonaut carve their name on it, with the name of their own protector.'

Jason's quick glance at me was a mixture of relief and amusement. 'Well, at last. At last! Excellent suggestion! A carved oar carved with names! You see? I knew I was right to persist on the subject of carving.'

'Anything you say, Jason.'

'Anything I say,' he agreed with a wry smile.

And he went back to the ship and persuaded the crew, as I'd known he would. He had an eloquent way with words.

The altar was finished and an oar three times the length of a tall man was carved, whittled, marked, then raised in the fire-pit by the ship. First a dedication was made to Mielikki, the

swan from the lake, an offering from lake to forest; then an
offering to Enaaki, a yearling reindeer, to pacify the lake-
guardian as we crossed his domain. When these respects had
been paid, Jason lit the fire. The flames took time to catch on
the oar, but soon they licked along the shaft, reaching sky-
wards, hissing, probing, tearing open the new wood, releasing
the flame, the warmth, the sap and sinew that would help
guide our journey back to the warm seas of the south, and
Jason's time-reaved son.

Now the order went out to 'stow your clothes and weapons'.
Supplies of meat and the fruit liquor that sustained the Pohjoli
through the winter were hauled aboard, and skins to make a
deckboard cover against hard rain. The Dacian horse would
have to clamber aboard from the shallows; Rubobostes had
already constructed a harness to hold the animal comfortable
and steady should the river run hard, or the sea swell dangerously. The creature would have to be fed from what we
found along the way, though Lemanku's people gathered together enough dry forage for a few days at least.

The Pohjoli, in their tall red hats and voluminous cloaks,
stood in a group and sang to us, melancholy tunes that occasionally broke into high-pitched squeals of laughter and
teasing. Gifts were exchanged, and Niiv brought me a small,
painted tooth. A little comforting *sedja*, she explained. The
tooth was human, one of the chewing teeth, and was hollow
and scarred. I had no doubt that it was one of her dead father's. She kept all his teeth in a small pouch against her
breast, below her clothes. This was a very valuable gift that
she had given me.

'Jason won't let me come with you,' she said with a frown.
'I've argued and argued, and my uncle would like to see the
back of me. Well, hear the back of me, now. But I don't think
your defrosted friend trusts me.'

The girl's eyes were moist with tears, though her mouth
was angry. She watched me for a moment, then leaned forward to kiss my cheek.

'Is this your father's?' I asked, holding out the charm.

She smiled coquettishly. 'Yes. How clever of you.'

'What can it do for me?'

'You'll only age a minute finding out. It won't do you harm, only good.'

'Hmm.' I wondered what she had done to the rotten piece of ivory, but assumed she had used a simple spell to allow her to see me, occasionally, in her dreams. A little 'comforting'.

'I'm going to miss you, Merlin.'

'I'll miss you too,' I told her, half thinking that indeed I would, since she intrigued me; half thinking that I was glad to be away from those eyes, those lips, that quizzical look, the sense of trickery.

She tried one more time, asking me to persuade Jason to let her aboard, but I knew Jason: he too had decided that there were already enough tricksters on his new Argo, and whilst he had no objection to a woman at the oar, he certainly didn't want so beguiling a child as Niiv.

I refused her request, and she shrugged. 'Well. Never mind. Sail well, and *do* wash occasionally.'

And she was gone, running through the fixed torches, back towards the stronghold.

Whilst she had been chattering to me, the mast had been raised and the cross-beam lifted aboard. The songs were at fever pitch and Jason had drunk a libation to the journey, a brew so strong that he was choking violently on the afterdeck of Argo, below the sinister leer of Mielikki. When the fit had died down, and he had thrown the flagon to the Germanii, who cheered him and passed the liquor among themselves, he called for two men at the ropes. He and I exchanged a glance across the distance, remembering Argo's impatience when she sensed her moment of freedom, but the ship was calm. The launch would be quieter, then . . .

I had admitted this welcome thought too soon.

The swans suddenly rose as one from the dawn-lit lake, a huge cloud of wings and flight that filled the sky. A mist had started to form on the water, rolling towards the shore from the centre of the pool. The air turned chill, a winter chill;

frost formed on the ground and on my clothes, and on the trees at the edge of the forest.

Ice formed rapidly on the lake, growing visibly, deepening and thickening with every breath.

'Launch!' I shouted at Jason. 'Launch at once!'

'My mind exactly, Antiokus! Cut the ropes!'

The ropes were struck. On each side of Argo, eight men hauled the ship down the rollers to the lake. The prow cut the ice and the ship made water, but ice like ghostly fingers began to creep across her hull.

'Aboard! Aboard!' screamed Jason. 'Get the ramp!'

Ramp down, the argonauts slipped and crawled their way to their oars. Rubobostes dragged his horse to the womb of the ship, securing the animal. Oars were used to crack the ice, which was rising like a living beast in the middle of the lake, blocking our way to the river to the south.

Niiv! I thought. This is your doing; your jealous act to keep us here. She was stronger than I'd thought and I looked for her among the silent Pohjoli, then called for her as I reached for the rope that would haul me aboard.

'Is this that damned girl's doing?' Jason shouted angrily.

'I think so.'

'Then counter it!'

I could counter it best by countering the girl. I called for Niiv and she stepped forward from the crowd, a torch held in her hand, a small pack on her shoulder. She called back, asking what I wanted.

'Is this your doing? We'll never sail through this ice.'

She was silent, her gaze steady and bright. 'Am I to come aboard, Merlin?'

I reflected the question to Jason who was furious. 'Yes! Yes! All right, bring her aboard.'

Niiv was on the deck before I could throw her a rope, tossing her pack below and skidding on the ice to a place where she could huddle. Oars were straining, breaking ice and pulling us from the shore, but that monster cliff of white kept rising ahead of us.

'Do something,' I suggested to her. 'Break it open.'

'Not my doing,' she said almost nervously, a half-smile on her lips.

'Then whose?'

'*Voytazi*. You're taking Mielikki from them. They won't let you go.' '*Voytazi*? I thought they belonged to the lake. Not the forest.'

'The forest roots grow into the lake. They form part of the roof of Enaaki's castle.'

I took a moment to absorb this information, then went to the prow and conveyed Niiv's trickery to Jason. 'Then it *is* up to you,' he said, slapping me on the shoulder and stepping back to take an oar himself.

The ice parted before us, the prow cutting through the white, Argo progressing in lurching lengths. I reached into my bones and melted a passage for us, aching and sickening as I saw into the heart of the ice, cracked it, shattered it, made it split wide enough for Argo to slip across the freezing water to the far channel which wound south, to the sea. I remembered hearing tales of a man who had parted a whole sea to escape a pursuing army. That must have taken strength of a sort that I could not summon, but this ice was the work of elementals, and I had learned how to deal with them over many circuits of the Path. And everything would have worked out easily had it not been for Jason.

Behind me, Niiv screamed. I lost my focus, turned to see Jason lift her bodily and fling her into the lake, between the walls of ice.

He saw me, shouted, 'Don't look at me, Merlin. Concentrate on getting us through this winter trickery!'

But I ran down the deck, shedding cloak and sheepskin jacket. Jason struck me a hard blow. 'Leave her! You didn't want her; I didn't want her; she tricked her way aboard.'

Niiv was screaming, then went under. The ice closed around us. 'Quickly, Merlin, back to the prow!'

'I'll not let her drown. Crack the ice yourself, Jason. See how easy it is!'

'Don't betray me a second time!'

'I didn't betray you a first! But now I might! For your cruelty . . .'

Whatever Jason screamed at me then I lost as I summoned warmth into my body and leapt overboard, swimming down among the *voytazi* towards the motionless, sinking form of the girl. Her heavy skirts were raised like dark waterweed above dangling white and naked limbs, a skeletal frame, a girl so gaunt she might have been a corpse. When I reached her she was on the verge of breathing out the last of life. I gave her some of my own life, then kicked to the surface of the lake. She screamed and gagged when we reached the air, then panicked. I held her close, keeping her mouth above the water. The ice had closed around Argo, flowing around her, trapping the ship in a frozen tomb. I could see Jason on the stern, leaning out towards me, timeless and motionless, reaching a hand as if to call me back.

'Let me go, let me go,' Niiv gasped, struggling again in my arms. 'Save Argo. Save your friends. I can swim back to the shore.'

She tried to push me away. I had lost concentration and the cold was numbing. Each time my grip loosened on Niiv her waterlogged clothes drew her down into the lake.

I watched Jason as he began to die for a second time, furious with him, and at the same time terrified of losing him.

I held Niiv in my arms, determined not to let her go. My life had changed, though I was too cold, too confused, to be aware of it at that moment.

I began to sink.

Nipping fingers lifted me. The lake swirled around me, hands held us, pike-faced elementals took the pressure off my legs and arms, holding me afloat as if I were straddled on a floating log.

The ice around Argo melted. Jason was shouting, 'Get ropes! Get ropes! Merlin, hold the water, we're back-oaring to fetch you!'

Ropes came down and I tied one around Niiv and one around myself, and Urtha and others hauled us, battered and beaten, up the flank of Argo, wrapping us in warm furs.

Oars were raised, lowered, and the ship lurched southwards again, towards that glowing, watching eye.

Urtha was all grins and tease as he helped me recover from the lake, his attention half on me and half on the brooding figure of Jason, now at the steering oar. 'There's more to you and that girl than meets the eye, then, is there?'

'No.'

'Liar. But I'm glad that this has happened. Your friend Jason is more dangerous than I'd realised. I'm telling you this, Merlin,' he touched a finger to my lips as he spoke, held my gaze, 'because, friends though you are with him, I wouldn't want you to think that his oarsmen are expendable according to his whim. We're in this together, this journey—for our different reasons, yes, but *together*—and if he tries again to throw away the unwanted, just because it suits him, it'll be Jason screaming for a spar in the sea while he drowns in our wake. I hope I make myself clear.'

Urtha spoke softly, a young man with a young voice, but his anger signalled itself clearly, and I nodded appreciation of his sentiment.

If not Niiv, or the *voytazi*, that had created this difficult launch, then who? Or what? The answer came as easily as waking from a shallow sleep. I went down into the underdeck, picked my way through the bales and ropes and leather packs, past the softly breathing horse, and came to the forbidden part of the ship, below the figurehead, below Jason, who still held the steering oar.

'No closer,' whispered Mielikki.

'You blinded her uncle, you tried to kill the girl, you tried to kill us all. Is this what we can expect from Mielikki, Argo's new protector?'

'The man was blinded because he came too close,' she whispered voice came back. 'The girl belongs to me. Yes, I tried to kill you all; why would I want to leave my land? What are you all, if not just cold spirits from cold lands? Yes, I tried to kill you all. But you saved the girl. The girl belongs to me. So I have let you go. And I will tell you two things. I will have her back in my own groves, no matter what she wishes, though you can have her for a while. And she is dangerous. You have rescued your nemesis. And one more thing: I am at the edge of the world this ship contains, not within it, and someone deeper is aware of you, and wishes you dead. This for the girl's life; the rest I will decide as we sail.'

I asked her more, this Lady of the Forest, but she was silent behind her half-lidded eyes. It had been Mielikki herself who had raised the ice, not Niiv, not the lake spirits, but the goddess, reluctant to be taken from her own land. Only to save her servant, the capricious Niiv, had Mielikki relented, releasing Jason to his southward quest. We were on our way, but it was clear to me, now, that we were as much in danger from Argo as under her protection.

And someone, hidden in the ship, wanted my death!

I avoided Jason, choosing to sit down close to Urtha. He was muttering vile oaths as he heaved on the oar. He suggested that I helped him, and when I refused he swore at me. But I felt comfortable in his presence, and Argo struck across the lake to the steady rhythm of the drum. Soon, the lake narrowed, stark winter trees crowding over us, and we entered the mouth of the river, the beginning of our long journey south, to freezing seas and hostile coastlines and then to the Island of the Dead, to Alba.

PART THREE

In Ghostland

CHAPTER NINE

—

The Hollow Ship

The ice storm, and the possibility that our ship's guardian was less happy to be on board than perhaps we would have liked, soon passed from consideration. We navigated carefully along the winding rivers, gradually getting used to the weight and rhythm of the stroke and to those sudden, urgent needs to ship oars, when a fallen tree or jutting rock loomed out of the darkness.

Tairon and Jason stood together at the prow of Argo, Tairon's nascent skills in 'walking-in-labyrinths' helping us find our way to the main waters, and not get caught in a circular backflow. Elkavar complained loudly about blisters, the Volkas seemed at ease with the task, and the *keltoi* told outrageous tales of the ships they had rowed, sailed and stolen in the past. Jason kept an attentive eye on everything, especially the stroke, instructing and criticising quite freely, and I noticed that this irritated the Celtic king, Urtha, who did not like him. I heard him mutter to Cucallos that it seemed quite wrong for a man, until recently dead, to so presume the role of captain.

But Manandoun counselled him wisely, and Urtha settled into his role on the bench, hauling on the oar. He also acted protectively towards Niiv, who was in great fear of Jason, and I took this careful kindness to be part of Urtha's culture as much as his nature.

Soon, Argo entered that part of the Northland which is more lake than land, and here we could set the sail and cut across the water at a greater, easier speed, Rubobostes on the steering oar when the wind was hard and Argo listed, the slimmer Tairon taking over when the breeze was gentle.

It would not be long before we reached the cold sea, and turned towards the setting sun.

One night, when we were moored below drooping willows, resting, Elkavar nestled down beside me on the hard bench, and wished me good evening.

'I don't wish to intrude,' he said, 'but I was wondering if I might ask you a personal question. I certainly don't want to offend you.'

'There is no harm in a question,' I reassured him. 'And I'm slow to take offence.'

'You see,' he went on, his brow furrowed, 'I'm not an experienced man, not at all well travelled. Except by accident, that is. Well, that's true. So I suppose you could say I *am* well travelled . . . but without intending to be. I wasn't paying much attention, and most of the time I've been more concerned with getting home than with asking questions about where I was. The underworld is a terrible place, especially for people like me who sort of stumble into it by, well . . . accident.'

'And your question is?' I prompted him.

'In all these *accidental* journeys I've made, I've met a variety of people. By the Good Father himself, some of them dressed in a strange way. And the food! I draw the line at eating the eyes of any animal, except a small fish. Disgusting. But as I say, I'd not really taken much notice of these strange folk, because I suppose, strange as they were, silly hats, curved swords, eyeballs for breakfast, I still recognised them as being . . . well, *sort* of similar to me. If you get my drift.' He looked at me sharply, then said, 'But not you. I don't recognise you at all. You're wrong. You're not right. You don't belong here. Anywhere. You make my guts crawl, in the same way as when I see a spider hanging above me in my bed. You're not taking offence, I hope.'

'Not yet.'

'You see, Merlin . . . it is Merlin, isn't it?'

'It is.'

'Though Jason calls you Antiokus?'

'That's the name by which he knew me. I made the name up. I've been known by many names.'

'I was going to say . . . the scuttlebutt on this ship is that you can defy Time itself. Is that right?'

'Not defy it. I'm just careful with it.'

Elkavar laughed approval. 'Well, indeed! That's a good thing to be. We should all be careful with our time, though for most of us that means using it wisely. The candle always burns, but more brightly when we're young. You, though. Your candles seem to burn without burning *down*.'

'They're burning down, but more slowly than yours.'

He laughed, as if in triumph. 'You see? This is what I mean. You don't belong here. You're like a man from the stars. A different light has warmed your skin. Different water pisses out from you. I knew it the first moment I set my eyes on you. How old *are* you, exactly?'

'Exactly? I've no idea.'

'You're not taking offence?'

'I'm not taking offence. All I know is, that when I was a child the world was quieter, the woods more vast, and the chatter of men as occasional as the chatter of a magpie. It was a big world and the sound of the wind and of rain was the loudest sound of all. There were drums and flutes, but they made a gentle sound. Now there are drums and horns in every valley, and the air screeches with pipes played by wind-bags and madmen. No offence intended, by the way.'

He shrugged. 'My pipes don't screech. And you always need a windbag. And I'm certainly a madman. But back to you . . . You're very old, then.'

'Yes.'

'And you have magical skills.'

'Yes.'

'May I know them? That was my question, really. The question I'd hoped wouldn't give you offence. What exactly can you do?'

For a man whose guts clenched when he thought of me, Elkavar was certainly warm and close, a man at ease with the confrontation. He looked much the same age as me, though I think the twinkle in his eyes was a touch brighter. He seemed easily inclined to laughter and mischief, perhaps in equal measure with his inclination to song. Even as I sat on the bench, wondering what to tell him, he had offered to 'compose a song about you in exchange. A good ballad. Completely flattering!'

Since Jason knew my skills, and Niiv was aware of them, and since they would certainly come to be used on this voyage, I decided that there was no harm in letting him know the truth. The truth, of course, was that only a fraction of my talents were yet in use, and they were the obvious ones of 'shifting' and 'travelling'.

I told him that I could summon the spirits of hounds, birds, fish and stags, and run with them through their own realms. I could look forward in time, but that was dangerous, especially if the vision involved myself. I could summon a corpse to glimpse the underworld, but that was to be avoided at all costs. I could break the lie from a trick, to expose the truth, as I had done for Jason, to let him see how Medea had confounded his senses and made him believe in the death of his sons.

Elkavar was silent and thoughtful as Argo drifted on that gentle river below the bright, night clouds. Then he said, 'Who taught you such things? Where do you go to learn such things?'

'That,' I told him truthfully, 'I cannot answer. All my life

I've walked a path, a road around the world, more or less circular. It passes through Gaul, and Greek Land and mountains to the east, and through the snow-wastes of winter and the mosquito-misery of summer of this country.'

'Are you alone?' he asked quickly, and with a frown.

And what a strange question that was! I tried not to show how deeply those words had struck. Because in my dreams I dreamed of others, old friends, children who had played by the same pool, beneath the same willows, and chased the same small deer as me in that land so long gone it was no longer on my bones. But that was my *dream*, the comforting story in my sleeping mind.

Was the question innocent? Looking at the dishevelled but bright-eyed Hibernian, lost in the world yet abundantly optimistic, I decided that it was.

'Yes,' I replied. 'Not now, of course. I have companions. You, for example. Elkavar, this is the second time I've pulled an oar on this ship. I've been a long time alive. A long time pulling rough-hewn oars. It is not a favourite way to spend my days.'

He looked at his hands, the skin already blistered with the effort. 'I couldn't agree with you more. Rowing boats is harder than I'd thought. Well, with all those great strengths in enchantment, can you at least summon a wind to take us south, Merlin?'

I told him that I couldn't.

'Much good you are, then,' he said with a quick smile, then leaned forward in an attempt to sleep across the oar.

Urtha suddenly whispered from behind me, 'I heard all that. Our druids are not as potent.'

'So I saw.'

He hesitated for a moment and then asked, 'Can you enter Otherworlds?'

I knew to what he was referring. 'Not easily. Most of them are closed against me.'

'Not *too* powerful, then.'

'It takes too much of a toll. I like being young. I like what youthfulness can add to life. I'm careful with my power.'

Urtha seemed amused. 'Would we all had that choice. But you know, in *our* land, when we die, it all starts again. Don't fear age, Merlin.' He laughed quietly. 'Let me foster you!'

The journey of lakes south from the land of the Pohjoli was behind us; and the freezing sea, with its floating ice and sleek, dark pirate ships, was also behind us; and we were about to enter the land of ghosts.

The land of Urtha's birth had been known by many names, most of them referring to the rugged coastline or the treacherous estuaries of the great rivers that led into its interior, or to the whiteness of the towering cliffs which the sea had carved along its southern reaches. Five-river-land was how a trading people, the *phoaniki*, had known of this northerly and inhospitable island, though there were many more rivers than that. I had met one intrepid trader of that race who had sailed its circumference and whose tales confirmed the well-attested belief that the land went down into the sea on its farthest edge, and that the inhabitants of that part of the island moved between the realm of ocean and forest as if there was no boundary.

Urtha called his realm Alba, and this was a familiar enough dialect name for what various peoples of the south called Albos, Albon, Hyperalbora and so on, invariably meaning 'Whiteland', though the name was not necessarily derived from the chalk cliffs so easily visible from the territory of the Nervii on the mainland itself. Long before Urtha's time, Alba had been shrouded in mist for more than fifty generations, a cloying, brilliant cover of cloud that had made navigation around its coastal waters a nightmare. That endless, timeless mist had concealed great storms that pounded ceaselessly at the deeper forests and mountains. The island had been a rainland of terrifying darkness, and there were accounts of 'ancestor trees' reaching high above the stormclouds, whose canopies were home to whole clans.

It was at the end of the age of the huge stone sanctuaries, however, those massive circles in the wildwood, that the most enduring name for Alba arose: Ghostland. I had journeyed on by then, back on the Path after helping with the building, but I learned later that this Otherworldly land had suddenly risen in the heart of Alba, an enormous realm of forested hills and deep, twisting valleys, connected to the clan territories that surrounded it, such as Urtha's, by mist-shrouded rivers and narrow passes.

In Ghostland, the shades of the ancient dead ran, played, rode and hunted with the spirits of those yet to be born, bright elementals who always took adult form and dreamed of the adventures and fates to come in their own far futures. For this reason, Ghostland was also known as the Land of the Shadows of Heroes.

Urtha's stronghold was a few days' ride to the east of this Otherworld.

'I've seen it from a distance,' he explained one day as we rested from rowing. 'And I've seen some of the Shadow Heroes, when they come to the edge of their world, close to ours. They have their sides of the rivers, their edges of the forests, their own valleys, which we leave well alone. They ride mostly by night. Some are like my own *uthiin*, bound to one leader, bound by their own codes of ghostly honour. But they are drawn from strange places, and they are mostly unrecognisable, though my wife's father, Ambaros, claims to have seen ancestor signs on some of them. We keep the border between their territory and ours as taboo. To cross the wrong river, take the wrong forest path, is to disappear as completely as a puff of smoke on a windy day, not even a footprint remaining. Though to be honest, it's an almost impossible task to enter their realm. They come into ours, though.'

Urtha made the crossed finger gesture that indicated both protection and danger.

No such concerns occupied Urtha now as he stood at Argo's prow, screaming greeting to the craggy cliffs of Alba. His *uthiin* rowed hard, the Germanii and the Volkas sang rowdily, the Cretan looked worried. Urtha could think of nothing but his wife and daughter—and his two fine sons (potential return had finally made his heart grow slightly fonder towards the boys he had described as 'twin demons'). Jason stood with him, while Rubobostes held the tiller, and as Argo rocked on the rising swell of this grey, grim sea, so they discussed where along the island's shores we had arrived. Gebrinagoth of the Germanii was helpful, having once rowed with a war party through the channel between island and mainland. He hadn't stopped to raid, he assured Urtha nervously. It was agreed we were too far north. To reach the small river inlet that led to Urtha's land would take two days, either rowing or sailing.

In fact, we hoisted the sail, since the wind suddenly got up, a useful northerly, and there was a great sigh of pleasure as the oars were shipped. Argo listed heavily in the current, but rode her way quickly south, standing off from the shore to avoid the rocks. At times, figures lined the cliffs, and where we passed the beaches, long-haired, masked riders galloped in parallel with us. There was often a clamour of horns and drums, distinct warnings. When Argo dipped too close to land, slingshot showered towards us; during the night, torches burned on high or on the shoreline.

Urtha was not happy with the omens, though he would not specify the nature of his concern. I had noticed, however, that many of the spear-shaking, horn-blowing guardians of this part of Alba were women, children and older men.

Then, in the dark of the night, a while before the dawn, we saw a burning figure in the distance, in fact two great wooden effigies in the shape of men, which appeared to be wrestling with each other across the mouth of a narrow river. As they burned they showered fire on to the water below. We could hear the screaming of animals, caught in these figures, being slowly consumed by the conflagration.

'Is this a sacrifice?' Jason asked.

Urtha agreed that it probably was. 'And a discouragement. Something has happened. Something has changed . . .' He seemed very worried, very confused.

'Why do you say that?' I asked.

'Because this is my river. My territory is a two-day haul along it. These people who live at the inlet are my allies at the moment. We trade cattle and horses and foster our sons. You'll remember me telling you, Merlin. I've never known the local king, Vortingoros, to use cage-burning. Something has happened.'

Jason dismissed Urtha's immediate worries, demanding, 'If that's the way to get to where you live, to fetch these great knights of yours you've promised me, how do we pass below this burning bridge?'

There was a long silence, then all eyes turned to me.

Elkavar shouted genially from his bench, 'I have an excellent suggestion. Let's back-row and forget all about it.'

Ullanna and Rubobostes cheered, and there was a ripple of laughter among the other argonauts.

'Is there another river entrance?' Jason asked. Urtha shook his head.

'None that I would trust. Besides, I need to know what has happened here. Have you noticed the strange thing?'

We all stared at the burning giants, their arms locked around each other's shoulders, fire dripping from their wood and wicker frames as metal pours from the cauldron. I realised, then, what Urtha meant.

There was no sign of Vortingoros or his elite; no horsemen, no chariots, no screaming women hoisting bloody spears, no raging druids calling down the fury of Taranas, no curious children waiting for the slaughter, no howling, foaming hounds.

There would always have been hounds, wherever there was fire and the presence of men, waiting with the shedding of blood on their minds. The element of surprise, second nature to Jason, did not feature in the thinking of the warrior castes of Gallia and Alba.

'There is something wrong,' Urtha said again. 'We should wait until those effigies have finished burning, then row fast through the mouth and into the river. I have a bad feeling about this.'

Jason was still contemplating Urtha's suggestion when Niiv whispered in my ear, 'Ask them why they're struggling. Tell them to stop the fight.'

'They're effigies in wood. Talking to trees is not a speciality of mine.'

'But not beyond your ability,' the devious Niiv whispered, quickly adding, 'But were they built by man or charm?' I sensed the point she was making. There was something about the sheer size and ferocious combustion of these giants that pointed away from the mere sacrificial. I had seen such structures burned before, and they quickly exhausted the wood and animal fat, dulling down to embers, which might glow for a season but without any real fire. These figures had been lighting the night sky for all of our approach.

I stared hard at the fire then passed through the flames and entered the wooden skulls of these embracing figures. The raging hearts of birds and the terror of rams made the place stink of fear; most creatures were already dead; a raven was tethered, calmly waiting for its passing. Crows screeched around the hollows as tongues of flame licked for them.

I came back. I had found no sign of charm, save, perhaps, for that quietly watching, tethered raven. And the pure size of these giants, vaster than any clan-made effigy that I had seen before.

Jason had called Cucallos to the prow; this was the man's land, and silent though he was, Jason had soon discovered he had the sight of a hawk; 'far-seeing', the *keltoi* called it. His cousin Borovos had a similar talent to do with hearing. At once Cucallos confirmed what should have been obvious: that the falling fires were burning carcasses. He also saw crouched figures some way up the river, beyond the giants. They were by the water's edge, quite motionless. Cucallos was sure they were by the landing stage, close to the village and high-walled stronghold which was his home.

Urtha was still inclined to wait, despite his concerns and curiosity as to what might be happening further along the river. He felt a sense of dread, he explained, and of terrible danger. It would be wise to wait. Manandoun and Cathabach agreed. They too felt they were being warned away.

Jason was in no doubt that this was exactly the intended

effect of this monstrous display, and he quickly made the decision:

'Lower sail, lower mast, get ready at the oars! Remember the clashing rocks, Merlin? We raced through those, didn't we? With no more than a dove-tail clipped!'

'You had a helping hand, I seem to remember.'

'Did we?' Jason challenged with half a smile.

'Hera herself summoned help to hold the rocks apart.'

'Or we dreamed she did! But it was oar-strength and courage that got us through the danger and on to that black ocean! This is just a night roast. Tairon, take the drum . . . a steady beat, then a fast one. Niiv, Elkavar, stand by with blankets to smother flames. Ullanna, prepare to treat burns on the arms. The rest of you, to your benches.'

We took up our oars and the beat began. As the mast was lowered the oar-rhythm was struck above the waves, then the blades dipped and Argo moved across the ocean. Pragmatic Jason found a boat hook, held it ready: 'I'll hook us a roast that will last this crew for seven days!'

Surging forward, Argo crested the waves, then cut more strongly. The drum rhythm pounded faster, oars dipping, Jason urging, the arch of fire rising over us, flame and burning beasts falling like thunderbolts. A ram struck the deck and Niiv quickly smothered it. Burning wood showered us and the argonauts set up a noisy howl, a protest at their scorching, but they kept heaving on the ash shafts and we passed below the burning giants with the speed of a swallow.

A great flaring carcass plunged into the sea to our side, a bull of enormous proportion. Roast flesh and fat was a welcome scent to men half starved and sick of fish. Jason swept the boat hook over the side, caught the bull below the jaw and shouted to me for help. We dragged the beast half out of the water to reduce the drag, then held firm until we were past danger.

Rubobostes added a third pair of hands and we pulled our supper into the ship, lowering it into the hold away from his restless horse, which was not happy with the smell of burning but which had remained secure in its harnessing.

The bull, I noticed, had discs of bronze sewn through its hide. Its throat was cut and its flanks were impaled with the burned shafts of arrows. It was one of the biggest of its breed that I had ever seen, and had almost certainly been both sacred and sacrificed.

Urtha agreed with me, then added, 'But this is not the work of the Coritani.'

Jason was also staring at the smouldering bull, at the blackened bronze. 'I've seen this sort of thing in my own land,' he said in a strange voice.

He let the thought fade away as Argo moved with the stroke and left this fiery gate behind.

Not long after, we came to the mooring place where Cucallos had seen the crouched figures. The bank had been cleared at this point to make a landing, a wooden jetty stretching out into the river, and shallow-drafted Argo could tie up against it allowing us easy access to the shore. The only boats to be seen here were three broken and rotting hulks among the reeds. A high palisade kept the forest at bay around this small and muddy haven, but its gates were now open to reveal a wide track leading inland, to where the tall thatched roofs of a village could be glimpsed.

The figures made an eerie sight, five at the river's edge, down on one knee, spears held forward, shields raised against chests. Every detail of face, beard, armour and clothing was clear to the eye, but these were oak effigies of men, stained dark and already blooming in patches with green moss and ivy.

One was shown wearing the ornate helmet of a chief, its crest carved in the shape of a small hawk, its wings spread. When Cucallos saw this one he gasped with shock and distress. He was staring at an image of his father.

Elkavar called to us. He had found more kneeling statues up against the palisade. Tairon, who had passed cautiously through the gate, came back to report that, 'They are everywhere. I count twenty in the trees, all different. It's as if a whole army had been turned to wood.'

He added, 'A funny thing: if it was not for their clothes,

they might almost be Danaans, from Jason's land. They remind me of Danaans.'

Cucallos and Borovos immediately returned to Argo and put on their colourful battle dress, keening their swords and selecting light throwing javelins. They came quickly back to land, followed by Manandoun, also armoured, and Tairon, whose dark eyes glittered from his face-clinging bronze helmet. Borovos tossed me a javelin. 'Come too, will you, Merlin?'

We ran quickly through the gates and along the forest track. Silent eyes watched us from the undergrowth, as Tairon had discovered, and at one moment Cucallos again stopped and sighed in bewilderment. The youthful features of his brother watched him from below its horse-crested helmet. These statues, too, like those at the shore, were down on one knee, spear and shield held at the ready.

It was clear to me that these strange carvings had a great significance for Cucallos and Borovos. I'd seen that each man had streaked his face with a red dye, and imagined this was a sign of mourning. They'd intuited what they were going to discover.

The village sprawled out before us, silent, not even the grunt of a pig disturbing the stillness. Beyond it the land rose towards the high banks and heavy walls of the fort on the hill where Vortingoros held court. There was no sparkle of metal from those walls, however, no flutter of banners, no wild galloping of horsemen along the winding road that came down from its massive gates to the river.

We divided into three groups. Tairon and myself explored the deserted village, while, with Rubobostes' horse slightly lame after the crossing, Borovos and Manandoun made the long run to the hill. Cucallos went alone, deeper into the forest, to search the oak groves and the rock sanctuary of Maganodons, the god to whom this tribe turned for protection.

The houses had become rat's nests. They had been abandoned at least a month ago, though there was no sign of pillage or destruction. Wildcats and wolves had probably taken the chickens, and there were signs that pigs had escaped their pens and were no doubt foraging in the woods. There was no armour or weaponry to be seen, but hoes, spades and ploughshares were scattered around.

Tairon and I returned to the jetty to wait for the others. Jason was impatient to row on, to get to Urtha's land. We were now heading *away* from the warm south where Orgetorix was to be found, and Jason hated delay.

Urtha was impatient too. I found him in a brooding, anxious frame of mind, wandering through the woods, close to the river.

'There is something very out of place here, Merlin. Not just these strange statues. I almost dread to say the word. I'll know for certain when I get back to my own hill.'

He was staring at one of the mossy effigies, this one of an older man, long-bearded, brooding-eyed, the jaws of the wood torque around his neck carved in the shape of snarling wolves. 'I knew this man well,' he said. 'He fostered me for seven years. But is this *him*? Or the shell that now contains his ghost? Or just a memory of a man who has been taken from the world? This place has been deserted. But what sort of energy does it take to carve an image of each man who has gone? Too much for the men themselves. There is only one thing that can have caused this.'

He refused to say more. He seemed almost terrified by what he was thinking. And for the moment at least, I did not see exactly what was there before my eyes. I left him to his business.

Borovos and Manandoun returned later in the day. The fortress was deserted too, no sign of life, no sign of violence, just empty houses and an empty royal hall, still laid out with what looked to have been a feast for a large party, though the food had long since been scavenged.

Cucallos didn't return from the groves, however, and as dusk grew deeper so Urtha's spirits fell lower. He was now desperate to get to his own land. Hot-tempered Borovos became almost frenzied with concern, and it was all Jason could do to keep him from running after his friend and cousin. We sounded the horn and Urtha called in his war-voice, a terrifying sound that alarmed Ruvio, grazing on the bank, more than our icy and violent departure from Pohjola. There was no answering call or cry and suddenly, when night had fallen, Borovos struck a torch and went ashore.

'I have to find him. I have to know what's happened here. Can you wait a while longer?'

'Until dawn,' Jason agreed. 'After that, we'll strike up river. But we'll stop on the way back in a few days and call for you again.'

Borovos nodded his thanks, then turned and trotted through the gate, a forlorn figure in his cousin's cowled cloak, disappearing into the gloom.

He had not returned by sunrise. Jason blew the horn five times, five long blasts separated by long silences. When no sound came back, when there was still no sign of the two men after the fifth blast, we hauled up the stone anchor, cast off from the jetty and rowed on in silence towards our destination.

CHAPTER TEN

—◆—

Earthworks

A tight bend in the river, flanked on each bank by rows of tall, grey stones painted with Sun Wheels, labyrinthine spirals and the images of lean, leaping horses, marked the beginning of Urtha's tribal land in the territory of the Cornovidi. Willows crowded the water's edge for a while, then the stream widened and became shallow. Argo dragged slightly in the weeds. Urtha urged us on, searching the woodland around us for any sign of life. There was an uncanny silence in this early summer, and a growing sense of apprehension among the crew.

Another bend, then Tairon, on the steering oar, pointed ahead of us in surprise. We turned on our benches to see the looming shape of 'Brigga's Oak', standing high above the drooping willows, hung with ragged cloaks and rusting iron, old swords and broken shields, slung from the branches in offering to the river. The woodland opened beside it, showing the road inland. The blackened, burned remains of a landing stage were half submerged in the water. On the bank, two magnificent mastiffs stood by the charred timbers, watching our approach in silence.

Then one began to bark, the other joining in, a tremendous row, teeth bared, eyes wide.

'Maglerd! Gelard!' Urtha cried. 'My hounds. My beautiful hounds! What's happened to you?'

We up-oared and dropped anchor and Tairon expertly used the steering board to turn the prow into the shore, catching it on the gravel bed. The landing ramp was dropped, just short of the bank, and Urtha crossed it, wading ashore. The dogs came at him, snarling in fury, the larger bowling him over and trying to reach his neck. Urtha was shouting the same name over and over—'Maglerd! Maglerd!' The muzzle drew back; the creature stood astride the fallen man, staring down at him; its companion growled, dropping to a low crouch, sneaking forward from the side.

Again the name, gentler now, and Urtha reached out a hand to touch the chin of the maddened hound. The beast drew back, crouching like its companion. Urtha slowly stood, holding his left arm where the teeth had broken skin. He leaned down, reaching out, and the two dogs went wild again, running at him then shrinking back, heads low, their voices more of a whine. After a while the bigger came to its master, let him pat its flanks.

I could hear Urtha whispering, 'What is it? Gelard . . . Maglerd . . . What have you done? Why are you behaving like this? Who gave you these scars? Where are my other fine hounds?'

Then he called to Manandoun and Cathabach, and to me. I followed the men to the shore. One of them tossed Urtha's pack to him, then they started to put on their battle dress.

Urtha beckoned me over and I approached the panting hounds carefully. 'Look at this,' he said, lifting the black fur on Maglerd's back. I saw terrible scars.

'This is sword, and this too. This is a spear. And look . . .' he touched the crusted stub of an arrow shaft in the dog's haunch. 'The other is the same. They put up a good fight; but who were they fighting?' He rose to his feet, then looked at me with a young man's dread of what he might discover. 'And what have I lost?'

'We'd better go and find out.'

'But arm yourself, Merlin. Take a spear.' I noticed that his hands were shaking. His mouth, below his heavy moustache, had gone quite dry. I could hear the fear in his voice.

Now he stripped off his shirt and pinned his short, grey cloak at his bare right shoulder, leaving his sword arm free. He drew a bronze torque from his pack and squeezed it round his neck, the two hound's-heads facing each other across his throat. He hung his scabbard round his neck, the blade swiftly sharpened. His men had dressed in the same fashion. Then each of them in turn went to the river, scooped up a little mud and smeared one side of their faces. As they did this, so they whispered words to the water.

This ritual complete, we left Rubobostes, Tairon, Michovar and his men and the Cymbrii to guard Argo, since the ship was a prize and Jason was distrustful of the apparent 'silence' all around. The rest of us took our weapons and followed the broad track through the woodland until we emerged on to a thin strip of open land, staring across the distance at the stark rise of the vast hill fortification that was Urtha's home and seat of his tribal kingdom.

Enormous, steep embankments wound around the hill, high palisade walls of dark oak rising rank upon rank to the highest wall of all, where tall watch-towers seemed to drift against the clouds. There were five gates along the winding approach between the earthen banks, the first capped by twin bull skulls, the second with the interlocking antlers of fifteen-summer stags, the third with wolves leering from their bones, the fourth with human skulls grinning from hollows carved from elmwood columns, the fifth with the long-bones of two horses, tied in bundles, wrapped in horse-hide and topped with the red-painted skulls of Urtha's favourite war-steeds. They had pulled his chariot in raids and carried his children in fun. On their deaths, in combat against Nervii raiders from across the sea, Urtha had elevated them to the highest rank of totem in his clan.

Long before we had reached this final gate, we knew the fortress had been pillaged and abandoned. It was silent, clearly deserted, and two of the gate-towers had been burned. There were no cattle or sheep grazing between the banks, nor dogs chasing them. And on the clear air there was the taint of corrupted flesh. The wind that gusted between the earthworks, as we ascended the steep road, seemed to breathe at us from the grave.

A while later, Urtha and his *uthiin* stood among the ruins of their lives.

Manandoun shouted with anger as he emerged from the *uthiin's* long hall, where he and Cathabach, unmarried men, were stationed.

'No weapons, no corpses! Were they even here?'

But there had been slaughter. We all found the grim traces as we searched the streets and houses, the stables and forges. We found remains scattered everywhere, even in ditches near the western gate, where the hill dropped towards the deeper, forested valleys that led towards forbidden lands.

And there were the bodies of several hounds, two of Urtha's among them, their shrinking maws still caked in blood, but killed by spears. They lay near the main gate, crowpecked and stinking. They made a dreadful sight.

The worst sight was to come. Urtha finally entered the king's hall, his own home, and after a long while called for me. I followed him into the long, gloomy house. It, too, had been ransacked, little remaining that hadn't been smashed, woollen hangings ripped, jars and vessels spilled and broken. The air was putrid with corruption.

In a stream of light, where the wall had been broken through, Urtha was crouching over the body of a mastiff.

'This is not Ulgerd,' he said, 'but he was once a fine companion. Urien loved him. They ran together after hares, just for the race. Now my son has killed him; and he has killed my son.'

He reached to the flank of the huge creature and pulled out a small, bone-handled sword, a child's weapon, a thing of beauty and delicacy, bronze-bladed and designed for play, not killing. It had done its work. Laying the little sword down, Urtha pushed the hound away from the almost skeletal corpse below it. He breathed hard for a moment, his voice almost breaking into a cry. From where I stood I could see a small clenched fist, the broken limbs, the hound-ravaged face and neck.

'Well, Urien. It looks as if you did your part. Well done. By the Good God, I'll miss you, despite your temper. I would forgive you ten times that temper if I could have you back.'

He choked up for a moment, his head dropped on his chest, then he took off his grey cloak and wrapped it round his son, standing and lifting the body in his arms. He looked at me through tear-bright eyes, asking in a whisper, 'What has happened here, Merlin? By the Crow and Wolf, what has *happened* here? The dogs have turned on their own. There are none of my warriors among the dead. The fort is deserted when it should be in the hands of the enemy. What has happened to the rest of my family? And where are my warriors?'

'I wish I had answers for you. I don't. I'm sorry for your son.'

'Brave boy. I should have known he would be such a brave boy. I'm proud of him. I can't go back to Argo until I've buried him and found the others.'

'I know. I'll wait with you.'

Manandoun was waiting outside the hall. He looked grim and sad at the bundle in Urtha's arms, then reached out to take the body.

'It's Urien,' the warlord said.

'The others?'

Urtha shook his head. 'I'll bury him in Herne's Grove, close to the river. For the moment, take him to the *uthiin*'s hall. And close him in. Will you stand watch outside?'

'I will, and gladly.'

The argonauts had continued to search the hill and the land around. By dusk one thing was clear: none of Urtha's *uthiin* were among the dead. Twenty-five men, left to guard this place, to maintain order among the lower ranks and to attend at sacrifice and festival in Urtha's absence, none of them could be found. And nor could the bodies of Aylamunda, Ambaros her father, nor of little Munda or Kymon.

Head in his hands, Urtha sat by the well, mourning, frightened and confused. I was about to approach him when Jason came out of the shadows, stared at the forlorn king for a moment, then reached below his jacket for a leather flask of wine. He passed this to the grieving man, then sat down next to him, accepting back the flask and drinking from it, then talking quietly.

Old warrior, young warrior, a Greek and a *keltoi*, stumbling with each other's language, perhaps understanding each other more through the language of loss than through that of war. Or perhaps it was a word or two of hope that Jason offered; after all, only one son was dead, and the rest of his family were not among the corpses.

Whatever they talked about, whatever passed between them, it was after dark before Urtha called for me again. He was drunk and angry. Gelard and Maglerd, his surviving hounds, were tightly, cruelly tethered before the king's hall, their eyes wide and bright by torchlight, watching with nervous concern.

'Why would my dogs have done all this?'

'I doubt if they did.'

'But there are no wounds on the dead except for teeth. My dogs turned against my clan and family, killed them, savaged them . . . Some died in the attack, but most seem to have escaped. Only these two survived and stayed, and not for long. Look at them: aware of their crime, terrified. Their heads will give me a certain satisfaction. I'll burn their carcasses to Belenos and ask for a vision of what happened here, and where I can find the other bodies.'

'No dogs did all this, Urtha. No pack of dogs, wolves or wildcat. Spare the hounds.'

'I can't. I once had twelve brilliant hounds. I would have given my left hand to save any one of them. They have turned against me. These two even tried to drive us back from the river. They're killers, I'm convinced of it.'

He sounded like a man talking himself into believing the

impossible. He needed a focus for the killing blow that might alleviate some of his anger, though not his distress.

Then a thought occurred to him. Angry eyes held my gaze for a moment before he asked me for the favour that I had already been considering.

'Merlin . . . you took Jason to Skogen's sanctuary and showed him his past, the truth of his past. Can you show me what happened here? Would that *sorcery* be too . . . difficult for you? I know it will cost you. I'll pay you back in any way I can.'

'I showed Jason the truth of something he himself had experienced and been blinded to. The magic came from his own mind. I can't do the same for you. You weren't here when your son was killed.'

He seemed crestfallen, but accepted my words. I probably could have seen through time for him, but I was more than reluctant to endure the age that would creep into my skin and bones. Such sorcery, as he called it, must be rationed with the greatest care.

'Never mind, then. We'll find the truth another way.'

There was one way I might be able to gain a clue as to his family's fate, however. By dreaming. I told him this, adding, 'In the meantime, spare those hounds. As for payment, put it from your mind. I believe we'll be together, on Argo's benches, for a long time to come. Favours will flow back and forth.'

It was a bright night and I could see the river in the far distance, a moonsilver gleam winding through the woods and round the hill. I always like to dream by rivers, especially in the embracing reach of an elderly elm or whispering beech. So I took a torch and left the fort, turning away from where Argo was moored, following the path that Urtha had told me led to Herne's Grove, close to a stream that led to the river itself. I had no difficulty finding it; the grove was edged with statues, indistinctly carved, and centred with grey stones. Among the trees were small mounds, the burial places of Urtha's kin.

I planted the torch, curled up against a trunk and summoned sleep.

Shouting ... angry shouting, and the sound of women crying ...

Dawn breaks, and a fresh wind begins to blow across the open land ...

After a while the land changes colour and complexion; this is winter. The river runs hard and strong; the wind grows keener, an easterly, smelling of the coming snow ...

Riders suddenly spill from the main gates of the hill fort, thirty or so, their horses laden with leather packs and weaponry. The shouting and wailing continues. Children chase the riders, throwing stones at them long after they are out of range. The men enter the forest, heading towards the river, leaving confusion and alarm behind them, older men in conference, women talking animatedly, youths fetching weapons and piling them at the gates.

They are the *uthiin*. They are abandoning the fort. The war band, Urtha's guardians of his home and family in his absence, are deserting their post. Urtha's realm is exposed and vulnerable ...

Why have they done this? Why have they betrayed their king?

I woke suddenly to the presence of a face close to mine. It was Niiv, breathing on me, peering at me curiously. She was beautiful in the light of the torch, but startled me so much that I almost struck at her.

'What are you doing?' she whispered, as if the grove might be listening.

'Dreaming,' I said. 'And you interrupted me. I was trying to see the reason for something, but you've broken the charm.'

She was suddenly excited. 'Let me dream with you. Please? Let me share the dream?'

'No! That's a dangerous thing to do. You must always

protect your own charm. Didn't your father teach you that at least?'

'You don't trust me.'

'That's right. I don't trust you. I wouldn't trust anyone who didn't guard their dreaming sight. Now go away, Niiv. I'm trying to help Urtha.'

She sulked and sat back, hunched up on the ground, pale face motionless as she stared at me. I had been trying to discover the reason for the *uthiin*'s leaving, but I'd failed. Nevertheless, I'd sensed the approach of danger and I wanted to go back, to watch what happened next.

I set up a simple defence against the girl's curiosity, then called back the dream.

Niiv had gone when I came back again to the world of night and the grove. I could hear voices, men approaching, and see the flare of torches. Dazed and confused, I stood and went to meet Urtha and the others, as they carried the shrouded body of Urien to this sanctuary, to bury him among the trees, in a shallow grave below a cairn of white stones. It was a sad little ceremony, and when it was over Urtha sought me out.

I told him what I'd seen clearly, the desertion of his horsemen; but I couldn't make sense of what had followed.

The raiding band approached from the forested valleys to the west. They came in the dead of night, below black storm clouds, visible at first only as torches. The horses thundered across the open land towards the poorly guarded gates. I had struggled to see their shapes in the night, but only streaming fire was visible. There was enchantment at work here. I could see neither shape or face of these riders, nor their horses. The sound was loud, the effect was devastating, but all was invisible to me.

The hounds behind the high walls were going mad, bounding in a great circle, led by the largest and oldest of the pack. Urtha's people had run to the walls, some with sling and shot, some with bow and arrow, most with no more than a handful of iron-tipped lances. They too set up a shout, a defiant roar, a scream of rage, rattling iron on iron to make a clatter that might have discouraged a skirmishing band, but not this ghostly host.

The torches flowed up the hill. The gates to the fort opened as if rammed. The desperate defenders scattered, fighting against men whom they could see but I, in my dream, could not.

A few minutes later, the hounds turned against their masters.

It happened so quickly that for a moment I didn't recognise the way they had been transformed. They stopped in their mad, circular flight, ears pricked, tongues lolling, all staring in the same direction, as if they'd been summoned. Then they turned, spread out like silent hunters, and leapt for their fleeing prey. I saw one woman dragging a boy and girl with her, screaming in terror and anger as two of the mastiffs bounded after her. Torches followed the hounds. This small party disappeared into the darkness towards the river, towards Herne's Grove.

There was mayhem in the king's hall. I guessed the boy, there, was fighting for his life.

A moment later, it had all gone quiet.

The torches streamed from the stronghold. As suddenly as the attack had come, so it had ended. Again I heard horses, and the cries of the wild riders; but enchantment still blinded my eyes.

Urtha had listened in silence to my brief and strange account. He was thoughtful and weary, as if he had expected no more than what he'd heard. I was tired and itching, and needed food. It was well after midnight. We went back to the fort and huddled in a morose group in the *uthiin* lodge.

Urtha said quietly, 'You know: I went to that cold place ... Pohjola. That lake ... because I was told I would find an answer to my fears for this land. But my *leaving* it was the answer.'

He was inconsolable for the moment, and I left him alone. Shortly after dawn, the ram's horn sounded three times from Argo, a summons to the ship. Urtha and I went up to the ramparts by the main gate. Rubobostes was cantering towards us. Ruvio seemed fully fit again. The Dacian dismounted at the foot of the hill and shouted up to us. An old man had arrived on the other side of the river, he told us, and was calling for Urtha; he had a bow and some fearsome arrows and was threatening to kill any man who swam across to him before he was ready.

'What did this man look like?'

The Dacian elaborately described the patterns of green and blue that covered the left cheek and left arm of the man; and that his scalp was shaved except for a topknot of whitened hair that stuck up like the stalk of a mushroom and flowed down like the mane of a horse; that he was missing two fingers, one from each hand, but none that would affect his archery.

'Ambaros!' Urtha breathed. 'Aylamunda's father. The canny old wolf! He survived this slaughter. But how much did he fight?'

He called the question down to the Dacian.

'From the look of him,' Rubobostes shouted back pointedly, 'and from the unhealed scars on his arm and neck . . . quite a lot.'

He turned and rode back to the ship, to continue his guard, the rest of us following on foot, all except Elkavar, who stayed in the fort to play and sing for the dead.

—

CHAPTER ELEVEN

Desertion of the Land

The man waiting for us on the other side of the river was dressed and equipped for single combat. Five thin lances were stuck in the ground beside him, blades upwards; two shields, one round one oval, leaned against each other; an axe with a double blade rested at his right foot and a sheathed sword at his left. He stood, arms folded, facing the jetty. His feet were bare and painted black. His face was shaven down to a grey stubble, his eyes hard, his grey hair tied in a horse tail, rising vertically from the crown and flowing round his shoulders. He wore a sleeveless leather jacket and green and red striped trousers, bound at the waist with a twisted rope.

'Well, Urtha, have you returned in triumph?' shouted this ageing apparition as Urtha stepped into the reedy shallows on our side of the water. 'Have you come back with Ignorion's cauldron, from which our first kings feasted?'

'No, I've not come back with that.'

'Or Llug's lance, which once thrown will not fall to the

ground until it has pierced seven of the enemy? Or his cloak pin which can sheer the heads from oaks if cast in the right way?'

'No, I've come home with none of that.'

'Then have you found and killed the first of all bristle-backed hog-boars, twice the height of a man, with the failed hunters of his past still bound to his flanks with their own rope snares? You bragged of doing it! Have you got his razor and his tusks?'

'No, father. I've come home with none of that. Though not for want of looking on the way.'

'Then have you come home with Diadara's silver shield, through which we can watch not just our fathers but our un-born children hunt in the Land of the Shadows of Heroes? That, after all, is what you went in search of. For the vision of your future kingdom.'

'No. I've not come home with it. I was falsely advised.'

'Then have you at least come home with wonders to tell your children, and tales to excite your *uthiin* and their broth-ers? Tales of adventure that will silence even the noisy dead from Ghostland on the night of wild winter?'

'No. I've come home with none of that either.'

'Nearly a year,' the old man shouted, 'nearly a year, Urtha. For none of that.'

'I followed a dream that was false,' Urtha shouted back. 'I've returned to a nightmare.' Then he softened. 'But I'm glad to see you, at least.'

'For my part, Urtha, I'll have none of *that*!' cried our chal-lenger, snatching a spear from the ground and jabbing its blunt shaft towards Urtha in admonition. 'You should have been here. You had no business deserting your fine fortress on the word of a dream. Terrible sons grow into men and can learn. Lost shields stay lost! *You* should have *stayed*!'

'I accept that. And my loss is all the greater for it. I'm glad to see you, Ambaros. But if it's a fight you want, a vengeance fight, then we should move to the shallows, below the hill.'

Ambaros was silent for a long while. Then he raised his left arm. Two raw cuts, still healing, circled the flesh between shoulder and elbow. Urtha sighed, seemed to stoop a little, then whispered to me grimly, 'They're grieving wounds. One for his wife, Rhion; one for his daughter . . . Aylamunda. My Aylamunda, Merlin. She's dead, too, along with Urien. But I suppose I knew that. So: my wife and son. And surely now there is no hope for little Munda and wild-haired Kymon.'

He called across the water: 'I would rather save my fury for their killers than for you. The choice is yours, father. For myself, I would rather grieve.'

'You will certainly do that,' his bond-father acknowledged. He was silent for a long time, staring at Urtha. Then he said, 'But not to the extent you imagine. Come across the river. Bring your friends. Cross at the shallows.'

'Is this to fight?' Urtha shouted. 'Because if it is, I'll come alone.'

Ambaros looked at him long and hard, then shook his head. 'No. Not to fight. Not yet. And not between you and me. But save your blood, Urtha. You'll need it in the time to come.'

The old man gathered up his spears and shields, slung them over his back and paced off through the drooping, pale green fronds of the willows towards the place where the river surged white and fierce over the black stones of the shallows.

Urtha and Ambaros met in mid-stream and embraced. I was introduced, then Niiv, who was still staying close to me, then Jason. The two grizzle-beards eyed each other cautiously, exchanging the merest of courtesies.

'That's a restless ship you've sailed up the river,' Ambaros volunteered. 'She aches to be away from here. And a strange ship, though why that surprises me I can't imagine. The world has gone more than strange in the last little while.'

'She's Argo. I built her with my own hands,' Jason lied. 'In Pagasae, the harbour of Iolkos.'

'And where is that?'

'South of here, on the warmest sea you can imagine. In Greek Land, as you people call it.'

'And you built her with your own hands . . .'

'And then rebuilt her by the light of the North Star, with the help of your son-in-law and this man here,' he waved in my direction, 'with frozen timber, and ice instead of bronze. But she still smells the wines of Makedon and the olives of Achaea, which is why she's restless.'

For the first time I realised that Jason was homesick, transferring his own desires and dreams to the ship. If Argo was missing anything at all, it was the snows of the frozen north and the stink of rutting reindeer—Mielikki's tastes—rather than the aromatics of Greek Land.

Ullanna had just crossed the stream, bow over one shoulder, arrows over the other. Ambaros exercised a greater courtesy with her than with Jason. She reached for his arm and touched the two healing scars in the flesh.

'I'm sorry for your loss,' she said through me.

'My wife and my daughter, the mother of this man's children.'

Ullanna rolled up the loose left sleeve of her jacket. A long scar ran from shoulder to crook; when she opened the hand I could see the mark of arrow shot. 'My husband and my infant son,' she said. 'Killed by Persians while I was hunting in the hills. We mark our grief in much the same way.'

Ambaros put a finger to the scar on her hand, between the smallest fingers. Ullanna drew an iron-tipped arrow from her quiver and made a quick thrusting motion through the flesh.

'We grieve for as long as it takes the wound to heal,' she said, and Ambaros nodded. 'Or so we pretend,' she added, and Ambaros smiled at her.

'Short, painful, practical,' Jason muttered to me. 'If I'd known how to grieve like that—to get it over like that, quick and fast—it might have stopped me rotting for twenty years.'

'Well, you've stopped now.'

'Yes.'

The ram's horn on Argo sounded a warning, but Ambaros raised a hand. 'They're friends. Some of the few faithful who stayed behind when your dog-horsemen quit the fort with Cunomaglos. The rest are dead. That's what happened here, Urtha. You went away, then the others rode off, down river and across the sea to the land of the *bolgae*, then further still.'

Four grey-cloaked horsemen, spears lowered ambiguously,

trotted evenly and easily through the river, cautious but relaxed, now that they saw Ambaros at conversation and not
engaged in defence. Urtha knew these men, but not well, and
they would not have been his chosen warriors. More important, though, he wanted to hear from Ambaros himself what
exactly had happened; who had done the slaughter. And what
had he meant when he'd said the world had gone 'more than
strange in the last little while'?

'Let's talk as we ride,' Ambaros suggested. 'Take these
horses. My friends here can do some foraging as they follow
on foot.'

The four *uthiin* seemed taken by surprise, but dismounted
politely, if not without black looks at Ambaros.

We mounted up and Ambaros led us through the woods,
towards the west.

After the attack, and his escape, he explained as we rode, he
had not returned to the stronghold. He had fled along one of
the river's tributaries, deeper into the forest, and into one of
the several gorges which marked the barrier between Urtha's
land and the realm of the Shadows of Heroes, that place of
timeless ghosts where Urtha and his clan expected to go when
they finally fell in combat, or to the years.

Ambaros had a very dangerous location for his hiding
place, but there were caves here, and the hunting was easy.
And since the rocks were marked with clear protective charms
from longer ago than even legend could recall, he and his
small band, and the other survivors of the attack—a few families and their dogs—had felt safer here after the destruction
of the fort. And the more so because of the treasure they
protected.

'Treasure?' Urtha asked.

We were just entering the gorge, now. Ambaros blew on a
short, bronze horn, and an answering call echoed down the
valley. Then he turned to his bond-son and said quietly,
'Munda and Kymon. They escaped the slaughter. I have them
safe, and will take you to them later.'

'Alive?' Urtha slumped forward on his pony, shoulders

heaving as he cried silently for a few moments, an unfathomable mixture of grief and relief finding instant and welcome expression.

We threaded our way across a rushing stream, then along a winding trail through heavy oaks, aware of the crags above us and the scudding clouds. Soon we had come to the narrow gorge where Urtha's people bustled about their tasks, and several horses complained as they were trained along the narrow banks of the shallow river.

And quite unexpectedly a strong and aching pang of memory surfaced, quite unbidden; it happened as I saw the heavy skins hung across the mouths of two caves, the crude coverings pinned to the earth with wooden stakes, painted with images to call only the Good God, and discourage the Crow. I had seen homes like this in my distant past, in places that were remote from here. I could remember the chatter of children and the baying of dogs, the crackle of fire, the swirling smell of smoke and the rich aromas of baking and roasting.

As if in a dream, I remembered bathing in a river, a girl next to me, throwing stones at floating logs, scoring points for each hit.

Where had that been? And when? My life was breaking open, like a dream, like a series of dreams. I felt anxious and tearful. Fond memories, forgotten for an age, were coming back, but I sensed they would soon twist into tragic ones. I wasn't ready for this release of my past life, and I felt irritation at Jason and all of them for making such demands upon me that my age advanced too much towards maturity.

Urtha was calling me from where he waited in the gap in the skins covering the bigger of the caves. 'I need you, Merlin,' he said as I slowly approached, still dizzy from this flash of the past. 'I don't know why, but I do. I don't feel unhappy about it. The crows have pecked my eyes and no mistake, but when your shadow passes by, the light sharpens slightly.'

He was staring at me searchingly. And at once I could feel Time weaving around us. I'd been waiting for this, half knowing it would come, not alarmed by it. I had felt the same thing with Jason in Iolkos. My dealings, my relationship, with

Urtha would extend into an as yet unknown and undefined future. Perhaps only through his lifetime, perhaps longer. The manner was not yet ready for revealing, and I had no intention of stealing a glance.

'We've never met before, have we?' he was asking.

I'd met his ancestors, I imagined. I'd met most people's ancestors. But I couldn't tell him so, not yet, at least. Not until I was more certain of what was happening to my own life.

Then Urtha changed the subject. 'You seem sad, Merlin. *Are* you sad? I have a certain cure for sadness.'

'Confused,' I replied truthfully. 'And yes. A little sad.'

He peered at me in comradely fashion, then slapped my shoulder. 'Then we'll take the cure together. But we'll talk about it later, if you'll forgive me.' He frowned as he said this, adding, 'The gods, Nemetona especially, should be enough. But Merlin, I need you by me. Is that strange? I'm going to face the truth of my wife and son's death, and I need to do it, and I need you by me when I hear it. There's a calm that comes from you, like childhood . . . or perhaps death.'

What did he mean by that, I wondered?

'I'm not intending to go anywhere, Urtha.'

'Don't. I need that calm.'

He was putting a brave face on despair, though the glisten of tears gave him away, but he blinked and sighed and stepped back into the warm gloom, sitting close to the blazing fire in the corner.

A deer's carcass and several birds hung from wooden beams that had been wedged into the rough roof of the cave. Lean, unsmiling faces, the tribal gods, had been hacked from stumps and branches and were positioned in propitiatory locations, each with a bronze bowl at its chin. Rough beds were further back, and there were piles of cloaks and furs, wood and weapons, jars and iron-cornered chests, all salvaged from the fort after the attack. This was a warm home, if a grim one, and meat was eaten for a while, and a sour, slightly poisonous ale consumed by all of us save Ullanna, whose first mouthful she instantly spat on to the fire, causing the flames to rage for a few moments.

'The land is deserted, Urtha,' Ambaros said eventually. 'It happened after you left.'

'I know,' Urtha said, standing as he spoke and dropping his head slightly, as if in shame. 'I saw it, father. And I believe I recognise it for what it is. The second wasteland from the Dream of Sciamath. I know what you're going to say, and I will agree with you until I know better. That it was by my leaving that this has happened. It is always the action of a king that blights the land.'

Ullanna and Jason looked at me for an explanation of Urtha's dramatic behaviour, standing stiffly in front of the older man, his arms crossed, his head lowered.

'Sciamath?' Jason seemed to be asking with his eyebrows.

Sciamath had been born from the union of mountain and wildwood. A wild man in every sense, he had hidden from the world until the flesh on his body was as hard as his father rock, and the hair on his body as abundant as the full canopy of mother forest. Tall, radiant-eyed, clothed in woven strips of softened bark, he had walked into the world through one of the valleys that led from Ghostland.

No ghost, but very much a seer, he had brought a warning, a dream, a vision of the future:

In his Dream, grown in the wilderness as he himself had grown, Sciamath had foreseen three destructions of the land, three 'wastelands', as he called them. The first would be a *desecration*; the second a *desertion*; the third would appear as *desolation*.

This Dream had arrived with the man at the end of the building of the stone-ring sanctuaries, many generations ago. The story, the Dream, had passed down the ages, and across the world to east, west and north, a warning to all the clans and kingdoms.

I remembered the first wasteland clearly, and with discomfort. For years, as I walked the Path at that time, it was as if the world around me had entered permanent night. Other worlds and other times spilled into the tribal lands. Indeed, perhaps this was when Urtha's Ghostland had arisen. King-doms all across the north had been affected. Trees were on fire in every forest, but not burning down. Invocations to the gods brought only misery, and strange, giant animals stalked the hills and rumbled through the woods.

It had lasted a generation, and I remember hastening away from those western countries of Hyperborea, hurrying to Greek Land where, after a while, my path crossed with Ja-son's and oak-hearted Argo, and brighter events began to oc-cupy my life. I never discovered what had resolved and ended the *desecration* wasteland, though stories of 'moonsilver ships' seen at the time intrigued me.

But was this truly the beginning of the *desertion*? Could one small king, leaving his land to sail north, bring so much misery?

As Urtha knew, and as I now remembered, Sciamath had referred to 'destruction of the forts by horsemen from the shadows; the sky darkening with four-winged birds; the land scattered with effigies in wood and stone and in the earth itself of those who have been lost; snow in summer; bees swarming in winter; a man who will come from nowhere, drawing the wildwood around him like a cloak . . .'

The list had been voluminous.

The strange sight of the crouching wooden figures in the land of the Coritani, and the events at his own fort, seemed persuasive indeed to the shaken young man.

I kept an open mind, however, as Ambaros requested the grieving king to sit down again, and began gloomily to re-count the events of the months following Urtha's departure for unknown snowlands, and his futile quest for a vision of the future.

'Almost at once, Vendodubnos and forty of his men from the Avernii made a raid on the fort. Cunomaglos and the rest of your *uthiin* drove them off without difficulty. The skirmish happened outside the gates. Vendodubnos had come proudly by chariot; he rode up and down like a man in triumph after battle, shouting abuse at our walls as if the walls themselves could hear.

'He had been misinformed about the strength of our fort. The look on his face when Cunomaglos and the others ran out in their shimmering battle dress, with only a shield and stabbing spear, was like the look on the face of a hog suddenly seeing the winter killing knife, all wide eyes, wobbling jowls and squealing. That was the chariot wheels! He went so fast the charioteer fell off, leaving the reins to the fat man himself. Cunomaglos ran so fast behind the chariot that he could casually prick out a pattern with his spear on the fat man's backside.

'It was settled quickly, after that. Cunomaglos brought the chariot and its two fine horses back in triumph. He was very proud. I watched him carefully; I thought he might develop the blood rage. The *uthiin* sang and gambled until dawn, but Cunomaglos stayed sober. I was worried about this. I watched him carefully, but he kept his own counsel and let the battle pride subside and his companions fall asleep. I should have recognised the signs.

'Another raiding party came from the south. I think they were Trinovanda. About thirty of them, very young. They stayed at a distance from the fort but killed some of our cattle in full view. Cunomaglos sent a champion. The matter was settled quickly, with fists, wrestling and skinning knives. Cunomaglos took four horses in exchange for the dead cattle, then allowed the war band to take their dead champion away. The head was not worth taking, he roared at them. But it had been a good contest, and the Trinovanda, if they are not part of the desertion of the land, should be reckoned seriously. They live far away, but they are probing other territory.

'After that, we had a month of peace. And then the emissaries from Brennos came.

'They came at night, five men, weary from the long ride from the coast. Their torches were so bright they clearly intended peace, and I opened the gates and admitted them. They were rank, wet and hungry. They had been recruiting along the river. They had heard of you, Urtha, and your *uthiin* horsemen. They were eager to talk to you, they said. They were also intrigued by what they called Shadow Hero Land. Their leader was called Orimodax.

'We set a good meal for them, considering the lateness of their arrival, mostly boiled pig, salt fish, soft bread and crisp apples, and a good flagon of wine. They were courteous at the feast; they refused the best cuts of meat, though I insisted they share in them, and when Cunomaglos arrogantly challenged them on their deeds in battle they simply stared at him, though Orimodax said, "That will make an interesting discussion for later."

'And though they continued eating, there was something unpleasant in his calmness.

'Halfway through the meal, Orimodax offered me a spear as thanks for the hospitality. I shall give it to you later. It has an interesting inscription on its shaft.

'As soon as they were refreshed and relaxed I explained that the man they sought was on a dream quest. I didn't tell him how foolish you had been to even think of it, nor what madness had descended from the air at the moment of your birth to make you a man of such selfish judgement. I made you sound better than you are. You were away in the north, that's all they needed to know.

'All Orimodax said was, "That's a shame. There's a bigger quest gathering under Brennos and the three clans, and he'll have to miss it." Orimodax cut more meat from the carcass on the table, then looked around him. "But there's no reason for the rest of you to miss this chance of glory."

'No man here is free to leave the fort,' I advised him, and perhaps I should have understood the scowl on Cunomaglos's face better, but I didn't. I assumed it was because I was suggesting the weakness of the guard on the stronghold, which indeed I was. I added, "Not until Urtha returns," and hoped that this courteous stranger would be satisfied with that. He certainly seemed to be.

' "I understand," he said. "When Urtha returns, tell him that we are recruiting men from across the northern world to join the three clans. We are of the Tectosages; the others are of the Tolistobagii and the Trocmii. You'll have heard of us, I imagine. We have certainly heard of you. We welcome all tribes, though there are restrictions and rules of behaviour which you will have to adhere to if you choose to join us. Our three leaders are Brennos, Bolgios and Achichoros, three great warlords, three fine champions. We are gathering the army along the southern banks of forest-edged Daan herself, the most wonderful river in the land. A thousand offerings have been made to her and she sings of success and triumph, of great battle and great glory; of great treasure to be found in the singing earth itself, in the heart of the caverns of a hot land where for all of known time a price has been paid by powerful men to see their future."

'He had our full attention now. He went on, "Among that treasure is hidden something that belongs to all of us, something that was stolen during the first wasteland. Brennos will reclaim it. He needs ten times a thousand warriors. Make your own ways there, when you can, and if you're in time you will be welcome to join the Quest. I would personally welcome you among my own Tectosages. We could continue that discussion . . ."

'He looked meaningfully, but with a smile, at dark-faced Cunomaglos, who nodded his head in acknowledgement of the compliment.

'I thought about what Orimodax had said, then agreed to let you know just as soon as you returned from the north.'

Orimodax and his men were quartered comfortably at the end of the long evening. Ambaros, guardian of the stronghold, went warily and worriedly to bed. He had every cause for concern. He awoke in the early dawn to the sound of horses leaving the fort. Bleary-eyed and dizzy with wine he stumbled from the king's lodge to see Cunomaglos and the rest of the *uthiin* riding through the open gates, fully armed and equipped, kicking their dark horses into a canter, following the men from the Tectosages. Only a few older men remained behind. The fort had been deserted.

Ambaros ran to the stables and untethered his own horse,

then rode like the wind after the deserters, catching them at the river, where the road to the coast began. He rounded on Cunomaglos, stopping the young man in his tracks, pacing his horse up and down in front of him while the others watched.

'Is this how you repay Urtha's loyalty? Is this how you exercise his trust in you?'

'I counselled him against leaving,' said the other man angrily. 'This is how I serve something greater.'

'Yourself! Your greed!'

'What else did Urtha serve if not himself? If not his greed? And all for a dream! Well, he should have been here. This quest of the three clans is a dream that will never come again. Orimodax has described enough of it, and what can be achieved, to persuade me that every man worth his shield would want to be a part of the greatest raid in the world. This will be spoken of and sung about when the sky *itself* lowers on the land. We *have* to go. And you have to stay. You are only half the man you were, Ambaros, but you have twice the wits. You'll find a way to hold the fort.'

The line moved on. The ten *uthiin* stared hard at Ambaros as they passed, blank, hard faces, utterly without remorse or regret at their treachery. These men had once been his friends. It was as if he no longer knew them. They had dreams in their eyes, like a winter's mist; they could see nothing but the unknown, and that unknown glittered with gold. Ambaros would have flung his short spear, but he was in no doubt that Cunomaglos would have flung it back with greater accuracy. And there were the children to think of.

Ambaros was shaking his head as he recounted this act of treachery, a desertion that I imagined was as bad, in his mind, as any wasteland. 'After that, the tragedy,' he finished. 'We guarded the walls as best we could, and made provision for a retreat into hiding. We expected raids, perhaps a night attack from Ghostland itself—the dead have come against us in the past; your stronghold was built too close to one of their paths, Urtha.

'But I swear on my shield, the riders that night came from

the place *beyond* Ghostland. They were our Shadow Heroes! Out of the night, from the Beautiful Realm, they crossed the divide on a raid of incomprehensible fury. Among them was a woman, urging them on, her face veiled, her movements quick, her voice harsh and strange. Why would they do such a thing? We have all seen them from a distance, we've all stood on Morndun Hill and looked into the Bright Land. We've admired the horses, the gleam of armour, the flash of weapons, the turreted enclosures, the shimmering woods. Why would they turn against us? We stood no chance at all. I'm sorry for your wife and son . . .'

Urtha raised a pacifying hand to the older man. 'I'm sorry for your daughter and your grandson. I know you would have fought like a madman to save them.'

Jason and Ullanna had listened patiently, understanding very little. When I had summarised Ambaros's dreadful tale for them, Jason said with a shrug, 'If this is that second wasteland that so worries you, then it was started by the man Brennos. This Dog Lord, who left you open to attack, would have gone with Orimodax anyway. You would still have been abandoned. This sounds like modern greed, not ancient prophesy, this desertion.

'You're back, now. You can reverse what has happened. You're the king, after all.'

Urtha acknowledged Jason's optimism. 'I can't reverse the death of my family and friends,' he said grimly. 'Though I shall certainly avenge them. Even my dogs turned against me. My three favourite hounds.'

'*Your* dogs,' Ambaros said with surprise. 'No. They were the only three which stayed true when the others were bewitched and turned into killers. Ulgerd tried to protect your son Urien, but the boy thought he was being attacked and stabbed the dog. Even so, Ulgerd fought against the others, but he failed and Urien was unable to leave the house. I fear he's dead. But Gelard and Maglerd carried Kymon and little Munda in their jaws, escaping up the valley. I followed. We were the only three to escape at that time, though these few sorry others limped after.'

Urtha was looking shocked, almost enraged. 'The dogs saved my children's lives?'

'Carried them for hours,' the older man said. 'Saved them and made them safe, as if they'd been touched by magic. I'll take you to them. Each child has a powerful protector in those dogs of yours.'

Urtha shook his head in despair. 'No. I'd believed them to be killers. Their heads snarl silently from the gates. But for that act of misjudgement I'll make amends.'

Ambaros was distressed. 'You've killed them? Each day, after the attack, those dogs waited by the jetties, watching for you. It's as if they could smell you coming home. They pined and cried for you, Urtha. They were ashamed of what had happened, that they'd been unable to save more than two.'

Urtha shook his head woefully. 'I took that shame for guilt. I'll make amends. But now, take me to my children!'

The older man hesitated only for a moment before saying, 'I'll take you to see them. That's all I promised. They are two days' ride away. Bring only who you need, we're short of horses.'

Urtha asked for me and Ullanna. Two of Ambaros's riders would come as well. Niiv and Jason returned to Argo, not without some argument on the part of the woman.

When we were packed and ready, Ambaros led the way from the camp to the river, but instead of turning back towards Argo, he cantered along a narrow track through the woods, going deeper into the hills.

CHAPTER TWELVE

—

Fierce Eyes

The tired, slack-eyed horse that was supplied to me for the ride was not just an abandoned grazer, too old for Cunomaglos and the *uthiin* to have taken with them, too useful, still, to sacrifice, but was also small. For a tall man like myself, the experience of riding the animal was only a marginal improvement on that groin-straining journey by reindeer. I do not like riding with my toes dragging in thistles. I was soon at the rear of the small, straggling column of riders and complaining to Urtha.

'I thought you *keltoi* were *proud* of your horses.'

'We are. The best horses come from the land of the *bolgae*, over the sea. We often sail there and steal them. We breed them and train them more for turning ability than speed, if they're to be chariot horses, and more for stamina than strength if they'll be ridden to raid. But when they're older, we let them roam free. They'll always find their own grove to die. To come across a horse-shrine is considered very lucky.'

'This one's already got a grove in mind, I suspect.'

For two days we headed west through a series of deep, echoing gorges andsilent valleys, crossing over sparsely wooded hills, finally entering a forest of enormous depth, a place of shimmering, misty light, a green chapel where restless, curious movement disturbed the shadows.

It was not necessary to ask where we were going. Only one place could lie at the end of this tortuous journey. Ghostland, the Land of the Shadows of Heroes.

By the third morning, Urtha had resigned himself to a simple fact: that he would see, but not touch, his surviving son and daughter. We finally came out of the forest to find ourselves by a wide, fog-shrouded and slow-flowing river. Dark woodland rose behind a narrow pasture on the other side. Creatures had grazed there, and slipped down the muddy bank to drink.

We camped. Ambaros used a bull's horn to blow a sequence of rising calls, repeating them throughout the afternoon. Animals came out of the dark forest to the river's edge, staring at us before bolting back to cover: giant deer, bright-eyed wolves, two brown bears, a playful group of grey-backed lynx, a sullen troop of stark-ribbed, snarling dogs.

When the children came, Urtha cried. I sat with him, watching through drier eyes as the boy and girl approached and crouched at the water's edge, staring at us as if they could only just make out our shapes. We were shadows to them, I felt sure of it. But they were curious, they could not resist the sound of the horn, and no doubt that curiosity had led them from their shelter to this limit of their new world. Behind them, staying close to the trees, I could just see the forms of three cowled, cloaked matrons.

'How did they cross the river?' Urtha finally asked. 'No one can cross the river to that place.'

'Your hounds dragged them there, and left them,' Ambaros said. 'Then crossed back as if the journey was as easy as a winter's forest hunt. I'd followed them, trying to slow them, so I saw it all. Those three women came from the trees and picked up the children, carrying them out of my sight. You had remarkable hounds, Urtha. More remarkable than you knew.'

'But I can't hold my daughter or mock-fight with my son. For all I know, they're dead and what I'm seeing are their ghosts. That's the land of shadows, over there, and they have no business running through its woods, not yet.'

I knew what was coming. I could feel the pressure of Urtha's thought, as if some winged messenger had flown from one head to the other, a silent portent preceding the moment at which Urtha articulated his desperate need: can you help me cross the river, Merlin? Can you use a little charm?

'Merlin . . . Is it in your power to take me over there? What would it cost you? I'll be for ever in your debt.'

I was about to remind him that he was already in my debt, for the dream-journey at his fort, but I said nothing. His suggestion had frozen my blood; even the suggestion that he was about to *make* the suggestion had frozen my blood. I couldn't cross this river, though the reason for the denial wasn't clear at that moment.

The three matrons called softly to the children. Munda and Kymon returned to the forest, their curiosity unsatisfied, but almost at once alert to other childish interests. I heard their laughter as they chased a hare that had suddenly exploded from its cover on the open ground, bounding ahead of them into the trees.

Urtha was gloomy.

Ambaros suggested that we should now return to the caves, but Urtha said he would stay overnight—it was a fine evening, the sky clear, a pale three-quarter moon hanging in the blue—and I settled down to keep him company. Ullanna slipped away to hunt, while Ambaros constructed a simple shelter and built a fire ready for whatever she might bring back.

The day turned as dismal as Urtha's mood, storm clouds sweeping across the sky, darkening the land. There was no sound of thunder and no sign of the storm, but that grey gloom over Ghostland flickered with lightning for a while and the ground shook, as if to the passing of riders. I sat with

Ambaros at the river's edge, sensing an approach from across the water but unable to glimpse more deeply into the realm.

Ambaros was uneasy. He carried a small horse-head amulet, a bone carving of Epona, and he rubbed it between thumb and forefinger, whispering to himself. Almost involuntarily, I did the same with the small ivory charm that Niiv had once given me.

The edge of the wood, where we had earlier seen the children, suddenly dissolved into the shapes of armoured men. They walked towards us, javelins and oval shields held loosely, short cloaks buckled at the shoulder. They were insubstantial and eerie, fifteen in all, one emerging at the rear—riding in a small chariot drawn by two ghost-white horses. This one rode the chariot to the water's edge, turned it to display its right flank (not a challenge, then) and peered at me.

I was shocked. I recognised him at once. The shock passed away into confusion and I peered more closely. There was no doubt about it, this was the same dark-bearded, dark-eyed warrior whose consultation with the oracle in Makedonia I had eavesdropped. I was staring at Orgetorix. Jason's son.

But this wasn't possible. Everything told me that Orgetorix was with Brennos. That had been his destination after consulting the oracle. Was it possible he had been ambushed and killed, and now rode in Ghostland? But he was a Greeklander, not *keltoi*, despite adoption. Acheron, Elysia, those were his destinations if Time chose to take his breath away. How could he have changed his path to the land of his death?

Or then again, was he dead at all? It was hard to tell. The Shadow Realm denied my efforts to enter it with charm, filling me with a dread of trying and a sense of disaster when I tentatively probed it.

This place did not want me near it. It was making it clear that I was not welcome. That too startled me. As I thumbed the *sedja* Niiv had given me, I felt a voice whisper: *you are still a small, small thing. You can't always have what you want.*

Ambaros was breathing steadily, peering hard across the river.

'Can you see them too?' I asked him.

'They are part of the force that raided and destroyed the fort,' the old warrior whispered hoarsely. 'I recognise several of them. They are the Shadows of Heroes, and yet they killed without warning. I can't understand why. But I can understand why they're in Ghostland. They're searching for Urtha's children. That *must* be the reason.'

His sudden glance at me was anguished and afraid. Urtha himself was unaware of the visitors. He was among the trees, lost in his own thoughts. 'How will we save them?' Ambaros asked finally.

I had no answer for him.

'They are not all the Shadows of Heroes,' I said. 'The man in the chariot is both a Greeklander and a dead man. I saw him alive nearly half a year ago. He must have been killed in that time. He's a ghost.'

Ambaros was puzzled, then told me something that again made me reel with confusion. 'No ghost, Merlin. He grew like the others. When I was Urtha's age I saw him as a boy. He was training in that same chariot. It has an odd decoration on its battle side. I constantly glimpsed him, growing into a youth, then a man. He has a brother in Ghostland. I've not seen him, though, for years. We called them "brother wraiths". Neither was part of the raid on Urtha's fort.'

Then this was *not* Orgetorix. The man's spirit could not have been in Alba's heart for twenty years, while the body roamed in Makedonia and Greek Land. Could it?

No, this apparition (still staring back at me) was *not* the same young man who had questioned the oracle about his father. It was the simplest explanation. But when he wheeled the chariot around, turning a full circle before whipping the reins and setting the horses galloping silently along the river's edge, so I saw the emblem painted on its battle flank: the head of Medusa! The same icon that had been on Orgetorix's shield as he had waited, grimly, in the shade of the olive trees in the village.

I itched to know, but I would need to be across the river and the river wouldn't let me cross. Or would it?

Taking a chance, I summoned the spirit of the swift, and looped and darted across the river towards Ghostland, turned back twice by its protective elemental forces before triumphantly flitting through to veer and swoop about the eerie band.

I brushed at Orgetorix with my wing, and he turned in surprise, following me with his eyes, his mind open for just a moment . . .

What turbulence! What turmoil!

This was no human mind; it was a screaming gathering of shades and wraiths, a jumble of memory, fragments of conversation, screeching and echoing like the forlorn hope of a dying man.

'Who are you?' Orgetorix asked, sensing my skulking presence within the darting bird. 'Kinos? Is that you? Still playing tricks? Where are you, brother? Where are you hiding?' There was an urgency in that whispered voice that matched the despair in the searching eyes.

And then the mind closed down, smashed into darkness, closed off in fury, like a blow that deadens all the senses. And I fled from the scene. Someone had driven me away.

But nothing could take away that brief, illuminating, terrifying glimpse of the spectral nature of what lay inside Orgetorix in Ghostland. All the memories of a life were there, from childhood to youth, from youth to manhood, from playing games to hunting games, to combat and the grief at the loss of a friend. But those images were collapsing into ruin, much as a dream dissolves into nonsense on waking, though in this case more slowly and with the confusion of a sudden flight of gulls, screeching, swirling, blinding in their panic. And only one strong thought remained coherent at the centre of this noise: where is my brother? Where is he hiding? Why has he drifted away from me?

I realised I had touched no human mind at all. But perhaps (I remember thinking at the time) perhaps that was not so unusual for an inhabitant of the Otherworld.

* * *

By twilight, the storm-skies had cleared. I had told no one of my encounter with the shade of Orgetorix. I was still quite shaken by the encounter.

Ullanna returned to the camp, carrying a sad-looking, white-feathered bird hanging from a noose and a plump fish still on the arrow. She looked disappointed, but simply shrugged as she began to prepare this meagre feast. 'I'm losing my touch. Too much time on that cramped ship, not enough on horseback.'

She had raised a knife, ready to behead the bird, but stopped in the action, staring at the river. 'Istarta's breath, what's this?'

Out of the twilight came a sleek, brightly decorated barge, gliding round the bend in the river as if by magic, her small sail half furled, catching the slight breeze, hull leaning gently in the water. She tacked towards us. The small figure of Niiv sat within her, resting her arm on the tiller, holding a single rope, staring ahead as if she were in a dream. Then she saw our fire. She dropped the tiller and waved to us. The barge rocked in the current, faltered, then seemed to anchor. No oars struck, no true wind blew. This small boat had come here by her own power, Niiv called softly, 'Merlin! Come aboard. This little boat has something to say to you.'

I waded into the river, all fear gone, and Niiv helped me into the barge. At once I recognised Argo, but Argo from the time of the stone sanctuaries, when elegant boats like this had carried the bodies of the noble dead, by night, by torchlight, along the winding forest rivers to the towering circles which lay at those forests' hearts. Argo had shed a ghost, to come and find us.

Niiv was now crouched in the fore of the craft, the forbidden place. When I joined her I was startled to see how grey she looked, as if ice had taken on her skin.

'Mielikki has been watching you. And watching Urtha. She will take you across to his children, but only the two of you. Fetch him.'

I called for the chieftain. He threw off his short cloak and stepped down the bank to the river, wading out to the barge and hauling himself aboard. He was curious and cautious as he crept into the narrow space where I crouched with Niiv. Niiv withdrew. I silenced Urtha's questions. The boat rocked and shifted in the water, slipping away from one land and crossing to the other. She grounded in the mud, but before I could stand to peer over the side, the forest opened up before us in the boat itself.

Urtha and I stepped into the Spirit of the Ship, walking into the heat and sunlight of a world that did not belong to us. Mielikki stood there in her summer clothes, her face veiled in grey against the biting insects that swarmed around her. A lynx sprawled playfully at her feet, half an eye on us as we walked towards the waiting woman. Mosquitoes plagued us. The land was restless and hot, the woodland disturbed by the grazing of reindeer.

'This is my place,' Mielikki said from behind the dark veil. 'The threshold place. I keep it as I like it. Walk on and you will have entered the land of your own shadows, and your children are there, Urtha.'

She was young. Her eyes gleamed from behind the thin veil. This was not the sinister crone who watched over the deck of Argo.

She added, 'And there is something for you too, Merlin, though I can't see it clearly enough to say whether you'll want to remember it.'

I didn't like her words, but curiosity was a tempting Fury in my head. I could hear, distantly, both the playful laughter of children and the cruel chatter of crows. Mielikki had allowed Urtha into the Spirit of the Ship, a gesture of kindness. But knowing what I knew about this birch-barked elemental I was suspicious, though I hid my concern from the warlord himself.

'How long can we stay?' I asked her.

'As long as you like. It will make no difference to the others.'

'Then we'd better not stay too long.'

'From the whispers I can hear, you've stayed too long already.'

Mielikki, I thought, smiled at me from behind the veil. Insects fussed with the sweat on my skin, and the scent of pine resin added to the heavy stillness of this summer gate. I dismissed Mielikki's words as a tease. I was certainly aware that Urtha and I were entering a place where the days and nights might be lifetimes in our own world—which is to say the world of Ambaros and the mysterious Great Quest—lifetimes; or perhaps . . . just moments. Though it would make more of a difference to Urtha than to me.

Urtha was impatient. He thanked Argo's protecting spirit and before I could counsel caution he had run ahead of me. I pursued him, passing from the insect-blighted summer forest of the Pohjolan protectress to the wilting summer greenwood of Urtha's land. A few minutes later we rushed from the trees into a clearing, where a group of children were playing an elaborate circle game, holding hands and dancing to right, then left. Four of their number stood in the middle waving cloth-headed sticks, the white material painted with eyes and grinning mouths.

Urtha's son, Kymon, was in the middle. His daughter was among the circling throng. The game went on for a while, then suddenly Munda was summoned from the ring. She joined her brother, who seemed annoyed with her, then suddenly saw her father standing in the shadows. Kymon and Munda screamed with delight and came running to us. The game was over, the other children dispersed, ignoring us completely. The surrounding forest seemed to swallow them up.

Munda flung herself against her father, crying now. Urtha picked her up and swung her round, planting kiss after kiss upon her forehead and braided hair. The boy jumped on to his father's waist and hung there until Urtha's firm hand shifted him higher. In a gesture somewhere between anger and delight, Kymon thumped his father's back until calmed by the man. I watched with a strange moment of envy as Urtha sat down with his children and talked to them of his adventures, listening in turn to their own excited chatter. I saw nothing in bright-eyed Kymon to suggest the unlovable brat of Urtha's Pohjolan description. Perhaps he had only been monstrous in the company of his brother, and there would have been nothing unnatural in that.

I'd thought that Urtha was closed to everything except his children and I started to wander back into the forest, but the man called out, 'Where are you going?'

'To have a look around. That's all. Take your time.'

'Don't go too far,' Urtha commanded. 'We're here by indulgence, not by invitation . . .'

Quite so, I thought. To Urtha and his kin, this ghostly realm was a place of legend, loss and fear; he would have grown up with stories of the Land of the Shadows of Heroes; he would be balancing his dread of the place with his delight in contacting his surviving family for a while.

As for myself, there was again that nagging feeling of familiarity. The shape of the high hills beyond this woodland, the way the crags cut starkly against the clouds, the echoing sound of falling water, the murmur of wind in the branches, the sense of peace and the pricking of danger combined.

I found a sunlit dell, tall with grass and purple flowers, heavy with the scent of oak, and sat down for a while in this silent place. Evening crept across the sky, and night shadows emerged from around me, figures that breathed softly, that crept close to explore me. I was not alarmed. I saw the glitter of twilight on a hawk's beak, the gleam in a hound's eye, the glimmer on a salmon's scales; moonlight shone from another face, and the innocence of a child from a fifth. The grass rustled with furtive movement. Sadness, then laughter, drifted through my head. I was suddenly stunned by memories of a past that was obscured from me, a richness of story and event, of people and families that made me cry out. Stories, shadows . . . as fast as those glimpses of my past had come, so they had gone, but three grim, masked faces pushed forward to peer at me before abruptly withdrawing.

All in all, ten: and they sat in a circle around me in the glade, whispering. I could see only the tops of their cowls above the high grass. Their voices murmured and urged, ten voices from a time I had forgotten; ten memories of my childhood; those same ten faces that seemed to dog my life, always appearing unexpectedly.

'What are you doing here?' asked one of them. 'You shouldn't be here. Not yet.'

'We weren't expecting you,' whispered another. The voice of the forest . . . Skogen! 'We are surprised to find you here.'

The grass before me parted and a sniffing hound peered at me; Cunhaval! Then the air around me was disturbed by wings and I remembered Falkenna. These were two of the forms that I could adopt to see and smell beyond my own body. To use the hound and the hawk was not expensive.

Then a child giggled and pinched my cheek—how could I not recognise Sinisalo?—but he/she had vanished before I could turn and look at its face more fully.

'I remember you,' I said to the circle. 'Some of you, anyway. You were watching me as I left for the Path. I was just a child. The world was so empty then.'

'You're still a child,' laughed one of them. I caught a glimpse of watching eyes and a name came to me, a dream breaking: Hollower. 'And you've left the Path too soon,' this Hollower went on. 'You're still young. You should be walking the world. I know you very well. I'm the one who watches you from the caves . . .'

'All but one of the others have almost finished walking the world,' whispered Falkenna. 'Not finished yet, but finished soon. You have hardly started.'

And a gentle voice I remembered as Moondream added, 'What is your name at the moment?'

I told them, and they burst out laughing. After a moment, Moondream explained, 'This is just a nickname, the name your mother gave you; *merlin* . . . a small part of the name you were given when you first played by the waterfall. It holds something of you, but not very much. Your full name is much bigger. Do you have any other *nick*names . . . *Merlin*?'

Again the laughter as the name was repeated.

I said that I didn't. I'd adopted many names in my long life; only now did it occur to me how regularly I returned to that simple sound. Merlin. There was comfort, if not meaning, in the name.

'You are still so young,' said Skogen. 'You should be older. But you always were the lazy one. Your mother had to tie your leather shoes for you. I remember you standing by the fall, the others already gone, and there you were, undone, unshod, uncertain, unburdened. You hadn't even caught your supper for those first nights on the Path. You hadn't stitched the leather to make your bag for carrying. You had to be helped. You haven't learned very much in all your walking, it seems.'

'Why do you say that?' I challenged the harsh-voiced Skogen.

'Because you've come back, Merlin. To have your leather laces tied again. If you'd learned what the others have learned, you would have known not to cross the river. You seem to be blind.'

'I'm helping one friend, the man who's here with me, with his children. I've been helping another, a man who is resurrected, a Greek called Jason.'

'Not helping them very much,' said Cunhaval the hound.

'All I can, without giving too much.'

'The others have given a great deal during their long lives,' said Hollower, his voice admonishing me.

'Then they're old and grey,' I muttered angrily. 'Old and grey.'

'And wiser by the day, and no less tired for it,' said Sinisalo, the child lecturing the child. I caught a glimpse of the fresh-faced youth darting through the grass, dark hood thrown back. Sinisalo's mask-face was my own, though without the wiry beard, without the lines, without the sunburn, and windburn and the scars of thorn and birdclaw. A moment later I felt fingers tugging at my boots. 'Laced up!' Sinisalo mocked. 'He's solved one problem, then.'

These shadows faded into the wood. The last words were from Hollower: 'I watch you when I can . . .'

'From the caves, from the oracles, I realise that now . . . I never recognised you.'

'I didn't interfere. I was just there to keep an eye on you. But fiercer eyes are following you and watching you, now.'

'Fiercer eyes? Whose?'

'The one who went astray, Merlin. That one, too, has left the Path and crossed the river, but is hiding from us, and hiding from you. You were the best of friends, once, when you were children. You played in the waterfall together, and learned together, and created your own language together. Have you forgotten?'

'Yes . . . though sometimes I remember . . . just a little. I loved her . . . I remember being sad to leave. So long ago.'

'But now she hates you. Her anger has transformed her.'

'Why? I've never in all the generations of my walking met *any* of the others. I even doubted their existence. I've always felt so alone.'

'All of you were alone. Until it was time to come home. And all but two of you are very close to home.'

'Then how can she hate me?'

'Search your past. But she's close, and watching. Stay still and you might get a glimpse of her. I can't help you more than that. You've learned how to tie your laces. Several forests grew, flourished and died before *that* miracle happened! Now to untie the other knots. And persuade you to grow old gracefully.'

The wind ruffled the grass. The shadowy presences had gone. I sat dreamily, aware of cloud shadow and the day turning cooler. My limbs were heavy. I tried to rise and failed. Then I heard the sound of falling water. I managed to turn and peer through the leaning trees at the sparkling pool, its surface calm for the most part despite the cascade of crystal liquid that tumbled from the high cliff above.

This was home, the place where I had played.

She sat there watching me, wearing the buckskin and lambswool dress, glittering with polished shell and painted stones. The small bow was drawn and she struggled to hold it taut,—

the arrow with the plum on the end nocked and ready to fire. Her hair, long and lankly black, blew across her face for a moment and in that moment I jumped to one side, but she sensed me, eyes closed, and the plum struck my chest and splattered. Her laugh was triumphant. She swept her hair away from her face. Her eyes gleamed with pleasure and teasing.

'Got you! Got you! You can't hide from me.'

I remembered being furious. And when I charged her, to push her with me into the pool, she had fleet-footedly moved out of sight. I hit the water alone.

But those mischievous eyes—peering down at me as I floundered . . .

Turning! Suddenly turning. Furious. Narrow. Old! Peering from above a glittering veil, full of anger, full of fierceness. Fierce eyes, hating eyes!

Gone suddenly, leaving me feeling sick and shaken.

A girl with arrows painted on her cheeks was peering at me. She was holding me by the ears and shaking my head, calling my name. I recognised her suddenly as Munda. When she saw that I was back in the land of the living, she bobbed down and picked up two coarse-skinned apples.

'For you,' she said. 'You need to eat. Daddy said so.'

'Thank you.'

'Who were you talking to?' she asked as I bit into one of the fruits.

Her question took me by surprise. How long had she been watching me? I stood up and looked around, then fumbled with the leather ties on my deerskin boots. The knots were fine, but almost self-consciously I unthreaded and re-threaded them. Munda watched me in bemusement.

I was being watched! By the one who had gone astray! I struggled to recapture another, any other, memory of childhood, but even the waterfall moment was vague, evaporating like a dream, leaving only those eyes, those terrible eyes. Had this been a true encounter? Or was it just that entering into Ghostland had called shades of my own past out of hiding, a tease, a provocation from myself to myself for having refused to let age take its toll on me?

I couldn't focus; I couldn't see clearly. *Had* I been home, albeit briefly? Or just seen a glimpse of home, a world within the world, made possible by passing through Argo's spirit heart?

It slipped away; the encounter became unreal. There was just Munda, staring up at me with a frown.

'Daddy said you were strange. You should eat more,' said the girl, shaking her head. Then she took my hand and led me through the woods, back to where Urtha and his son were wrestling for possession of a small, bronze sword. The three dark-robed women stood silently at the other woodland edge, the eldest smiling as she watched the antics in the field.

'I have to go,' Urtha called to me from below the weight of his determined son. 'I have to go to the east. I need to get moving, and you must come with me, Merlin.'

He suddenly tossed the boy over his head, turned and roared a warrior's-kill roar, overwhelming the smaller knight.

'First lesson in life: never trust your father to fight fair!' he laughed.

Then he picked up both children by the waist, slinging them under his arms like pigs. He came over to me and said, 'You're right, Merlin. Children *are* more of a burden than I'd realised. Do you think our Scythian friend Ullanna could paunch, joint and roast these little boars for us?'

'I'm sure she could. But she might be offended that she was cooking something she hadn't caught herself.'

Urtha grumbled as his children squealed and squirmed. 'That's a wise thought. I suppose you're right. When we come back, perhaps.'

'Certainly. If they're really that troublesome, I'm sure we could cook up a feast.'

'I'm nobody's feast!' Kymon shouted, half in alarm, half in hysterical laughter as his father's fingers probed his ribs.

'You're *Nobody's* feast? Nobody was a good man, according to the story. We'll invite him to eat with us too.'

Abruptly, Urtha swung the children into his embrace, holding them one on each side. 'Well, daughter, give me a kiss,' he said to Munda.

The girl grimaced, pulling back. 'You're too hairy.'

'Kiss me anyway.'

'Too hairy,' she insisted.

'Kiss me anyway,' Urtha said, squeezing her tightly.

She searched her father's face and finally planted a kiss on his forehead.

'Take hold of my moustache,' he said to his son, and the boy grabbed the two looping strands of hair. Urtha let him fall, bracing himself as the boy's weight was taken by the voluminous growth. After dangling for a moment, Kymon let go suddenly.

'Who said you could let go?'

'Didn't it hurt you?'

'Of course it hurt me.' Urtha reached for the lad's topknot and hauled him from the ground. Kymon cried out, then hung limply in the painful embrace, angry eyes on his father. 'Does that hurt?'

'Yes.' The boy folded his arms defiantly. 'But as long as you can hold me, I'm happy to dangle here.'

'How much does it hurt?'

'Very much.'

'Only very much?'

'Very much,' the lad said grimly. 'But never mind that. Your arm is certain to tire long before my neck breaks away.'

'Well spoken, you little bastard.' Urtha let him drop. 'Pain hurts; it's in the nature of pain to hurt. Limbs tire; it's in the nature of limbs to tire. The hurt, the tiring, aren't the point. If the hair on our heads and on our lips can be so strong, how strong are our hearts?'

'Very strong,' said Kymon, massaging his scalp.

Urtha crouched down and gathered his children to him. 'Stronger than hair, make no mistake. Don't forget that. Either of you. Before I see you again I will have encountered a strong man and sent him to wander the poisoned marshes, where the dead have no bones, no memories and no song.'

'Cunomaglos!' Kymon cried out furiously.

'Indeed. Cunomaglos. He has a strong beard too. But how strong is his heart?'

'A chicken has a stronger heart!' shouted Kymon.

'True enough. I'll use his beard for rope, though. Never waste good hair.'

'When he dies, others will sing from Ghostland,' Munda announced proudly.

'Yes. Your mother among them. Your brother among them. Now then, both of you, go over to the Mothers. You're in the safest hands possible.' He kissed each child, hugged them, then pushed them towards the three waiting women. 'I'll be back before next spring,' he called after them as they walked away, sadly, reluctantly. 'And we'll go home together. I promise you both!'

He had seemed loving and gentle as he'd played with his children. But now, as we walked back to the edge of this world, to waiting Argo, his face had become like death.

'I will not smile, nor laugh, until my bastard, betraying *uthiin* are all on lances, beheaded, bloody and bewildered. This will be a terrible time, Merlin, a winter time, even though it's summer. You will share your life with a nightmare. But I promise you a fresh start in the spring, if you will just stay by me.'

'I'll do what I can for you, Urtha. As will Jason.'

Urtha glanced at me with a frown. 'Jason? He'll do what's necessary to achieve his own dream. I don't trust him. You, though, I don't know what to make of you, Merlin. I trust you. But you puzzle me. When we came to this place you were fired with excitement. Now . . . well, you look as if you've seen your own ghost.'

'I did. Eleven of them. A rich dish of ghosts.'

'Eleven? No wonder there's blood in your eyes. Who were they?'

What should I say to him? What could I say to him? What would it mean to him, to hear a man like me talk about a time when the world was almost silent, and the earth itself was making forms and shapes that would wander its veins and passages, unknowing, enchanted, and with no other goal, it seemed, than to live and age and watch the passage of the generations.

I had glimpsed where I had come from. I had no idea where I was going. I lived and acted only for the moment through which I passed, rarely venturing elsewhere either for myself or for others. I wore my life like a shroud. The reason I was haunted was not that I had glimpsed the beginning of my days, but that I was now aware of their pointlessness.

With the exception of the one who had gone astray, and now watched me with fierce eyes.

Who was she? Why was she so angry?

'Never mind,' said Urtha, seeing that I was confused. He turned back to the river.

CHAPTER THIRTEEN

——

Moongleam

Mielikki, Lady of the Forest, was waiting for us close to the river, at the edge of her threshold. When she saw us approach she turned and walked towards ancient Argo, moored fore and aft. The veiled woman stepped among the willows and disappeared for a moment, consumed by the shimmering arms of the trees. Then she stepped briefly into view, watching me, and I said softly, 'Thank you. For Urtha, and also for myself.'

But the woman said only, 'Something sour has passed by me and is in the ship, hiding.'

I felt a chill at her words.

Then Urtha and I hauled ourselves aboard the decorated barge. The vessel turned on the water and drifted away from the Land of the Shadows of Heroes, across to the far bank. We came quickly back into twilight, to find Ullanna singing a song, while her fish grilled over burning wood. Ambaros hailed us. We stepped ashore. Niiv embraced me: 'Tell me what you saw. Tell me everything. Are there really ghosts over there? Ambaros says the ghosts are not only of the dead but also of unborn champions. My child is there perhaps. Did you see my child, Merlin? Was it a boy? Did he look like you? Tell me, tell me . . .'

I disentangled the pretty leech from my waist and neck. I have seen jewels shine, but none so brightly as that woman's eyes as she bludgeoned me with her curiosity and her teasing.

'Later,' I said.

'Fish!' announced Ullanna. 'Not much left. Not much to begin with, mind you, but we've saved you a morsel or two. Eat it quickly, or it'll scorch to nothing.'

Urtha picked at the fish on the spit. 'Not bad,' he said.

'Better than the fowl. Just feather and bone. How can you bear to live here, Urtha? The hunting in your country is like searching for shit on the tundra!'

'Hard to find?' I ventured, picking at the moist flesh of the fish.

'And days old and dry when you find it,' Ullanna concluded. 'Still, the apples here have come into fruit strangely early. We won't starve.'

Urtha stared at the Scythian woman for an uncomfortably long time. He was clearly annoyed at the insult to his country; I could imagine him seething in his need to tell the woman that the hunting here was normally very good indeed, but we *were* at the very edge of the Otherworld, in the name of Belenos! And besides, there was every indication that one of the three wastelands of the realm had arisen . . . Though if he had made this case for the poverty of the hunting, no doubt Ullanna would have reminded him of the deer we had seen a few days before, which had seemed perfectly fleshed and easy prey.

He kept his counsel, muttering only, 'Apples are always in fruit, this close to Ghostland.' But then asked quite brazenly, 'I've heard a lot about women from your land. Traders bring stories with them, as well as cloth and wine. Is it true you cut off your left breast so that you can draw a bow?'

Ullanna stared at the man with an expression of disdain. After a while she picked at her teeth with her small gutting knife, responding, 'Is it true you Celts are so clumsy with horses that you have to cut off your balls to make riding easier?'

'Clumsy with *horses?* Are you mad?'

Ullanna laughed. She unbuckled her leather jacket and drew back her blouse on the left side. A small, red-tattooed, hard-nippled breast was revealed. She cocked her head then quickly covered herself again.

'Don't believe everything the Hittites tell you.'

Urtha frowned. 'The Hittites?'

'Gossips. Liars. When I met you I was sure you had no balls. You see? Hittite lies. Though you do ride awkwardly,' she added with a smirk. 'More fish? Quick. What you don't eat, I'll eat. I caught it, after all . . .'

Urtha picked at the carcass. I noticed he'd adjusted his patterned trousers slightly and that Ullanna was amused. Urtha might have been more responsive to the woman's smile, but the shadow of his dead family had confined him, now, to a gloom that would not be brightened until he found the men who had abandoned him. Perhaps Ullanna was aware of this too; she turned away from him, occupied by her own thoughts.

In the late evening, after dark, Niiv suddenly stood and said, 'Argo is going back to the jetty. She wants me to sail with her. Are you coming, Merlin?'

Had Argo spoken to Niiv? I'd heard nothing. Perhaps the two were closer than I'd realised.

I looked quickly at Urtha, thinking of what I had agreed earlier; if the man wanted me to ride back with him, then I'd do so, but he waved his knife dismissively. 'Go ahead. I'll see you back at the fort. I have something to do here before I rejoin Argo. Tell Jason I shan't be long, if he can wait.'

I stepped through the shallows and clambered into the boat. Niiv was snuggled down among the decorated drapes and I lay down beside her, feet to the fore. This eerie, older craft then slipped her mooring and caught the current, rocking slightly as she took the bend in the river. We came below the great sweep of trees that would shade us for at least a day as we sailed back to Jason.

In this moon-streaked silence Niiv worked on me, with all her charms, her laughter especially. Tell me this, tell me that: she wanted to know more about the Path, more about my magic, did it hurt to keep my enchantments so tightly bound inside my skin? Why not share a few simpler charms? And anyway, where had I come from, how could I possibly never age? I should be like a tree, gnarled, broken, lightning-burned and clinging on to life.

She stroked my face, kissed my lips. She took off her clothes in the moonglimmer through the trees and like some silky, silver upright fawn swam in the water, holding on to a mooring rope; I leaned over the hull to watch her glide elegantly in the stream, aroused despite my caution.

'Come in, come in,' she cajoled me. 'You'll love it. This river runs through everything, mind, body, it's like *being* the river . . . it feels so strange! Come in, Merlin, come and taste the water . . .'

I couldn't resist. At the end of my own rope I swam naked with her, letting Argo pull us further to the east, holding that cool, vibrant body against my own, Niiv sprawled on my belly, her nose brushing delicately at mine, lips just touching, tongues just touching.

When we clambered back into the boat she shivered, wrapped a drape around our bodies and curled against me, her hands rubbing me dry and warm.

'Is this the moment?' she whispered through a kiss. 'Please let this be the moment.'

If I had weakened for a while, I found my strength again, removed the arousing fingers (kissed them) and separated our bodies in the confining cloth. An owl swooped silently overhead, its wingbeat touching my hair. For a few minutes I could see its gleaming eyes, blinking and watching me from the branches as it followed our gentle course through the night river. I concentrated on the bird and Niiv grew weary of trying to seduce me.

'This is the perfect opportunity,' she murmured sulkily.

'I'm too old for you,' I answered tiredly, but of course she didn't see me as such.

'The child in me longs for a father; are you afraid that some of your charm will escape from you into the child? Or into me? Is that why you hold back?'

Truthfully, I didn't know. In all my time, in all the worlds of the path I had walked, I had enjoyed myself with abandon, and there were almost certainly many sons and daughters of this roving enchanter, most long dead, but leaving behind sons and daughters of their own. I had never experienced any diminishing of my powers or my insights, only my back and breath. But I had been careful never to fornicate with the mad, moonstruck, overly merry, mysterious or miserable, and whilst the daughters and wives of powerful men held an unhealthy interest for me, I had certainly never wittingly lain with a known enchantress; Niiv's ancestor, Meerga, had been my only lapse. And it was that thought, yes, that kept me at a distance from the Pohjolan girl. Whatever I might pass on in any act of sex or love would be welcome to die in its *own* time; but I didn't want it following me through Time itself.

I was reflecting on this at dawn, watching the crows fly through the airy realm between the branches and feeling Niiv's mouth gentle and sullen on my body, taking a little pleasure now that she had been denied love itself, when the air turned icy, the boat shuddered as if passing over rapids, and I sat up to see the misty shape of a Greek galley before us, prow looming over us, vast in my perception.

The oak barge slid into that hull as easily as dye into water, mist into a forest, absorbed and devoured, leaving Niiv and me wrapped together in the hold of the bigger ship, among the bales and sacks and stowed oars.

Then again we moved on the river, and within a day had come back to the mooring by the track to Urtha's fortress home, to be greeted by Jason and the rest, who for the time of our absence had been living in the fort, burying bodies and building protective talismans and totems to keep the place safe for the next few months.

*　　*　　*

Urtha and Ambaros rode to the gates at sunset of the fourth day. Niiv and I were waiting for them. Ullanna was leading a cow that she had poached from the wilderness, and shouldering a spear laden with hares. She had broken taboo, but refused to listen to Ambaros, who was still sulking at the woman's dismissal of his pleas that hares should not be killed in early spring, when the corn spirit mated with them, and scattered them through the fields, protecting entities until the harvest.

'Meat is meat,' she had said to the outraged older man, 'and a little added "corn spirit" would do no harm either . . .'

To pacify Ambaros I pointed out that if this was indeed a wasteland, then all taboo was suspended for the duration, since there would *be* no harvest. I tried to sound convincing, but it was hard to remember what had happened so long before when it came to taboo.

'Is it?' Ambaros muttered. 'I suppose that might be right. Brigga's blood! We need a poet or druid to make this clearer, but they've all gone over the river,' (he meant to the Otherworld), 'so I'll have to trust your word.'

I believe he was glad to be persuaded.

Urtha had dismounted and stripped to his trousers, flinging down his sword and squeezing the thin gold torque from around his neck. He walked to the two sharpened stakes where the bodies of his mastiffs had been impaled alive. He called out their names, a howl of pain: 'Maglerd! Gelard! Wait for me where the children play. I'll follow you and we'll hunt again, and never again will I doubt you, faithful dogs! I could use you now; there are other dogs to be killed, they walk on two legs, and you would smell them before I could even see the sun on their foulblooded lances!'

It suddenly occurred to him that the stakes were bare; where the shrivelling corpses should have been dangling by the throat, there was just fresh wood.

One of his men told him that the hounds were now in the Shield Lodge.

'You took them down. I'm glad of that. Now I'll give them heroes' funerals, before we leave for the gathering on the river

Daan. Help me, Merlin. I'll need all the Corn Spirits from those hares to do this!'

Grimly he walked to the Shield Lodge. He entered alone and a moment later howled again. And the sound of hounds barking was loud and terrifying. From the noise they made they were struggling with the man, bearing him to the floor, and it was a long time before Urtha staggered from the round house, face wet, hair dishevelled, skin scratched by claws, his eyes, just briefly, alive with delight.

Maglerd and Gelard came after him, pushing at him, standing shoulder high to receive his affection. 'My hounds!' Urtha roared. 'Merlin, they're back from the dead!'

'Never went there!' I shouted at him as again his animals forced him down to a playful struggle. Niiv was laughing, hands covering her mouth. She had been nervous those few days before, when she had used a simple charm to stay the swords of the men who were about to kill the dogs. 'I couldn't let them do it. Something about the hounds . . . I knew they were innocent.'

Sticky and bloody, hair plastered over his eyes and nose, Urtha brought his hunters to heel at last, then walked with them to where Ambaros stood, grinning broadly.

'I'm taking them with me, father. I'm confident Jason will have them aboard. They can't row, but they can fight like demons. Though with Cunomaglos gone, I don't know who will be their guardian.'

'It was the girl who saved their lives,' Ambaros said. 'Merlin has told me everything.'

'Which girl? The Pojholan? Niiv?'

'Yes.'

Urtha tossed Niiv the two coiled leashes. 'Thank you,' he said. 'Meglard, Gelard, go to Niiv.'

The huge hounds obediently crossed the ground and dropped to rest, one on each side of the delighted girl.

'I'll love them with my life,' she avowed, resting a hand on each panting head.

'Time to sail,' Urtha said, rubbing a hand across his grazes and scratches. 'Close the gates behind us; if any man not of this clan is living here when we return, we'll kill him. This is my home. I will not have more of my life stolen! Do you hear that, Scaithach? Morrigan?' He shouted this to the skies, where the crow-queens flew and watched events below. 'This is my home. Guard it for me.'

We closed the gates and Urtha 'crossed' them with two swords from among those found in the ruins. He wrapped each in a strip of the grey and purple cloth that was the clan colour. This done, we returned to Argo and her impatient argonauts.

Jason had set up two braziers before the figurehead of Mie-likki. There were traces of burned flesh and vegetation, and deep cut-marks on the planking of the hull. Jason himself was in a dark mood, heavily and darkly cloaked, and unshaven.

But he brightened slightly as we came aboard, and even approved the hounds, though he was concerned as to what they would consume.

Should I tell him what I had seen? That shade of his son? In the absence of an explanation, it seemed prudent not to do so, but he quizzed me anyway. He could always read my eyes. He knew I was disturbed.

So I told him of 'fierce eyes'.

His only comment was to approve of the fact that I, too, seemed to have a hidden past.

Within the hour we were rowing downstream to the sea, there to cross to the marshy outlets of the Rein; and begin the long river journey to find the Great Quest, which had now been gathering for more than two seasons under the watchful eye of Daanu.

CHAPTER FOURTEEN

—◆—

River Song

With all the argonauts back on board, keen-hearted Argo slipped her tethers and turned in the stream, catching the current and drifting, oar-guided, back through Urtha's land to the blighted land of the Coritani. When we came to the place where Cucallos and Borovos had gone ashore and disappeared, Jason dropped the stone anchor, turning Argo's prow to the shallows where she was held fast. Manandoun and Cathabach went ashore to search for their brothers-in-arms, while aboard the ship we blew horns all day long until the land seemed to echo with our futile calls. The two men returned later, shaking their heads. They clambered back on board.

Niiv saw a solitary swan and snared it; she used her own talents to whisper to the bird and sent it flying low over the woods and hills, circling wider, searching for the lost men, but at dusk it too came back to the river and flopped exhausted into the reeds.

Soon after, to a cheer from Argo's crew, Borovos came out

of the wood and stood at the river's edge. He was tired and dishevelled, his face grimed.

'I agreed to sail with you, Jason, but I ask to be freed from that promise. I'll continue to search for him. Modrona alone knows what has been going on here! If I find him, I'll try to catch up with you, to keep my side of the bargain.'

Knowing well that in the absence of his cousin's body, Borovos could not possibly abandon his search, Jason agreed readily. 'Is there anything you need?' he asked.

'Faster legs, stronger sight,' Borovos answered. He raised his spear, then turned and ran back along the path in the wilderness. Niiv released the swan from its spell. Then Jason ordered torches lit and the anchor weighed. Argo drifted on, Elkavar at the prow and Rubobostes at the tiller. By the next evening we were passing below the rotting forms of the wicker giants and hoisting sail to fight against the grey swell of the sea before us.

Soon after this, Pohjolan Argo entered waters that would have been familiar to the hidden Spirit of the Ship, memories of old, from Jason's second expedition, when his sons had still been infants. On that voyage Argo had hugged the cliffs of Urtha's ancestor's land (Jason not daring to enter what all Greeklanders believed to be the realm of the dead) before crossing this same sea to the estuary of the river dedicated to Reinu, mischievous, dangerous, seductive Reinu, who waited in different guises at each bend in the stream, below each rock overhang, at each tributary, ready to snare the unwary.

Broad waters and wooded banks gave way to towering cliffs, and foaming rapids that tested Argo prow and stern, keeping Rubobostes, on the tiller, taut and tired as he guided the ship between the leering, looming stones. On the shore-line, the grey, the great and the grim watched us from their thatched sanctuaries, but as in Alba, this land was deserted. Nothing but mist, wraith and the haunting, singing voice of Reinu herself gave evidence of life.

Urtha's mood darkened the further east we sailed; each burned-out village, each silent jetty, added to his desolation, enhanced his anger. The man who had been such rowdy, cheering company on the first part of our voyage now rowed or sat in silence, often in his battle kilt, stripped to the waist, face and chest smeared in spirals of the blue dye that marked him as a man approaching combat. Sometimes, when the oars were shipped, I saw blood on the wood where his hands had gripped more tightly than was needed to haul against the flow of the river.

Ullanna, I noticed, kept a cool and careful eye on him, and insisted he accompany her to the shore when she hunted. Invariably, though he might leave grim-faced, he returned laughing, even bragging at his prowess in the chase, a touch of the wilful exaggeration that must have played its part in elevating him, during his combative youth, to the noble rank he now held.

It was to Ullanna that he talked about Aylamunda, though I eavesdropped at every opportunity. I think he knew I was listening. No doubt he assumed I wouldn't want to hear it all again because to me he talked of his sons.

No mention of the 'twin demons' now; no mention of his sons 'tearing the land apart'. Behind the invective had been admiration, and a certainty that his boys, when men, would have overseen the land with fairness and ferocity in equal measure, with an eye to beauty and a mind to necessity. And what more could a father ask, he asked me, though he needed no answer.

Urtha could have been describing himself at that moment: in his heart, the beauty that had been his family, and all his hopes for the future. In his mind's eye, the grim necessity to avenge the death of so many dreams, and of two people in particular. It would be a short, fierce hunt: for Cunomaglos and the others of his *uthiin*, even now greedily waiting for the spoils of Brennos's quest.

And he was envious of Jason.

'He has come back from the dead with a chance to find a son who's still alive. Lucky man. I must die before I see my son again.'

'But there will be a new lifetime, after this. In Ghostland.

Urien will be waiting for you. And Aylamunda will be there.'

'Yes. But perhaps on different islands.'

He was too gloomy, and the ghostlands of the Celts too complex, for this conversation to have continued with any confidence.

The Germanii, Erdzwulf and Gebrinagoth, recognised the river now. They scanned the water ahead of Argo, shouting instructions to Rubobostes and the rowers. They knew where there were safe havens, and where it would be wise to put up our shields. But the call from Brennos to join his Great Quest had largely stripped this waterway of danger, and we berthed on mud banks, hunted inland from gravel shores, and risked very little except the tusks, teeth and claws of the creatures who freshened Michovar's copper cauldron.

With Erdzwulf and Rubobostes, Jason prepared a map of our journey, using charcoal and sheepskin. He called me to the bench where he was marking our route.

'I know you travel a circular path. I also know you often veer from it. Have you veered down this river before?'

I told him that I hadn't. He gave me a long, hard, disbelieving stare, then shrugged. 'Nevertheless, you may recognise a part of the land, and you can correct us if we get it wrong. Now . . .'

And he proceeded to mark our journey, starting by drawing the island of Alba in the west and the ocean he called the Hidden Sea in the east. The Hidden Sea was circular. Colchis, where we had stolen the fleece and Medea had entered Jason's life, lay on its farthest shore.

'From Alba to the Hidden Sea . . . a lifetime's walking: a hundred mountains, a thousand forests, marshes that could swallow the moon herself. But two rivers cross that land. Is that correct, Rubobostes?'

'Indeed,' replied the Dacian thoughtfully, 'though I have only ever heard of this Rein, never seen it.'

Jason drew the two rivers, the Rein flowing west towards Alba, the Daan flowing east towards the Hidden Sea, but each river rising in marshes and forests in the heart of the land.

'And passing close together only seven days' walk apart.' He stabbed a finger on the crude map. 'That is the task for us. To carry Argo across that bridge of marsh and forest, between the waters dedicated to angry Reinu and fragrant Daanu, and then we'll be there. Sniffing at this Brennos's heels! We carried her before when we were beached on the Libyan desert, do you remember, Merlin? A giant wave,' he explained to the others. 'It struck us and carried us two days inland, leaving us high and dry and at the mercy of the sun. We nearly died. But the desert gave up its own dead, long enough for them to visit our dreams, to mock us into *living* again. We found the courage to drag Argo back to salt water and continue our journey home.'

I remembered the incident well, though the huge wave that had swept us inland had not displaced us by two days, more like half a day; and no desert dead had visited *me* in my dreams. I said, 'Argo was smaller then and you had more men on board. We had more shoulders to help the dragging.'

'We'll do a count of shoulders later,' Jason said with irritation. 'Now: for the details . . .'

And between them, they sketched what they remembered of the curves and rapids in each of the waterways, and I watched and became confused, because Time changes even hills, and I realised that much that I had once known had gone, though it lived in my memory.

'Cheer up, Merlin,' he said to me suddenly, with a wide grin, interrupting my dream. 'Can you see any flaw in the plan? Have we missed anything, do you think? You can see what I propose for our ship.'

To row as far up Reinu's river as possible, then carry Argo overland for seven days, maybe more, to where the waters of Daanu began to deepen and could take the draft of our vessel. Then to row with the current, south and east in the direction of the Hidden Sea, until we came to the forest where Brennos was gathering his warrior horde, ready for invasion.

'You'll need wooden rollers,' was my feeble contribution. 'To drag the ship.'

'Rollers . . .' Jason scratched his beard. 'Well, yes. We'll have to get them from trees, I suppose. The round trunks should be useful. Are there any trees in the forests between the headwaters of our two rivers, Rubobostes?'

'I'm told there are,' the Dacian answered, 'though of course, this could just be rumour.'

And they all laughed.

Jason furled up the skin, half watching my forlorn features. 'Don't look so concerned, Merlin. I'll have you back on the Path before long. This isn't the first time you've ventured away from it, after all.'

As ever, with Jason, I revealed too much of myself, putting into words a thought that had been lingering with me since Ghostland.

'Something tells me my time on the Path is coming to an end.'

'*Something*, eh?' Jason and Rubobostes exchanged an amused glance. 'Well, there's certainly no arguing with that.'

They'd probably been drinking. There was no other reason I could think of at that moment for this levity.

But he came to find me later, where I crouched in the hold, as close to the entrance to the Spirit of the Ship as I dared without invitation. The moon was full and high and Argo glowed silver as she rolled on the current. Cathabach was singing quietly as he held the steering oar, waiting for dawn, for up-anchor, for the deepening journey.

'How is she?' Jason asked as he hunkered down beside me. He proffered a flask of wine and a sweet biscuit, which I declined.

'Who? Mielikki?'

'I'd expected her to be more troublesome.'

'She doesn't own the ship,' I reminded him. 'And she's aware that there is something else aboard, something she doesn't like.'

'Probably me,' Jason muttered. He was in grim mood; but in a way that was not like Jason. I was curious. We stared at the darkness in the hull, smelling frost and summer mixed and fluid, the seepage from that other world.

'I'd have thought you could come and go as you please,' he said provocatively.

'I guard my life, and bide my time,' I reminded him.

'Ah, yes. Staying young. Not too many favours.'

'Not too many favours,' I agreed.

'Hera limited her favours to me,' he rambled on, 'when we went for the fleece, for Medea, when we fled and killed that poor boy. Remember? When we travelled the world. Limited her favours.' His brow deepened as what he remembered caused him pain. 'But you know, she always made it clear what she would do, and she didn't trick us. This Pohjolan witch . . .'

'Sssh! Witches can hear, and witches do damage. Mielikki so far has been a good guide, and a good help.'

'For you, perhaps,' Jason said sharply.

He was certainly drunk, though our supplies of wine were very low. He was brooding; and yet also concerned. And there was a strange gleam in his eyes.

His references to Hera were accurate (but then they should have been, since for him they were only twenty years in his past!).

Hera, travelling in the Spirit of the Ship, had advised and directed our first journey, and had told Jason no lies. She had helped us through the clashing rocks, guided us to the harpy-tormented blind man, Phineus, put words of love in Medea's ears to help her betray her father and her people. But when Jason and Medea had dismembered Medea's brother, throwing the pieces of his body over the stern to delay her avenging, pursuing father, Hera had withdrawn from the vessel. That had been an act of violence too much for the goddess whom Jason had persuaded aboard. Argo was ice-hearted at that moment, without a guardian, but she was a ship of memory, and older memories, older guardians, had come back to her. Argo loved her captain, no matter who that captain was, no matter what deeds were done from the shelter of her womb.

And no deed had been so badly done as that killing and cutting and savaging of the youth, his sister contriving the plan to keep her father at a distance since he would have to bury every piece of his son he found, while Jason and she fornicated and frolicked their way to freedom, along the winding flow of the Daan, the river we were soon to join again.

Jason threw the remnants of his wine into the darkness. As he stood, Ruvio struggled in his harness, disturbed by the angry mood close by. Above us, clouds rocked against the moon.

'There's a libation for you, dear Lady,' Jason said. 'Here's another.'

He opened his britches and pissed against the bulkhead.

He had stepped into the place where even I dared not go except by invitation. He crouched there, below the struts and knotted ropes, and banged his fist against the double hull, but not in anger, more as if summoning.

Lemanku had been blinded because he had breached this threshold, in his enthusiasm to build a new and better ship. Jason, drunk, had entered Argo's heart with impunity, but Argo remained silent. Had a new threshold been crossed, then? Just as I began to need the ship in a way I had never anticipated, was Jason now signalling his desertion? His words seemed to suggest so:

'So many old ships are buried here,' he whispered as he stroked the wood. 'So much *time* creaks and complains in these old and new timbers. So many forgotten worlds, but worlds still here! Though perhaps not forgotten by you, Merlin,' he added, glancing at me quickly. 'But worlds still here, if only in the shadows. Each ship was built with timber, skill, adventure and purpose—and was guarded by a spirit from its age. And they're all there still, those spirits, that's my belief. They're all alive there, behind this birch and oak, and the right words can bring them back. Your new witch doesn't scare me, Merlin.'

My new witch? Did Jason think I was responsible for Mielikki's presence? I'd done nothing more than attend at the forest rite, when the birch was cut.

'My old witch helped me when I needed her,' he was rambling bitterly. 'Hera! She'll help me again if I call loud enough. This ice-hearted crone has done nothing yet. She's given me no sign at all of what lies ahead!' He stared up at the leaning figurehead and Forest Lady stared back, grey and hard-eyed in the moonlight, slash-mouthed and lank-haired, watching Argo's captain with almost challenging indifference.

I wondered if I should tell him that I believed Hera and her ghostly predecessors had abandoned the ship, so much time having passed as Argo, lay frozen on the bed of the lake. Argo had felt dead on rising through the ice. But I couldn't be sure. And I was afraid it would cost me too much of my life to make the journey and find out.

'Have you asked her for help?'

'Twice. When we were moored by Urtha's fortress.'

So that's what he had been doing!

'What did you ask her for?'

He seemed surprised by the question. 'A sight of my *son*, of course. Or a direction to someone who might help to find him. Anything! Hope! What else? A dream to hold, to concentrate my mind while we sail.'

'But you *know* where he is. He's with Brennos, among the army gathering on the shores of the Daan, waiting for whatever madness Brennos has in mind.'

The empty wine pouch was slapped against my face, a reprimand. 'I had *two* sons, Merlin. Do you imagine that I've forgotten Kinos? My little Kinos? If Thesokorus is still alive, why not him? But you're right.'

I'd said nothing to be right about, merely watched him.

'You're right. One son at a time. Thesokorus should be in my mind first because at least he's in my grasp.' He rose unsteadily to his feet. 'You can have the ship, Merlin. Take over as captain. You have the eyes of a hawk, the ears of an owl, you're older than mountains, but I know you're human because I've seen the way you look at that girl, half in lust, half in fear. Only men are confused by those two feelings. You can have your little confidences with the Frost Bitch, old Lady Gnarled Wood. Fuck her in her knot-holes, for all I care. I'm sure you'll find she has more than one. But I'm sorry I pissed on her.' He turned unsteadily away. 'I'm sorry I pissed on you!' he shouted to the figurehead, again disturbing Ruvio and several of the slumbering argonauts. 'It won't happen again!'

He slumped down beside me, eyed me carefully, then shook his head.

'I need to ask. I have to know,' he whispered. 'Not knowing claws at me.'

I knew what was coming. This was the real reason for his drunken fury. He had put off asking for too long. Now he needed to know about Medea.

He said, 'She taunts me in my dreams, running from me, a bloody head in each hand. The image haunts me, Merlin. She turns, laughs, and tosses the trophies to me, and I catch them. Cold, bloody balls of flesh and bone, young faces grimacing at me. A terrible dream—'

'But just a dream. We can break that dream.'

He turned to me, tearful and anguished, the drink taking its hold on him. 'What happened to her? Did she have a long life?'

I could only tell him what I'd heard, though the news wouldn't please him. 'She lived to a great age. After her father died, she returned to Colchis, safe again, and set up her sanctuary. Her tomb lies in the Valley of the Crow, north of Colchis. Though it has been desecrated several times.'

'That was me,' Jason muttered with a hard, bitter smile. 'Reaching from the lake! Or if it wasn't, it should have been.'

Then he looked into his empty leather flask. 'Well. That's that. Now I know. And it doesn't help. Perhaps we should find some better wine . . . less *sour*!'

We rowed on, the days marked as different only by the changing colour of the forests and the rise and fall of the crags and cliffs that towered so silently above us as the river narrowed. We saw fires burning, one day at dusk, and Argo slowed while Jason and Gebrinagoth studied the low island in the water, a long spit of land, heavily wooded, its shores partially stockaded. A line of youths waited there, watching us, some of them armed.

When Gebrinagoth called out, asking if we might put ashore, children of several ages appeared suddenly and curiously, peering round the cloaks and trousers of their elder companions.

'No!' came the answering call. Older men appeared now. One of them called to us, 'If you're looking for the other ships, they passed by more than a month ago.'

'I counted more than forty,' came a second voice. 'Drumming hard. In a hurry.'

Suddenly Gebrinagoth realised the nature of this island in the river.

'It's the Place without Mercy,' he said. 'Among the families who rule along the north of the river, when a father suspects the legitimacy of his newly born son, he casts him into the water. Legitimately born children swim ashore, saved by Reinag, Reinu's dreamy, kindly husband. Illegitimate ones are swept away to the sea and drown. A few, I've heard, find the strength to swim against the flow, to this haven. Reinu doesn't allow them to leave the island, but she keeps them alive. These are those survivors.'

Not long after, we found the forty ships. Most had been drawn up on to the shore, roped down and covered; a few had been scuttled and lay drowned in shallow water. One had been burned. Its charred hulk was set apart from the rest, inside a shallow trench. The blackened corpses of several animals lay within it.

The war bands who had beached these ships had continued their journey to Brennos by cart, chariot and horse over the southern hills, following a wide path through the forest. The route would take them weeks, but they had not thought to drag their vessels as now Jason organised the dragging of Argo.

There was an hour of delight among those of the argonauts who knew about these matters, since the rollers for the ship could be cut from the masts of the beached vessels, saving time and effort in the woods. The covers were thrown off and the stocky masts thrown down, trimmed to make them level along their widths, and of manageable lengths for three or four men to carry them forward as the rolling road was laid.

We would have to follow the forest path for a day, in the wake of the war bands, but then turn east again, ascend and descend a sequence of hills, and cross a dangerous expanse of marsh. On our own, twenty men and women only, we would need a month to haul our boat, our supplies and ourselves across that land.

But we had Ruvio, the Dacian horse, and he would prove to be tireless.

Niiv and Rubobostes returned on Ruvio from their sortie up river, assessing its accessibility to Argo. The Dacian was looking confused.

'Rocky shallows and rapids is all I can see. I'm not surprised these ships were drawn ashore here. But the girl disagrees.'

Niiv was excited. 'There are fingers of water everywhere,' she told me in front of Jason. 'They fan out. Some of them are deep. I can smell them. They come from the hills and woodlands. All we have to do is find them. I'm sure we can find them—with a little help,' she added meaningfully.

I thought for a moment she meant from me, but she made it clear she was referring to Argo herself, in particular to Argo's guardian.

'Old Lady Forest can open ice and split open the log-jams of rivers. She could *lift* Argo through the shallows. We can get so much further by water. Less dragging,' she added.

Erdzwulf confirmed that several rivers poured into the flow of the Rein at this point, and that yes, if they *were* navigable, then indeed they could bring us to the edge of the Wolf Marsh, and only one mountain pass away from the headwaters of the Daan.

'But they're not. Not navigable, I mean.'

'Not yet,' Niiv volunteered, her eyes sparkling. 'Let me talk to Mielikki. Merlin, come with me? Please? She seems to favour you.'

I agreed, though I felt apprehensive after Jason's rude re-

jection of the ship a few nights before. Mielikki had exacted
no revenge for the old Achaean's drunken heresy, but I remembered her sudden violence at our departure from Pohjola
as much as I remembered her kindness in showing Urtha his
surviving children, and warning me of a shadow presence
watching me from the Spirit of the Ship.

Alone, on board, I rested in Ruvio's harnessing while Niiv
sang delightfully to the goddess, her long hair liquid in the
torchlight as she weaved her shoulders and head in the rhythm
of her song. Frost-faced Mielikki watched her with no softening of the features on the wood, but after a while Niiv was
silent. She drew her cloak about her shoulders, her hood over
her head, stood and turned to me. When she stepped towards
me I saw more bone than flesh in the beautiful face.

'Put out the torch,' the girl said. 'Get them all on board.
Row according to my directions.'

The voice was Niiv's, but her breath, as it reached me, was
of stinking swamp.

The argonauts were roused from a sleep induced by feasting. Muttering and complaining they dragged aboard the rollers we would need, then took their places at the oars. But
Niiv instructed them to blindfold their eyes.

'Rowing blind and at night? And in rocky water? This is
madness,' Manandoun complained, but Jason silenced him.

'You too, Jason,' Niiv commanded. She had taken the
steering oar and stood there, braced against its shaft. Her
faced glowed with frost and moonlight. Jason was obedient,
a man humbled, perhaps, by the recognition that Argo was
going to assist our passage despite his harsh words.

He tied a cloth around his eyes and took over my place at
the oar. I went forward. Niiv shouted to me: 'Don't look too
deeply, Merlin. But you may look a little.'

She knew I would understand what was happening, but she
was showing off a little, and there was no harm in that. I'd
let her use her own enchantment.

She commanded the moorings loosed and the oars to strike.
Argo lurched on the river, then seemed to glide, the oar blades
tickling the water almost in silence.

The shore crowded in on us and the river ran fast and white below the prow, but Argo kept moving forward, into the hills, always turning left where two streams joined. Sometimes the vessel shuddered, sometimes shook as we grazed over gravel beds. The branches of alder and willow raked the deck. The men rowed steadily, though, their pull directed by the rhythm in Niiv's eerie song, which she called a *northsong*. She swayed on the shaft as if the steering oar was as light as a feather.

'Don't look back!' she commanded when I glanced at her, and I obeyed, but not before I had seen the distant glow of sunlight behind her, as if we moved through a tunnel. Above us, the moon was horned and bright. Jupiter gleamed steadily, four tiny golden birds dancing attendance on it. The river narrowed further. Not even a coracle could have floated here now. But Argo slid like a swan in the night, a seemingly endless night, moved by song and guided by magic.

I left her to her own devices.

'This is a long stretch,' Elkavar announced after several hours. 'Has the day come up? Might we rest? Might we sip something?'

'No rest,' Niiv said. Again I glanced back. Mielikki loomed above the girl, a frightening silhouette against that ruby sun.

'Then perhaps a different song,' the Hibernian insisted, but Niiv hissed, 'Silence your tongue. A different song is a different spell!'

She picked up the *northsong* again. Argo pressed on, along streams and channels that could not possibly have taken her draft.

Creatures moved through the woods that crowded round us, heads raised curiously against the stars, eyes gleaming as they stared down at us. If the argonauts had not been blindfolded I believe they would have panicked. I saw a wolf's maw and the muzzle of a stag. Bright-eyed owls blinked as the frail craft passed below them, and for one terrible moment the sky darkened as a crow flew from its nest, swooped low above us and decided that we were too strange to devour.

'This is as far as we go,' Niiv suddenly announced. 'Ship oars!'

This was done, but the exhausted crew remained at their seats, still blindfolded as Niiv instructed. She ordered them ashore and they stumbled from the craft, crawling up the steep bank. Rubobostes, working in the dark, tethered his horse round the stern of Argo and with the rest of us pushing the beast heaved and laboured, drawing the ship from the water, dragging Argo a hundred paces through the undergrowth, where she slipped slightly to the side and rested.

Rest came to us all, then, and we slept until dawn. I awoke to find Niiv curled into my body, her face as peaceful as a child's. While the rest of us stood, stretched and sought relief from that long and arduous night, Niiv slept on. Mielikki had left her and her beauty was back.

Jason called to me and I went to the thin, fern-fringed stream that ran down from the mountainside among rocks, scrubby oaks and twisted thorns. 'Did you do this?' he asked. 'Did you bring us up this impossible stream?'

'Not me. I just looked ahead and discouraged predators.'

Indeed, my back was aching and my eyes sore. I'd been using my talents without realising it and could think only that Mielikki must have had a bony hand on my heart during that river trip. It was too worrying to imagine that it might have been Niiv influencing me.

'You look concerned,' Jason said.

'I'm always concerned around you,' I replied. 'You piss on goddesses and stalk the world, seven hundred years dead, as if nothing had happened. That's a concerning sort of man.'

'Seven hundred years?' He laughed quietly. 'I don't even want to know what might have passed in my sleep. And that's how it feels, Merlin. I've been asleep. Now I'm awake, but what's changed? Trees look the same, the stars look the same, you look the same. Women look and smell the same. The sea smells the same. And I'm sailing with one young man who's out for revenge, and a lot of others who are searching for things that only the gods are prepared to give them. What's *different*? On board is a man who sings like a dying cat rather than a skylark and plays an instrument that sounds like Hel giving birth, rather than the lulling strings of Orpheus's harp. But what's different? When I see my son I'll know him by his eyes; he'll know me by mine; he'll want to fight me; he'll be angry; he's lived without me as long as I've lived without him; it will take time for the embrace, it always does when love has been denied a father and his son. What's different?'

He stared at me, waiting for an answer.

'I don't know,' I said at last. 'But something is.'

I was thinking: *the ship. Something in the ship. Something sour* . . .

Jason shrugged. 'New gods, new philosophies, new metals, new kingdoms. Is that what you mean by *something*? It would take me the rest of my life to understand *those* differences. All I crave is to fill in the gap in my sons' lives. I'll do anything. I'll sit down by the fire, I'll do as I'm told, I'll let them mock me, rage at me, call me seven kinds of monster . . . just so long as I fill that gap of twenty years. I'm haunted by that silence, Merlin. Can you understand that? Where did they go? What did they hunt? Who did they love? What jokes did they share? What did they learn? That's all that interests me. That's the only difference in my life that I wish to be made recognisable. Can you understand that?'

'More than I can understand how a ship built for forty men can have been rowed by twenty up a stream too narrow for a swan.'

'But it was you who did it. Admit it, Merlin.'

'Not me. The ship.'

'Not the ship. Not the ship! I no longer need the ship. You were right to say she died when I came back from death. I will not have help from that ship, only you. You, however, can take help from where you can. And pass it on if you need to.'

And with a wave of his hand, a dismissive, angry, ungrateful gesture, he stormed back to where his argonauts sat huddled around the fire, yawning, murmuring, trying to come to an understanding of their dreams.

Later in the day, Rubobostes galloped back to Argo, his face red with excitement.

'It's a long haul up the hill here, but then it's a free ride down to the marshes. I saw horses and deer grazing in the distance. Riding *and* eating! A Dacian's dream! It looks rank and dangerous, though, and there are heavy forests on the horizon. Where's Ullanna? She could hunt blindfolded and still bring us our supper.'

Niiv slept on. No amount of shaking or calling to her could rouse her, so I wrapped her carefully in her cloak and carried her into the belly of Argo. She was in the Death Sleep, a place I'd been to myself, though being so much younger than me, and being inexperienced in the using of the power of charm, she would take longer to walk back from that realm.

When she came back, though, she would be stronger.

It was Elkavar who brought a note of practicality to the situation, as we began to unload the contents of Argo's hold.

'We'll never haul this ship over that hill,' he said. 'Not with so few of us. Fifty or sixty, maybe. But not with so few.'

'I've carried this ship before,' Jason growled at him irritably, 'I'll carry it again.'

'Not with the sort of knots you use to harness her,' Rubobostes put in quietly. 'They'll snap, or rip her keel from ribs. A hundred paces was fine. But not that distance.'

We all looked at him. He seemed surprised by the sudden attention. 'Grease, rollers, ropes, pulleys, it would take a lifetime without a hundred men. What you need is Ruvio, old stump-puller there, and *Gordion knots*.'

A number of blank faces stared at him, waiting. Then Jason raised his hands: well? What are they?

'A Gordion knot is very clever. A rope pulled through the tangle of the knot is helped by the knot itself! It seems to pull on itself. It reduces effort greatly. It's been known since time began, but only certain men can master its complexity. A Makedonian warlord tried to untie it and failed—'

'Alessandros,' Tairon whispered.

'Iskander,' Ullanna muttered. 'I remember now.'

'The same. A generation ago, when he was leading his army east. He was ordered to either untie the knot or worship publicly at its sanctuary. He wanted to prove himself and so spent days struggling with it. But the knot defeated him, and in a fit of rage cut it through with his sword. An act of defiance. The knot fell apart, the cut ends dropped away, leaving two smaller, identical knots. A very clever device.'

'And of no practical use to us at all, by the sounds of it,' said Jason, still irritable. 'Since we don't have one.'

'I should have mentioned: I know how to tie one.'

'Well, well, well . . .' Jason breathed, with a great, approving grin at the Dacian.

'I told you I'd be useful.'

Jason and Erdzwulf lashed lengths of mast along each side of the keel, to broaden the base of the ship and make her easier to roll. Then the tired but willing Dacian horse took the strain as Argo, propped on each side by eight of us, pushed by eight, with four argonauts running the rollers from stern to prow, was inched along the rise of the hill, a labour that soon became a matter of routine. Ruvio snorted and steamed, but he was soon in his stride and had reached the first of two summits before his shaking head and whinnying objection told his master that a rest was needed.

Rubobostes fussed and stroked his steed, even sharing his water. I heard him murmur, 'I hope we never run out of meat. I'm sure they'd slaughter and consume *me* before they considered *you* for the spit!'

When Niiv finally stirred from her deathly sleep, we were on high ground, looking into the misty distance. The first stretch of the Daan that was navigable lay only two days away, now, across a lake and marshes in the land that Erdzwulf was sure was the tribal territory of the Sequani, a land which stretched before us into evening oblivion.

PART FOUR

Hawk Watching

CHAPTER FIFTEEN

—

Hawk Watching

The ice on the great river Daan had begun to crack. Swirling flights of cranes and crows circled the vast sprawl of camps and enclosures that stretched along its shores and through the forest. Spring would soon burst from winter tree and frozen ground. Already the air was quickening, and the gathered hordes were stirring from their winter quarters. The fires burned brighter and clan colours were added to the high totems that marked each separate army.

Here were kings of the Bituriges and Avernii, warlords of the Senones and Ambarii, chiefs and champions of the Carnutes and Trocmii, large clans and small, some each other's bitter enemies. But all enmities and discourtesies had been put aside on pain of death, though early on Warlord Brennos had allowed some settling of hostility by champions. No claim for slaves or territory was allowed after the combat, however, merely an agreement for the losing party to pay from the spoils of the Quest.

Foraging parties went out again into the largely deserted

country around this stretch of the Daan, searching for stray cattle, sheep and horses and forgotten fields of winter roots. Corn would be gathered on the way, later in the year from the fields, or sooner from the storehouses of villages.

With the end of winter, war parties with their own supplies came in from their camps to the north or east, the last of the tribes to join the Great Quest. Each was a long train of riders, chariots, men on foot, women and children, wagons and carts, and what remained of their oxen, goats, geese and salted joints of pig.

These new arrivals were assigned to one or other of the armies under Brennos's two commanders, either to Achichoros or Bolgios, and taken to find ground to camp and forage in the woods. Their leaders were instructed on their position in the forthcoming march to the south, the direction of the march being the only available information at this time.

The three warlords rode through the swarming camps, Achichoros in his grey wolfskin cloak and falcon-crested helmet, red-bearded, jade-eyed Bolgios in his iron-studded leather armour, Brennos, narrow-eyed, narrow-featured, heavily moustached, his helmet made from the tusks of boars, his short green cloak embroidered with the bloody muzzle of this totem beast. They encouraged and promised, congratulated and reassured (their destination was not yet known to any but these three commanders). They made sure that the baggage trains were organised and ready, the order of animals, the order of horsemen. They settled the petty squabbles of rival bands, meted out justice in the presence of druids, exacted life where their rules had been breached, and all the time noted numbers, supplies, strengths and weaknesses in this wild and unwillingly restrained horde of glory seekers.

Only the envoys who had journeyed to the west remained to return, those who had gone to recruit in forested Gaul, among the Remii, and in misty Alba and mountainous Celidon. Each day, watch was kept for their dark shapes to appear on the western hills, but time was running out for them.

While they waited for their numbers to reach the final figure for warriors and champions, which had been told to Brennos in his glorious dream, games were held at all hours of the day and night, tribe against tribe, champions in combat, youth against the old. Chariot races, running contests, javelin contests and feats of memory enlivened the waiting. Now was the time for head hair to be shaped and stiffened with lime-water, for chin hair to be cut back to a stubble, for bodies to be daubed with dyes in clan colours, and for bronze to be polished, swords given their edge and votive shields painted and cast into the water, dedicated to Daan, Teutates and Nemetona, the protecting gods. Cloth, woven during the winter, was cut and shaped, leather was stitched, the winter dead were given careful, sorrowful burial in mounds built on the northern banks of the Daan, in the shelter of groves.

Dogs roamed and scavenged. Horses were broken, trimmed and harnessed, given names, a few sacrificed, their haunches cast into the flooding water, the rest distributed to the elite among the horsemen.

Everything was restless, nervous, a suppressed energy that would very soon burst out into the land around like water from behind a frozen wall of ice. Brennos sensed the urgency of the need to make a move sooner, rather than later.

But a moon waxed and waned.

Then horns and trumpets, sounding a distant din from the western hills, signalled the final arrival of the Gauls, and the Albanii from the Island of Ghosts, and the fiery Celidonii with their wild running-dancing way of moving. It was evening. Orange light glinted on what seemed a thousand raised spears and shields, and then a thousand more as the tribes spilled over the crests of the hills and down towards the river, wildly yelling, racing their small horses, pursued by a horde of barking dogs and shouting children.

As these last arrivals were greeted, fed, numbered and divided between the armies, away from the mayhem a small band of skirmishers from the south rode quietly to the gates of Brennos's enclosure, six men in all, wrapped well against the chill, well provisioned, well armoured, totally exhausted. Lord Bolgios, wine flask in hand, came out to meet them.

'We'd given you up for dead.'

'The dead have given us back,' the dark-eyed man who led them answered. 'We've been in Hell, and no doubt about that, but it seems we're not welcome there. But the route you propose will work. There are watch stations at the heads of most of the valleys, easy enough to overcome. Only the pass in Thessaly will cause difficulty.'

'You'll be able to tell us all about it later. But first you need sleep. Welcome back, Orgetorix. And well done.'

A day later, Brennos lit five great fires in the sprawling royal enclosure he had constructed at the heart of the gathering, and sent for the kings, warlords and champions of every tribe to come and feast and learn the details of the quest ahead. They came dressed for ceremony, high-crested helmets, bright-coloured cloaks, shimmering bronze and gold at their necks and arms, riding the best of the horses, which shone behind their armoured masks. The smell of roasting meat and hot, honeyed wine was rich in the air. Four hundred men feasted for a day, and not one was allowed the best cut but rather all who had come to the feast were given a portion of all cuts; fighting and abuse were limited to the verbal kind, though a few jugs and plates were thrown. But a guard of men with throwing spears stood around the feast with instructions to strike down any man, no matter how high in rank, who drew sword from scabbard.

Truth to tell, it was curiosity as much as anything that kept these champions on their best behaviour.

Early in the afternoon, a pair of hawks appeared, hovering above the fires in the enclosure as if watching the events below. When, later, drunk, Tungorix of the Avernii used slingshot to strike the male on the wing, bending back the feathers, Brennos ordered him to leave the enclosure. He had taken the birds as an omen of far sight and good luck. That luck had been wounded

'Nemetona has sent them. Hawks like those can see both danger and their prey as if by magic. In the same way we shall see danger ahead, and spot our prey as if with the eyes of hawks. All birds are good omens.'

A while later, though, one of the hawks flew down to get

a closer look. But a raven dropped suddenly from the sky in a panic of spread wings, chasing the hawks back to the blue before landing on the table where Bolgios and his commanders were seated in brooding silence. It raised its wings to cast shade over the weary face of Orgetorix, seated at the same table. Then it snatched a bone from the wooden platter from which Bolgios himself was eating and launched itself into the air, but rather than departing back to its rook, it attacked the hawks again, which dived and veered and fled the scene, though they returned soon after to continue their hovering observation.

After that, Bolgios's mood darkened, though he refused to refer to the counsel of a wise man in order to correctly interpret the sign.

Brennos now decided to call an end to the feast and finally declare the nature of the quest to which he had dedicated two years of his life, and for which he had sent riders to the ends of the known world.

He pinned a red, rough wool cloak at his shoulder, climbed the ramp to the watch platform inside the wall, and looked down at the gathered host, smiling as he saw the mess of bones, bread and spilled wine that covered the long tables. The mood was good. He had carried a small oval shield with him, and this he now placed at his feet. There was nothing on the shield but polished wood and a small bronze boss. In effect, he was stripped of status. And with this humility he addressed the assembled kings, chiefs and champions.

'I am Brennos! I have a clan, a family and land. But as of this moment I have *no* clan, family or land. *You* are my clan. *You* are my family. And my land is the dream that was sent to me from Ghostland—to summon and lead a great army of the best of us, the most courageous of us, the most feared of us!

'I am nothing without you. When the dream is fulfilled, I will be nothing more than a man who once dreamed. But until then, I am Brennos! And you have answered my call to arms. And now you need to know the reason for the call.

'Is there any man here who does not know how our ancestors were robbed by brutal pillagers, murderers and mercenaries, people who were strangers in our land? Armed men who came without thought of peace or trade, but only with thoughts of destruction, despoliation, desecration and the plundering of our sacred groves and the high, proud tombs of our forefathers! If such a man is here, then he was born without a past. But there are no such men here, I am certain of that.

'Those strangers took away our chariots, our shields, our heads and our hearts. And they took all that was shaped from gold and silver, and was sacred. All that had been fashioned from bronze and obsidian, all that was sacred to us because it held the richest part of the life of our clans—our ancestors! Those precious objects were the vessels from which the dead were able to move among us. They were stolen. To be offered to the blind caves in the mountains of the south, where windy voices and wine-sodden gods and goddesses tell lies about their futures. These places are called *oracles* and they are stuffed with infamy. And filled with treasure. And that treasure is our stolen heritage.

'Is there any man here who has not heard the wailing of our ancestors, now that their lives of adventure, of feasting and of combat in our ghostlands has been blighted? Their worldly memory is not in its place in our houses, but locked away in those temples of lies, the sick booty of men who are strangers to us. Every man here has heard those wails, I am certain of that. Looking at you, I see the tears in your eyes. We have all suffered.'

He was silent for a moment, then went on, quietly at first:

'When I was a boy, I watched my father fight for honour in single combat. Five times in as many years. What man among you has not done the same at some time in his life? Not one of you, I am sure of that. Five times in all, my father fought: in each fight using chariot and our swift, short, throwing spears; then on foot with sword and the long stabbing spear; then in water with axe and shield, and then in the racing, running, jumping way. Four times, in these challenges, he was the victor, and the fifth time he gave his head, and it was honourably given and honourably taken. I was older by then. Two years later I raided his killer and took back the head. I did it swiftly, fairly, decisively. Honourably! If any one of you has taken back the head of a father, a brother, an uncle, a foster brother, strike the table! Strike it now!' he shouted.

'By the Lord of Thunder himself, that is a frightening sound you make. Even iron-striking Teutates, Lord of Lightning, would quake at that sound. Yes, as you have made clear by that clamour, we have all done it. We have all seen a loved one killed swiftly, fairly, decisively. Honourably! And we have taken vengeance swiftly, fairly, decisively. Honourably!'

He looked up to the sky and pointed. 'We are like those two hawks that hover over us. Do you see them? They are still there. They are from forest-loving Nemetona, or perhaps from battle-hungry Badb, Queen of Slaughter, what does it matter? They are no ordinary hawks, they are watching us, and listening to us, and we are the same, ready to watch, to listen, and then to strike, suddenly, swiftly, decisively!

'You saw the raven that pecked at the bones on Bolgios's plate. That was not an omen of death. Cheer up, Bolgios, good friend! That raven was a lesson. It struck without honour; it is a carrion bird; but it will steal good meat if it finds it; the strangers who came to our lands were carrion seekers. They found something precious and took advantage of our infighting and our weariness of war. They stole our ancestors.

'After a day's fighting, we are all weak. Our spilled blood turns rivers red. Wolves could bloat on the flesh we carve from each other's limbs. But in the morning we are strong again, our strength returns, and the fight is on.

'The strangers struck when we were weak. They stole our memories, they stole our lives. Now we are strong. Now we will take back our lives, our gold, our silver, our masks, our chariots, everything that is precious to us, everything that was looted from us, everything that is hoarded by those strangers.

'It will be a long march, and a difficult passage. But the further we go the warmer and brighter that march will be. Why? Because we are going to Greek Land! We are going to raid Greek Land! We will take back everything that is ours, from the land of the Illyrians, and from Makedonia, where Aleksandros kept his spoils. But Greek Land is where we will find the glory of our ancestors! At a place called Delphi, where a snake guards the cave where most of our past lies stored. We will cut the head from the snake, rip the hearts from the so-called priests who collect the tribute, then break open the earth itself. And take back our fathers' lives!'

These last words, almost screamed, drew a clamorous response from the guests in the enclosure. As they cheered and drummed the tables with their fists and swords, Brennos again looked up at the hovering hawks, and for a moment, so fleeting that only Orgetorix at the feast noticed it, there was uncertainty in his eyes.

As Brennos came down the ramp, Orgetorix came towards him, bringing him his boar's-tusk helmet. Brennos watched him carefully but kindly.

'That was a fine speech. I'm impressed by this gathering, Lord Brennos. Aleksandros, as you call him, raised an army and conquered half the known world and much that was unknown. But this horde is countless. You could conquer the gods themselves. And you called them here on your word alone. I'm impressed.'

Brennos accepted the compliment humbly. 'It still remains to be done, Orgetorix. I'm making a claim for more warriors than I actually have. Sometimes what seems like a thousand is only a hundred. So several thousand can seem tens of thousands. And I have no intention of conquering the gods themselves. Except for that snake at Delphi. For the rest, I'll leave the Greeklanders' gods alone. This is about plunder; and the return of a plundered past.'

'The past can be robbed in many different ways, Brennos.'

The warlord tugged at his moustache as he digested this impertinent observation. He smiled thinly, then agreed. 'Yes it can. And one day I shall ask you about your own plundered past. And why you, a Greeklander, pretend to be other than you are, and call yourself "King of Killers". Orgetorix! But for the moment, you are my guide into Greek Land—your land!—and I trust you.'

'You trust me?'

'Yes. I choose to trust you. Only Lords Bolgios and Achichoros know our true strength. Yes, I trust you, and I suppose I must trust those grim-faced vagabonds who guard your back. What I don't trust is those hawks.' He glanced up at the hovering birds. 'They have watched us for too long. They are not natural.'

'Nor was the raven,' Orgetorix agreed. 'It upset Bolgios, but it was *my* face shadowed by its wings.'

Brennos considered this carefully. 'Yes. It frightened Bolgios. And Bolgios is not an easily frightened man.'

'It took his food. That's what frightened Bolgios. But ravens do that. They scavenge. This raven scavenged. But the scavenger was only the bird in the raven. There was something else in the raven, something that raised its wings to block my eyes from the evening sun. Or perhaps from those hawks.'

'More than a bird, then. A ghost.'

'More than a bird,' Orgetorix agreed. 'Perhaps a ghost. But not frightening. Almost . . . protecting. Those hawks trouble me more. We are being watched, that's certain. All my life I've been watched. And suddenly I feel I'm being hunted. I don't know if those hawks are watching me, or you. But even if you do not have the one hundred times a thousand men-at-arms your dream insisted on, by my count you have a good quarter of that number—the Greeks are good at counting, this one at least—and I can lose myself inside that fierce-raging horde of iron.'

Brennos said, 'Lose yourself if you must, but don't lose sight of me, or where we're going as we flood into Greek Land, and bloody it. When it comes to those mountains, and the narrow passes—those Hell's Gates—I shall need your counsel.'

'In my short life I have never met a Celt who trusted a Greek as much as you seem to trust me,' the young man said.

Brennos smiled coldly. 'But you are more Celt than Greek. Everything about you tells me so.'

'I was born in Greek Land. I was stolen from Greek Land. My brother, too. I miss my brother. I am *lost* from Greek Land, Brennos. I am betraying it to you by guiding you there. But Greek Land is in my heart.'

'*Lost* land is in your heart,' Brennos observed, with a quizzical stare at the other man. 'Your father may have been a Greek, but from what you say, your mother rattled with coloured glass and bright bronze, drank ram's blood and stank of bitter herbs. An enchantress. In other words, not from Greek Land. You know it and I know it. King of Killers? You would be better named King of Ghosts. Though the Scald Crow alone knows which ghosts clasp their cold fingers around your heart. But I've promised to help you with that, and I will. First, though, help me south! Help me to the warm land where my father lies. The warm embrace. Not my father's embrace alone, but the embrace of *all* my fathers, and my mothers, my brothers, my sisters—all the stolen dead, carried away by your ghosts, all that time ago, so long ago that perhaps even the stars looked different.'

Orgetorix smiled, then looked to the evening sky again.

'*Do* the stars move? Except to fall, I mean. If they do, I'll not live long enough to see it. But birds . . . look at those birds . . . How they move!'

The hawks had stooped, turned, and suddenly were flying west. Orgetorix watched them, noting with a moment's puzzlement—indeed, fascination—the way they vanished from the dusk-stained clouds, like puffs of smoke struck by a sudden wind.

'I won't let you down, my Lord Brennos. But the truth is, we all need ghosts inside us, and I am short of ghosts. If I can find them, if I cage them, I will not answer for anything that has to do with Greek Land coming back to me.'

'You'll betray me.'

'Certainly not. But I will turn against you. But in the day! Not by night.'

'Fair enough,' Brennos said, reaching for his cloak.

* * *

At dawn, all camps were struck and the first of the armies began its ponderous march to the south, Brennos and his cavalry at its head. For two days all that could be heard was the sounding of horns, the rattle of carts and the shouting of orders. In three great waves the shores of the Daan were cleared and left in smoking silence, save for the wolves and dogs that fought for scraps among the smouldering fires and rubbish pits.

Even this activity had ceased by the time dream-driven Argo drifted into view, sail slung low, grabbing the breeze as she followed the eastward flow of the Daan.

Desolation and desertion greeted Jason and his crew, but the course of the Great Quest was easily apparent. The horde, Brennos's legion of vengeance, had cut a swathe south through wood and country that would remain for a generation.

CHAPTER SIXTEEN

Out of Time

I have woken from the Death Sleep many times, but never to find a woman laughing in my face with delight.

'We did it! We did it!' cried this fair-haired vision, her blue eyes wide and radiant with excitement. 'We flew together!' She was straddling my body, her hands slapping my cheeks as she roused me from the haunted passages of death.

'Wake up! Merlin! Wake up!'

When she saw that I had come back to consciousness, she leaned down and pressed her mouth to mine, a strong, hard kiss, hungry and consuming. Her thighs gripped me powerfully, her fingers stroked my closed eyes, celebrating the sights we had seen, perhaps.

Now she started to tremble, hugging me, soft cheek against mine. 'We are strong together, Merlin. My father never flew like that. I didn't think it possible: to fly through the days and weeks. We could fly through the years together!'

I pushed her away and stood. She looked annoyed. I was

shaking too, and was giddy and nauseous with the sense of being high and looking down. I felt like falling. And my right arm was bruised and aching.

What had she done? What had this northern charmer done to me?

'You look tired, Merlin. And older,' she murmured, propped on her elbows as she watched me. I held up my hands. The skin was grey, and where wrist joins arm there were ridges and creases that had not been there before.

'You made me fly through time! That was a dreadful, dangerous thing to do.'

'But it was wonderful!' she said, the excitement returning. She jumped to her feet and tried to hug me again. 'It was the best thing I've ever done in my life. We saw the whole army, all of them. And we saw where they're going! Why are you so angry?'

'Because it was the most dangerous and dreadful thing to do!' I shouted at her again, stunning her momentarily. My face was sore. My sight still hadn't returned to normal, I still seemed to be staring down from a great height.

Niiv reached a finger and touched my temple. 'You *are* older,' she said, then added teasingly, 'but you look good for it.'

This coquettish behaviour infuriated me; I was in a state of panic and shouted, 'I've lost years because of you. You dangerous witch! I ought to kill you now . . .'

'Why?' She was outraged. She couldn't understand why I was angry; she had no idea what she had done.

All I could think about for a moment was: how had she done it? I had intended to use a little flying magic to go south, to see how far the expedition had journeyed, to eavesdrop and spy on the chieftains; to try to learn their destination. Distance flying is hard, harder than running (as a hound, say), though not as hard as swimming, which in any case I dislike intensely. But distance flying advances age very little, which is why I had agreed to it. Niiv had begged me to let her come on the wing as well, and knowing her origins, and curious to see more of her own skills at work, I had agreed.

And the cunning little creature had flown us back in time. Her own body could take the ravage of that act (though not on too many occasions). Mine felt shattered by the effort. Somehow she had joined her charms to mine, spied the method of flying through the seasons, and copied it, blinding me to my own inadvertent use of it. There are marks on my bones—so I was told—that key for these dangerous enchantments. She had seen, stroked and copied the signs; she had entered me deeply. And I had not felt her doing so!

She chased after me for a while, crying out, as I walked and ran in confusion, trying to lose myself in the forest. A horn sounded, and I could hear the dogs barking. I supposed that Jason was as alarmed by my departure as anyone, and was coming to find me. I soon shook off the girl. Those damned dogs, though, Urtha's faithful hounds. They nosed me out in the narrow overhang where I huddled. Their barking turned to sympathetic whimpering as they stared down at me.

They seemed pleased to find me safe. And soon Jason's brawny silhouette towered over them, chasing them away, stepping down to sit beside me, wine-soured breath labouring from the run, chest heaving.

'You run a good race. You look ill, Merlin. You look grey.'

'That bitch stole my soul. Just for a moment, but she stole it. You have my permission to kill her.'

'Last time I tried that, you rescued her. And Argo's protectress nearly froze our balls!'

'Times have changed.'

'Well, before we discuss the future of the nymph, tell me what you saw. You *did* see the army, didn't you?'

I told him that I had. I decided not to mention that I had seen them shortly before their departure, some weeks ago, from the exact location where Argo was now beached, and the argonauts resting after the long river journey. I described the scene in detail, the three armies, the gathering of champions, the nature of the quest itself, namely that they were on the biggest raid in history, to return the sacred objects of their tribes, their ancestors' death tribute and totemic presence in the living world. Naturally, there would be a great deal of looting on the way, and there was no doubt at all that the blood fury was close to the surface in just about every man at arms, and the women too.

This would be a savage journey south, and it would leave a trail so easy to follow I saw no point in searching again for the precise position of the army on this warm, early summer's day. The faster we moved, the sooner we found them.

'How big is the army, did you say? Jason was asking me.

'Three armies. Brennos leads one, one is led by Bolgios, the third by Achichoros. Some years ago, Brennos had a dream, as far as I can make out. He was tasked, by the angry spirits of his ancestors, with bringing back the sacred objects of their race. They were looted to give as offerings at any and all of your many oracles. In the dream he was charged to raise one hundred times one thousand men-at-arms, champions all. I don't know who or what sent the dream, but it seems he's done it. Brennos has a powerful friend behind his dreams.'

Jason scratched his beard. 'One hundred times one thousand men. By Apollo's bright cock, that's a lot of men. One hundred times one thousand . . . how many *is* that in total?'

'One hundred thousand. In total.'

He held his hands in front of him and wiggled the fingers. 'That's ten. Ten fingers. So if ten men sat here, that would make one hundred fingers. So one hundred men makes . . . one thousand fingers. So to make one hundred thousand . . . Gods, that's a lot of fingers.'

'If you're counting fingers, you need to talk about ten times one hundred thousand.'

'I'm not good at numbers, Merlin.'

'And fingers are the least of our problems. The baggage train is huge, probably half as many women and children again. They've saved stores and animals over winter. They're equipped for a big invasion of Greek Land. Your land, Jason. And there'll be plenty of forage and pillage on the way. This is well organised.'

He watched me for a moment, then furrowed his brow.

'And where are they heading?'

I hesitated before saying, 'To Apollo's shrine, at Delphi.'

I don't know what reaction I'd expected from Jason—outrage, perhaps, or insult—but I had not anticipated a brief look of astonishment followed by a roar of laughter. He stood up, threw a long stick for one of the dogs to chase, turned and looked down at me.

'To Delphi? Then they're mad! They'll have to squeeze through one of the narrowest mountain passes in the known world! The Hot Gates! Thermopylae! Delphi? They'll fail. Gods or no gods, bronze or iron, they'll fail! Twenty men can hold that narrow gorge with nothing but pointed twigs and piss. One shout out of place as you tiptoe through its chasm and the walls come tumbling down. Do you remember that hair's breadth miss when we rowed through the clashing rocks? On our way to Colchis? They crushed the tail feathers of a dove, and clipped the wood from our stern. The Hot Gates are a hundred times as bad!' He suddenly realised what he was saying. 'Yes, that's right. So if we're going to catch them, we need to catch them before the pass. Otherwise there'll be nothing to catch, my son included.'

He dropped to a crouch. 'On that particular matter . . . did you see him? Thesokorus?'

I told him that I had. 'He's with the army, and has a rank that brings him close to Brennos himself. The two men seem to be friends.'

'How did he look?' Jason asked after a moment.

Like you. So like you. I didn't see it in Makedonia. The sun was too bright, perhaps. But he is the image in fierceness and far-seeing that you were, when you were young and hungry.

'Strong,' I said. 'Young. Eager. Handsome. But he is missing his brother.'

'Yes. Yes, of course. The little dreamer. But one son at a time, eh?'

'There is something else,' I went on. 'Something else that disturbs me. Niiv, in her own hawk form, didn't see it, or if she saw it, the sight didn't matter to her. But a raven suddenly dropped to the feasting table. It stole food from one of the commander's plates, but it seemed to be watching Orgetorix. Your son. Orgetorix. He was sitting at that same table. That raven came from nowhere, just as Niiv and I had come from nowhere. Jason, I know that raven! For the moment, I can't recognise it. But we *are* being followed.'

'You've told me this before . . .'

'Then I'm telling you again. We're being followed, watched . . . and I suspect we're all in danger from that follower.'

Jason agreed with me, then hauled me to my feet. 'We have twenty-one times ten fingers to poke in old Black Bird's eye if it tries to scavenge on Argo. That's a lot of poking.'

I felt it necessary to point out to him that: 'If I knew whose eyes we were poking, I might be better able to judge how useful two hundred and ten fingers might be!'

He responded angrily. 'It's just a bird, Merlin. A big black scavenging bird. There is nothing you can teach me about scavengers. Now brighten up. And tell me more about my son. Did he look like me? Did he have a spark in his eye? A swagger; a nobility? Did he look like the grandson of Aeson?'

I walked with Jason back towards the dogs, and to Elkavar and Tairon of Crete who had led the hunt for me. I could not fully comprehend this man, this resurrected man, this dead man living and walking in a land seven hundred years or more distanced from his own. He seemed to have no feeling for the lost time, only concern for a face, a gesture, a wink or grin that would remind him, in one small piece of flesh and blood—his son—of himself! Was it that he was anxious to see no Medea in the boy? Or just that he wished to see the boy and know him as his own. Jason was a struggle within himself, at one moment angry, at another focused; and again, dismissive of everything he believed in, yet a day later a man who would sacrifice to gods long gone.

He was truly out of time.

So was Orgetorix.

And yes: so was I.

'Your son looks nothing like you,' I lied, and Jason seemed disturbed as we walked.

'Really?'

'He looks like himself. But I have no doubt that he's yours.'

'And why is that?'

'There is something about him that doesn't care. He's bold, brave, foolish and self-centred.'

Jason laughed. 'Well, that's certainly a rich mixture of poisons. But like any medicine, poisons, in small doses and in proportion, can make or break the illness!'

I stared at Jason for a moment, mystified by a metaphor that seemed quite inappropriate; and yet: I had not told all the truth about Orgetorix; I had not mentioned the feeling of loss and bewilderment in the young man. And I wondered if Jason had intuited that omission, and was simply saying that through the right combination of those strong traits, his son might conquer the fear of his own displacement.

The young Celt's face haunted me. Hovering above him, on the wing, I had seen both the shadow and the fire in his eyes as he had gazed up at me. He had known there was more to the hawk than just idle predation. He seemed to call to me across the days that separated us, and I was intrigued.

And even as I thought this, so the shadow of the raven seemed to darken the sun.

Argo was tied hard to the shore and had been unloaded. Ruvio grazed and cantered among the remains of the great gathering, the earth banks and enclosures with their ragged palisades and ash-stained earth. The argonauts were searching the deserted camp for anything of use that had been left behind or overlooked, whether grain, or salted meat, or canvas or clothing. They scavenged among several packs of dogs, that snarled and growled as they scraped at the ground. Urtha's two hounds stalked among them, giants among their kin, and the wild dogs kept a respectful distance.

Rubobostes pointed to the woods, however, where until recently I had hidden. Sure enough, narrow eyes and grey muzzles told of the wolf pack that watched silently from the trees.

'There are more than ten. They are very quiet and very patient. I hope they're waiting for us to leave rather than waiting for us to sleep.'

The king's enclosure, where Brennos had addressed his commanders, had been tidied up, the gates restored and made suitable for the short rest all of Argo's sailors felt they needed. Rubobostes and Ullanna had prepared a succulent mix of foods from the meagre supplies on board, and from local scavenging. Michovar had created bread out of grass, it seemed.

'Anything can be used to make bread, if it can be ground into powder,' he instructed us. 'Even skulls!'

Elkavar and the two Cymbrii, Conan and Gwyrion, had re-broken seven horses that had been gathered from the forest's edge and the river bank, older animals that had been long abandoned, had returned slightly to the wild, but which were perfectly usable for the journey south.

Erdzwulf spent his time poring over the new maps of the land. Tairon of Crete, though unfamiliar with the mountains to the south which led to Greek Land, a country that partly impinged upon his experience, seemed to have a talent for interpreting labyrinths; and since mountain passes and winding river valleys were the oldest labyrinths of all, his slim, gold-tipped fingers traced several routes by which we might pursue and overtake the lumbering mass of men and horse that was seeping through the hills to Makedonia, as flood-water through fields, gentle at first, then overwhelming.

We would now have to abandon Argo. We faced a long trek through increasingly difficult mountain passes until we reached the eastern edges of Illyria; then a winding passage through Makedonia to Thessaly, before the Hot Gates, the narrow gorge, and the tramp across hostile and unwelcoming lowlands to Delphi.

Jason was torn between a certainty that it would be better to intercept the army before it reached Thermopylae, reasoning that there would be a dreadful slaughter there, and his son would be caught up in that killing, and an instinct to wait until Delphi, which was a much smaller place. But if the Celtic army successfully entered Achaea, the horde would spread out widely, easily arriving at Delphi in a number of swirling formations, falling on the oracle like so many storms. And Orgetorix might become lost among them, perhaps not completing the mission through a memory of affection, or respect, for the sacred place itself.

Urtha sympathised with the thinking for his own reasons. He did not want Cunomaglos to fall to a Greeklander's spear. The intercept must occur before Thermopylae. We should hasten our departure.

The question arose who would tell Mielikki that Argo was to be put under cover, hidden from sight, and deserted for a while.

'I pissed on her,' Jason said. 'I dread to think what she'll do to me if I go to her.'

All eyes turned on me, but I shook my head. The hawk-flight had been tiring, and I had other things on my mind. But Ullanna reminded me of my own special relationship with Argo. I had no choice but to agree.

She kept me waiting. I hunkered down in the empty ship, conscious of the smell of the horse, whose droppings, scooped and scrubbed away, were still a lingering presence in the air, and called softly and repeatedly for the Old Lady of the Forest. The grim face watched me from the stern, and I felt cold. The smell of winter drove away the smell of horse, and a snowflake settled on my cheek, an icy touch.

Old Lady Forest was not happy. It turned out she had heard us talking.

'You have sailed me this far, and now intend to leave me!'

The sudden voice from the Spirit of the Ship startled me. I was encompassed in a frozen woodland, crouched in the thick snow, the sun on the splinters of ice and layers of frost that adorned the landscape so bright that I had to squint.

Mielikki, clothed in black bear-fur, face hidden below a voluminous red-green cowl, stalked towards me, kicking up snow in angry clouds. Her lynx growled and spat at me. I rose to meet her.

'We have to go south, through mountain passes. We can do it fast, on foot and horse. This is the end of the river journey. You're not being abandoned, just moored in dry dock for a while.'

'Sail to the sea,' she said. 'Then south through the narrow straits, then through the islands to Iolkos, or even to Thessalon. Argo sailed there once before.'

She was referring to the journey Jason had taken, the straits being the dangerous neck of water at the Hellespont. The ship herself was feeding that memory into its protecting goddess. I remembered the length of that journey as if it were yesterday, the long haul around the coast of the wine-dark sea, to Colchis, and across the wide ocean to the treacherous navigation where the mouth of the Daan spread out through a landscape of mud and reeds; then the heavy rowing against the flow as we had struck inland, towards the mountainous land, south of Hyperborea, where now Brennos and his Celtic kin ruled over the world. And my experience of walking the Path around the world told me that the land journey _would_ be shorter, though this certainty would have to be tempered by an understanding that on the sea we were at risk only from pirates and such of Poseidon's malformed sea-creatures as he should be inclined to send against us. On land, we faced tribal warlords at the least, and the spirited and well-armed Makedonians if we were unlucky.

The Greeklanders themselves were weak, and had been for some years. Only at Thermopylae could they hold, and Brennos had already outlined his strategy for storming the pass:

'We move through it like the hot spill from a volcano, burning everything that gets in our way, the living running over the cooling dead! We'll overwhelm every blade of grass, every blade of iron, every young life that tries to block us.'

He might just do it. These Celts were less mindful of death than the Persians who had stormed the gates four generations ago, and been held back by a small force of Spartans.

Times had changed. When a warrior's death simply meant

a continuance of fighting, albeit in the Otherworld, fighting tended to continue after death.

'We will not abandon you,' I said to Mielikki. 'But the land journey will be faster. After that, we'll return to you and sail you home.'

Mielikki was angry; and as she paced through the snow in front of me, making a strange sound, like a low song, under her breath, I thought she seemed frightened. At length she came back to me and pulled back the cowl. Her face was almost death-white, the eyes like ice, the mouth thin-lipped; lines of age and experience patterned her skin, and crystals of tears gleamed where they had frozen. She was lovely, but I could see how this woman could turn hard and violent.

'The one who was here before,' she said, 'only visited. She was not always here. She came at her whim, or when this one you call Jason summoned her.'

Mielikki was referring to Hera; Hera had only promised limited advice to Jason, on that voyage. She had been part of a bigger, tighter game being played beyond the mortal realm.

'Some of the others who were here before, the very old ones, were like me, bound to the ship. They, like me, had no escape. The ship was their world, and the world they had once belonged to was denied to them. The further I go, away from my land, the colder I become. You cannot simply abandon me. I will freeze you all where you stand if you think of doing such a thing.'

I shivered and shook, breath frosting. The Lady of the Forest covered her face again. I said, 'We can only haul Argo a short way, even with Ruvio. And we are about to move through mountains. The ship must stay.'

'The ship can stay, but the Spirit of the Ship must be taken,' Mielikki insisted. 'It's only a small part; your carpenters can remove it. It will always be useful to you, Merlin; wraith-ships can be summoned. And besides: you might need to use its spirit again.'

The words were very meaningful. 'Might I? Why?'

'The *fierce eyes* that watched you have fled. She left the ship almost as soon as we came ashore. She fled on the wing.'

'As a raven,' I breathed. When Mielikki didn't respond I asked outright. 'As a raven?'

'A dark bird. She is very angry; and she is very dangerous.'

'And she hates me. I know.'

'She is afraid of you. She is afraid of Jason.'

Mielikki's words were tantalising.

Afraid of us? Hating me? That girl from my past? If Mielikki could know this much, she *must* know more. I begged her to tell me more. All she said was, 'I am not like the one who sailed with Argo in Jason's day. That one—'

'Hera. A goddess.'

'That one, by whatever name, was stronger than me. She could enter the Spirit of the Ship. She played a game with the men who rowed Argo. Older guardians were more respectful of this ship, and I will respect her too. But, Merlin, I can only glimpse the shadows that move, this way, that way, across the threshold. If I could tell you more about Fierce Eyes, then I would. If you abandon me, I can't help you. If you won't sail me, carry me with you. The land beyond the threshold goes in many directions. I'm useful.'

I left Argo and sought out Jason. He listened carefully to what I told him and together we again estimated the sailing time to the ocean, then along the western coast, through the narrow straits, the clashing rocks, and across the island-studded ocean to Thessalon, Artemisium, or anywhere on that coast where we might put ashore and make our way inland to intercept Brennos.

We would be with the flow of the Daan, not rowing against it, we agreed, but it would still be best to go by horse. We had seven horses, not including Ruvio, and Ruvio could haul a loaded wagon easily.

Everything indicated that a land journey was the most practical. But I was concerned for Argo, and, to my surprise, so was Jason.

'If we abandon her, she's right: she might fall into the wrong hands. She might even be broken up for winter fuel.

And I hadn't known we would have to return this freezing Lady to her homeland.'

He folded his arms on the table where the crude map of our journey was still spread out. Rubobostes was singing loudly as he added wood to the fire in the enclosure, and beyond the gate the horses were being cantered through their paces under the watchful eyes of the Cymbrii.

'I agree,' he said at length. 'We'll hide her well. In the woods, there. We'll return and sail her again. That makes a lot of sense. Bring Argo's heart if you must, but cut it lean when you cut it from the ship. Wood is heavy and we're not going to be riding across some summer pasture.'

He tapped the map with a finger, thinking hard.

It took me a moment to realise I had been dismissed.

CHAPTER SEVENTEEN

—

Blood Rage

The hounds sniffed me out again. I was huddled in a new hollow, cold and confused, my arm still aching where the slingshot had struck it, my joints stiff with the sudden surge of age that my body had taken.

Gelard nosed up to me, wetly, its breath reeking of meat. I was ready to shout abuse at Niiv, the beast's designated handler, but it was Urtha himself who leaned down through my feeble screen of branches and leaves and grinned at me.

'So there you are.'

'Go away. I need time to myself.'

'Your lover is sulking. She's frantic, looking for you.'

'She's not my lover!' I shouted furiously at the warlord, before realising I was being teased.

'Too skinny, eh?' he laughed, then pushed through the foliage to step down into the hollow.

'Too dangerous.'

The dogs panted and watched until ordered to sit and be

quiet, an instruction which they promptly obeyed. 'But she's got under your skin, all right. I can tell that.'

'Deeper than my skin,' I confided, and Urtha nodded as if he understood what I meant. He sighed.

'Ullanna's the same. When I'm in a blood rage I'm aware of her, close by, keeping quiet. Then suddenly her hands are on my face, or my shoulders, and the blood rage subsides. Then she sits with me and banters on about the *tundra*, whatever the fuck that is, and the hunting, and the winters in the hills, waiting for war against some stinking band of horsemen I've never heard of, and repeats the sort of jokes they tell each other to while away the time, the women, who are as wild and wicked as the men, if not wilder. And I laugh, Merlin. She makes me laugh. And if one part of what she claims to have done in her life on horse and with spear and sword is true, then she could silence a poet in my household every night for a full cycle of the moon! I like her. I like her very much. She makes me laugh.'

'Well, that's good. Isn't it?'

He looked at me sharply, almost painfully. 'I can't afford to laugh, Merlin. I need that blood rage. Nothing can continue until Cunomaglos is silent on the hard earth, open-breasted, crow-feasted. Do you understand? Aylamunda is in my heart. She shouts to me in my sleep. In my sleep. I put my arms around her. Do you understand?'

I told him that I did. For the first time in a long time Urtha had shaved his cheeks, trimmed his beard, and cut his neck hair short. It was a smart look. The hair on his crown was stiffened slightly, ready for the application of limewater, to make that odd spine of spikes that these warriors considered an appropriate design for battle.

This young man looked clean and handsome, and there was a sparkle in his eyes that told less of hate than of interest.

He was not ready to lose hate, however. And he was at risk of losing it.

As if he had intuited my sudden awareness, he repeated, 'I *need* the blood rage.'

He was asking me to help him. To help keep him angry.

To keep reminding him that his wife and son had been abandoned, slaughtered, were to be avenged.

I nodded agreement, and he seemed satisfied.

'I need the blood rage.'

'I know you do. And Cunomaglos will encounter it. Jason will hold your spears. I'll tend to your wounds. We'll both abuse Cunomaglos.'

'Only while he's alive.'

'But of course.'

'When he's dead, the abuse is all mine!'

'Of course.'

'Thank you.' He turned to me again and grinned, once more teasing. 'So she's got under your skin, then?' he repeated, prodding my shoulder. 'A little bit of Niiv in the young-old man's heart?'

'Deeper than that. It's not my heart that worries me. There's a blade of ice in my heart, and I can use it well.'

Again: I was opening my mind to this brazen, brash young Celt.

'Ah,' he said, slapping his hands together. 'Of course. Those bones. Those old, carved bones of yours. She got that deep, eh?'

'Yes. She did. And I don't see why you are so amused.'

'Perhaps because I don't understand. In fact, I've been meaning to ask you for some time. About your bones. If I understand you correctly, your bones are patterned with spells and magic and enchantment and various recipes for all that woodbark, leaf-mould, red-ochre shit the druids pretend to know about and usually don't, though I have to say it often works ...'

'My bones are marked with charm, yes.'

'Charm! Yes, of course. Well, what I wondered was: when you die, and all of this ugly flesh rots away,' he patted my cheek and pinched my arm, 'this ugly, ageing flesh, scavenged by rats and wild dogs, and carrion birds, and all the rest, all those creatures that aren't too fussy about the meat they eat, and just the bones are left, just the magic bones, poor old dead Merlin's bones ...'

'What are you trying to say, Urtha?'

'Well, will they be of use to someone like me? If I kept them for *personal* use?'

I stared at him. Was he joking? Was he serious? I was beginning to realise that with Urtha, a substantial part of life was a game. The difficulty was, a substantial part of life was also to be taken deadly seriously.

'Why are you asking me this, Urtha? Are you planning to kill me? If so, think again. There's a curse built into the magic I hide below my flesh.'

Urtha was delighted at the idea. 'Could you build such a curse into me? That would be wonderful. To die honourably is one thing, but too often we die with a spear in the back. A curse that stalks the killer would be a wonderful gift. I leave you to decide, of course.'

'Why are you asking me all this?' I demanded again, increasingly irritable with this inquisitive intermission in Urtha's blood rage. 'Are you trying to cheer me up? If so, go away. I have other things to think about. And the last thing I need is for you to start considering my skeleton as trophy should I catch the wrong arrow.'

'I wasn't being serious,' Urtha said softly, half smiling, then looking away. 'I was simply curious. Like you, I have other things on my mind. I've been thinking a lot about my boys, and Munda, and what comes after me now that . . .'

He stopped speaking, scratching at his newly trimmed whiskers. He was thinking of Kymon. And I was sure he was thinking how things had changed, now, how his concerns for the future had been based on a false dream. He had imagined a squabble between his sons, developing into a war that would divide the ancestral land. Fear of that had driven his passage north. The event could no longer occur, since one of his sons was dead. His fears for the future had come through that mouth from Hel which the Greeklanders called the Ivory Gate.

Nevertheless, those dreams that came through the Ivory Gate—by tradition, lies, falsehoods, deceptions—usually had a twist about them. Nothing was ever as it seemed. Urtha might one day have a third son by another woman; or young Urien, dog-feasted, might come back from the dead. Nothing could be discounted. Only Time herself could answer for the truth or falsity of dreams, and I was not in any mood to enter into a costly bargain with Time for a glimpse of Urtha's future.

My skin was loose, my beard showed flecks of grey, my eyes were tired, my self was sorry for itself, and all because of bright-smiling, smile-caressing Niiv. Like a worm, she had burrowed down to my bones and grazed the pulp of magic; like a wolf, she had howled her triumph after the feast; like a cat, she had realised her mistake and watched me carefully, with cat-wide, cautious eyes. And with all of this hovering over me, I was not, now, in a generous frame of mind.

And besides, I was only guessing.

'Why have you come to find me?'

Urtha struggled to his feet, brushed the winter decay from his trousers, snapped the mastiffs into silent obedience again, and helped me up, a firm hand on my wrist. He looked me in the eye. 'Because I've found something. I wanted someone else to see it. Come on, let me show you.'

We struggled out of the hollow. I took hold of Gelard, Urtha wound Maglerd's leash around his wrist, and we ran with the hounds through the sparse trees. There was a warm and fragrant scent of wood smoke on the air, and the sound of building. I glimpsed activity among the argonauts. They were preparing for the long haul in pursuit of Brennos and the horde.

The dogs led us to the steep bank down to the grey flow of the Daan. In the high sun, in this crisp day, the water gleamed. The dogs struggled and whimpered, looking nervously to the west.

'They have a nose for death,' Urtha said, and after a few minutes' trotting along the ridge above the water, we came to the open grave where two grey-faced corpses lay in awkward rigor, bodies turned down. There were no weapons with them. Each half-exposed back showed blood. The dirt had been clawed from them, no doubt by Urtha's hounds. It was hard to see clearly.

Urtha said, 'These were two fine men. They were my friends. They were my *uthiin*. They betrayed me. And Cunomaglos betrayed them in turn.'

He reached down and tugged at the split fabric of one of their shirts. 'Stabbed in the back.'

'Who were they?' I asked.

'I know them, but I'll not tell you their names.' He threw a handful of cold turf on to each of them. 'They deserve to rot with the beasts. I'll remember them, though. They were once friends. And I'll remember them for the good fights and the wild rides. Cunomaglos has done this. I imagine he doubted these two men's solidarity. He was right. I can imagine they had grave doubts about what they were doing.' Urtha looked at me, steely-eyed. 'That leaves nine. Nine in all.'

'A lot of men to challenge.'

'I'll only challenge one, Merlin. Dog Face himself. If I lose, that's an end to it. If I win? That's when the difficulty begins. They'll come for me one at a time. They'll be fresh and fierce. By about the sixth I'll be quite tired. It won't be easy.'

I squeezed his shoulder like an old friend, hiding my smile. 'Well, at least you have arrogance on your side, and that will help.'

He nodded. 'I do hope so. But the first is all that matters.'

'Merlin. *Merlin!*'

There are times when I feel like a tree, rooted to the ground amidst a swirling flock of chattering crows; they nestle and fight in my branches, flap and feed, and I can do nothing to chase them away.

Jason, Mielikki, Urtha . . . and now Niiv, challenging me from a mound at the edge of the camp, arms crossed, pale skin flushed, her frown making her seem to pout, though it was only her eyes that flashed such irritation.

'Merlin! What have I done? You mustn't ignore me. Is it true that you told Jason to kill me? Why?'

My anger returned. 'Stay away from me. Latch on to Tairon; he's as twisty as you.'

'Twisty? What's twisty?' she screamed in frustration. 'I don't even understand you any more. What did I do to make you so angry?'

'You know what you did! You stole knowledge from me! You weakened me!'

'I did *not* steal from you,' she shouted, wagging a finger for a moment as if addressing a child. 'You were *always* in the saddle, *always* holding the reins. I just . . . I just jumped up behind you. And held on to you. I felt safe with you . . .'

She was pleading with me, trying to warm my heart. She thought I was simply angry with her. How could she know that I was terrified of her?

'You charmed me,' I countered. 'And you stole from me.'

'That's not true. You're a liar!'

'I don't need to lie when it comes to tricky whores like you.'

'What? What did you call me? How dare you!'

'Do you think I've not met your kind before? You carry a half-child. You're the worst kind of witch! Do you imagine your many times great-grandmother Meerga wasn't into the same game? I fucked her and she tricked me. She tricked me and I had her killed.'

Shocked for an instant, Niiv said grimly, 'She died in the lake, trying to contact an ancestor. She didn't take the right precautions and was taken by Enaaki. The same thing would have happened to you if I hadn't warned you.'

'She died *on* the lake. In a boat. Naked. Bruised around the neck. She paid the price of prying! Enaaki gobbled her remains. I ate the half-child. I took it back. I rowed back to shore.'

'Liar . . . *Liar!*'

'I know what you carry, Niiv. I know you have a half-child inside you. Don't come near me. What more can I say to you? How much more can I give you?'

'Everything! You can give me everything!'

I took unexpected pleasure in staring at her for a long time before saying, with calculated coldness: 'Leave me alone, Niiv. I'm too old, too careful to let a frost-sprite like you, a nothingness like you, a breeze in the storm of charm like you—too wise to let you trick me twice.'

'Nothingness?' she echoed, and for a moment she couldn't speak, upset or outraged, it was hard to tell. 'If I'd tricked you once, I'd be able to trick you again,' she complained. 'But I didn't trick you once. And I promise I'll never try. And I don't believe you killed Meerga. And I don't believe you want Jason to kill me. Tell me it isn't true.'

How wonderful to see such beauty dancing to my tune. How like her ancestor Meerga she was, but without that woman's bitter selfishness. Meerga had been carrion in my hands, though it had not been my own hands that had killed her. I couldn't see Niiv with the same hawk's eye.

'Believe what you want,' I taunted. 'If Jason lets you live, just stay at the other end of the ship to me.'

'This is all to do with that other one, the one who came ashore! Isn't it? The one who smelled of blood and burning leaves.'

Blood and burning leaves?

Now it was my turn to be shocked. I'd heard the expression before. Perhaps Niiv took my sudden silence as disbelief. She elaborated, angrily:

'The one who rattled with green-bright metal. Knife-eyes!'

'Mielikki?' I asked cautiously, though I didn't mean the Forest Lady at all. 'Mielikki has left the ship?'

'Not her. The other one!' she cried. 'The one who went ashore while you were preparing to hawk-fly. She didn't know I was watching. If you look for her you can't see her. But it's her, isn't it? You're hiding her; and you don't want me to know.'

Niiv's voice was like a howling wind. She stood at the centre of her own storm, angry and abandoned, intuitively jealous of an affectionate friendship from my past. The activity at the camp, and around Argo, might have been at the other end of the world.

Blood and burning leaves?

It couldn't be!

I said to Niiv, 'Were you hiding in the ship, then, when this knife-eyed woman went ashore?'

'Mielikki is my spirit-mother,' the girl reminded me. 'Which is why you'll never have me killed. I am her *child*. She would never let me come to danger.'

She had been in the Spirit of the Ship! Mielikki had protected her. Why was I so surprised? Forest Lady and young *shamanka* were of a single heart. It was only natural that Mielikki would wrap her cloak around her kin.

But what had Niiv seen? And how much would she tell me?

'I don't know this knife-eyed woman,' I shouted. 'Did you hear her name?'

'I only glimpsed her. She was like cloud shadow. But she was predatory. *Terrifying*. I hope she didn't see me. And you *do* know her. I can tell.'

'Perhaps you're right. But for the moment, leave me alone!'

'No!'

I turned away from her. She screamed at me: *who is she, then?*

She screamed my name, then crossed her arms, dropped her head and wailed bitter curses, which bounced off my skin, green acorns striking the hide of a mule.

What to do?

Jason was running towards me, sword in hand, alarmed at the sound of shouting. I could see Elkavar and Conan the Cymbrian trotting cautiously in the same direction, looking nervously at the black-robed girl standing on the slope above me.

'What is it, Merlin? What help do you need?'

'None,' I called to him. He looked at Niiv and the sword flashed in his hand. She shouted in fury and indignation, turned and vanished down the other side of the rampart.

I looked at Jason, saw the curiosity and concern in his strong features. He was waiting for me to speak to him, but

I could think of nothing else but *where has she gone? Where is she hiding? It can't possibly be true . . .*

And I could not tell Jason what was in my heart. Not yet. Not yet.

'Keep that girl away from me!

He said pointedly, 'Permanently?'

'No. Not permanently. I wouldn't try harming her. She has a powerful friend in Argo.'

—

CHAPTER EIGHTEEN

The Hollow Hill

I needed to find Fierce Eyes. I needed to know the face behind that veil. But where to look? Where had she gone when she had slipped ashore? How to call her to me? This time I took precautions.

I must have made a strange sight in my filthy sheepskin jacket and baggy woollen trousers, long hair unkempt, running, running to the edge of the woodland, then along it, avoiding those watching wolves, smelling and searching for some path, some passage, any hole or nook in the forest through which the woman might have slipped after her escape from the ship.

I ran and walked for several hours, towards the south, along the side of the wide road that Brennos's army had ploughed through the land. I came to a stone-walled house, its roof fallen in, its door ripped off for use as firewood, no doubt. It had long since been ransacked and abandoned, but there was a pile of coarse sacking in one corner and I drew this around me as I hunkered down and summoned my skills in dream travelling. I entered the Death Sleep.

First I flew. I am most adept at flying as a hawk. I soared and swooped, rose above the land, saw the spread of forest, the huge clearing with its smouldering fire and patterns of enclosures, the glitter of the river, the rolling hills to the north, the rising mountains to the south where soon Jason would have to ride hard and fast. I called for Fierce Eyes, for the girl from the waterfall. I hovered on the wind, calling, waiting . . .

And she answered my call. Suddenly! She came out of the sun, a broad-winged raptor, claws out, dropping on me with a screech of fury. I stooped to avoid her, but her wing struck me. She turned and came for me again, savage eyes, bright eyes studying me, curved beak slightly open and ready to tear out my throat.

I dropped again and flew fast down to the forest. She followed for a few terrifying breaths, then turned effortlessly on the wing, rising back against the sun, and in so doing became lost to me.

I summoned the hound next. I nosed my way through the woodland, through thicket and along cold, leaf-clogged streams. I howled for her. Again she heard me and came to me in hound form, but again she surprised me.

She growled from a high rock. As I looked up, catching the star-gleam in her eyes, the flaring of nostrils, the opening of the muzzle, so she leapt on to me. I bounded backwards. She fell hard, struggled to her feet, then came for me in two elegant and powerful bounds. We struggled and snarled, claws taking their toll, canines bloody but managing to tear only thick-furred hide, not throats.

And this time it was she who broke the struggle, *hounding* away along the stream, a quick glance backwards, then gone into the gloom of the wood.

Below the sacking, in the ruined house, I licked my wounds.

One thing I knew, now: wherever she was, she knew I was looking for her. And she was answering my calls.

More hurt than tired, aware of being hungry—how long had I been here? I had lost track of time for the moment—I tried a softer form. The child I had once been, that part of us all that is *sinisalo*, the child in the land, the child that never goes away but always walks with the man or woman the child becomes.

I sent my ghostly child back through the wood, running until he came to the stream where the hounds had fought. The rivulet ran into the Daan, its shallow flow taking it through the area where the army had camped, close to the king's enclosure where Brennos had addressed his warlords. But I went deeper into the wood, until I found a place where the stream curved round a small hill. Here, a rocky outcrop concealed a narrow, sheltering cave. I called for the Other and perhaps she had been waiting for me.

I watched from across the brook, and she emerged from the overhang, a small girl, skin-clothed, wild-haired, armed with a sling, which was loaded with a smooth oval pebble. As I started to rise from where I was crouching in the undergrowth, she slung the stone and ran. The stone struck my shoulder painfully. I followed after her for a while as she darted from glade to hollow, over rock and under fallen tree, scampering from thicket to muddy stream, always ahead of me.

This was no game. There was no laughter, no taunting, no sense of pleasure.

After a while I gave up the ghost and let the child in the land return to me through my dream.

It was night and there was a man standing in the broken door of the house, looking round. Startled, I gave myself away and the man's head turned to see me in the moonlight. I managed to throw back the sacking and draw my iron sword, struggling to stand.

'So there you are,' Elkavar said. 'Put it away. Scaithach's smile! but you're a hard man to find. Fortunately, you haven't washed for a while.'

He tugged on a leather leash and Maglerd appeared, barking twice at me in recognition and welcome.

Hound-nosed again.

'I'm glad to see you, Elkavar. But why have you been trying to find me?'

'Because I've understood a little of what and who you are, and who you're looking for, and I've found something I think you should see.'

What I had failed to discern, perhaps because she knew how to blind me to her traces, Elkavar had discovered by instinct and that Hibernian-born talent of his for finding the ways-under, even though on his own admission he was equally adept at getting lost once the ways-under had been located.

He had nosed out a narrow passage in what appeared to be an outcrop of rock from a small hill which rose deep in the wood. Indeed, from the moment we had beached the ship, he had been convinced there was a way-under somewhere close.

'I have a feeling for these things,' he reminded me. 'Though I have no sense of direction, as you know.'

He had tried and failed to find it. Then tried again; and found it. As soon as I saw it, I recognised the mound where I had encountered Fierce Eyes in hound form.

It was soon clear that this hill was old, and made by human hand, though the narrow mouth was roughly hewn.

It led down into the earth, quite steeply at first. Elkavar was very satisfied. 'The *brughs* of my own land are of superior workmanship, but then the people who lived in my land in the days of the Danaans were the most skilled in the world at shaping the face of a stone.'

I know, I thought to myself. *I remember*.

The passage wound intricately for a while and then divided, beyond an arching gate of petrified oak, between human earth and the spirit land. It didn't reach far into the underworld, we discovered. The light there was gloomy on a heavy, silent lake, full of frogs, haven of silent wading birds, a place that stank of marsh gas. Occasionally, dead water splashed dully against slippery rocks as some creature surfaced or prowled at the edge.

I saw no ghosts and decided that this was an abandoned place, a blind road to the underworld.

'There's nothing here,' I said, disappointed.

'Is that right?' he teased.

I looked again, then urged him to tell me more.

'Well, for a start, lakes like this, lakes like the one where we met, in the Northland, they change as you walk around them. If you're not looking for it you don't see it. That great lake in Pohjola is one of the gathering places for these ways-under, as perhaps you knew.'

I'd suspected exactly that, especially when Elkavar himself had appeared. It probably explained why so many dream-journeys, so many talisman-hunts, could arrive there. But that great ice-lake had seemed very different from this stinking pond below the small mound by the Daan.

'If you continue round the shore,' the Hibernian continued, 'there's a wild wood, and a clear path through it. And some-one has been there recently. They've tried to hide the way from other eyes. I sat there and smelled the air coming back through the wood. I think it goes south. Sometimes it smells scented, like those herbs we love from the southern seas. Sometimes there's just a hint of blood . . . '

'Blood?' My heart raced. I watched Elkavar carefully. 'Blood and what else?'

'A smell. Like burning.'

'Fierce Eyes! So that's where she's gone! She must have nosed out the path while I was flying in time with Niiv hanging on my neck. Elkavar, you're a hero.'

'No hero,' he said modestly. 'I was born with the ability to find these passages. Though as I've said before, I can as easily get lost in them. But that and singing are about the only things I'm good at. I'll wait for you here.'

I had just started to walk on, round the dark lake, when a thought occurred to me. 'How quickly can you learn a tune?'

'As quickly as you can sing it,' he replied with confidence. He had clambered up one of the grim, grey rocks, where the

dark gnarled trunks of winter thorn reached out to the starless
vault. The lake swelled gently, but as I sang the song I wanted
him to play on his pipes, so its surface erupted, shedding
black forms on the wing, which circled for a few moments,
a cloud of activity that finally settled back with a soft splashing to return the lake to silence.

Elkavar laughed, 'If you can do that, think what I can
do . . .'

He blew up the bag for the pipes and squeezed it firmly;
the drone set the lake alive again, but again it settled, and
remained so as he thumbed the pipes and produced the melancholy tune to a song that I had once heard a mother singing
softly to her children, as they drifted into sleep, rocked in her
arms.

'What were the words again?'

I told him, and he sang them gently, the pipes mellow and
warm, almost sad.

> *I am the exile,*
> *returning, returning,*
> *to the Hollow Hills,*
> *to the Shining Ones,*
> *I am the exile*
> *who is walking home.*

The lake shuddered. The gloom seemed to deepen across
the water and the trees trembled, as if a storm was coming.
A cold breeze blew against me. But everything in this eerie
place was silent, then.

Elkavar intuited my feelings and sang again. The notes and
the words seemed to drift as if sleepwalking, across the edge
of the lake to the dark gap in the trees where Fierce Eyes had
gone.

Silence again, save for the lapping of lake water on the
shore and the gentle breathing of the wood.

And suddenly she was there, a tall, dark figure in the darkness, veiled in the night, standing like a statue at the mouth
of the path, watching me.

I walked towards her. The Invocation, sung by the Hibernian, had called her back from her journey, turned her round almost certainly out of curiosity, of fond but hurtful memory. And I was quite certain, now, who watched me from behind the veil.

I stood before her, close enough to reach out and touch her, not close enough to kiss. She kept me at that distance. I could see her face behind the veil, year-worn, far more than year-worn, but beautiful, not part of this world, untouchable, and like me, lost in time yet bound to it.

Medea! Daughter of Aeëtes. Priestess of the Ram. Of *none* of this! Because she was older than this by uncountable generations. She and I were part of the same heart, that ancient, ever-beating heart.

'Who *are* you?' she breathed. 'Who *are* you, to know my secret song? You sail with *Rotten*bones . . .'

I had believed Medea dead. The oracle at Arkamon had told her son she gave too much to hide you. 'She died in great pain.'

Of course she did. I saw it now. She died for seven centuries. I'd been blinded by my own refusal to use the talents I possessed. The oracle had spoken the truth—a guarded truth.

Medea hadn't died. Medea had lived through time. Medea had walked the Path, and I hadn't recognised her when our own paths had crossed. I hadn't recognised the girl who'd been my childhood friend.

'I was nicknamed Merlin,' I said, hardly able to summon the words. 'As children, we swam in a pool by a waterfall. You took pleasure in shooting fruit-tipped arrows at me. We had ten guardians; they still watch us, waiting for us to come of age, though I don't know why.'

She studied me carefully from behind the veil. I sensed her mind as the buzzing of insects—frightened, confused, intrigued, unwilling to accommodate the truth that was on the way.

'I was called Antiokus when Jason first recruited men for Argo and sailed to sack your sanctuary at Colchis. I was on

Argo. I was in the palace when you mimed the murders of your children.'

With a scream of horrified recognition—breath reeking of blood and burning leaves—Medea tore away the veil and stared at me. She half believed, because she half knew the truth.

But the look of recognition and sudden comprehension quickly passed, and anger took its place, deepening the tracks of tears and pain around her eyes, hardening the sculpture of her brow and mouth.

'What *is* this?' she hissed at me. 'What trick? He will never see his sons! Tell him that. I've worked too hard to hide them. He will never see his sons! They are the only thing in my life that matters to me. They are growing strong. I'm proud of them.'

'He's close. He'll find Thesokorus.'

'Will he? I stopped him on Alba. I raised the dead on Alba. I helped *waste* the land to keep you back. And I can stop him here. I poisoned his mind on that ship. And I *can* stop him here.'

She could not take her eyes from mine. I could hardly cope with the implications of what she was saying. I thought of the huge bull that had plunged from those wicker giants. The touch of Medea's hand. And that frightening presence, that canny raven's presence, in the giants' heads as we had bobbed on the water, finding our courage. She had been that close. How much of that wasteland had been this woman's doing, I wondered?

I could not take my eyes from hers. The blur of grey images, the rotting accumulation of so many centuries, was beginning to sharpen: for us both. She shook her head, remembering. Memory was a flood, rushing back, cold and fresh. It hurt to watch her. She had been in Ghostland with me, not knowing who I was, what we had been in the long past, even as I was recoiling from Fierce Eyes, not understanding Fierce Eyes at all. I longed for her again, or perhaps for the childhood we had shared.

She cut to the quick, speaking softly, deliberately, breaking the spell.

'This trick will not work. You are a clever man, Antiokus, a friend of that rotten man. But I see through the trick. You are *not* like me. I was always *one alone*. The others were false memories. I walked the Path alone. And Merlin . . . Merlin was just a gentle dream!'

Why, then, were her lips trembling? Why was she cold? Because, of course, she too was beginning to understand.

'I thought the same,' I said. 'I thought I was one alone; with only gentle dreams to make me feel there were others like me.'

'No!' she snarled. 'This is a cruel deception. Somehow, you've picked my memory like a crow. But Rottenbones will *never* feel the touch of my children. I've waited too long to be with them again. Hecada! Hecada!' she howled suddenly. 'How is he here? How can he be here? The earth itself seems to turn against me!'

And with that wild and wailing cry, that angry moment of desperation, she turned and ran, swallowed by the path and shadows.

But the sound of her running suddenly stopped. I was still standing, staring after her, conscious of darkness, the stench of the pool, and the distant drone of Elkavar's pipes as he quietly practised. I couldn't see her, but she had come back, and called out to me.

'How many guardians?'

'Ten.'

'Tell me a name.'

'Cunhaval. The hound that runs through the forest.'

'Too easy to guess. Tell me another.'

'Sinisalo. The child in the land. Like you and me.'

'And another.'

'Skogen. The shadow of unseen forests.'

There was silence; then once more the sound of running. I went to follow, but again her voice came back, almost plaintive. 'Leave me. Leave me, Merlin! Please. I can do you harm.'

And I realised she had reached far deeper into her bones than I had. She had used more charm. She was far stronger in charm, and that was dangerous.

She was gone. I went back to Elkavar, who was waiting for me where the rocks met the water in this grey and silent underworld, his pipes slung casually over his shoulder, his face a mask of curiosity and mischief.

'Well, that didn't last long,' he commented. 'I hope it wasn't something I sang. I can take criticism . . .'

'You sang perfectly,' I assured him.

'Thank you. I thought so too. But I'd thought you might have had more to say to each other. You've clearly shared a past together.'

'We have,' I admitted, off my guard. 'Far more than you can imagine. We've both been caught by surprise.'

Elkavar sighed as if he understood exactly what I meant. Then he shook his head as if he understood exactly how I felt. Then he offered me advice. 'I'd compliment you on your way with women, Merlin. But I'm afraid there's nothing to compliment. You didn't take the upper hand. You let her get away too quickly.'

'What you've seen here is not the end of it.'

'You're going after her? Good man! The way she looked at you, it was obvious you've once been lovers. That flame can be rekindled. And I'll write the song! What was her name?'

'Elkavar . . .' I started to say, but discovered I had no words to either reprimand, disabuse or compliment him. If he had seen something, with his talents for exploring the ways-under, then who was I to doubt his intuition? My past was a series of moments, vivid experiences in a void of walking the Path. Most of my life was as obscure to me as a landscape on a misty day; sensed but not seen; coming into vision only when approached closely.

Lovers? The man was a romantic. She and I had been children together before Time began. No more than that.

Our paths had separated. (*And yet . . . and yet . . .*)

The love between Medea and Jason, however, had been startling in its intensity, shocking in its vigour, tragic by its betrayal. I had not recognised Medea for who she was when I had helped in her escape from Colchis and the furious king who regarded her as his daughter. (How had she crept into *his* life?) I had not recognised her on that day when she had fled from Jason, her sons in hand, her knife in hand, her tricks ready to block us from further pursuit as she trapped us in the tunnel behind bronze gates.

I remembered how powerless I had felt, that day in Iolkos. Jason's cry: *Antiokus! Use your magic!*

I can't!

It was Medea herself who had stopped me. But I hadn't known, then, how much I *knew* this woman, I wasn't looking for it. She had just used the very words that I would have used: *you were just a gentle dream. I was always one alone . . .*

Medea, I now was sure, was the 'one who went astray' in the words of the spirits of my past, in Ghostland. I was the one who couldn't tie his laces. The others were home or almost home.

Medea and I, left alone on the Path, though each of us had escaped the consequences and necessities of our lives in a different way.

I had to find her again. I needed to gather her back to me. From the moment she had stepped from the grim wood and peered at me from behind the veil, I had felt an overpowering need to reclaim a part of my life that had been taken from me: its beginning.

CHAPTER NINETEEN

— ✦ —

Dreams and Memory

Argo was meshed in the net of ropes once more, and Ruvio harnessed. The willing horse hauled the ship up the bank and across the deserted camp to the woods.

'Where have *you* been?' Jason asked suspiciously. 'You have a bird-look about you.'

'Later,' I said. 'I'm still giddy.'

In fact, I was looking nervously around for Niiv. It was a relief to see no sign of her.

Michovar and his men, and the Germanii, had prepared a hide for the vessel, a shallow trench covered with branches. Argo was wrestled and nestled into place. She would not be safe from anyone foraging in the forest, but she was certainly invisible from the river.

Now Jason cut through the girth-lashings on the stern, and he and Rubobostes eased out the figurehead of the Forest Lady. This was wrapped and laid out in the larger of the two wagons that had been repaired. Jason alone entered the Spirit of the Ship and under Mielikki's guidance hacked out the heart. The chunk of blackened wood looked no more than a lumpy, raw-edged piece of shipwreck as he carried it to the wagon, but it echoed with ancient days.

Figurehead and heart were covered with two layers of canvas before planking was nailed over them. The rest of the cart was filled with supplies, ropes and weapons. The axles of the four broad wheels were greased. Two spare wheels were mounted at the rear. Ruvio would be able to haul this small vehicle without difficulty.

All of this preparation took only a day; we overnighted by the fire in the enclosure, enjoying Michovar's food and bowls of a rough wine that Elkavar had discovered in a clay jar, in a waste-pit by the river. There wasn't much of it, but the Volka spiced it and mulled it, and the mood of tiredness and irritation among the argonauts lifted to one of humour and storytelling.

Tairon told us a version of the tale of Icarus and his brother, Raptor, whose father had pulled bronze tendons through their bodies to hold pairs of mechanical wings. Elkavar sang for us, to Urtha's delight, though to Jason's grim-faced tolerance. Michovar and his men danced for us to the rhythm of a drum, accompanied by animal grunts and tuneful chanting: a dance in celebration of the successful hunt of a tiger and the stealing of its spirit. The tiger, we learned, was a creature that appeared rarely in their country and brought great change and good omens.

Then Ullanna wailed a lament for her homeland, mercifully short, and Conan and Gwyrion hummed in harmony, an unusual sound that they explained 'related to the unspoken need of all men and women to nestle safely in the land of their fathers'.

Michovar was not impressed. All too sentimental. 'You wouldn't want to nestle in the land of *our* fathers,' he grunted. 'Snow up to your neck, frost-bitten arse, and mink-rats eating you from the toes up. At least our song was about hunting and catching things . . .'

The fires began to die down and Conan went around them, stoking them and feeding them, bringing new life and new warmth. Cathabach and Rubobostes tended to the horses. Manandoun and Urtha huddled away from the rest of us, talking quietly. Then Manandoun rose and left the chieftain, shaking his head quickly at Ullanna who had been standing close by, watching.

She settled down, drew her cloak around her, carefully positioned her spear and sword and stared at the stars. She didn't move when, after a while, Urtha stood up, gathered his own cloak around his shoulders and left the enclosure. I followed him at a discreet distance, until I saw that he was going to the river. He was a motionless shape against the starbright water, staring at the vault of the heavens, deep in thought.

I wanted to talk to him, to explain that I had decided to go ahead of the rest of the argonauts, but this seemed an inopportune moment. Before I could return to the enclosure, however, another man loomed out of the darkness, alert and curious, despite the heavy scent of wine on his breath. He came up to me and put an arm around my shoulder.

'I've been talking to that wailing Hibernian. He's told me to talk to you. Let's walk. I know you're leaving us; the least you can do is tell me why.'

Jason, as ever, was both straight to the point and diplomatic.

We walked away from Urtha, along the river. 'He can smell those betraying bastards,' Jason said, with a last glance at the forlorn figure of the Celt. 'He's summoning a Titan, I expect. Assuming these Celts raise Titans. To help when the moment comes.'

'We'll all be there, when the moment comes.'

'Will we?' Jason stopped and looked at me closely. 'Will you?'

I wondered what Elkavar might have said to the Greeklander. As if intuiting my thought, Jason said, 'Elkavar says you've found a way to scout ahead. I was asking him where you'd slipped off to. I was worried about you, since the Pohjolan girl has disappeared as well.'

Niiv? She'd be around somewhere, watching from the nightshadow.

'He's right,' I told Jason. 'There's a way through the world that leads ahead of us, perhaps ahead of the army. I'm going to leave you for a while, to explore the way. I can't tell you more than this: that a part of my life has caught up with me, and it needs resolving.'

Jason shrugged. 'Every one of us is catching up with their past. Why not you? But you should have told me earlier, Merlin, before we prepared the cart and the horses. We can all go south through your tunnel.'

I quickly disabused him of the notion. No ordinary man could breach the gate to the underworld, not until his death. Elkavar, in his own words, had been 'born' to such travel, though inclined to go astray. Like several of the argonauts, he was half legend, half human: Tairon with his labyrinths, Rubobostes with his great strength, Ullanna, the echo of the Huntress. But none of them—perhaps Tairon excepted— would be able to enter and pass through the earth.

'Where does your unearthly road emerge?' Jason asked after a moment.

'Certainly in the south,' I told him. 'And I have an idea *where* in the south, but I can't be certain. Elkavar will help me if we should get lost.'

Jason frowned for a moment, then caught the smile on my face and laughed a little. 'Yes. Well, good luck with that.'

What I didn't tell him was that it was Medea's pathway, or at least, a Daanian entrance that would connect with her pathway. As I'd truthfully told Jason, I couldn't be sure, but all sanctuaries have their own smells—sweet, sometimes, like honey, or acrid like sulphur. And the hint of cedar and rosemary, strong despite the sulphur, as she had returned to confront me, suggested a place I had visited before; an oracle, yes; one particular oracle if I wasn't much mistaken.

'I notice you're not wearing that little tooth amulet the girl gave you,' he said suddenly.

The *sedja* had been sewn into my sheepskin jacket. I'd almost forgotten it was there. But after the incident when Niiv had entered my hawkflight, over the army, I had removed the token. I suspected she could 'fly' to it and it was essential that she didn't follow me.

It lay hidden in denuded Argo, below the ship's branch roof, deep in the hold.

'I'm going to miss you, Merlin,' Jason said as we turned back to the fires in the distance. 'I'm aware that I'm here because of you, because of your certainty and belief in me, because of your powers of enchantment, because the world—my world—has gone mad! Is mad the right word? A son and a father, alive again seven hundred years after their deaths.' He nodded to himself, thoughtfully. 'Yes. I think madness is the appropriate way of putting it.'

I almost told him, then, what I now knew: that Medea too was alive in his mad world. Indeed, that she must have *always* been alive, walking her path, walking the years down, wearing them down, until . . . strange thought . . . until her sons appeared on the earth, again, stepping from dark to light, from one era to the next, unaware of the loss of Time.

But every instinct told me it was too soon to mention Medea. He would lose his focus. He needed to think of nothing but his son, and the way to find him.

My experience on the shores of Ghostland, however, and Medea's words—*I stopped him on Alba, I can stop him here*—were sufficient for me to tell him something else; something to keen his appetite.

'What is it?' Jason asked, staring at me. I'd been looking at him strangely.

'I believe I know where Kinos is hiding,' I said, and his eyes widened.

'Kinos? Little Dreamer?' His face was suddenly alive with surprise and wonder, and he gripped my shoulders. 'How do you know? How *can* you know? You only saw Thesokorus, you told me. Did you see him? Was he visiting an oracle as well? Why didn't you tell me before?' Now his gaze became suspicious, and he repeated quietly, 'Why didn't you tell me before? Merlin! Where is he?'

I eased his hands away from my shoulders; his fingers had dug so deeply I thought he would crush my precious bones.

'He's on Alba, hiding within that place called Ghostland. The Shadow Hero Land. He "lives between sea-swept walls". Remember what I told you of Thesokorus's visit to the oracle? The sea-swept walls are the cliffs of Alba. But Ghostland is a complicated country. It's more than just a place of the dead. It's a place of the unborn. And somehow, Kinos has managed to enter the realm.'

Somehow? Medea sent him there! But I couldn't say this to Jason.

He was deeply quizzical. After a long moment he shook his head and drew back from me. 'You work in strange ways, Merlin. You are a strange, unearthly creature. So why I should doubt you makes no sense. But I do doubt you. Only because I want it to be true, and I can't bear the thought of disappointment. One son at a time, you always tell me, and I am tearing apart inside with the need to see my little Thesokorus. I can hardly wait to hold him again.'

I couldn't help laughing. 'He's not your 'little Thesokorus', Jason. He's a big man. He's nearly as powerful as Rubobostes. And he's called King of Killers. I'd be wary, if I were you.'

He nodded dismissively; he knew all that; that wasn't the point. The point was, to *see* him; to be reunited.

'How can you be sure?' he repeated. 'About Kinos?'

'I saw a ghost of Orgetorix when I visited Ghostland. I didn't tell you before because I'm confused myself about why he would seem to be in two places at once. Ambaros, Urtha's father-in-law, knew that same young man from his own time spent spying on Ghostland. And he said there was a "brother" with the man. He was certain they were "brother wraiths", as he called them. I have an idea what has been going on; by the time I see you again, I will try to *know*. One son at a time, Jason; but we'll find them both, before too long. Hold that as a "wonderful" thought.'

'It will be wonderful when I've held them both, and seen their eyes,' he murmured darkly. 'Then I'll know this isn't just a dream. Sometimes I think I'll come to my senses suddenly, and ice water will be in my lungs again, and my shade will be screaming from the lake.'

'This is real,' I told him gently. 'You'll find out.'

He nodded, a sort of thanks, then drew a quick breath, resigned to my departure. 'Well, off you go then, Merlin. And may Poseidon guard your arse for you as you go under the world.'

Jason agreed that the others would be told of my departure only after the event.

I had thought that with the ship abandoned for the moment, some of the argonauts would also decide to abandon the journey south, Michovar and his Volkas especially, since they had only joined Argo as a circuitous way of getting home. They were hotly debating the issue, but thoughts of the warm south, and intrigue as to Brennos's quest and the secrets of oracles, had persuaded all the rest of the crew to stay together. On horse and foot, a few in the cart pulled by Ruvio, they would form a land Argo.

Urtha was still by the river. I approached him cautiously and told him I was leaving. He looked at me, scowling in the night. 'You were going to abuse Cunomaglos for me, before his death. Your own words.'

'I expect to be there to do just that,' I replied. 'You won't catch the army for several weeks. And then you have to find your enemy. It's a big army, spread out through the hills.'

'I'll find him,' Urtha said with utter confidence. 'That bastard's stink is in my hounds' noses. When they start to slaver and go red-eyed, I'll know he's close. Travel safely, Merlin. Where's that girl?' he added as an afterthought. 'My dog-handler?'

Where indeed? I told him I didn't know, but that if he saw her to be gentle with her, and to persuade her to stay with the group and not to try to fly in pursuit of me. She would not find me in Poseidon's realm.

'I think we all know, by now,' Urtha said pointedly, almost wistfully, 'that you go where you choose to go.'

*   *   *

Elkavar had gathered together our provisions as we had discussed; food, water, small amounts of the bitter herbs I had located at the woodland edge, strips of bark from the oak, ash and hazel that flourished in the forest—these were precautionary, to be shaped into talismans should the need arise—and weaponry, not to fight the forces of the underworld, but to protect ourselves in the world of men and warriors at the other end.

We would each carry a sword, a knife, and four thin throwing spears with lean iron blades. Elkavar also had his sling, and a small pouch of tiny 'fairy shot' as he called it, which I recognised as the little stone arrowheads of a much earlier age.

Thus equipped, we slipped away from the enclosure and found the stream, following it through the night, through the wood, to the high mound where the people of the Daan had buried their dead, at the edge of the world beneath.

CHAPTER TWENTY

—◆—

The Ghost in the Land

The Greeklanders had a word for it, the confusion and disorientation that follows arrogant certainty. I had been so sure that to pursue Medea through the underworld would be as straightforward as following an army of tens of thousands of men. But there are trails and trails, and an army leaves a land reduced to waste; in the chthonic realm where Persephone and Poseidon flew like bats, where the paths divided between one gloomy passage through rocks and another down to a black lake, where no hint or scent of her who had gone ahead remained on the stale air . . .

We were soon lost.

'This is all my fault,' Elkavar said grimly, as he cast his line again into some dark water or other, hoping to catch a fish, drawing in only a clammy clump of weed. 'I've not been paying attention to the signs.'

What signs?

Alas, he didn't know. If there'd been signs, he'd missed them. He'd not been paying attention.

Even his pipes were useless. He inflated the bag, squeezed it with his elbow and fingered the holes on the wooden pipes themselves. No sound came from them but the sad exhalation of dead breath.

Poseidon had stolen his music. Without his pipes, he couldn't sing. His voice was as dead as dust. He could not sing any song of summoning, or lament to the dead to come to our aid; he could not sing for the wind from the world above, or for the sound of thunder to roll through the caverns and allow us to follow its echo. He could not sing Medea's secret song and hope to entice her back sufficiently far along the path to give the clue as to our direction.

'I don't suppose Orpheus ever had this trouble,' the glum Hibernian muttered. I reminded him of Orpheus' fate, ripped apart by the women of Lemnia and thrown into the river.

'That's true,' Elkavar nodded sagely. 'It's the fate of musicians to occasionally fall out of favour. Perhaps I'm lucky after all. But I miss my singing.' He looked at me darkly. 'How about your own?'

I broke the news to him that Poseidon had stolen my voice as well; or rather, I was aware for not the first time in my life that to enter these underearthly realms was to lose most of my abilities with charm. I had always survived such journeys into the underworld, but the visitation had the effect of blocking me from my skills. I had never questioned this fact, just acknowledged it.

Earlier, I had tried to 'sing' to summon Medea again, and discovered the absence of harmony. I had also tried to summon the hound, the hawk and the fish, without success. To have been able to sniff further down the passages would have been useful, but like a scroll that has been locked away in a clay vase, I could not reach below my flesh to the patterned clues and guides that normally would have helped me.

'You're just a man,' Elkavar said, disappointment heavy in his voice. 'Just an ordinary man.'

'Well, for the moment. When we reach land again,' I added sarcastically, 'I'll be the same monster I was before.'

'I do hope so.'

But now a thought occurred to Elkavar. 'The scuttlebutt among the argonauts is that you can fly and swim, and run and things like that, as an animal, as it were. Indeed, didn't I find you in that sacking, in that ruined house, looking more bird and dog than man? You'd been doing it, then, you'd been *shifting*. Don't tell me I'm wrong, now. I know shifters, and I know shifters, and some wear the marks of the beast on their faces all their lives, and others just smell of it. And, my friend, when I found you so distressed, you smelled of bird shit and dog breath.'

'Thank you.'

'But you did. And the scuttlebutt—'

'I know about the scuttlebutt. And you're right. I have often flown as a hawk. It's demanding, but useful. But in answer to your question, I've tried everything I'm aware of—bird, hound, fish, child . . . I've even tried to become the root of one of those trees there . . .'

Above us, the vault of our world was a tangled, eerie mass of root and fibre, tendrils of the upper world draped like shrouds across the sky. Elkavar stared at the vault for a moment then looked at me as if I were mad.

'Why?'

'The roots of the forest connect the world. We are enclosed in a net of forest.'

'I see. I didn't know. But to get back to what I was saying, the scuttlebutt among the argonauts is that you have more up your sheepskin sleeve than you're letting on.'

Who had he been talking to? Or was he just wonderfully intuitive? I guessed the answer was: Urtha. I had confided a great deal in Urtha, and the Cornovidian and this Hibernian, despite a history of warring against each other, certainly had become friends during our river journey.

'What exactly has Urtha told you?'

Elkavar looked slightly embarrassed. 'That you are haunted by ten faces from childhood; that they are present on your bones; that your bones can open worlds; ten worlds, and if I'm not much mistaken, you open them in the form of birds, and dogs . . .'

I stopped him with a finger raised, alarmed by his knowledge of me, not angry about it, just reluctant to think too hard about the life inside my flesh that I was increasingly using, against my generations-long better judgement.

'And your point?'

'What else is down there, Merlin? There must be something that can be summoned to help us find the way. If not a hound . . . how about a bat? A worm would be too slow.'

I silenced him again. I was tired of his persistence, his nagging at me. And he was right. Ten *shifters*, as he called them, were indeed in my power.

I reached for the one I was always reluctant to use. The only one that could work in this underworld.

Morndun.

The ghost in the land . . .

I had forgotten how much it hurt to raise the ghost.

Life, which should quicken, suddenly slows to black cold. Ice creeps through the limbs, and despair begins to shriek inside the head. Time stretches endlessly, bleak, harrowing, wasted, a wasteland of days and years. The shadows that watch are the shadows of the lost. They shuffle, they cry, they abuse, they curse. Joints seize up; walking is difficult. You stumble through mud; there are no fresh smells, only rank decay. A mother calls, a father shouts, a brother wails, a sister calls from afar. These are the lost-from-life; alive, we can learn to live with grief, to focus on the day, and the days ahead. But to summon the ghost is to summon what has slipped away, never to be reclaimed.

It hurts to raise that shade.

So think of me: older by far than any corpse that lay in the black lake before me. To raise the ghost was to open gates to moments of happiness and pleasure that stretched back beyond the forming of hills themselves.

I cried for a long time, huddled on the shore, the flesh hanging from me in rancid folds, jaws of ice chewing on my guts.

Elkavar fled, to watch from a distance.

I called for the dead and they rose from the lake, not many, some of them too long gone to do more than lift a head above the water. A few dragged themselves towards me, bent forward, hands clutching at chests, as always happens with the dead, staring at me through hollow eyes. The closer they came the more I could see how keen they were to hear my voice: was I here to take them back? How wrongfully they had died; how prematurely they had passed away. This young messenger was surely sent to lead them out again, out into the bright day, out into the quickening year . . .

How quickly they shrank back in disappointment when I used the words, 'I'm lost. I need a guide.'

After a moment a voice called, 'I fell at Plataea, fighting for the Spartans. Did we win the day? We tried so hard.'

Then another voice, 'I saw fire on the walls of Tiryns with my last eyes, before that spear struck me through the jaws. Did the city burn?'

And another, 'My friend Agamnos was in mortal combat with Hektor in the spring, at Troy. I was cut down from behind before I saw the outcome. Is Hektor dead?'

I answered that Hektor was dead, but that I didn't know the answers to the other questions.

A calmer voice came from among these shuffling, watery shades. 'Where are you going?'

'South. To the mouth of an oracle.'

'In what land?'

'Makedonia. The oracle at Arkamon.'

A woman stepped forward, heavily cowled, arms crossed tightly over her stomach. 'I am not long dead,' she whispered. 'And I still have strength. I know where you wish to go. Follow.'

She stepped from the lake towards me, but suddenly crouched down at the pool's edge, and with withered hands wrung the water from the lower part of her filthy clothes. She squeezed the water from sleeve and girdle, as if trying to shake off her shroud for just a little while. Then she came towards me again, and I thought she would walk past, head bent, but she stopped and looked up at me, haunted eyes in a shrunken face.

'Is my husband happy?' she asked in a ghostly whisper. The drawn flesh of her brow creased into a frown of anguish. She stared at me, a corpse regarding a corpse, but with such need to know the answer to her question I almost choked.

'I don't know. I'm sorry.'

Her grim gaze held me. 'We had two sons. Bright boys. They went to war. For ever. It's a hard thing. To die of grief. It's a hard thing. To leave a good man. I hope he's happy.'

Her head dropped again and she began to walk, back along the path to a place where Elkavar and I had taken the wrong turn.

We followed at a distance, not stopping for rest—this corpse never stopped—and soon our limbs were weary, and our senses dulled with tiredness. But she walked and walked, that slow, shambling ghost-gait, and we passed through forests and valleys, along the edge of streams and through the ruins of ancient towns, whose stone walls glowed with soft luminescence, though there was no moon to illuminate their heights.

And then we smelled the earth again, and herbs and sun and summer.

And fear! And blood!

Between one step and the next I could hear the sound of a savage fight, the shrieking of men, the sharp ringing of sword on sword, the laughter of Furies.

Our spectral guide stood for a moment, face lifted to the thin light from ahead of us.

'Thank you,' is all I could think to say. Still she stood, staring at that sun-gleam, that life-gleam, remembering. Then she slowly turned and walked back along the dark path.

I watched her go until she was out of sight. Then woke from the Death Sleep, startling Elkavar who saw the ashen hue of my face suddenly flush bright with blood and life again.

'I was about to bury you,' he muttered brightly and with

some relief. 'I've spent the last little while terrified out of my life. You make a convincing corpse!'

As Brennos's great army had swept slowly down through the mountains, towards the plains to the north of Thessaly, war bands had ridden to east and west, prowling the country for spoils, forage and adventure. There was no controlling them. As long as they returned to the main body of the army, there was little Brennos or his commanders could do.

This band, two hundred or so, had sniffed out the oracle at Arkamon, ridden up the passes, through the woods, and poured over the rocks to confront the small, determined band of kilted soldiers dispatched to protect this isolated sanctuary. Older men for the most, this protecting force carried spears and heavy swords, wore iron cuirasses and greaves, and yellow helmets that curled forward at the top.

They were not winning the day.

I estimated a hundred raiders were involved in the combat, stripped naked to the waist, their red-green trousers belted tightly. They had painted their faces white to match their hair. A black stripe ran across each man's torso, from heart to groin. They were almost laughing as they fought, whirling and kicking, leaping from rock to rock, slashing at the defenders with a speed and ferocity that was dizzying. Impaled on a spear, they crawled away, or stood, arms raised, sword in hand, shouting noisy challenge to their assassin, falling on him with a death rage that finished one or both of them quickly.

Just inside the wood I could see the glint of spear points, and the shuffling of horses. These were chariots, waiting for the outcome.

If I had been inclined to move down through the fray, and cross to the woodland, Elkavar made the wiser decision. 'They're all marked the same, if you notice. This is a big raiding party, all from the same clan—Tectosages, I think—and you and I are as different from them as those poor bastards with the funny hats. They're in no mood to start checking our credentials. These are the swordsmen. But there are spearmen up in the woods. They're called *gaesatae*, and they can throw four spears in the time it takes you to clap your hands.'

The stench was stomach-turning. The noise like the feeding frenzy of gulls. I glanced to where I had hidden once before and listened to this oracle, that concealed cave in the cliff, and saw a figure watching, furtively, from that same sanctuary. And distantly, slumped in the saddle, six dark-cloaked men on heavy horses, watching the affray from safety.

One of the raiding band, a tall man, young and lithe, one of the few to be wearing a bronze torque necklet, suddenly somersaulted over the thin, desperate rank of Makedonians, and jumped to the rocks that led to the main entrance to the oracle, where Elkavar and I watched. But as this man came bounding up the path towards us, so the tall, dark figure slipped from his hiding place in the crevice, coming up behind the Celt and quickly impaling him on a spear. The man arched backwards, face a grimace of pain, fell back and twitched.

I recognised his killer at once. Orgetorix!

Jason's son looked quickly round, then made to move back into hiding. But his action had been seen from below. A warrior came leaping towards him, sword ready to strike, the sound of his approach lost in the din of the skirmish. He was moments from the kill. I grabbed a spear from Elkavar, raised it, gave it wings and flung it.

Orgetorix saw my action, saw the spear come towards him, was frozen with the surprise of it and more surprised when the shaft tickled his neck. He turned quickly to see the weapon embedded between his attacker's jaws, as the man flew backwards, squirming and struggling with the shaft. Then the young man bolted: not back to his previous cover, but up to the oracle, through the narrow gap between the rocks, and into the fragrant space where Elkavar and I crouched, watching the mayhem.

Orgetorix said nothing for a moment, though his quick, fierce frown as he met my gaze suggested instantly that he recognised me.

He looked at Elkavar, looked him up and down, saw all the signs of a man who might be from among Brennos's gathering and asked, 'Are you defending this place? Or attacking it?'

Elkavar almost understood the other man's words, but not quite, so I intervened.

'This is Elkavar of Hibernia. I am . . .' what else could I say? 'Antiokus . . . the name you once called me as you chased me with a catapult in your mother's palace. I'm known as Merlin, now. And we're neither defending nor attacking this sanctuary. But I'm afraid the sanctuary is lost.'

'I'm afraid you're right.' He glanced at the fighting. 'This place is very special to me. But those bastards want their spoils, and there's nothing I can do.' He paused for a moment, then studied me again. 'A catapult? In my mother's palace?'

'You were just a child. Your aim was good, though.'

What a look he gave me. For a moment he was running through those marbled corridors, pursuing the shadow of bird and hound—a little trickery to avoid those small clay pellets!—laughing with the tease of it as I vanished, and with the surprise of it when I loomed up behind him, with the small triumphs that I'd allowed him as he caught me.

But the memory was too fleeting. I could see it fade from his eyes, though his interest in me burned on. It was more important to attend to the business of slaughter.

The last of the Makedonians fell below the swift blades of the war band. The bodies were looted and trophied, then flung face down. Blood-smeared men poured into the cavern and began to search the passages, coming very close to where the three of us were hiding.

There was not a great deal to loot. The oracle at Arkamon had not been in great demand. It had had a strange reputation for all the centuries I'd known of it, which is why, whenever I had been able, I detoured from the Path to come and see it.

This was not a place of pilgrimage so much as of last chance. The voice of the oracle had come and gone at a whim; it had no great reputation. It was unusual in that fact, and curiosity had often brought me here, and it was through curiosity that I had found Orgetorix.

Who sat here now, watching his special place be looted by half-naked, half-crazed, bragging warriors of the Tectosages, men who were increasingly irritated to find nothing but walls of rock painted with ghostly images of animals, stinking passages that led down into an even more rank and unwelcoming earthly bowel, and a few items of gold and silver that were plucked from the alcoves where they had been carefully placed, stuffed into sacks and taken away.

With their departure, the world outside settled into crow-feast and silence. The Tectosages' dead had been gathered up and carried away. The Makedonian dead had been left where they lay and would soon begin to rot.

There was nothing the three of us could do, so we slipped out of the cave and found our way back to the ransacked village. There were crows here too, but Orgetorix's friends as well, holding his horse. They had stayed clear of the raid; they had kept quiet during the pillaging of the village. They had been with Orgetorix too long to question his instructions: do not participate in the raid on this oracle!

One of them, though, recognised me. He leaned forward in the saddle as we gathered in the square and said, 'You were here before. You were sitting over there, watching and waiting.'

Now Orgetorix too put a face to his suspicions. 'That's right. The scruffy man, with his two scrawny horses. You sat eating olives and goat's cheese, watching us. You followed me up to the oracle. The oracle knew you were there.'

In the middle of a murdered village, Elkavár and I were surrounded by seven men on horseback, all of them, fortunately, more quizzical than threatening, but one of them, Jason's son, watching me with an intensity that was almost burning.

'I don't deny it,' I said to him. Elkavár was looking edgy. His elbow-pipes kept making nervous little wails.

Orgetorix asked me, 'Who was my mother?'

I looked him straight in the eye, those dark eyes, those eyes that had once shone with laughter as he had scampered through the palace among the guards, playing his games of hide-and-seek, Little Dreamer following, Jason prowling, Antiokus, Jason's friend, calling out: we can *see* you!

'Your mother was Medea.'

He considered that answer for a long time, without expression, perhaps because he had not expected me to know; perhaps because he had been unsure himself.

But from his horse, looking down at me, he asked, 'Then who was my father?'

'Do you want me to answer: Rottenbones?'

The answer startled him. His horse reared up and backed away, distressed. He reached forward to calm the animal, still staring at me.

'What was my father's name?' he asked carefully.

And I told him: 'Jason, son of Aeson. He was a man who voyaged half the known world to claim back a land stolen from him; and a man who loved his sons—'

'And betrayed those sons. And betrayed their mother. And betrayed everything. Rottenbones! A terrible name, but the right name for a man as hateful as my father.' Curious, he asked: 'Say his other name again? Let me hear it . . .'

There was something about this young, aggressive man's behaviour that wasn't right. And then I recognised it: he was *unable* to say his father's name. Medea had put a lock on his tongue. I was certain of it. What crueller way to block a father from his son's heart than to make his father's name an unspeakable curse.

'Jason,' I whispered. 'Jason.'

Orgetorix looked down, half slumped on his horse. His men were edgy, quick glances flashing between them.

Then Orgetorix said quietly, 'Find horses for these two. Quickly. We have a long ride.' He nodded to me. 'We'll have to follow those bastards, back to Brennos. With luck, they won't remember what you did; or what I did. There's an invasion going on, as you'll soon discover. I remember you now. You appear in my dreams. I was just a boy; you showed me simple tricks; I teased my father. You told me wonderful stories . . . I remember you.'

'I'm glad to see you again . . . Thesokorus.'

'Gods!' he said, surprised but not threatened. 'You know I was called that? My childhood name? I'll not turn my back on *you*!'

CHAPTER TWENTY-ONE

—

King of Killers

The six men who rode with Orgetorix were a squalid bunch, mercenaries who had failed to keep their temporary bonds of honour to the chiefs whom they had served in various lands, and who had escaped justice by the skins of their teeth; if the stained, broken pegs that graced their mouths could be called teeth. Two bull-jacketed Iberians, a sour-faced, nervous Avernian, a half-faced Tectosages of age and wisdom who watched me constantly, and two men who had been lone-wolf for so long they had forgotten where they were born.

They had adhered to the young Greeklander as shellfish to granite at the ocean's edge, perhaps because Orgetorix promised adventure and spoils; men such as these, ferocious and ferociously independent, still needed a path to follow, and a dreamer like Jason's son—unaware of who he was, determined to find out where he had come from—was a little touch of magic in that dark, decaying night of their lives.

They were not happy now: Orgetorix, intrigued by my

knowledge of him, was keeping my company more than theirs, though he asked nothing further about me for some time. All that relaxed them was Elkavar's singing and pipe-playing. The music, and his mellow voice, opened up the gates of memory for these men as they sat around the fire, chewing tough, half-cooked meat and drinking very sour wine. Every so often one of them would stand and sing, a fondly recollected drone from childhood, and Elkavar would do his best to follow the melody, and add some rhythm.

'I find it very difficult to summon enthusiasm,' he confided to me at some point during our journey, 'for a song that mourns for the shade of a murdered mother, wandering in the barren hills of her homeland in search of a husband who has abducted the daughter of a man who sells donkeys.'

Orgetorix kept his own counsel for two days, as we rode south and east in the wake of the raiders. All I learned in this time was that he had heard of the plan to attack the small oracle at Arkamon, and had followed not so much to attempt to stop the ransack, but to ensure that nothing of its spirit was taken. He believed that a little piece of his past lay within the caverns. Why else had the oracle called to him to find it?

We moved through the land in quiet, cautious harmony.

Then, unexpectedly, we felt the rumble of the earth itself.

The low murmur, the tremble of an army on the move. To look to the east was to see the tell-tale sign of haze, the dust that a hundred thousand horses threw into the air, the rippling of twilight and dawn that comes from the rising heat of so many bodies.

Brennos was close to a series of valleys, running towards Thessaly, which were likely to be heavily watched. I rode with Orgetorix to a point on the hill where we could just make out the distant glitter of arms and armour. The raiding party, travelling at the wild gallop, had almost certainly rejoined the main body of men.

'So there it is,' the Greeklander said wistfully. 'A horde dedicated to ransacking a part of the country that I should hold dearer to me than life itself. And I have done my bit in

bringing them here. I have skulked and scouted the hills north
of my country for them. I have led the invader to the city
gates.' He shifted in the saddle, arms crossed on the stiff
pommel, dark eyes picking out my own attention. 'You seem
to know a great deal about a great many things, Merlin. Do
you know where that horde is going?'

'To Delphi.'

He nodded absently, clearly not surprised by my knowledge. 'Some of them will make it, no doubt. Brennos believes
that his ancestors lie in the oracle there, prisoners of past
plundering. I suspect that all he has done is created a wonderful story as an excuse for looting the sacred place. The
pity of it is, I can feel neither for the truth nor for the lie. I
don't care either way. That little shrine behind us meant more
to me than the whole of Greek Land, and I watched it raped
and could do nothing about it. There is something dead in
me. And why am I telling you this? Because there is something dead in you. We are dead men on a vibrant earth. We
are out of place. Or am I wrong?'

'We are not so much out of place as out of time.'

Orgetorix laughed. 'Well, well. I'll sleep easier with that
as a comfort for my dreams. Out of time? It's time to talk.
Let's eat. Tomorrow our lives will change completely.'

The coarse band of men were impatient with Orgetorix, and
had lost patience with Elkavar, who had been consigned to a
solitary position at the edge of our rough camp. The mercenaries were keen to rejoin the army. Though Brennos was
forcing the pace, we could see his fires in the distance, and
these men could imagine a better spread of food being offered
at the clustered camps than the dry rations we chewed on in
our rocky overhang, more exposed to the night than sheltered
from the cool wind.

'I recall you more and more,' Orgetorix said from his blanket. He was stretched out and propped on his elbow, the position he adopted both for eating and talking. He waved his
small knife easily as he spoke, cutting chunks from a coarse
loaf and swallowing quickly.

'There are two faces I remember, from the palace dream. Both are staring at me from behind thick golden bars. One is black-bearded and the man is screaming; the other is not bearded at all and he is anguished. I can never remember enough of this dream to remember the words being shouted— angry, certainly; frightened; begging—but there is always a terrible smell of stinking blood—and then a knife goes into me.

'And another strange thing. This happened soon after. I'm sure this happened to me in real life, though it feels vague. I remember being huddled in a boat with Little Dreamer. Little Dreamer was my brother. The sea was rough and a cowled woman was barking instructions to an armoured man who was rowing for all his worth, the sweat pouring from him. A ragged sail was flapping, torn and useless, and we came ashore. And this man picked me up under his arm and carried me to a cave. Little Dreamer screamed. The woman stalked about us, pacing up and down against the light, cursing in a strange language, while outside the weather changed to a black storm. It still makes me shiver to remember how the sea came crashing into that cave, sucking at us, trying to claw us back to its waves.

'My little brother was crying; and I was terrified. Something was raging at us; Poseidon, I expect. We were out of favour with the gods, there was no doubt about that. It was almost a relief when the woman took us in her arms at the back of that cave, safe now that the tide was receding, and told us to sleep. I remember those words so clearly: you must go to sleep now; as boys. You will go to sleep as boys. You will wake as men, and you will care for each other, and you will be cared for.'

Orgetorix stared at the fire for a moment, then suddenly sheathed his knife, stood up and walked to a tree that clung to the rock face with three bony roots. In the distance, the summer night was scattered with tiny fires.

'That anguished man was you, Merlin,' he said without looking at me. 'I see that now. And the bearded man—'

'Yes,' I agreed before he could say it. 'Your father.'

I walked over to join him. His arms were crossed and he was staring down the winding path that would take us over the nearest hill and into the bosom of the army again.

'Rottenbones. A terrible name for a terrible man. He betrayed his family. He caused Little Dreamer and myself to be cast into exile.'

I kept silent for the moment. When hate and anger flushes through a man there is a certain stench; Orgetorix was confused about many things, but hatred for Jason was a rope around his heart, pulled strongly by a heavier horse than I was prepared to break at that moment.

He sighed suddenly, glancing at me. 'And my mother, I'm sure, was the woman in the sea-cave. Though why she spoke in a strange tongue . . . I can't fathom that.'

'Medea.'

'Of Colchis.'

'A different land. With a stranger, older tongue than yours.'

'Is that right? Then that would explain it. It was never explained to me. She was the daughter of a king called Aeëtes. I could never find anyone who had heard of him. A storyteller talked once of a ram's fleece that bled gold and had come from that place, that Colchis. I'd thought it was on one of the islands. But a different, older land, you say. Yes, my brother and I must certainly be a long way away from home.'

They had woken from a deep sleep and walked hand in hand from the cave; but the cave was no longer the sea-cave, where Poseidon had tried to destroy them. This was a place in the hills, warm, scented, a system of caverns through which a wind like a gentle voice blew constantly.

And as a man, he had just watched it sacked. The children had emerged from the oracle at Arkamon.

Orgetorix suddenly brightened. He turned away from the valley, hoisted himself into the crook of two branches, and regarded me with interest for a long, lingering moment. Then he nodded, as if something had become plain to him. Indeed, he went on:

'After that, memory is much clearer. There were fruit trees and olive trees and we fed like mad things, two little scavengers in the middle of nowhere. After the horrors of the sea, and those nightmare days, this was Elysia. We hid in the woods and watched people coming and going and talking to the cave. We thought that was very funny. Sometimes they brought cooked meat and left it there, and after they'd gone, several men came and took it away. We managed to steal some of it before they came, and they left wine as well, though we didn't know it was wine, and one day we got so drunk we gave ourselves away. A raven dropped on us, a huge creature, and drove us into the woods while these strange men were pursuing us. We got away, but we were out of our heads, and very sick. I recall a man on horseback riding down on us. He had a helmet like burnished gold, with a bird of prey, wings spread, rising from its crown. His horse was masked; a terrifying sight, like a demon. But this man was Belovisus, descended from a great king of the Bituriges, and he took pity on us at once. What he was doing at the oracle I have no idea—we *keltoi* get everywhere, as I'm sure you've noticed . . . but he took us north, to his fort, and we trained and grew up as his foster sons.'

He slipped down from the tree and rubbed his hands together as if chilled, though the evening was warm and still. I had the impression he was glad to have talked to me.

'And that is that, for the moment . . . Merlin . . .' he said with a half-smile. 'There are a few questions I'd like to ask of you.'

'If I have the answers . . .'

'I'm curious to know about my brother. You saw me at Arkamon. You are a part of my life, clearly. I just wonder . . . have you ever seen my brother?'

He searched my eyes, not with suspicion, but with need. He was like the dead, I thought. I decided to lie; I was not sure of what I believed and I saw no point in building some false hope in him. I'd already made the mistake of doing that with Jason.

Jason!

Where in the world was he, I wondered quickly. How long had Elkavar and I been lost in the underworld? Perhaps the other argonauts were already with the army, madly seeking the ghosts and guilty of their lives.

'If I remember, the oracle told you he was between sea-washed walls; the ruler of his own land—'

'Though he doesn't know it! Yes. I remember the words of the oracle. And I *knew* it was you in the rocks, listening that day. I knew I was right.' He laughed. 'Though I didn't know who you were. Are you following me, Merlin?'

'No. I follow a particular path; don't ask me why. Sometimes I find it crosses my past. That's all that has happened here.'

He shook his head, ignorant of my meaning, confused by my words. 'What an odd man you are. I wonder: did you love my mother?'

'I never loved Medea,' I answered truthfully. But his question had been like a blow between the eyes. That look of Fierce Eyes' in the underworld; that sudden shock; the memories that we shared at that instant, of softer, kinder, closer times. Before Colchis.

Unaware of my confusion, Orgetorix persisted with a sallow smile, 'Then did you love my father?'

'Yes. I loved Jason.'

'You loved the man I hate. How strange. How strange. That we should be standing here like this, knowing now what we know, and I'm still opening my guts to you.'

Should I tell him that I knew where his brother lived? Should I tell him what I suspected about the brother he had hunted with, had ridden-to-raid with, had trained and grown with, under the watchful, caring, yet unseeing eye of Belovisus?

I was put out of my misery by Orgetorix himself, who suddenly said: 'I lost him. He disappeared. It was so strange, Merlin. Little Dreamer. One day we were riding through a deep valley. It was very quiet. We were recovering from light wounds received on a cattle raid. It had been a good raid; ten head of shorthorn blacks, and a grey bull; and four horses. War trumpets were being sounded, but there would be no retaliation for a while. They weren't strong enough, a small family on poor land, so a few of us went hunting. My brother thought he'd spotted a fawn, a perfect catch. I saw him ride down through the bushes, and heard his sudden laugh: I've seen you! That sort of laugh. And he never came back. I found his horse grazing a short way away, but no rider. I searched the valley for two days. It seems impossible that he could have vanished so completely. If he had been killed, the river could not have carried him far. I am haunted by that loss. No caves, no passages, no twists in the valley, no dreamy orchards or overhanging oaks, no shrine, no stone-mouthed hill . . . nothing that could have snared him. I missed him and I missed him. We had been exiled together; and to lose him so suddenly, and so mysteriously . . .'

He watched me carefully, thinking hard, clearly in pain with the memory. Then he added quietly, 'I suppose that is why there is something dead inside me. This is not my life. I have lost my life. A valley in the land of the Bituriges stole the last fragment of it. Until you . . .'

I took a deep breath, ordering my thoughts.

But a slow drone on Elkavar's elbow-pipes stopped me from responding. We looked round to see one of the Iberian mercenaries standing a short way away, spear held low and pointed towards us. His suspicious gaze flickered from Orgetorix to me and back again. Behind him, the other men were mounted, the spare horses on rope leads.

'What's this, Madraud?' Orgetorix asked softly.

'You do a lot of talking in the night,' Madraud answered. 'But you'd stopped to sleep. We wanted to ride on, but you wanted to stop. To sleep. We wanted a fight at that speaking hole. But you wanted to watch from a distance. There is something of the game animal in you, we've decided; to be hunted, not to hunt. So this is goodbye.'

'Then goodbye it is,' Orgetorix said evenly. 'But leave those horses.'

'The horses come with us,' Madraud murmured with a meaningful shake of his head, the spear lifting in his grip.

Then I found out why young Thesokorus had perhaps earned the name 'king of killers'.

He moved so fast I was scarcely aware that he had left my side. He pressed suddenly and fatally against the Iberian, using a technique I had seen practised by the Greeklanders themselves, a body charge that risked all and claimed all. Madraud gasped as his leader gripped him by the back of the neck, pushing aside spear, pushing in the lethal, leaf-shaped iron blade that he had slipped from its scabbard with the sound of metal dragged against a sharpening-stone.

At once, one of the other mercenaries jumped from his horse and ran at me, spear raised to throw, eyes like a wild dog's. He was suddenly struck by a wailing sack. Elkavar had flung his pipes. The man, startled for a moment, staggered back as Orgetorix struck him a lightning blow through the heart.

The other riders turned their mounts and started to canter. Orgetorix raced after them, jumped nimbly on to the trailing horse, ran along its back, on to the back of the Avernian's horse, knocking aside the spear that was stabbed at him, struck down through the man's skull, then leaned over the panting head of the animal and grabbed the reins, tugging it aside with the three spare horses. The other riders galloped down the hill. The jerking body of the Avernian was pushed to the ground where it continued to thrash wildly for a few moments. Orgetorix trotted back, leading our mounts, frowning.

'I wasn't expecting that,' he said, with a grim glance at Madraud's sprawled corpse.

'I wouldn't have known,' I replied. 'You fight like a cat, but without the screaming.'

'Screaming wastes breath. Merlin, I'll ask you to strip these bastards when they've stopped twitching. Madraud's leather jacket looks better for the battle ahead than that filthy sheepskin you're wearing ...'

Once again my clothing was being criticised!

'And their boots and belts are useful.'

He dismounted and inspected his own clothing for blood.

Elkavar was inspecting his pipes. Two splits in the bag, from my attacker's sword, had taken away their breath.

'Like a stuck pig,' he reflected sadly. 'No more squealing for a while. But easy enough to repair when there's a moment, you'll be pleased to hear.'

We rested, then, until that darkest hour which signals the sudden burst of sun, and a fresh dawn. At some time in the night Orgetorix had hauled the three naked bodies of his erstwhile companions to the trees at the cliff, and hung them from the branches. This was not an act of vengeance, but an expression of hate, it seemed to me; and not hate for these men . . . Their sad corpses were just the machine by which Orgetorix could cry his silent fury. And it was my own arrival that had opened up the gates.

I watched him move about the rough camp, pale and ghostly, silent and determined. If he was aware of my watching, he didn't show it.

I was certain I knew, now, not just the nature of his hate, but the source of it; and by implication the falseness of it. But for unfathomable reasons—which is to say, reasons I did not wish to address within myself at the time—this was not the time to talk to this brash, bold, inquisitive and lonely young man.

One reason was not unfathomable at all, however: I was wondering where his mother lay hiding. She might have been watching us now, from some rookery, or crevice in the rocks; from the sky or from the burrow of a subterranean scavenger. I was certain, though, that she would watch us without revealing herself. And I wondered when that revelation might next occur. And why she was allowing me so close to a son she had so jealously protected.

In my heart I felt that she was as shaken as was I by the discovery of our own ancient history. Neither of us knew exactly what to do; and both of us had preoccupations, the consequences of a long life and the occasional lapse into involvement with the more spirited of the men and women that we met along the way.

* * *

Wary of ambush by the dead men's companions, Orgetorix led us down the hill and along a stream, riding hard when the land was open to get ahead of the column. We soon met the silent line of Brennos's slaughterers, shooting down the panic of game animals that fled ahead of the army, mostly small animals and birds. These men were experts with sling and arrow, and as soon as the earth began to tremble they piled their kill and rode silently and swiftly to the south, to wait again for the disruption of nature by the approach of the vast gathering.

Soon the army appeared, led by twenty heavily armed men on black horses, walking slowly, wary eyes on the hills and surrounding woodland. When they saw us, four of them came galloping forward, spears lowered, shields high. They were helmetless and flaxen-haired; I couldn't read their clan signs. They barked words at us and Orgetorix understood the language easily. One of them seemed to recognise him, asked the names of his companions, gave Elkavar and myself harsh appraisal before nodding to us curtly, then the four waited for the column to catch up. We were allowed to pass back through the lines, a point of some two hundred men, then the mix of men-at-arms and ox-pulled carts, laden with booty and supplies.

The slaughtered game was gathered enthusiastically. The slow march flowed past us, the eyes that regarded us not so much curious as weary. There was talk of heading for the sea coast, and the thought of it was clearly a source of enthusiasm and relief. Anything to escape these endless mountain passes and boggy woods.

'I have to go straight to Brennos,' Orgetorix advised me. 'I'll need his protection if those marauding bastards sight me. Enough of them will have seen me strike down one of their chiefs. They might apply for single combat, by way of revenge. I should take him a gift. High Kings like gifts.' The young man appraised me coolly. 'I don't think you're much of a gift, though he might like Elkavar's singing. The trouble is, this is silent marching.'

Silent marching? The very hills were shaking with the

steady rhythm of their advance. He meant, of course, no war
cries, no trumpets, no drum-beating, or shield-beating, no
screeching skirmishes at the head of the column. And as few
fires as possible. Inasmuch as so many thousands of men and
their train could advance noiselessly south into hostile territory, this arrogant, magnificent army was attempting it.

Hence the slaughterers, culling the game alarmed by the
movement in the earth. And the selected men who rode more
distantly, taking over the watch stations. Orgetorix had spotted most of these outposts when he had 'skulked' for Brennos
in the autumn and winter.

But he had not seen them all.

We were close to a valley that wound between five hills
and would take us to the heart of Makedonia itself. I had
overflown this place, when I had been searching for Fierce
Eyes, before I had settled to the flight; and before Elkavar
had found me in the ruined house.

I had rested briefly and seen the danger, though it was only
now that I calculated the extent of that danger.

I had something of importance to impart to the leader of
this endless legion.

I had a gift for Brennos.

PART FIVE

The Hot Gates

CHAPTER TWENTY-TWO

—

At the Watch Station

The watch station had been built just below the ridge of a hill, overlooking the wide valley known as the Run of Wolves which led south towards the fertile plains of Makedonia, still a warrior-nation to be contended with, despite the continued grief over the distant, ritual-death of its young king: Alessandros, also known as Aleksander, Iskander . . .

So many names in so many tongues for one small-boned man with an eagle's eye for finding the edge of the earth itself. How quickly and persuasively his shade must have bargained with Time to let him take so much of legend hostage!

The house nestled in a copse of young cedars and pines, and with its dark-painted walls it was almost impossible to see from the valley below. Even eyes that knew of its presence would have been hard put to distinguish its walls below the crest of the wooded ridge.

Cloud shadow swept across the hills as the man who lived in the station went about his business, one day in early summer. He was cautious in his use of fire, never cooking until after dusk, and only when the wind would carry the scent of smoke to the south, away from danger. Towards the memory of Alessandros!

He had been so young, then, this watchman, just a boy, really. And too weak-chested to make that great journey to the east, to find Ocean herself, the end of the world. But the young king had liked him and made sure how to use him. 'When you've grown up a little, you will be a watchman at my northern frontier!'

He was certainly grown up now. So much so that he was the oldest man he knew. Sometimes he thought that Death had lost sight of him. The years came and went in tens, and soon he would have seen eight such tens. He had learned to be good at counting. And yet he was as spry as a spring fawn. He was white-bearded but still hawk-eyed, a small man who could scamper from rocky outcrop to pine-scented copse like a hare darting from its form to deep cover.

Four times each day he passed like a ghost, like that same cloud shadow, around the hill where he lived, scanning the valleys and ridges for signs of danger, for the tell-tale signs of war bands, for the deep rumble and sky-haze that told of an army on the move.

And how he longed for there to be an army on the move! He could still remember, with an inner gleam of bronze and colour, the sight of the young king's war-quest moving off to Persia. But no armies moved, now. These valleys were wasteland.

Behind the house, his precious pigeons were caged and calm. There was space for sixty. He flew them south in a special way. Each moon, the pigeons were returned to him by four riders from the fortress which they knew as home. When one of his birds failed to return—taken by an eagle, most likely—he felt sad. He knew them all. But there was always the pleasure of getting to know new birds.

Four times a day he scouted the mountainous land around his post. Once a day he wrote the same message on a piece of parchment: *Everything is as it should be.*

Every day, the way this message was written and attached

to the bird was changed; a little extra security for the men at the outposts, three days' ride away, where the hills flowed down to open land.

A cautious man, he always varied his route, and routine, though in more than fifty years at this station nothing had occurred to make him urgently change the message to the south. But he always stopped for a while at the marble urn, hidden among its own small copse of thorn and pine, where his late wife lay in ash.

They had liked to dance; on the silent hill, they had danced to remembered music; and still, each morning and evening, he picked her up and danced with her. She had been happy here, despite the isolation of the station, and the regular difficulty in getting food, especially if the Makedonian winter was particularly hard. She had cried when their two sons had gone away. When no further word had come from the boys, his grief turned to stone. He had abandoned the memory of the brash young men, though two small, polished shields lay beside the urn, a token of hope. It had not been the same for his wife.

Alone for more years than he cared to count, the watchman lived for the day, as contented and clear of eye and mind as he had been when a child.

Everything is as it should be.

And sometimes he would write: *Several horsemen and pack animals, weary, lightly armed.*

Or: *Migrants; a wagon train. A family; two oxen and five horses.*

But usually nothing more than: *Everything is as it should be.*

And this man, this whitebeard, might have lived happily until he died, to be placed in an urn beside his wife by the men in the south whom he guarded, had it not been for a moment of madness, when he left the cover of his house to chase a hawk.

The hawk had landed on the ridge. Fearing for his birds, he had flung two stones at the raptor. Hard eyes had turned to see him. A hard mind had realised where he lived, and how his house was disguised. Sharp wings had lifted the bird away and to the north.

It was that man's misfortune, that breezy summer day, to have chased off a bird of prey, and by doing so, to have run into me.

Everything is

He stopped writing. The pigeons had fluttered suddenly in their cages, a brief moment of alarm. Had that hawk come back? The sun slanted in through the small window to the east, picking out the stone bowl of olives and dried fruit that was to last him for the day. Then a cloud passed over the sun and for a moment the small room, in the station, became gloomy.

Was it a wild cat? A lynx, perhaps?

But the birds were settled again, just the odd flurry of wings and the gentle 'coo' of the carrier pigeons as they watched the shadows from their cages. He turned back to his nook and completed the message:

as it should be.

He signed and carefully marked the small strip of parchment, then looked up again. The birds, now, were unusually silent. Perhaps there *was* a predator.

He picked up his sling, stretched it, rubbed the pouch, loaded it with a rounded pebble, then rose from his seat. But before he could take a step to the door, the door was pushed slowly open. The light from outside was blocked by a tall, cloaked man who stooped to peer into the room, then stepped forward, finger to lips, and closed the door behind him.

Behind the watchman, the shutters of the window creaked open. An olive-skinned man peered in, grinning. 'Good morning,' he said, in a dialect of the old man's language. 'My name is Thesokorus. I wouldn't use that sling, if I were you.'

'Excuse me,' said the other man, his accent awkward. 'I'm forgetting my manners. I am Bolgios, a commander in an army that wishes safe passage. I also wish you a good morning.'

And they both laughed.

The tall man took off his iron helmet and scratched at a beard that was flame-bright. His eyes, in a face that was dust-encrusted, gleamed as green as jade. His cloak was black, bearskin probably, and the stink of horse and human sweat flowed like a miasma from the patterned shirt and trousers below.

This green-eyed man was holding three pigeon cages, the six flustered occupants very much alive. 'For today,' he said to the watchman, 'for messages.' Then he pulled back his cloak to reveal ten birds, broken-necked and hooked into the fabric. 'For supper,' he added with a little laugh.

The olive-skinned man at the window hauled himself through the narrow gap and picked up the note, reading it carefully and nodding his approval.

'Everything is *indeed* as it should be. Do send the message.'

'Who are you?' asked the watchman, terrified, eyes wide, his hands shaking as he held them defensively before him.

'We are friends of what lies deep in Delphi,' said the olive-skinned man. 'Though in different ways.' He put his arm around the old man's shoulder. 'Now attach the message. And send it.'

The watchman did as he was told. The bird flew high, circled the hill once, then disappeared to the south. The man called Thesokorus, watching from the window, blew it a kiss to speed it on its way.

'Very good. Now write the next five messages, exactly as you would normally do, and attach them to the birds. And write down when the birds should be released.'

The watchman did as he was told, hesitating for a moment as he stared at the pigeons in their cages. He looked up, met the hard green gaze of the taller man, then sighed. Perhaps he had decided against the trick he had planned. He slowly inscribed the messages, marked them, then tied them to his birds.

He felt sick with the betrayal.

'Well done,' said gentle Thesokorus. 'These birds will live.

Hold that in your heart. There will be someone here to send them.'

When all of this had been done, the green-eyed man, the gruff northerner, put his arm around the watchman's shoulder and led him outside. The other birds all lay dead below their cages, and Thesokorus scooped them up into a leather bag; more flesh for the pot.

'I didn't see you coming,' the watchman muttered nervously, as Bolgios led him towards the edge of the slope. 'How could I have missed you?'

'We knew you were watching. We'd sent a bird to find you. He says you threw a stone at him.'

'The hawk? That hawk?'

'The hawk. We took precautions. It wasn't easy, my friend. Look . . .'

'Mercury's cry!' the old man wailed. 'How could I have missed *that*?'

He stared in shock and bewilderment at the great swathe of horsemen, soldiers, women, wagons and oxen that filled the two fingers of the valley round the Hill of Artemia, a crush of bodies, a restless army, stationary, heaving in the ranks, watching the hill above them, waiting for the signal to move on, down the pass, towards the ocean's edge. The green-eyed man raised his hand high, waved it to the right, and the earth trembled as the horde was mobilised and began to flood to the south.

'It's not possible . . . not possible . . . I looked here only an hour ago.'

'We were not here an hour ago,' the olive-skinned man said. 'And your eyes and ears had been . . . distracted, shall we say?'

'I would have felt the trembling of the earth.'

'We came on tiptoe.'

'It's not possible.'

'It has been done. Thank you for your help.'

The watchman looked into the dark eyes of the young man who spoke his language. Softly he asked, 'What happens to me now?'

'Come with me.'

Thesokorus led the watchman to where the marble urn was cool in the shade. 'Who lies here?'

The old man crossed his arms over his chest and started to shake. 'My wife. She died many years ago. That was the only time I left the station, to attend at her funeral. I carried her ashes here. I needed to be close to her. Don't touch her!'

'You loved her?'

'Very much. I still do. Our two sons went south, to war. For ever. That was the last we heard of them. It's a hard thing. To watch a loved one die of grief. I miss her very much.'

'Well,' said the other, 'that is a love that must be respected.'

A while later, the watchman's heart was placed with great reverence in the urn, rested on the ashes, and the urn sealed carefully again, and left in peace between the brazen shields of two lost sons.

CHAPTER TWENTY-THREE

Against the Makedonians

For a few days, after the silencing of the watch station, the great army continued south in the shadow of hills, spreading out between the narrow valleys, the columns squeezed thin. It was a time of nervous silence and gloomy anticipation. The sound of our progress seemed to swell in the gorges, doubling and doubling again in volume. But the word had spread, like a summer fire in an olive grove: the watch station is silenced. There is nothing to fear until we reach Thermopylae.

Even Brennos was confident. Bolgios's triumphant story—how he had tricked the old man at the head of the valley, a story repeated twenty times, in the saddle, at camp, at meal times—had so numbed the war chief's sensibilities that he could scarcely believe the enemy had ever existed. So it was a surprised and rather confused warlord who led us from the valleys and on to a narrow strip of open land which rose steadily towards misty hills, there to find a force of fierce and heavily armed Makedonians waiting for us, barring our route to the south.

They had occupied a ridge and made a grim and threatening sight. Their lines stretched as far as the eye could see across the horizon ahead of us, facing every wood and the tumble of tall, grey rocks through which the Celtic army was slowly emerging.

Brennos sent riders back to stop the columns moving forward. He snapped quick orders: bring up chariots; bring up archers; get men on to high ground to see what these troops might be hiding behind their front line.

But then he fell very quiet, holding his boar's tusk helmet and idly polishing the ivory with the palm of his hand.

On his left, Achichoros, stripped to the waist in the heat, left leg casually drawn up across the saddle, was peeling and inspecting an orange. On his right, dark-eyed Orgetorix, now in his bull's-hide battle kilt and leather vest, leaned forward on the high saddle of his own war horse and scanned the army that was spread out before them.

The Makedonians were lined up in phalanxes, eight men deep, iron breastplates shining, sandalled and metal-greaved below loose, red tunics, strangely shaped yellow helmets on their heads, very unpleasant bearded faces below. They all held spears: long spears at the front, longer spears behind, and very long spears indeed at the back. The sun picked out the rising ranks of points. The blades looked lean and mean. These spears were slowly lowered and raised to the steady rhythm of a low, sinister chant from the warriors who bore them.

Pigeons, circling above the pristine field of encounter, sometimes landed on those slowly moving points and struggled to keep their balance. The only ripple of disorder in the orderly ranks opposed to us was the quick waggle of a spear, dislodging its unwelcome avian visitor.

'Of all the sights I expected to see when I came out of that fucking valley and on to this plain . . .' Brennos said suddenly.

Orgetorix stayed silent and Achichoros considered it diplomatic to stop his juicy chewing, watching the other warlord and waiting for the sentence to be completed.

When, after a while, no further words had been spoken, Achichorus ventured: 'You didn't expect to see four thousand Makedonians waiting for you, clearly knowing you were coming? Is that what you were going to say?'

Brennos gave him a sour look. 'Words to that effect. How did they know? One of those pigeons must have been wrongly messaged.'

'Probably the watchman's, at the head of the valley,' Orgetorix ventured. 'The message upside down; a wing-tip feather bent; some subtle signal. We Greeklanders are good at that sort of trick, and these Makedonians learn quickly from their neighbours.'

'That damned watchman!'

'Damned?' Orgetorix shook his head, amused. 'I doubt it. He's walking arm-in-arm with Alessandros even now, laughing at us. That old man knew he was going to die and he made a damned good job of persuading us that he'd sent the message we wanted him to send. Well, he's dead and out of it, and we're here and in trouble. So what shall we do, Lord Brennos?'

Achichoros waved his half-eaten orange at the enemy. 'I suggest attacking, Brennos. It's bloody, but it tends to keep things moving.'

'Go ahead,' Brennos said. 'Full frontal. You and your elite spearmen. We'll watch and follow later.'

'I thought oranges were supposed to be sweet,' Achichoros commented studiously. 'This one is quite sour.' He threw it over his shoulder.

Now Bolgios and his two-man guard galloped up, red hair streaming below his helmet, limbs glistening with sweat. He was in his battle leathers and carrying five javelins and his oval shield.

'Is there a reason for this delay?' he barked at Brennos.

'About four thousand, in case you hadn't noticed.'

'Seventeen hundred and eleven, to be precise,' Bolgios declaimed, with a grin at Orgetorix. 'It's not just the Greeklanders who are good at figures.'

'Well counted,' said the Greeklander.

'Thank you. And just to remind you, Brennos, we are tens of thousands against that seventeen hundred. If we were the sort of people who feasted on our enemy's guts in triumph, we could be belly-full with Makedonian liver before the day is half done! What *is* the reason for the delay?'

'Strategy,' Brennos said irritably.

'Strategy?' Bolgios looked confused.

'Why are they making it so obvious how little they've lined up against us? And their tactics. Chanting, spear lowering and raising, threatening to rip our horses open . . .'

Bolgios seemed even further confused. 'Spear lowering? Horse ripping? That's tactics?'

'They're making it very obvious, good friend Bolgios, which suggests to some of us that they're hiding something else.'

'Perhaps they're just . . . How can I put this without seeming to be impertinent, good friend Brennos? . . . Perhaps they're just . . . *obvious*.'

The two men glared at each other.

'I accept your criticism,' Brennos said quietly. 'But there's more to it. Not everything is as it seems.'

'Where have I heard that before?' Bolgios muttered. He suddenly looked up at the morning sky, his black horse rearing to take the great weight of its rider as it moved backwards in the saddle. He turned on the spot, still staring upwards, removed his ridge-coned helmet and laughed out loud. 'Yes! You're right. That cloudless sky! I see it now. It's just deceiving us by staying up there. It's about to fall and catch us all by surprise! Excuse me, my lord, I must go and instruct my legion to raise their shields above their heads!'

He cantered off, shouting violent abuse at the Makedonian force.

Brennos stared at the enemy grimly. 'He's right, of course.'

Orgetorix laughed out loud. 'That the sky will fall on us?'

'That we should cease this delay. All I can think of is that they're hiding chariots, or archers, behind their rank. They're well hidden. If Bolgios was able to count their numbers, he must have been higher up, and still he didn't see the concealed force . . .'

'I suspect Bolgios was joking,' Achichoros said with a quick smile, stretching in the saddle. 'Don't get me wrong, I don't doubt his courage, but I do doubt that he can count above the number of horses he could steal in a raid. That would be a high number, certainly, but not that high. He was trying to cheer us up. We're looking at three times a thousand men at least.'

'Yes. I suspect you're right.'

'Seventeen hundred or three thousand, that's a massed rank of them,' Orgetorix pointed out carefully. 'And they are blocking the exit from this pass. And we're not even at Thermopylae.'

'Bugger Thermopylae!' Brennos said with passion. 'One pass at a time. Where's that enchanter? The one who warned us of the watchman . . .'

'He's behind you.'

Brennos turned heavily in the saddle and stared at me. When he glanced down at my horse, the animal shied slightly, as if this man's fierce eyes were as frightening to the equine world as they sometimes could be to the human. But even powerful men can be curious, and curiosity softens fierceness.

'Does your far-sight see men beyond these men?'

I answered quite simply, 'There are more, but not many more. They want you to think they're hiding nothing by pretending to hide a legion, to discomfort you. They seem to have succeeded.'

Brennos's face glowered for a fleeting moment, then relaxed, and a small smile touched his lips. He turned to Achichoros and said something and both men laughed. Achichoros moved away, riding steadily back to the head of his own army, and the spearmen who stood ranked at its head. Brennos sent a rider to Bolgios, on the right flank. Behind us, the chariots began to rattle in anticipation. Again, Brennos looked round at me. 'I would like you to leave the field; find a vantage point and watch from safety. You too, Orgetorix. I would like to keep you safe. I want to send you south again, ahead of us.'

'As you wish,' the Greeklander said, rather gloomily.

We rode forward to canter along the line, a dangerous manoeuvre if the Makedonian phalanxes were indeed hiding archers as well as several hundred cavalry, but we had hardly left the commander's group when, with a great shriek, a war cry of howling anger, a small chariot, drawn by two long-maned black horses, raced from behind Bolgios's front line of horsemen and streaked across the level ground towards the rise where the Makedonians waited, still uttering their growling chant, still raising and lowering their spears.

They seemed as surprised as the Celtic army at this sudden, singlehanded attack on them.

There was something familiar about the two protagonists of this small but noisy raid: the charioteer, leaning forward, whipping the horses ferociously, was a lean-bodied woman, clad only in a thin, green vest, bare-armed, and ragged leather britches. Black-faced, her dark hair streaming, she exhorted the animals to greater speed as the chariot came almost up to the line of pikes themselves, before turning tightly and racing down the hill.

Not before the passenger, tall, stripped to the waist, holding a short throwing javelin, launched that weapon with incredible strength, bending almost double as he flung the shaft, straight into the Makedonian lines, impaling a soldier so deeply through the chest that the man seemed transfixed, and probably was: to the man behind.

A long javelin was thrown back at him, and this lithe figure actually ducked and *snatched* the shaft as it grazed his shoulder. The charioteer turned the horses back towards the Makedonians, and that heavy spear was returned with vigour. But now arrows and slingshot began to hiss and clatter through the open ground between us, and the couple, struck and hurt by stones, ducked and turned for safety, the man hanging on to the chariot rail, his arm raised in meaningful farewell, his voice a piercing, taunting torrent of abuse and insult.

Urtha could certainly summon words of insult!

Ullanna was a wild and handsome charioteer!

Their attack had precipitated action in the ranks of Brennos's army, and as Ullanna steered the horses back to safety so our lines were broken by chariots pushing through, to sweep towards the Makedonian phalanxes, throwing spears at the ready, a noisy and exuberant charge at the enemy. Horsemen followed, earthshaking, shield-striking as they drove towards those deadly spears. Achichoros and Bolgios had launched attacks as well. We all raised shields to defend against the sudden rain of arrows that fell upon us, and Elkavar was hit in the leg, though the narrow point only skinned him. He was too busy trying to protect his pipes.

I shouted to Urtha. The man had a fierce look on his face, and was deaf and blind to anything but the attack. Ullanna had been hit on the shoulder by a sharp-edged slingshot, which had sent her flying from the chariot. She was crouched on the ground, now, plucking grass and rubbing at the bloody split in her flesh. There was a lot of blood. Urtha saw me and acknowledged me, but then Ullanna was back in the chariot, awkwardly turning the panting horses, and they returned to the battle. From the grim look on her face, she was clearly in great pain now.

Behind me I heard a man say, 'That damned bird again! That raven.'

Orgetorix was watching the sky. High above us, a raven was falling towards us, but it suddenly turned on the updraught and flew over the seething mass of men and murder. Elkavar and I withdrew to higher ground. The valleys were alive with restless men, waiting for orders to attack, kept still only by the steady nerves of the three men who led this horde. Riders raced along the columns, and the hills flooded with figures, anxious to see what was happening ahead of them. The wind was to the north. They could smell the stench of this frenzy and hear the noise of it, like the high-pitched shrieking of carrion birds at this distance, and the strident blasts of trumpets, keeping everything disturbed, on edge, and in endless fury.

* * *

A king of Makedonia died that day, with over a thousand of his loyal troops. The rest scattered, a broken army. We didn't know at the time that we had claimed so great a head, but the head was brought to us by the scavengers who had stayed behind to strip and bury the dead. They brought this king's trophy, and his armour, and the rings still on his fingers, including a royal seal. They had looted the fallen generals as well. Brennos gave them the armour from the generals, all the rings except for the seal. He sent the trophy back down the line, for oiling, preservation and eventual display.

The losses from Brennos's army had been huge. It was hard to say whether they would have been lower if the action had not been so compulsive, following Urtha and Ullanna's wild challenge to the Makedonians. What was clear was that, despite grieving for many of the dead, the Celts were in a state of elation. They had skirmished all the way from the Daan, but this had been the first significant confrontation, not expected, and won by sheer force of numbers and determination.

It seemed to many of the men who had fought that nothing, now, could stand against them. All pretence of silence vanished; fires were lit at night, game roasted, and trumpets were blown each dawn and dusk, and there was certainly no lack of singing and mock combat.

As many wounded as dead had been sent north again, under escort. The Celtic dead had been buried with great ceremony, the day after the battle, below five huge mounds that had been raised above them at the end of the valley. Whether time and wind would preserve those tombs was another matter. Brennos, practical to the last, recognised the need for ceremony among the grieving followers of the lost, and using his own wiles, with a wonderful eulogy by torchlight, sent the spirits of the men on their way to Ghostland, and urged the army to hasten south without further delay, since all in Greek Land would be rising from their beds, ready to confront the invader, now.

So we buried, feasted, sang to the Gathering God, who sent

darkwinged birds to assist the ghosts back to their homelands . . . and then we marched through the night.

To make up time.

Orgetorix had quietly disappeared, travelling ahead under Brennos's direction.

It wasn't long before Brennos sent for Urtha. Ullanna was in great pain from the strike on her shoulder, and Elkavar was at the reins of the chariot, the Scythian woman curled up in a fever, wrapped in blankets, inside the light wood of the vehicle. Her illness would soon pass.

Urtha and I met up with Brennos, and introductions were made. Urtha explained that, on his way to catch up with the army, he had found the chariot abandoned in one of the narrow passes. Brennos remembered several skirmishes and presented the vehicle to the man without hesitation.

'I've heard a lot about your land,' he said. 'My father told me that beyond its shores there is a place where the shadows of heroes ride, waiting for their time on the earth. Not the dead, the waiting-to-be-born.'

'That place lies close to my great fort,' Urtha declaimed, puffing himself up in the saddle. 'Yes. My great fort looks down to the river that separates our worlds. Sometimes I see the glowing boats that sail those waters. We light fires and sacrifice in the willow groves. When the shadow of a hero crosses the water, he first steps on my own land, although where he then goes, to settle, to quest, is his own business.'

'I very much like the sound of your land,' Brennos said thoughtfully.

Urtha could hardly restrain his pride. He said, 'I would be honoured to have you as a guest in my fort. My house is entirely at your disposal. The hunting in Alba is swift and clever, unsurpassable; and close to the river there is an orchard that is always in fruit.'

'And if I came with a hundred men, you could accommodate us all?' Brennos asked. 'Without thinking we had come to invade?'

'Come with a thousand,' Urtha bragged. 'We'll feast on deer-flesh and partridge for a full cycle of the moon, and then raid to the south for some of the strongest bulls you'll ever have seen. Southerners are not up to much, but they do breed wonderful bulls.'

'Your fort must be one of the largest I can imagine. I'm impressed by the sound of it. When this jaunt is over, I'll bring that thousand men, and enjoy your hospitality. Thank you. And thank you, again, for the spark that lit the fire. That charge. I will always acknowledge when a good action, spontaneously taken, breaks through my own uncertainty. That was a charge to remember. And your charioteer was like a screeching owl, but more desirable. The memory of her will linger the longest. Is she your sister?'

Urtha said nothing, just stared ahead as he rode next to the warlord. Brennos glanced back at me with a quick smile, realising that he might be straying on to delicate ground. In fact, I realised at once that quite a lot of the conversation was a typical tease. Brennos would have known that Urtha was exaggerating the hospitality and size of his stronghold. And a thousand men, crossing the sea to ride to Urtha's land, would certainly have been seen as an invasion.

But Urtha needed something; and if Brennos knew it, he was making it as easy as he could for the brash young Cornovidian.

'She is not my sister,' Urtha said after a while. 'She is from east of here, where according to the Hittites . . .'

'Hittites?'

'Gossips. Liars. They claim the women of her race—the Scythians—cut off their breasts to facilitate the use of a bow.'

'Now *that* is something I've heard about. But though your charioteer wasn't plump, from what I saw—'

'As I said, Lord Brennos. These tales are lies. Ullanna— that's her name—has been aiding me in a very personal task. There is a man, riding somewhere in your army . . .'

Brennos reined in and waved a warning hand. 'If you're going to say you wish to kill someone, the answer is no. Gods, we'll have a hard enough time getting to that snake hole, Delphi, without stopping every hour for some combat, some revenge joust, over the taking of a horse or the killing of a dog.'

The two men glared at each other. Urtha was red-faced and furious. Brennos was white-faced and cold.

Riders and chariots continued to stream past us. Somewhere, a wagon turned over and dogs barked fiercely as they darted for some of the spilled meat. A man rode up to Brennos, took one look at him, turned and cantered away.

Then Urtha said, very quietly, 'His name is Cunomaglos. He is somewhere in this horde.'

'There will be a hundred men with a name like that. In this horde.'

Undaunted by the cold suppression of his unspoken request, Urtha said, 'I was afraid for the future of my land. I listened to false advice, and abandoned my fort. I looked for answers in the world when I should have looked for the truth in my family itself. Does this mean anything at all to you, Lord Brennos?'

'It does,' the warlord answered with the merest nodding of his head.

Urtha said, 'When I was away, Cunomaglos and others came to join this expedition. They left my fort unguarded. I live at the edge of Ghostland. Not everything in Ghostland is friendly to the living. Does this mean anything to you, my Lord Brennos?'

'It does,' Brennos answered, leaning on his saddle, looking down. 'More than you might think.'

Urtha said, 'My wife is dead, my son is dead, killed by a force of evil that I will not understand until I can return and seek it out. But I cannot return until Cunomaglos has answered for his desertion. If he had stayed true to me, my family would now be mocking me, for being a fool, and laughing at my blustering apology . . . not waiting by Ghostland's river for news that their deaths have been avenged, so they may creep back into the world of shadows.'

Brennos stared at me for a moment, an unnerving gaze. Then he said to Urtha, 'Did you seek out this army to find *me*? Or to find this Cunomaglos?'

'Cunomaglos. All other considerations, for the moment, are in winter hibernation.'

'How will you find him?'

'Two old friends will sniff him out,' Urtha said, and he raised his arm. I heard the growl and bark of hounds, and suddenly Gelard and Maglerd appeared through the moving ranks, restrained on leashes by a sallow youth, cropped hair, pale-faced, dressed in brightly coloured trousers and shirt.

'Is that a man or a woman?' Brennos asked with a laugh as this slim, solemn figure stood beside him, whispering quiet words to the panting dogs.

'Neither,' Urtha said. As he said the words, fierce-eyed Niiv glared at him, but for a moment only. Her frosty, angry look was saved for me.

Brennos called one of his captains to him, a squat man, cheerfully featured, his face covered with a ginger stubble, though his moustaches were preened and sharp, reaching below his chin. He was wearing the colours of the Tectosages.

'This is Luturios,' Brennos said to Urtha. 'This is Urtha,' he said to Luturios. And then again to my friend: 'Find your Cunomaglos. Sniff him out. Do you think he knows you're here?'

'He soon will.'

'Well, I can't afford to have men watching their backs all the time. Find him, and Luturios and his squad will cull him from the pack. In a few days we'll reach the sea. I will make a single exception for you, Urtha. At the sea, if you've found this wife-killer, you may fight him. And I'll not stop that combat. And I'll wait until that combat is finished. If you try to finish it before we reach the sea, Luturios will have a say in the matter. Luturios is very efficient at having such "says" in the matter.'

'I'll cut your fucking throat,' Luturios said, by way of clarification, though he smiled as he said it.

Urtha bowed in the saddle, then turned his horse and rode away from us, following Niiv, who was running with the hounds down through the column.

CHAPTER TWENTY-FOUR

The Combat of Urtha and Cunomaglos

Urtha sought me out later, trotting beside me on a fine black horse as we clattered along a dry river-bed.

'I want to find him myself,' he said. 'It may sound strange, but I need that moment of recognition. I need to see the look in his eyes as he sees me, and realises that I've come for him. If I know Cunomaglos, it will be fear, not mockery, that greets me.'

I hadn't been about to offer my services, beyond helping ride through the lines, but I guessed that Urtha was dissuading me from doing him a favour with charm.

I nodded my agreement.

'Why fear?' I asked him.

'Because the man was a man of honour, and he loved me as a brother. And betrayal will have been a spectre on his back from the moment he left the land.'

There was no arguing with Urtha's certainty. 'You must ask me for whatever help you need,' I said.

'Search with me. Stay close. The dogs will sniff him out.'

Niiv had slipped away again. She was keeping at her distance. When Urtha had found the abandoned chariot, still harnessed to its horses, he and Ullanna had used it to get ahead of the others, but had taken Niiv with them—she was so light she hardly troubled the animals that pulled them. The dogs had scampered behind.

After the day's pause, to confront a local army, however, the others of our crew had caught up, and Maglerd signalled their discreet arrival with a cheerful series of whines and howls. Rubobostes and Tairon came to our fire sometime in the middle of the night. The Cymbrii arrived soon after with the cart and Argo's heart. Then Manandoun and Cathabach and the Germanii. Michovar, it seemed, had turned back after all.

And Jason?

'We lost him about two days ago,' Manandoun said. 'He took the strongest horse and rode towards the west. He seemed excited about something.'

'That rider,' Tairon added. 'The young man who called to him. He seemed to know him.'

A rider had appeared on a rocky ridge, among wide-branched pine trees, and called to Jason. Jason had been transfixed by the vision, then powerfully determined to find out who the young man was. He had taken very little, apart from the horse, and galloped up the slopes. That was the last they'd seen of him.

I asked an innocent question: concerning the sighting of birds at the time.

Tairon frowned and shook his head, but Manandoun scratched his jaw, thought hard, then answered, 'A few sparrows, or whatever passes locally for sparrows; and a rook, or some great black bird, a solitary thing. I've seen it before. I think it's following the army, probably feeding on the dead.'

I smiled at that.

Feeding on the dead? Protecting a young life from the *risen* dead, more like.

Urtha could see that I was unnerved by this news. When everyone was settled he whispered, 'Is Jason in difficulty?'

'He's been tricked,' I answered. 'He thinks he saw his son. The question is, how quickly will he realise the fact; and where will he go next?'

'To Delphi?' the Celt suggested.

Yes. Probably to Delphi. If Medea didn't lead him to destruction first.

Urtha drew his polished sword, rested it in his hand. 'I remember thinking that I would use this without hesitation on that strange man, your old friend, old Lake Corpse. I was angry with him. But once the business with the dog-bastard is over, I'll use this iron to help him in any way I can. This is not wholly altruistic, I hope you'll understand. I've invited Brennos and a thousand of his men to come and stay in my stronghold. To feast on deer-flesh and partridges, if I remember myself and my large mouth correctly. That was a little rash, I think. Jason might be useful to have around.'

'He certainly was, seven hundred years ago,' I said, and Urtha nodded, as if nothing could have been more obvious.

The earth began to shake. The night sky was black, star-speckled, and the air filled with the scent of cedar and lavender. To wake in such a land is to wake as if newly born; there is a blossom of dew on the cheeks, cold wind in the head, and a vigour in every limb. That hour before dawn! If dark Hades was as charged with life as this moment in the day, no Greeklander would ever regret dying.

The sun spread like fire to the east, above the tree-lined hills, picking out the shapes of rock and ridge, the old face of the world. I welcomed it, I remember welcoming it on that second day back with Urtha, as if there was a new season to the heart.

I kicked him in his blanket. The Cymbrii were up and ready. Niiv was silent, pale face glowing in the dawn below her shorn head. She watched me like a cat, but turned her gaze away when I threatened anger.

Earth shaking!

After a night on the march, we had had a night of rest. Now the ten times ten thousand men and women in the army of Brennos moved again through the land, towards the promise of sea; to the certainty of death for many of them at Thermopylae; to the promise of rescue at Delphi.

And as this great horde moved sluggishly to the south, Urtha and I, and Rubobostes on a lighter horse than his adored Ruvio, and Manandoun and Cathabach, faithful knights, rode steadily in the other direction.

Looking for a hound with the face of a handsome man, and the heart of a bastard.

If we had had a jug of milk for every time we heard the words, jokingly expressed, 'You're going the wrong way. Delphi is south . . .' we could have covered Greekland with cheese.

Day after day we rode through and across the ponderous mass of mounted men, and men on foot, and trailing beasts, scampering children and lumbering wagons.

Wherever we went it was assumed we were bringing information, or instructions, or orders for battle. Those at the back of the three columns had already created a great exaggeration from the fierce battle that had occurred at the front. They had seen the burial mounds, and smelled the fires. They had been aware of the dead. But they had passed, belatedly, over the bloody ground and only imagination had been their guide to what had happened in the distance from them.

Maglerd and Gelard scampered and prowled between the creaking wheels and tired legs. They were popular dogs. Whole platoons of heavily armed men would suddenly stop, crowd around the great beasts and start to play. They were missing their own animals. Maglerd and Gelard relished the attention, until Urtha's hard voice cut through their fun, and with slightly guilty, lolling looks, they returned to the hunt.

It was the dogs that made us accepted and welcomed as we searched through the clans, and asked for passing hospitality.

Then the day came, as I'd known it would, when the hounds looked fierce, their shackles rising, their red maws flecked with spittle. I could smell them, even though they were standing a hundred paces away, staring down the line. Maglerd had dropped to a crouch and Gelard was so tense that I thought the poor beast would crack across the ribs. A hundred or so horsemen were riding past us, and from their shields I guessed them to be Avernii, from western Gaul, close to the sea that separated them from Urtha's land. They were drooping and tired, dragging five cows and some weary horses. But among them, shrunk into their own horses, were a group of men who seemed to carry no colours at all. They had streaked their hair white, though the spines had collapsed slightly. They all seemed ill. Their cloaks were dark coloured, and it was strange to see them wearing them, because the days were hot, now, and most of the army rode or walked in very light dress indeed.

Urtha stopped one of the Avernians.

'Do you know the names of the other men who ride in your ranks?'

'From near to Ghostland,' the warrior said, looking Urtha up and down suspiciously. 'They brought some fine horses, and some excellent cows. We've traded in the past. They are fine men. Why do you ask?'

'I'm searching for an old friend. Cunomaglos. Of the Cornovidi. He looks after my hounds.'

The Avernian looked down at the two stiffened beasts, then again at Urtha, shaking his head. 'Why do you ask me such a question when your dogs have told you all you wish to know? And why do you lie? He's no friend of yours.'

And he snapped words at his compatriots; forty men on horse turned to look at us, scowling, then all of them drew away from the column, leaving the bedraggled troupe ahead of them exposed.

The dogs began to bark, hackles rising. They were watching one man among the small party of warriors.

Cunomaglos looked over his shoulder. He was just as I had imagined him, heavyset, umber-haired, mean-eyed and grim. He was wearing a mail vest over green linen, and short, striped trousers, his tattooed arms bare, his calves a mass of scars. He seemed shocked, then reined in, turned and suddenly screamed a curse towards us. He was unkempt, his dark beard untrimmed, his hair hanging thickly from below an un-decorated leather helmet.

I had walked the Path for lifetimes; I had seen the way fear and fury can mix in a man's eyes to give him the appearance of something so wild that he will give pause to the strongest-hearted contestant in combat. I cannot describe in words what I saw in that man Cunomaglos's eyes at that moment—murder and desperation, perhaps. Had he dreamed of the wreckage he had left behind when he had ridden away from Urtha's family? Had the spirits of Aylamunda and Urien taunted him from Ghostland? Had the dead among his companions, the *uthiin* who had remained faithful, ridden him down and whispered abuse at him? *Spectres on his back.* Something had happened to this man, and he was now confronting the dread moment of his dreams: vengeance had ridden up to him and said quietly, 'I've come to kill you for killing my wife and child. You stole my life, as I see from your eyes you already know. I've come to take it back.'

Cunomaglos stayed as motionless as a statue, his pale eyes not blinking as he stared at Urtha, who abruptly turned and rode back to me.

'*Got* him!' the young king said with a quick smile. 'And did you see the look on his face? He knows what must have happened in the fort. He's frightened. Now, how far is it to that ocean? Charm me to it soon, Merlin. I cannot wait to rub sea-salt into that bastard's wounds!'

As the ocean came in sight, a distant shimmer, specked with islands, the Celts began to break ranks, whipping horse and chariot ahead of the main army, bands of men exuberantly seeking the best beaches for games and races. By the time we were riding along the cliffs, not a single strand was in pristine condition, churned up by wheels and hooves as clan challenged clan to every conceivable competition; including swimming races to the dark rocks that rose, like a broken reef, at a distance from the shore.

Throwing-games abounded, using lances, rocks and bulky

pouches; the Iceni, from south of Urtha's own land, and the Belgae from across the water had formed into two teams of forty players, and were reinventing gwdball, a kicking, jumping and punching game using an inflated bladder.

Now Brennos gave instructions to throw up earthworks on the land side, and set up picket stations. For two days another army had shadowed our own. They were spread out across the hills behind us, and moved south in parallel with us. Their intentions were unclear. Brennos had established a very large force of heavily armed men at the rear of the column.

Luturios and his keen-weaponed brigade escorted Cunomaglos and his own men inland, to the far bank of a river that curled and rushed through the rocks towards the edge of one of the beaches. They found a place where there was grass and wood on both banks, backed by craggy rocks, and where the water was waist deep.

Urtha and Ullanna arrived on the near bank, with the other Celts from Argo. Tairon and Rubobostes had stayed behind to guard the Spirit of the Ship.

Luturios and his men withdrew seawards, along the shallow river, and set a fire, sitting down to watch from a distance. If this combat was conducted in the proper fashion, they would be no more than spectators.

Urtha and Cunomaglos laid out their weapons, then approached the river. Cunomaglos had shaved his cheeks and waxed his hair into a single, thick braid. Trousered, naked to the waist except for tattoos, he was formidable. All that earlier weariness and fear had vanished. His arms were huge, ridged with veins. His eyes were so deep in his skull it was hard to tell where he was looking. Perhaps everywhere.

Urtha wore a kirtle and a short blue cloak, drawn around his body and pinned at the shoulder with a hound-faced brooch. He had slung his father's gold *lunula* on top of this, and it was clear that Cunomaglos was aware of that family totem, as it glinted. Was he wondering what it was doing on Urtha and not on the druid, whose ended life had given it up?

It was time to negotiate. The Celts adopt the battle-talk

when facing single combat, formal and laconic; and they indulge in exaggerated metaphor as well as insult.

Arms crossed, each man examined the armoury that was opposed to him. Then Cunomaglos shouted, 'I see you have begged, borrowed and stolen a fine array of weapons. Those big shields are impressive, but they won't hold me back.'

'I'd be surprised if you came with that array of weapons all the way from your home. You've been doing some begging yourself. Is that a stone groinplate I see? You must be truly scared of the strength of my blade.'

'I will lend you the stone with pleasure, if you promise not to use the unfair thrust.'

'Only a coward like you would contemplate the unfair blow. Keep the stone. I'll use it to weight your dead body in the sea, when I bury you.'

'In fact,' Cunomaglos retorted, 'I had planned to carve it in memory of a brother, and lay it on the earth over your cold, blood-drained corpse.'

'Then don't concern yourself with practising with hammer and chisel. On the matter of the fight, this ground is wrong for chariots.'

'I agree. I would have enjoyed challenging you by chariot, but it would be unfair on the horses.'

'I would propose only two weapons at a time, the choice to alternate between us.'

'I'm quite happy with that. We must decide on whose side of the river we begin. And I propose that we keep the river itself for the fifth encounter, though that is just to be clear in the rules, since you will be crow-feast after the first.'

'Four on land, then the fifth in the river until it's done, until the death. Yes. And no matter what is happening, how far the fight has gone when we fight on land, when the last edge of the sun disappears behind that hill, the fighting is ended for the day.'

'I agree with that. Clewvar, who has sharp eyes, will stand the watch for me. Only if we reach the river will we fight to the end of it. Lexomodos will guard my weapons.'

'Cathabach will watch on my side. Ullanna of Scythia will watch my weapons.'

Although two of Cunomaglos's men laughed quickly at the suggestion that a woman would supply weapons and armour to a man in combat, it was taboo to insult a woman relative at such a time, and Cunomaglos stayed silent and stiff until the inappropriate insult had been silenced.

Urtha went on: 'And one further thing: since Brennos's man Luturios brought us to this place, neither of us can be considered to have arrived first at the ford, and therefore have the right to decide the weapons. I suggest we decide by throwing a spear at that olive tree, growing up the stream, by the grey rock, there. The winner whose throw comes closest to the point where the lowest branch divides.'

'I agree.'

Each man took up a light spear. They threw together. The shafts came close to touching, but each point found the tree unhindered, and Cunomaglos had made the more accurate cast.

'I choose the heavy stabbing spears with those wide blades, and the round shields of oak and leather with the bright bronze rims. And to fight on your side of the river.'

'Agreed.'

Just when you think a combat is going to spring into action, the Celts stop for contemplation and insult. Each man selected five spears and two shields, and Ullanna and Cunomaglos's weapons man, Lexomodos, met in the river and agreed that this set of arms was equally matched. Urtha ate a meal in silence, sitting cross-legged by the open hearth, staring at his foster brother. Cunomaglos glared back at him.

At dawn they were still sitting by the dead fires, staring at each other. Whether they had slept or not is hard to say, but they rose as one, seemingly fresh, stripped naked and went to the river to wash at the crouch.

'Today I will kill you, for Aylamunda and my son, Urien. They died because you abandoned the fort.'

'I expect you will give a good account of yourself for half the morning,' Cunomaglos replied. 'You'll tire after that. I'll be certain to tell you when the killing blow is coming.'

'I promise you that the echo of those words is the last thing you'll hear.'

Urtha pulled his battle kirtle around his waist, made of light material with a purple hem. He tied a leather kilt over this, with a hand-sized circle of metal to protect his groin. He chose sandals for his feet, tied a thin stone across his heart, then cut the ends of his moustache, giving them to Ullanna. He tied his hair into a top-knot, then quickly went away from the view of his enemy, crouched and let go of his bowels.

Thus refreshed he came back and tried each of the heavy spears, for weight and balance. The huge round shields seemed an encumbrance, to my uneducated self, but he tossed each of them into the air to demonstrate how easy they were to use, then went down to wait for Cunomaglos.

Cunomaglos was carried across the river—it would have disadvantaged him to have wet sandals. He was similarly attired, though his kilt was black and he had a strip of metal hanging loosely down the middle of his chest, tied by flax around his shoulders. He had not bothered with the groin-stone.

They put down their weapons and embraced, each kissing the other three times before pulling away and picking up their weapons again.

Cathabach whispered to me, 'The Three Unavoidable Embraces: for a past shared; for kind words shared; for a future when they will ride the same valleys in Ghostland.'

'And when do they get around to fighting?'

'Now, I think . . .'

When they charged each other I felt sure they must both fall at once. I have seen feral creatures attack each other, or pounce upon prey, but I have rarely seen such animal distortion on the face of men who were at one moment handsome, at the next like creatures from the Greekland world of Hel itself. Red-flushed, foam-mouthed, their voices like high-pitched, one-note horns, they smashed and stabbed and jumped and kicked at each other, whirling, twisting, darting and rolling away from the ferocious blows that were directed to every inch of their bodies.

Urtha's spear shattered and Cunomaglos backed off, chest heaving, as Ullanna brought him another, and they went to the fight again; and when Cunomaglos's spear broke behind the head, Lexomodos tossed him another. Spear by spear they cracked and splintered their way through the morning, and when Urtha's fifth spear shattered they flung shield and weapons aside and went to the river, side by side, plunging into the water and letting the blood flow away from them.

They rested until the middle of the afternoon, each on his own side of the river.

Then they faced each other again, patched and stitched by their helpers.

Urtha called out, 'I choose the heavy-bladed swords with the ivory hilts, which I see you have, stolen, I believe, from the Trocmii.'

'Donated!' Cunomaglos said with an expression of mock outrage.

'And the small, light shields of ash and leather. We need to get closer to each other to do some damage!'

'I agree. You danced so far from me, I began to wonder if I would ever see your face.'

'You'll see my face this time, and I promise you a kiss on the lips as your spirit departs.'

'The thought of a kiss like that from lips like yours is the first moment I've felt afraid!'

Both men laughed, then gathered the appropriate weapons, and Urtha was carried across the river.

This was a bloodier contest. By the end of it, my ears were ringing. Iron on iron, when struck with such force, creates a sound that lingers in the air, building in volume until the very rocks seem to shriek and shudder with the echo. The shields were splintered and discarded. Urtha took a deep wound to his side, but severed one of the small toes from Cunomaglos's left foot. They had broken three blades each when they decided to stop and mend their cuts.

It was still a long time until dusk.

'He's fighting strongly,' Manandoun said, as Ullanna applied moss to one of Urtha's more superficial wounds.

'Men who know they're in the wrong always fight strongly,' was Urtha's grim comment.

Ullanna said, 'You're fighting strongly too. I didn't know you had such turns of speed in you.'

'Men who know they're in the right always fight strongly,' Urtha agreed.

It was the end of the conversation.

Urtha drank a hot concoction of herbs, and ate a small amount of honey. Across the river, Cunomaglos was testing his foot, making sure he could run and leap with the bandaging about his severed toe. He was clearly in discomfort.

He came to the water's edge and called for Urtha. 'If you will agree to no leaping or other foot-attacking, I'll agree no striking at the flank, where I see you've been deeply cut.'

'I accept those terms,' Urtha shouted back. 'And now it is your choice of weapons.'

'No weapons but what the river can give us. We fight in the river. No quarter. We fight to the death. An end to this, Urtha. That is what I propose.'

'I will meet you there shortly,' Urtha called back. 'I accept those terms.'

He came back to us and put his hands on my shoulders. He said nothing, but turned to Ullanna and gently held her face. 'You've stuffed enough moss into my body to stop my heart. If I die, send reindeers to graze on me. Thank you.'

'Your heart will hold,' she said. 'Pick sharp stones if you can find them; avoid large stones. They're too heavy to deliver the best blow.'

Now Urtha discarded the stone tied across his heart and hung the gold half-moon around his neck.

He embraced Manandoun and Cathabach, then went down to the water. The light was going fast. Cunomaglos met him in the middle of the stream and the struggle began for the third time.

*   *   *

Watching them strike at each other with stones, then struggle, arms entwined, then fall and flounder, surface and spew water at each other, watching this desperate test of strength was like watching such feats of power from the beginning of Time itself. I have never enjoyed witnessing death. I have certainly seen enough bloody outcomes to satisfy any lingering lust for death I might have savoured.

They might have been wearing the skins of mammoths, or the sharp cuirasses of the Achaeans, who had fought so vigorously on the shores of Ilium. They might have been wild cats squabbling, or kings testing each other to win the favour of a fleet of great ships that spread out across a bay not unlike the bays close to this testing ground, where the chariot racing, and the foot racing, and the ball games, were quiet now.

It made no difference to me. I had seen too much of it before. I felt sickened by it now. And except for the fact that I had a soft spot for Urtha, I might have turned away for ever.

As it was, I turned into myself, curled up, let the grunting drift across me.

Elkavar would have sung that they'd pounded enough rock to fill a cove on the coast, as they struck at each other. Ullanna would have said they should have slept through the night; nothing would come of such blunt brutality.

I could smell the stuff of skulls. Both men had battered each other horribly. Neither would survive.

Ullanna's wailing cry 'Not fair!' roused me. It was twilight. I jumped to my feet to see Urtha staggering before the strike of a spear.

The river was full of spears!

'Anything the river offers!' Cunomaglos crowed, as he waded after the retreating king.

I realised at once that somewhere, inland, there must have been a skirmish; weapons and bodies came flowing through the stream. Ullanna had dropped to a mourning crouch, her head down.

'Anything the river offers!' the cold and bloody man screeched again, and stabbed again at Urtha, striking the *lu-*

nula, piercing the soft gold, driving him down below the water.

I saw my friend's hand struggle to the surface and grip on a piece of wood, a broken shaft, pointless, ragged, jagged.

He came up from the river like a man renewed and impaled his aggressor on the shattered wood. Blood pulsed from both men's chests. Cunomaglos seemed to fade.

Then Maglerd barked, ran to the river, leapt into the stream and dragged the man who had once been his handler down to the river's bed, down below the flow. The great hound savaged and roared, nose coming up for air, blood on its maw, eyes keen: then down again, to finish what Urtha had started.

Dog and Lord of Dogs slipped towards the sea, a dark struggle passing below the small fire where Luturios kept his careful watch.

Urtha crawled to the bank. Ullanna and Elkavar raced to help him, pulling his beaten body into shelter, wrapping a heavy cloak around his shuddering limbs. Ullanna pulled a narrow-bladed knife from her boot and thrust it through the open flesh of his chest wound, then slapped a great handful of herb-infused moss on to the gash.

'Still food for reindeers,' Urtha whispered, with a smile.

Ullanna, tears streaming from her eyes, leaned down and kissed him on the mouth.

'They won't dare try,' she told him gently.

Urtha reached out and gripped her arm, struggling to rise. 'About the other matter . . . I must be sure . . .'

'That he's dead? Cunomaglos? Dead and devoured. Your blood rage was enough. And now your hounds are enjoying a good meal. Even Luturios let them go after him. He said, "In my judgement, that is not quite fair. But fair enough." Urtha, Cunomaglos is gone. Now the others of your *uthiin* are waiting for you.'

'I thought they might be,' Urtha said wearily. He was clutching the *lunula* in his arms, running fingers around the gaping split in the gold. 'Tell Luturios that I'll discuss combat terms at dawn tomorrow.' He was paler by the moment. He smiled at me. 'Merlin will discuss them on my behalf. Nothing too heavy, Merlin. Nothing too sharp,' he said, trying to joke.

Ullanna took his face in her hands and shook him gently. 'They are waiting for you to say it's *ended*. They want to go home. They are in disgrace.'

For a moment Urtha couldn't speak. His breathing was shallow. He didn't have long. He was keeping me at a distance, I noticed. This was the way he wanted it. He had fought honourably; he would die peacefully, and in mortal arms, not with some enchanter trying to stem a bleeding in his body that only an enchanter's eyes could see.

I couldn't have helped him, anyway. A man's death is not my business.

Goodbye, Urtha.

'They must *not* go back to their own land,' he whispered angrily. 'Not to my fortress. Anywhere else that will have them. But not there.'

'Luturios will tell them,' Ullanna said.

'As for me,' said the wraith-like man, 'I do want to go home.'

And Ullanna said, 'You'll go there now. I'll take you. Let anybody try to stop me!'

We lit two fires by the river, and Bolgios donated one of his fine-sided chariots and six excellent horses, plus provisions, for Ullanna's long and lonely journey. The warlord was exuberant from the recent battle, away in the hills, where a second army had been defeated. None of us had the heart to tell him that the spoils of that skirmish had floated down the river, and interrupted, fatally, the meeting of the two foster brothers.

Manandoun and Cathabach looked grey-faced and troubled. They wanted to accompany Urtha home as well, but were aware they had made Jason a promise to stay with him until his own business was finished.

I assured them that Jason would have understood. They fetched their provisions, and each took one of Urtha's hounds.

Ullanna came over to me and gave me an arrow she had

made, a small thing, with its flights fashioned from a feathered necklace she had made during her weeks of 'provisioning' Argo with her skills, but had never worn.

'I know you have several things on your mind at the moment; but I expect you'll find the moment to remember an old friend.'

Her look was ambiguous and intriguing; but all I could see were the tears in her eyes.

I might have left it at that, clutching the arrow and already missing the young Cornovidian king who had become important to me briefly, and was not lost. But nothing is ever as simple as letting go. Time shiplashed me once again, reminding me from her hollow groves and gaping caves, and from her ten, watching faces, that my life was not my own.

The cold, nervous touch on my shoulder startled me. Niiv was behind me, pale in the night and apprehensive. 'Don't run from me,' she whispered urgently; and then again, almost angrily, 'Don't run from me. I know I was wrong before. I didn't mean any harm by it. I'm confused about what I can and cannot do. Don't punish me for my ignorance. Please! But you *must* do something for him.'

'For Urtha?'

She was still dressed in trousers and padded leather jacket. Where once frost had crystallised around her eyes and mouth, now I thought it might have been tears that were frozen there. But her young face had hard lines about it, and though her hair was still thick and full, it had that wispiness that always tells of ageing. And that was not a sign I wished to see.

'Why must I do something for him?'

'You know why!' she shouted, almost in pain. 'You must know why! It won't cost you much!'

Stunned by this outburst, aware that only Elkavar had seen it (and he discreetly turned his head away), I led Niiv to the river. The water flowed clear and bright in the stars; no more dead were floating down; several broken shafts of weapons had clogged the far bank, and weed stretched away from them, like mourning rags.

It would be the work of moments to push her down and hold her there, and let her slip in Death Sleep down to the sea.

'I ask again. Why must I do something?'

She hugged her own body, saying nothing. Guilty! My heart froze. I could hardly bring myself to utter the quiet words: 'You've looked ahead . . . You've looked ahead . . .'

'Just a little,' she confessed, and seemed to shrink even more. Then she turned to me, pleading, 'Only a little! And I didn't use you. I didn't look for you and me, only for Urtha. It's all shadows.'

'Of course it's all shadows!' I remember hissing at her. 'What did you expect?' I turned from her, my chest thundering.

What had she done? Had she taken from me again? She said not. Was it possible that she had such power herself? No! It was not possible. She couldn't be inside me still. But if not using me . . . then whom?

I heard Niiv say, 'I can see that I hurt you before. This time, I promise . . . it's only because you need to look after Urtha. Don't abandon me . . .'

I ran from her.

No screaming, this time, but she watched me from the dark, by the water's edge, a small, hunched figure, lost in the blossoming of a power that was overwhelming her without her knowledge.

I ran after the chariot, a child chasing his father, a dog scampering after his master on horseback.

Wait for me. Wait for me.

The hounds and the *uthiin* were foraging ahead. Ullanna, riding one of the horses pulling the forlorn carriage, was unaware of me until I clambered in and crouched beside the dying man, holding his hands in mine. The carriage came to a halt. Urtha was deathly cold. He watched me through half-lidded eyes, then frowned.

'Merlin? What are you doing? You look a little tired.'

'It's been a tiring day. Not all of us can afford the time to rollick around in rivers.' He smiled. 'But you look a little better,' I told him truthfully. 'And I'm certainly surprised by that. I believe you're in good hands. And I don't mean mine.'

'I believe I am,' he agreed. There was fire in his eyes, though he was paler than the shroud. 'It's an odd thing: earlier, after the river, I felt like death. But I didn't feel like dying. This will be one of the Three Recuperating Journeys that all men must take in their lives. So you can go back to Jason, knowing that I'll be telling lies about you to my friends before next summer.'

There was nothing I needed to do. I felt elated. His steady gaze followed me as I climbed down from the chariot and stood in the darkness, watching its slow departure to the north, through hostile territory.

He called out, 'And I expect I'll see you in Ghostland. One of these years.'

'Sooner than you might think!' I shouted back. 'And I'll expect deer-flesh and partridge when I come. Don't forget.'

'I won't. But when you come . . .' he added with a choking little laugh, 'do come alone!'

The last thing I saw was his pale hand, raised towards me.

CHAPTER TWENTY-FIVE

—

The Hot Gates

I have rarely in my life felt as melancholy as in those few hours after Urtha's departure on his long journey home. Elkavar kept me silent company, and Gwyrion and Conan joined us by the fire, close to the river. Niiv, devious Niiv, sat on the high rocks, a huddled shape against the crescent moon, as still as an owl. If she was watching me, I didn't want to know, although I was again intrigued by her. Her urgent words, at Urtha's departure, were a nagging reminder of the growing talents of the woman.

For the last two days I had been preoccupied with Urtha. Jason had disappeared south, in pursuit of what I was certain was a piece of Medea's trickery: the image of his son on horseback, beckoning to him. But Orgetorix, too, had slipped away, towards Thermopylae, scouting the land for Brennos.

There was a degree of disarray in the army. Achichoros had had his own 'vision', and decided to ride north, along the coast, and cross into the eastern lands, in the footsteps of Alessandros, where he believed there were easier spoils than at Delphi. He had taken several thousand men and their families, to Bolgios's fury. Brennos had been philosophical about the action. He was aware that he still had forces enough to press through the narrow pass and further down into Aetolia.

Gebrinagoth and Gutthas had gone with Achichoros, however; and Rubobostes was also becoming restless, I was told. The sweep of Achichoros's break-away army would take it close to his own land, and he was unhappy with this development, imagining that they would not hesitate to forage and pillage the country of his birth.

He sought me out, looking uncomfortable and depressed, and hot in his black, bearskin cloak, though he refused to remove it. We shared some wine. He told me he would have to take Ruvio, but would ensure strong horses to carry Argo's heart in wood.

'Although I'd agreed to sail with Jason only as far as my own land,' he said, 'I would have stayed longer. I would like to see him happy. But these armies are more interested in pillage than in the sacred dead . . .' he glanced at me carefully, 'as I imagine you already know . . .'

I told him that I did, and he went on, 'And my land has been burned once too often in the last few generations. I will have to persuade Achichorus to keep looking east, and not to the north and east.'

'You'll need a lot of Gordion knots to hold them back.'

Rubobostes grinned. 'I can fashion them faster than a man can empty a flagon of wine.' He passed me the flagon. I tipped it to my mouth and drank deeply. I couldn't finish it all, but when I dropped my head and wiped my mouth he was holding a small, exquisite knot towards me, made from a leather lace.

'To remember me by, although something tells me that my small path and your large one will cross again.'

'I hope so.'

He rose to his feet, bid me farewell and walked back towards the ranks of men massing behind the standard of Achichorus.

The argonauts were dispersing faster than summer rain. But

Tairon and Elkavar remained intrigued by what the oracle at
Delphi might reveal, though neither had any intention of con-
tributing to the looting of the place. These two men, hardly
able to exchange a word, were so alike in their strange talents
with ways-under and labyrinths that they might almost have
been siblings. Their minds worked in the same way. Looks,
gestures, glances and the odd shared phrase were more than
enough to have them laugh at some shared cryptic joke.

The Cymbrii were fired by thoughts of their ancestors.
Talking to one of Brennos's captains, they had heard the
whole saga of the invasion of their tribal lands, and the looting of their dead. Whatever Brennos's true motives for this
assault on Greek Land, he had inspired outrage and ancestor-
revenge in a great proportion of his army. Gwyrion remembered stories from his childhood that echoed and reflected
everything that Brennos had claimed, that day by the Daan.
In truth, these men's lands *had* been pillaged, and the memory
of that event—three hundred years in their past—was still a
source of anger and pain in their family homes; it might be
no more than story, now, but it was story that struck at the
heart itself. They were very keen to strike at Greeklanders.

At some time, during one of the nights that followed, Elkavar
murmured, 'Do you think you might have misjudged her?'

'Who?'

'Who? Frost Lady's favourite! Who else? Anu's kiss, Merlin, the child is raw; and infatuated with you. In case you
hadn't noticed. That's a child's sulk, there on her face, not
an adult's connivance. May the Good God whisper some
sense to you. You're a hard man, a cold man, an empty man.
You're as dead as that corpse you summoned underground,
the one that took us to Arkamon. You don't deserve the
warmth of your own blood. No wonder flies never bite you.
If your heart had feet, it would be halfway back to the Daan
by now, running, glad to have given you good riddance.'

'Do you mean to give offence?'

'On this occasion, yes. I do.'

'Then consider offence taken. Now go to sleep.'

Elkavar was angry, though. I could tell from his breathing in the starlit night.

'You are no more capable of taking offence,' he muttered after a while, 'than you are capable of feeling loss. Such simple touches of the human hand have been worn away by wind and rain. You truly *are* a dead man, walking this world with the mask of a smile and the mask of pain and the mask of laughter. I don't like sleeping close to dead men. They have a smell about them. So why I choose to stay close to you I cannot answer. Maybe for the glimpse of a single drop of water from your eye. We call them tears, where I come from. To you, they're probably an ingredient for some potion or other . . .'

He went on in this vein for some time, then fell quiet. But a while later added, 'Will you think about what I just said? About the girl?'

'I've been thinking about it for days,' I told him.

'I wonder if that's true,' Elkavar said sourly, pulling his simple cloak about his shoulders as he embraced sleep. 'If it is, then I'm glad for you. A little touch of human . . . at last . . .'

Sleep? Impossible. I rode in the dead of night to the sea, to stand by the starlit ocean, letting the restless surge of the waves sweep around my feet. A warm, still sea, glowing from within.

At dawn, a bird came flying from the ocean, its wingbeat slow and steady, its direction purposeful. I soon recognised the creature as a swan. It came out of the glow of the rising sun, silent and sinister, flying so close to me that its wing-tip struck my head, knocking me down. It veered in flight, recovered, and rose over the low cliffs, heading inland. The bird seemed ill.

Elkavar rose from behind a rock, tugging his clothing back into place. I had not been aware of him following me.

'Good morning,' he called cheerfully, then glanced in the direction of the swan. 'You know—I think she's trying to tell you something.'

I asked him irritably what he meant and he shrugged.

'She's going home, Merlin. I imagine she wants to say goodbye.'

His words struck me more deeply than I would have expected. The forlorn look on Niiv's face last night seemed less a posture, now. She had craved my understanding and I had blocked her through fear of the wild, juvenile use of her inherited talent.

The Mistress of the North had a lot to answer for, giving such strength to Niiv without controlling the child's use of the charm she now found, playfully, at her fingertips.

I followed the flight of the swan for half a day, and finally found Niiv, settled in a grove of almond trees, by a shallow pool among the ruins of a farm. It was hot and silent. She was singing to herself as she plucked feathers from the swan, which lay across her lap, limp-necked and dead. She had put wing feathers in her fair hair; they stuck out at odd angles. She was wearing the bright skirt she had taken from Pohjola; her small breasts and shoulders were bare and gleaming with perspiration.

Around her: the shells of almonds and the downy feathers of her swan. 'He flew a long way from the north for me,' she said as I dismounted. She stroked the dead bird's neck. 'He flew so hard. He flew so far. I know, I know. You don't have to tell me. I shouldn't use my charm before I know its limitations.'

She had summoned the swan with the intention of riding it home. Poor swan. Poor Niiv. The bird had been flying for days. She must have wanted to go home so badly.

Now that I looked at her I could see the damage she had done to herself. Her eyes were bruised with fatigue, lines beginning to stripe the skin. Her mouth was pinched. Her neck was narrow and lined. There was a touch of water in her gaze, not tears, not the swell of sadness, but the moisture of effort and age. Her hands shook slightly as she pulled the white feathers from the bloody skin of the valiant bird.

Her appearance disturbed me. I went to the pool, stooped to drink water, and stared down at the pale reflection of a man who was similarly ageing. My own appearance shocked me. For the first time I saw the change happening, and yet . . . and yet I was more concerned for the girl.

I went back to her, pulled the feathers from her hair, took the corpse of the swan and threw it away. She slapped me hard but made no move to reclaim the dead creature.

'Niiv . . . you *must* slow down. You'll be dead in a year if you don't.'

'Dead of what?' she whispered angrily. 'What can kill me? I am protected by the Northland Lady. And Mielikki has her own eyes on my well-being.'

What a fool she was! I could have laughed, agreed, and left her there and then to die in agony, old bones crumbling in young flesh. But I couldn't do it. (Niiv was not the only fool!)

'Mielikki is away from her world,' I insisted, 'and guarding Argo. Argo is a spirit in a ship, and your guardian has her hands full. The Northland's Lady gave you talent in charm, enchantment, but no talent in wisdom. You are killing yourself by using what she gave you so fast. Too fast.'

She spat in my face, looked sorry for what she had done and reached to wipe the mess away from my beard. But then she grabbed the discarded wing feathers of the swan and arranged them in the pattern of a fan, stroking them, a strange act of defiance.

'Leave me alone. You don't care for me. If I've aged it's from helping you. Or trying to. You've discarded me. Leave me alone.'

Once more I almost laughed; then I felt despair. What to say to this silly child?

'You will never work your charm on me,' I said. 'If you can understand that, you can start to be free. I believe you when you say that you meant no harm by flying with me through time. I do believe you.'

'It's true. Why did it take you so long?'

'Because you frighten me.'

'I frighten *you*?' Her laugh was almost sinister, her eyes like ice as they met my own. 'You *terrify* me, Merlin. I gave you a small part of myself. I made a mistake. Now I live in fear of what may be brooding behind that corpse-white face of yours!'

I couldn't tell whether she was innocent, and honest, or playing games. Terrified of me? It made no sense. I'd treated her to no more than anger and rejection for what I'd seen as her trickery.

One at a time, she stitched the swan's feathers back into her hair, an act that was both deliberate and ridiculous, a mime, a distortion of her features that pretended to have some significance.

'You frighten me,' I said again, softly. 'Because I'm frightened *for* you. You yourself. The damage that you're doing. Niiv, when you flew through time, only a little time, those few days into the past to see the gathering by the Daan, you wasted a year of your short life. For me, the effort was far less costly. You're not in the *least* like me, though I don't deny your talents. But you must nurture those talents as you would tend a rose. You can clip a bloom, but you must never harvest the whole flower.'

She stood up and screamed at me. 'Roses? Roses? You talk to me of *roses*? While I talk to you of *Time*? I saw you, Merlin, why don't you accept that I've seen you? I saw the man you will become!'

'And killed yourself in the seeing!'

She ran her hands over her slim body. 'Do I look dead to you?'

'You're dying!'

She was still defiant. 'Then I'll die knowing that you will become so powerful! I've seen that power!'

'Don't tell me!'

I ran at her and put a hand over her mouth, but she struggled away, determined to speak to me of that flight of fantasy, that nightmare flight into the future. One of her hands stayed linked with mine, even though the other fought me. Her eyes were furious. Her mouth a grimace of triumph.

'I don't wish to know,' I repeated desperately, and she

calmed, then mellowed, the fierceness gone from her face to be replaced by confusion.

We sat down together, hands together, and she seemed suddenly aware of her naked breasts, drawing her discarded cloak around her shoulders. 'I know I shouldn't have done it,' she said. She played with a swan's feather in her left hand, though her right hand kept a grip on my own. 'Oh, Merlin, I know I did the wrong thing. But didn't I tell you I knew that? I did try to tell you that I'd been foolhardy. You were so angry. So frightened . . . I hadn't realised how frightened you were. And the last thing I ever wanted to do was frighten you.'

She stuck a feather in my hair, laughing as she put it into place, then rearranged it. Her breath was soft but sour on my mouth. She whispered, 'Feathers suit you. But you know that. In your long life, you've worn more feathers than could cloak a flock of gulls. Haven't you?'

'Yes.'

'And danced to thunder.'

'Yes,' I agreed.

'There will be thunder and feathers in your future, though the forest will be more your cloak in times to come. Don't you want to know what I saw? Is there any harm in telling you? The act is done. The vision is in my mind. I can't put the rose back on its stem, Merlin. I can't put what I know back in Time's cauldron . . .'

'Then you'd better tell me.'

She was delighted, clapping her hands together as at last she shared her vision.

'You are as tightly weaved together with Urtha as the threads in this cloth skirt I'm wearing. Tightly knit! He will die, you live on. But one of the sons of the sons of his son will be the reason for your life, and the death of everything you love. His name is Arthur. Oh, Merlin, you will reach such heights of power! Your land is a forest. You live in its centre. When you move, the forest flows around you like a cloak.'

Did she notice my start of shock as she described that scene? Could she *truly* have seen such a thing? That echo of Sciamath? She babbled on, unaware: 'A great man, a great king, sits within great walls of earth and wood, turrets that touch the clouds, a fortress built on cliffs of shining rock. The king *fears* you. The forest flows around that fortress like an army, and Merlin, older, wiser, whiter, is at its heart.' She sat back, eyes glowing, hands clasped to her chest. She added, 'And a small shadow runs with the Lord of the Forest. That shadow . . . not me, of course!'

She said the last with a laugh, throwing herself upon me, forcing me down, her tongue licking at my lips, trying to force my mouth open. Her breath was stale, her hands urgent and probing, lifting her skirts to bare her thighs, tugging at my britches to open my belly to her rampant embrace.

She pulled back, disappointed, pouting in that playful way of hers. 'I've felt you hard, on that spirit ship from Argo. You did nothing. Now you're soft. You can't do anything.'

'And soft it remains.'

She rolled away from me, sitting up, huddled. 'I told you what I saw. Could that shadow in the forest be me?'

'That shadow in the forest could never be you,' I told her as I stood. 'Not even if you lived across five generations. The oldest you can expect to reach, even great age—withered, toothless, sightless—still would never take you to a time when the forests follow in *my* footsteps!'

'Then I'll stay here. Until I die. I like this place. This is my special grove. I like the nuts. And there are olives over there, and the water is sweet, and I can call bees for honey and small birds for the cooking pot. This is where I will stay. This is my Swan Place. When you need me . . . and you *will* need me . . . this is where you must come to find me.'

She watched me angrily and in silence as I untethered my horse. I gave her a last glance and a half-smile, then cantered down the slope towards the valley that led back to the sea. But Niiv wasn't finished. Not quite yet.

'Did you kill my ancestor? Meerga? Was that true?'

She was standing on an outcrop of rock, the dead swan clutched in her left hand like a toy.

'Yes,' I shouted up to her. 'But by accident. I didn't mean to. Truthfully, it was an accident.'

'What accident?'

Why not tell her? She had half guessed already. She would only help kill herself more by trying to find the truth through enchantment.

'She was full of our child, Niiv. We both knew the child would be dangerous. We had gone out on the lake to deliver it and drown it in Enaaki's water. But your ancestor died in the act of delivery, and for reasons I will never understand, I couldn't kill the new-born. I brought the girl back with me. I left her with your people.'

'So then: we *are* related!' She cast the dead bird away from her.

'Yes. We are. Alas. And you: your half-child. Do you still carry it?'

'Oh yes,' she taunted, though the taunt fell short of its mark. 'But it's very small. And very patient! You *will* have need of me, Merlin. There are exciting times to come.'

Not if I had anything to do with it, I thought as I rode grimly down the valley, only once looking back to see a dark tree on the hill, its branches raised above its head, waving side to side as if in a wild wind.

Goodbye, Niiv. For the moment.

But still she had the last word, her voice drifting to me down the defile as I rode back to Brennos, a voice carrying a message that would haunt me.

'I didn't tell you *everything* I saw, Merlin . . . not everything I saw . . .'

The earth began to shake again. Men on horse and foot, ox-carts and rattling chariots covered the hills, cut noisily through the river, some even following the coast, a double defile of laughing warriors, riding through the dawn swell of the gleaming sea.

In two days, we had reached Thermopylae.

The land had been rising steeply for some time, the valleys narrowing and heavy with tall cedar and pine, a heady swathe of green that deadened sound and made passage difficult. A pristine azure sky was almost blinding to look at. Tumbling streams covered dangerously slippery rocks, and horses struggled and stumbled, slowing the column. Brennos's army was dispersed widely through these hills, and if the Greeklanders were waiting for us here, they would have been able to cut us to shreds.

In fact, this was deserted land. The game had fled before us, or perhaps had never existed. When at last we emerged to face the stark ridge of mountain, we found ourselves at the edge of a narrow plain, shining with the crushed white bones of men. These were the dead of previous attempts to penetrate Thermopylae, dragged here and left to rot, scavenged and dispersed, then crushed by winter rain and the hooves of passing animals.

The mountain range stretched to left and right as far as the eye could see, so sheer in places that it was falling under its own weight. Trees hugged the cliffs in desperation, leaning out towards us. The sky was so bright that to scan its high edges was to lose sight for a moment. Frothy clouds scudded over that stark line, and hawks hovered.

But these mountains were split, a vertical cut so narrow that it might literally have been cut with a knife. It took time to focus on that gorge. The pass twisted out of sight only a short way beyond the mouth; all light seemed to drain from the passage. A mournful wind flowed from it. Of more significance was the spear that rose from the ground to guard it: immensely tall, hewn I expect from a single pine, it carried a wide, green-corrupted bronze blade that if it fell could have covered and crushed a hundred men. The trunk-sized shaft was tied about with thousands of fluttering rags: the kilts and cloaks of the dead.

Brennos's army spread out along the edge of the plain of bones. All attention for the moment was on the spear. But then a man on horseback rode slowly from the narrow pass and came to a stop beside it.

He watched us from the distance. His helmet covered half his face like a half-skull. Dull shining iron, no plume. He was armoured in the Etruscan style, short trousered, iron cuirass over a loose short-sleeved black shirt, shield on his left arm, throwing javelin held low. I could see a trimmed grey beard on the hard face.

I knew who it was at once. Indeed, soon after this steady appraisal of the army ranged against him, Jason removed the helmet and shouted my name across the plain.

Four horsemen rode suddenly and swiftly towards him. He drew back, turning shield-side on, and again called for me. The towering spear cast its shadow over him. A barking command from somewhere along the front line of the army brought the attackers to a halt. They turned and rode back and a while later a chariot clattered down the line, a man shouting, 'Merlin! Merlin! Go to the horseman!'

I edged forward and halted the chariot. 'He's calling for me.'

'Brennos says to go and talk to him. He seems to know you.'

'Tell Brennos that this man is my friend; that he is Urtha's friend; that he poses no danger.'

The Celt in the chariot laughed out loud, no doubt amused by the suggestion that one man could ever pose a danger to such a horde as was opposed to him.

I cantered across the crushed bone and trotted up to Jason, who held my gaze coolly. Behind him, the cleft in the mountain gusted and moaned with an evil wind. This close, I could see that no more than four men abreast could enter it on horse, six on foot, perhaps.

'I've been waiting for you,' Jason said. 'I've been chasing a ghost.'

'I know. Tairon told me.'

'Did he tell you whose ghost it was?'

'Thesokorus.'

'He called to me, Merlin. And as I approached, he turned and rode away, like an angry man. I rode as hard as I could but I could never catch him. I should have realised then, I suppose, that he had been sent to betray me. The question is: where did that ghost come from?'

'Where do you imagine?'

What should I say to him? That Medea was alive and in the world? From the look he was giving me I was sure he suspected that I was keeping a secret from him; and if it had not been for my discovery of Medea's true nature, I would have told him. But the woman's face, that look of recognition, that flash of soft, fond memory. I felt I would be betraying her.

Jason said, 'You saw a ghost in Alba. Could this have been the same ghost?'

'Perhaps. Jason, I am certain that when Medea hid your sons from you she hid them separately, one in Greek Land and the other on Alba. And each was given the spirit of his brother, to keep them comfortable; to keep them happy. When they reached a certain age, the ghosts disappeared.'

His frown deepened. 'That's a strange idea. How can you possibly know this?'

'Because Orgetorix told me the story of his childhood.'

'He told *you*?' Jason was both astonished and outraged. 'When? When did he tell you? You've been with him?'

'He was with this army. While you were chasing shadows, I met him at the oracle at Arkamon.'

'And where is he now?'

'I think he's gone ahead of us.' I nodded to the pass.

'Did he ask about me? Does he know I'm looking for him? Did you tell him?'

'Not yet . . .'

Jason was so canny. A half-smile touched those thin lips. His horse struggled, responding to his tension. 'What are you keeping from me, Merlin? What aren't you telling me?'

Before I could answer, Elkavar rode noisily across the plain, signalling his advance with punctuated wails of his elbow-pipes; Tairon was close behind him. The wall of Brennos's army stretched behind them, nervous, restless, waiting for orders. They were keeping at a distance in case the Greeklanders appeared on the high crags above them.

Elkavar reared up and grinned. 'A message from Bolgios.'

'Saying what?'

'What do you think? I have to tell you that there was some

very strong language in it. In essence, I think he needs to know what, pretty please, is going on, why, with your kind indulgence, are you sitting here talking, and if you have a moment—when it's convenient—could you possibly let him or Brennos know whether the pass is clear, secure or dangerous. I think he's assuming that you've just come through the gates . . .' This to Jason.

'I haven't. That Greeklander did.' Jason nodded to a naked corpse, curled up and bloody behind the towering spear. I hadn't noticed the dead man before now. That was where Jason had got his new armour. 'But there was only one of him. I don't know the answer to the question.'

'We could find out,' Elkavar suggested. He looked up at the imposing rise of dark, gnarl-wooded cliff. 'There's no way over, and no way under that I can smell.' He winked at me, then grinned. 'By Nemue's breasts! A while ago we sailed up a stream narrower than the flow of piss on a cold morning after a night of no drinking. I'd have thought we could ride through a cut in the hills like this with impunity. What do you say, Tairon?'

The Cretan's implacable features didn't change. He glanced up at the craggy skyline, shrugged, and muttered, 'Let's just do it.'

'Where are Gwyrion and Conan?' Jason asked.

'God knows,' Elkavar said. 'Drunk, the last I saw of them. I'll call for them.'

'And Rubobostes and that huge horse, and Urtha and his faithful *uthiin* too,' Jason added.

I explained to him that Rubobostes had turned north again; and the situation with Urtha and Ullanna, and Urtha's combat, had taken the Cornovidians away as well.

It was the first time I had seen Jason sad. He was pleased that Urtha had won his day in the field. 'I should have stayed,' he said quietly. 'I should not have chased ghosts. Urtha's meeting with that bastard was something else; but I should have stayed for the others. We needed to be together. Damn! Damn!'

'We have to go forward,' Tairon said, with a steady gaze at the old Achaean.

'Yes. I know. Get the Cymbrii.'

Tairon and Elkavar rode back to report.

Four of Bolgios's men came with us, ready to ride back to the main army if we encountered trouble. And with Jason at the front, we entered the pass. It was cold between those rocks. We seemed to make the cliff faces echo, every stumble, every murmur ringing loudly. The pass wound to right and left, sometimes widening, sometimes narrowing to scarcely more than two men's widths. Above us, the sky was a thin strip of azure, broken by twisted branches.

'This is a death trap,' Elkavar observed unnecessarily. 'There is certainly movement above us. We are being watched.'

I was sure he was right.

'Take the reins of my horse,' I whispered to him, 'and keep an eye on me.'

He nodded, fully understanding.

I summoned the hawk.

I rose up through the narrow pass, wary for slingshot or arrow. I could see ahead, see how the valley widened, emerging on to a plain, where the Greeklanders waited in massed ranks. The sun was bright on their helmets and shields and horsemen raced along the lines. They knew we were coming. They had created a false forest of pine between themselves and the pass, so that as the first of the Celtic horde emerged they would, for a few moments only, be unaware of what waited for them.

Along the edges of this narrow split in the hills, however, I saw only loose rocks, bushes and wind-stretched trees. A few deer grazed calmly on the wild thyme. Sleeker, faster animals prowled the cover, many of them aware of me as I hovered.

I was surprised, to say the least, that no Greeklander was waiting above us. So what had Elkavar seen?

I took back control of the reins, kicked forward and spoke to Jason.

'We're expected. These men will never make it through; and old Achaean that you are, you're still too strange to these new Greeks. We should turn back and warn Brennos.'

Jason rode on for a few more moments, clearly angry at what he had heard. He wanted to get on. He wanted to catch up with his son. His mind could accommodate no other vision, now that he was so close. And so close to his old home.

But he turned suddenly, nodded curtly, 'You're right,' and Bolgios's four guards galloped back along the pass, as if pursued by Furies, while the rest of us nervously cantered the return.

We had only just emerged back on to the plain before the first crush of men came pressing in. These were Remii, good horsemen, but with a poor reputation for fighting. Nevertheless, they were eager to clear Thermopylae, and they rode grimly past, shields ready to raise above their heads if the cliffs should start to tumble, long stabbing spears erect.

Brennos had sent them to the sacrifice, hard, calculating man that he was.

Hard behind the Remii, he sent the specialist spearmen of the Tectosages, the *gaesatae*, that same vicious cohort of men who had so brutally sacked Arkamon. They didn't like the confined space, and pushed hard, shouting loudly for the Remii to shift their horses.

And in this way, they were hastened to their deaths.

I realised, too late, that Medea had blinded my hawk's eyes, in much the same way as I had taken away the senses of that old man at the watch station. How could I have missed *that*, he had cried. I wonder if he had died still wrestling with the fact that he had felt nothing at all as the earth below his feet had shuddered with the coming army.

And now, I had missed the lines of Greeklanders who occupied the top of the cliffs. The rockfalls that descended upon the crowded army crushed them and broke them, panicked them into riding over each other. The cut in the mountain filled with the dead.

But Brennos pressed on, and men poured into that valley, shields raised high, pushing aside the wounded.

When the rockfall ended, the javelins came down, and the arrows, and the slingshot.

But what a force this army was! Brennos had anticipated problems at Thermopylae. He had given training instructions. As the men from the rear ran forward, they laid shield bridges over the dead. For every man who fell in the pass, five raced on, regrouping where the valley widened, forming quickly into phalanxes of warriors, all clan association forgotten now, just the task ahead on their minds. Weapons were distributed, shared and exchanged; the best with swords took swords from those who were best with spears.

I followed later, but Brennos and Bolgios went through Thermopylae at separate times, to ensure that there was a greater chance of one of them surviving.

They both got through, though Bolgios had lost a finger to a javelin, thrown from high above, that had cut through his hand into the saddle.

As we waited gloomily on the plain of bones, Elkavar cast me a look of despair and irritation. 'I told you there were men up there . . .'

'I was deceived.'

Jason overheard this exchange. 'Who deceived you? Who could possibly deceive a man who can raise a dead ship from the bottom of a lake? A man who doesn't age? Who doesn't die? Sometimes you make no sense. Are you playing games with us, Merlin?'

'No. I was deceived.'

The argonauts had gathered round me in a semicircle, pain on their faces, or perhaps confusion. Jason said, 'Remind me what my son said to Brennos. About betrayal. What was it again? You were listening.'

I made no response to that. Jason was pushing the blade home. He knew. I was sure he knew. He was waiting for me to agree that I would not betray him in the night, only in the full light of day, his son's words to the warlord.

Again, before I could make any answer at all, Jason said,

'She sent my sons through time. Seven hundred years through time, if you're to be believed. And now you tell me she sent them with a ghost for a brother. And I see ghosts on the horizon, and chase them. And you speak to my son behind my back!' He kicked his horse towards me, came up close.

'Tell me the truth, Merlin. She's alive, isn't she? She followed them through time herself. She came with them. It's the bitch who is causing all this difficulty for us. Tell me the truth . . . please . . .'

I noticed Elkavar watching me carefully. He had known, of course; but he had said nothing.

'Yes,' I said to Jason. 'Yes. She is alive. She tried to bar your way into Alba, where Kinos is hidden. Those gigantic statues, the fear we felt, perhaps even the wasteland, though I can't be sure about that. She poisoned your thinking on the Rein, souring your words, hoping to turn Argo against you.'

'She was on Argo?' Jason roared.

'Hidden. She's clever. Not even Mielikki knew she was there.'

'The gods know everything.'

'Alas. No. Or, perhaps, fortunately no. She sent spectres of her sons to keep the living sons happy. She sent a spectre to tease you and trick you. She blinded my eyes to the Greeks on those high cliffs. God knows, Jason, she may have blinded me on other occasions. I wasn't expecting her; so I wasn't watching for her.'

'She came through time with them,' he echoed. He was asking, not stating. He scented that this was not the case.

I said nothing. Nothing was all I needed to say. Jason was one of those few men in my long life who seem to have me opened like a carcass on the table, every curl of innards exposed and glistening to their gaze.

'You're a liar!' he breathed. 'By the Sacred Bull, you've been lying to me. I don't know how, or in what way. But you've betrayed me! Something is up.' And almost in pain, he repeated, 'Something is up. Leave me alone, Antiokus. Our time is finished!'

He turned from us and rode into the ranks of men still

squeezing into the narrow valley, preparing themselves for the assault at the far end. Gwyrion challenged me: 'Are we going to let him go alone? Didn't we come here for this?'

Tairon shouted, 'Whatever is between you and Jason, I strongly suggest you put it behind you for the moment. We have to get through this pass, and besides, didn't we agree to help Jason in return for passage on Argo?'

'Come on, Merlin,' Elkavar called to me, carefully. 'These may be called the Hot Gates. But their heat is nothing, I think, to what you'll be finding on the other side!'

What I had failed to see from 'on high', looking into the distance at that rank of Greeklanders, was how poor an army they were. They glittered with iron, and screamed their taunts with vigour; but they were fewer than they seemed, they were not the best; Greek Land had not recovered from earlier wars. It was a land where gates were closed against the enemy rather than opened to allow their forces to pour out and attack. They squabbled; they argued; they disagreed.

By Jason's Sacred Bull, they sounded almost like the *keltoi*!

Brennos lost more men than even a Greeklander could count that day. I have heard that their corpses were left in the pass for a hundred years, so compacted with time and the weight of the dead that men rode over them thinking they were on the path itself. And eventually the sea herself, Ocean, pitying, compassionate Ocean, rose and cut away the hills, and dragged those stones and the bones into her dark waters.

But on that day, when Jason rode away from me, the Greeklanders fought until night, and then broke ranks and dispersed, leaving their slaughtered to be butchered and displayed, horrifyingly abused by the triumphant horde, used to invoke certain gods of an underworld that I have always feared, and always avoided.

A beauty that does not age or fade
is lost in time
not part of this world
and always untouchable.

from *A Flower* by R. Andew Heidel

CHAPTER TWENTY-SIX

—

Sanctuary

If Brennos had expected further resistance from the Greeklanders, he was to be surprised. The army fell back before us, assimilated by the hills and valleys like cloud shadow.

For the next few days we had easy passage south and then towards the setting sun, following a route drawn from the vaguest of memories from the oldest among our host: myself. We found deserted villages and barren fields, but animals are harder to destroy than crops, and trees heavy with fruit, nuts and olives were in abundance. Brennos's horde had shrunk considerably by the time we came within sight of Mount Parnassus. This land was so open, so fragrant, so easy, that clan after clan had split away, with apologies and due ceremony, and gone to find pastures of their own.

Achichoros had already departed for the east. Now Bolgios took a census of the clans loyal to him and broke away, to ride to other sanctuaries and the western shore. The fierce man's decision shocked Brennos, but again he was diplo-

matic. The long march was halted and a feast prepared for all
the commanders, and each clan's champion. The ceremony
lasted until dawn, and it was decided, in serious discussion
during the revelry, that the two armies would link up again
in the land of the Illyria, at the northernmost point of the
western sea, where the mountain passes led directly back to
the Daan.

To show each other that they would abide by their word,
each war chief sacrificed a favourite horse. The entrails were
burned and the mane and its strip of hide cut from each,
scraped of flesh and presented to the other as a belt. This
bond in horse-hair was a powerful one. The carcasses of the
horses were quartered and salted, the food for kings for the
next few days.

The dust from Bolgios's train clouded the sky until twilight, long after the earth had ceased to shake. We settled
down for the night, but Brennos sent riders to rouse us all
before dawn and we ate and drank on the hoof. Each day was
the same, until the gleaming slopes of Mount Parnassus lit up
the horizon, a beacon, beckoning to the invader.

The last time I had seen Parnassus was during the year of
its first inauguration as a sanctuary. Being in Greek Land,
where numbers mattered, I entertained myself by working out
precisely how many years ago that had been. Eighteen hundred! Eighteen hundred years in the past of my life. The valleys had echoed and shuddered to the wailing of bronze
trumpets and the thunder of skin drums. The slopes of the
mountain had crawled with screaming women; the air had
been heavy with the blood of butchered goats and rams. I
remembered how the river that flowed between the hills had
been tinged with pink, and had smelled of death.

It was silent, now, save for the rumble of horses and chariots turning slowly towards the deep pass that guarded the
oracle of Apollo. We had crossed the wide plain known as
Crisa without difficulty. Old traps and defences, scattered
over the foothills, had proved no problem either. I rode ahead
of the main column, with Elkavar and Tairon, and felt the
first cool flow of breeze from the snow-capped mountain of

Parnassus itself. It had seemed small in the distance, but its steep slopes now towered above us, and the air echoed with each movement of our horses.

We rode carefully, skirting the great mountain's flanks, and came into the gorge that led to Delphi itself. Sheer walls of shining rock almost blinded us. The land ahead might have been cut in two by a sword. Gloom and shadow were all that could be seen against the sparkling brilliance of the cliffs. The river curled through stands of ancient olive trees, themselves shimmering silver as if with frost.

At dawn, part of the hills glowed rose-red, and it was there that Apollo had carved out the caves that would become his sanctuary. I knew where to look, which winding path to follow between the marbled shrines and sacred groves, and soon, as we rode ahead of the main army, we could see another strip of gleaming metal. This was not the ancient rock of the cloven gorge, however, but the last defenders of the oracle, two hundred Greekland veterans prepared to die for their god.

A report came back that they were all wearing the bull-hide belt. They would fight to the death, then; no retreat was possible for them in this world. They had taken an oath to that effect.

A storm cloud suddenly swept across the edge of the cliffs, darkening the gorge. The hoplites clattered swords on shields, a sound that rose in volume as it echoed through the valley. They seemed to slip like trickles of water in all directions, taking up defensive positions.

They would not hold against the ponderous horde of men which even now was riding slowly into sight of its goal.

Brennos fell upon the oracle at Delphi in a fury of iron, with a thousand elite horsemen and *gaesatae*, and forty wagons to carry back the 'dead in gold and silver' who were imprisoned in the mountain.

The steep valley was fragrant with burning censers. Every path, every statue, every deep entry into the hill, every tree had its own smoking tripod, an invocation to Apollo to protect the sanctuary.

Brennos had them smashed; he hacked branches from the trees and made them into burnt offerings; he pulled down marble figures which had stood in their niches for a thousand years, watching the valley and the mountain crags. He instructed his men to shout abuse at the snakes they couldn't see but which he assured them were worming just below the surface of the earth.

He had bragged that he would cut the head from the Pythia, as she was called, the terrifying old woman who sat, veiled, in front of the sulphurous clefts in the rock and pronounced the oracles from Apollo. To hear him talk was to summon an image of the mistress of the oracle as some form of gorgon, endlessly spitting snakes from her twisted mouth. In fact, the Pythia—more likely a young woman, and vulnerable, easily influenced by Delphi's corrupt priesthood—had fled long before the army had raised its dust in the north. Disappointed, but undaunted, Brennos cut the head from a youthful hoplite, shaved its cheeks with his knife and plaited its hair, then daubed ochre on lips and eyes. He presented the trophy to his commanders, later declaring how her 'age' had been shed like the skin of the snake she was; then he oiled and bagged the gruesome cut before the stubble could grow through the skin and give away his trick.

Now Brennos found the truth to the story that the Persians had looted the sanctuary before him. Almost all of what he had come in search of had long since gone east. It might still be found in the temples and palaces there. More likely, Alessandros of Makedonia, who had destroyed the Persians soon after their invasion of Greek Land, would have melted down the treasure for spoil and payment of his army. All of this, a generation ago; Brennos's dream of bringing back the Sacred Dead—if truthful dream it was—now corrupted into the cash and coin of the living.

He sent riders to Achichoros with this news; Achichoros would almost have reached the Hellespont by now, the narrow gulf between the two lands at the southern extreme of the Black Ocean. The ruins of Persia lay beyond. His crusade would be broader than he was expecting.

Bolgios was not at Delphi either. He had taken several thousand men and turned north and west, to the oak sanctuary at Dodona, looting the land on the way.

The Greeklanders were in disarray. Their small armies fell back across the straits to Achaea, Jason's land of old, to wait for the shaking of the earth to cease.

Apollo did not protect his oracle that day, though the Greeklanders would claim otherwise long after Brennos was food for ravens. But only two carts were filled with what, clearly, had once been looted from the lands of the *keltoi*. Four other carts were filled with further spoil, but in truth, it was a mean treasure with which to reward so vast an army.

Brennos knew it, and sent word to Bolgios to 'take everything and anything', silks, sapphires, polished stones, bronze, even ceramics.

'Everything that glitters!'

There would be a great many hungry eyes scouring the treasure carts for their share.

I watched the pillage of Delphi from across the valley, in the airy ruins of a small building that had once served as the quarters for the soldiers who guarded the priests and the Pythia. Elkavar played softly on his pipes, trying to compose 'a haunting song that will illuminate the heroic and tragic nature of this place'. And failing.

Conan returned quite quickly with the news that there was little to pillage. And Tairon, it seemed, had entered the caves of the oracle itself, more out of intrigue than greed, and when he later found us on the hill, he was puzzled.

The air was warm. The shouting from across the valley was shrill but distant. It was almost peaceful.

Tairon tethered his horse and crouched down beside me, rubbing his arms as if he was cold. 'There is a labyrinth of great complexity inside the mountain,' he said. 'Chamber after chamber, passages spiralling inwards, but leading outwards. It's a wonderful place! I feel completely at home. It connects with other oracles, I'm sure of it. I hear different winds blowing, and the creaking of oaks, and the smell of pine resin. And it connects to a place in my own land. I know the fragrance of my own land. There are traps and blind alleys. And a great deal of poor quality gold and fine obsidian, beautiful carvings, all stored in deep niches. Those bastards will haul it off, I expect, but they will never find it all.'

Elkavar asked if he had seen any sign of Jason, and the Cretan nodded, taking off his green-plumed helmet and pointing along the path close to which we crouched, to where it ran deeper into the valley.

'I think I saw him. He's wearing *keltoi* armour again. He was fighting two Greeklanders.'

Two dying hoplites, crawling into shelter, suggested where Jason might have gone. We ran quickly to a row of white columns which marked an entry into the mountain and found the man. He was standing, sword in hand, gaze fixed on the faraway, across the valley. He was wistful, perhaps sad. He was indeed wearing the colourful clothes of one of Brennos's army who had failed in the quest. A third Greeklander lay curled at his feet, shaking slightly as the spirit was drawn away from him. Jason himself was bleeding from a cut to the arm, and Elkavar used a short length of leather to bind the wound. I kept at a discreet distance.

'I don't know what my son looks like,' he whispered absently, then glanced at Elkavar, narrow-eyed and fierce. 'Does he look like me, I wonder? But then, what do I look like? I have no idea of my face. I leave that pleasure for those who can't avoid it. You must help me search for him, Elkavar. He's somewhere on that hill. I feel it strongly.' He laughed, though without humour. 'I'm anxious. Can you imagine that? After all this time: to be so close to my son . . . and I'm anxious. What if he doesn't recognise me? What if he's inherited his mother's anger? You must stay close. You were there when that betraying sorcerer talked to him. You'll recognise him. He'll talk to you. And you can perform the reintroduction. It may take him some time to believe who I am.'

'Merlin is here,' Elkavar said softly.

Jason cursed, glanced at me furiously, the sword pointing to my head. 'I will never understand! What games are you playing? Stay away from me. Nowhere near me! I no longer know who you are.'

The valley had become quiet, the long morning of fury finished. The sound of horses galloping back to the main army was still a rumble in the ground. Light caught the armour of the invaders as they ran back, carrying whatever they had found. The white tunics and bright horse-hair plumes of the dead Greeklanders scattered the hills. Cries of greeting, hailing and newly discovered trophy echoed briefly, the answering calls like distant music.

Delphi was almost silent.

And it was against this sudden stillness that I saw Orgetorix.

He was with another man, also dressed in the patchwork leather armour of the Hyperborean Celts. The two men slipped from the deep cover of rocks, across the valley, and ran lightly up the winding road to the complex of marbled buildings that contained and masked the oracle itself.

'There!' I shouted. 'Orgetorix. And one other.'

For a moment, Jason stood as still as one of the shattered statues, staring across the distance at the remote figures, drawing in every detail as if this might be his only glimpse of the young man who had crossed Time and yet was again almost in his grasp. Then he barked an order to Elkavar and Tairon and ran down the rugged and thorny hillside. If he was aware that I followed, he made no comment at that moment. He was blocking me from his mind.

'I knew he'd be here!' Jason shouted as we waded across the river, and with Tairon leading—he was the swiftest of us—ascended the cobbled road to the gates and courtyards that in turn opened to the barren cleft in the mountain's face. Here, the stench of sulphurous gas was strong; it gusted from the slit of the cave like a gorgon's breath. Indeed, perhaps remembering Perseus's account of Medusa, Jason picked up a discarded, round shield, kissed it and raised it to cover the lower part of his face.

Jason led the way into the cave. With Tairon, I listened for the sound of movement other than his, but there was only the kiss of the sour breath of the hill. Tairon seemed as puzzled as was I, but he had already briefly explored this system of dimly lit passages and led us to where the coiled statue of the Python guarded the way deeper.

We went deeper, and for a while the loudest sound was Jason's laboured, excited breathing.

A sudden movement in the unlit gloom of a tunnel to the left of us startled us all. A torch flared brilliantly and Jason growled in his throat as a woman stepped towards him, breasts and belly bared, eyes shining above a black veil, hair tied in long, sparkling ringlets.

Something in the way she moved, perhaps, or the glimmer in her eyes, but an echo of memory, at least, blew sudden insight and horror into Jason's mind.

In that moment he half knew, half sensed who it was who came towards him, and recoiled at the thought, taking an involuntary step backwards, shaking his head. I heard him murmur, 'No. Oh no . . . Not here . . .'

And then he cried out like a wounded animal, a wail of pain and fury as Medea tore away her veil to expose pale, ageing features, her cruel grim smile.

Without looking round at me, Jason stabbed his sword towards me, shouting, 'You knew! You must have done.'

Once again I had no answer for him. I suspect my tongue was tied again, as it had been tied all that time ago in Iolkos; and as my eyes had been confused at Thermopylae.

Medea was in her element, relishing the stunned and shaking man before her. 'Go back, Jason,' she shouted in a hollow voice, made all the more ringing by the cavernous system of passages. 'There is nothing for you here. All that you see is mine, still mine to love. You will *never* claim your sons.'

'Try to stop me!' Jason roared, but at that moment the two young men stepped from behind her. Jason gasped, hesitated in his step, then half lifted his hand towards them. The flame from the torch cast a flickering, eerie light on their solemn faces. All I could think was: Kinos? Here? This was not right.

My stomach tightened in nervous anticipation. I called quickly to Orgetorix. He should have recognised me, but he was silent: blank.

Then Medea turned and ran, extinguishing the light, the two young warriors pacing effortlessly beside her into the darkness.

Elkavar grabbed one of the fluttering, poorly charged torches that smouldered nearby. And in an echo of that dreadful pursuit through the palace in Iolkos, I ran again with Jason to save his sons from their mother.

She led us deep into the mountain, racing through the branching passages as if these were a natural home to her. Her laughter echoed and taunted. And her voice was an agony of insult:

'You should have stayed in the lake for all the good this chase will do you. I made a promise, Jason, that you would never touch your sons again.' There was a moment's silence. 'But you can have their ghosts,' she finished eerily.

She was suddenly there, framed in the darkness of the corridor, the torch again alight, held high into the narrow cleft above her head. Orgetorix and his brother stepped in front of her, each face a mask of hatred.

'Go to daddy,' Medea said, and this time her laugh was furtive, almost sad. Flame streamed after her as she ran further into the labyrinth, leaving the two young men.

Jason said, 'There's something wrong. What is it, Merlin? Use a little of your magic to tell me . . .'

'I can't,' I whispered, almost in despair. My thoughts swirled and blurred as I tried to summon a little enchantment. But Medea knew how to cast the net that blocked my charm.

'Of course you can,' Jason murmured with a sneer. The words hurt. The next words struck me like a hammer. 'But then, why should you? You and she are cut from the same heart. Too long in the lake. The gods blinded me to your deceit.'

'No!' I whispered. 'No deceit. I swear.'

My own words rang hollow. I had not told him what I knew. But why? Why had I kept quiet about Medea? *It's for the best. For the best*, I remembered telling myself.

A second later, his sons took two more steps towards us and Jason, despite his confusion, involuntarily moved to greet them. Then, like snakeskins, the gleam of illusion fell away to reveal Medea's trickery. The two dead Greeklanders, faces fish-belly white and gaping, stood for a moment or two more, then crumpled in their own gore, the last breaths whining from crushed lungs.

Jason sank slowly to his knees, fists clenched, eyes closed, the scream of disappointment that was so near to his mouth suppressed by pure will. Blood came from his lips; and then words, softly spoken, 'O gods, damn her! Damn her for ever! Father Zeus, burn her bones inside her; Lord Hades, hang her with her own bowels!'

He fell forward, then seemed to come to his senses. I heard him mutter, 'Apollo! Mielikki! Argo! Let me see him. Just for a few minutes. Then I promise the lake can have me back. Mielikki. Mielikki . . . if you have influence in the heavens, speak for me now. The lake can take me I back . . .'

He had begun to draw into himself, to hunch down like a dying man.

I stepped towards him, wanting to reach a comforting arm, but I drew back, afraid to touch him.

Still 'blind', I couldn't see the source of what happened next.

Jason seemed to hear a voice. He stood up, clutched sword and shield tightly, leaned forward into the darkness and began to breathe heavily, as if in anticipation. A heartbeat later the tunnel of rock closed around him a mouth consuming a piece of meat. A gust of sour air made me turn my face away. Elkavar and Tairon had their arms across their mouths, staring perplexed at the place where Jason had disappeared.

The tunnel was normal again, though we could hear the echoing sound of a man running.

Elkavar turned to me. 'Should we follow?'

There would be little point. The Apollonian spirit of Delphi had aided Jason. It would have no reason to aid us as well.

But Tairon was a 'walker-in-labyrinths'. He met my gaze,

perhaps thinking just what I was thinking—that he might pursue Jason far enough to discover where, among the many outlets of this oracle, the resurrected Greeklander might emerge.

'Wait for me outside,' the Cretan said briskly, taking up his sword. He turned from us and ran quietly into the darkness.

It was not long before Tairon came staggering from the mountain, breathless from the acrid fumes and with running. His lean features poured with sweat and he squeezed perspiration out of his lank, black hair.

I waited patiently until he had recovered, and was disappointed when he shook his head.

'I failed. I'd hoped to emerge with him at the other end, but I lost him, though I could hear him running. The only thing I noticed were the smells of honey and the breeze that blows in an oak forest. There's a special odour to it. But that could be anywhere . . . couldn't it?'

He looked at me, then smiled as he saw the expression on my face.

Tairon's words were a revelation—a blind man had suddenly seen the light.

Orgetorix was not here in Delphi. He was at the Oak Temple: Dodona! The sanctuary sacred to Zeus, where young Jason had travelled and begged for a branch of the sacred tree to build into the keel of Argo. Afterwards, his wish granted, that shrine had become Jason's spiritual home. He would be as attached to it as any child to its mother. I doubted if he even knew it, but I had known it, when I had sailed with him, long years ago. The oak that had been crafted so carefully into the ship had claimed her captain as its son. There were a thousand spirits wandering inside Argo, and Jason was one of them.

A fact Medea knew too well. She was leading him there, not *away* from her son, but *to* the confused and lost young man.

She had confounded me, and blighted my vision; she had

poisoned her son's mind to his father, and performed feats of enchantment that were stripping the years from her faster than a hunter can paunch the entrails from a deer.

She had tried to keep her son from his father; now she was certainly bringing them together. That she had done this was as clear to me as Elkavar's shining, ready, uncomprehending face. What better way to rid herself of Jason, than to have his own son kill him?

'He's at Dodona!' I said to Elkavar, and the Hibernian replied, 'That means as much to me as that he's on the moon. But whatever it means, just tell me when, and when not, to sing.'

'Sing to your heart's content,' I said to him. 'I have to go separately from you, now. Jason is in danger. I can't afford to get lost again by going through the underworld, though you and Tairon may fare better. But for the moment at least, this is goodbye.'

'Not for too long, I hope,' the Hibernian murmured with a frown. 'I was beginning to get used to you. And you are my best chance of getting back to my own country.'

'I'm capable of becoming as lost as you, I assure you.'

'And where exactly are you going now?' Tairon asked curiously.

'To find Argo and ask to sail in her again.'

Gwyrion was camped alone, a small fire burning, his weapons around him. He seemed nervous, too small a guard for so precious a burden. The ragged lump of Argo was in its cart, below the skins. The pale-featured figurehead lay exposed, face to the sky as if resting. The Cymbrian watched me through tired eyes as I approached him.

'She's not happy,' he said to me in a dark voice. 'It's all I can do to pacify her. Jason must take her back soon to the north. This is not going right.'

I agreed with him, then climbed into the cart, uncovered the heart of ancient wood and crouched before it.

'Mielikki. Argo. Spirit of the Ship! I need to go to Dodona, where part of you still lives . . .'

For a while there was cold silence, then the Spirit of Argo flowed out and embraced me. I was crouching among grey, hot rocks, yellow gorse and the gnarled trunks of olives. Mielikki was there, young and bright-faced, sitting in her summer guise a little way from me. She was unveiled, her fair hair tied in a topknot, her dress no more than a thin tunic. She sat cross-legged below a vast, spreading oak; beyond her, the hills were hazy with heat, green with bushes and woods, scented with herbs.

'This place frightens me,' she said. 'I am not used to such warmth. Do you recognise it, Merlin? This is where a part of the ship came from, lifetimes ago. This tree. Isn't she beautiful? So old, so old . . . you can see the scar where Jason cut her limb to make his ship.'

I could see, then, the wide oak, canopy so full, was scarred a hundred times, a hundred Jasons who had taken their fill of this special wood when their prayers had been answered.

So almost without asking, I had already been allowed through the ship to Dodona. She had treated me kindly.

As if sensing my thought, the Forest Lady said hungrily, 'Yes. You're there. And the army has not reached it yet. It is unsundered, but almost deserted. You can search safely for Jason, but promise me, Merlin—that when you've found what you've come for, you will take me home. I must go home. Who will take me home?'

She was pleading, her fair face creased with anxiety.

'I *will* take you home,' I said to her. 'Jason and I both. I promise you on my great age.'

'And with the unreliability of youth? I *must* go home,' Lady Forest hissed at me again. 'This place is too strange. I am out of my world. Where is the girl? Where is that impetuous girl?'

'I left her by the ocean. She expects me to return to her. I don't anticipate fulfilling her wish, though I don't think she'll follow me, now. But like you, I feel frightened of something.'

Mielikki shuddered and looked around.

'Yes. Fierce Eyes,' she whispered. 'Yes. She's somewhere close. I smell her. She has murder in mind. Come back to me when you're finished, Merlin. And if you *do* see that girl, tell her to come to me. Remind her she belongs to me.'

Murder in mind?

Medea had moved through and over the world with impunity. What a shock it must have been to sniff the wind, one morning, one winter, and smell Jason's stench again: the lake-wracked man, dragged up from the deeps, tied to his rotten ship by weed and rags. Had she seen his dead eyes open? Had she heard the gurgling of water in his lungs, the spilling of the water from those lungs, the surge of air and life back into his frozen corpse?

What feverish, frightening dreams she must have had that night!

Cold face, fish-belly white, the black-grey hair matted around his skull; eyes opening to her in that dream.

You killed my sons. The lake has given me back. The hunt is on again, Medea. The hunt is on again!

Her dreams only, I imagine. But after all that time, living in a world empty of what she loved, chasing the years, watching each winter give way to spring, counting the summers, counting the passing of the lives of those around her, running, running, hiding in the shadows, waiting for that moment, that wonderful, blissful moment . . .

When one of her sons stepped, blinking, out of the cave in Arkamon, little ghost-brother by his side . . .

When the other woke in some damp dell in the heart of Alba . . .

To whom did she go first, I wondered (as I searched for her at Dodona, running through the valley, sniffing the air, using what was marked on my bones to stop her blinding me again). Whose hair did she first stroke, invisibly, secretly, a wraith in their lives, a dream in their lives, sucking their life, their pleasure, their innocence, a mother more ancient than the caves they lived in; a mother, greedily drinking their new experience?

Did she clutch them in her dreams? Did she dance as if they knew her, holding their ghosts to her breast, singing of her triumph? *My boys. My boys. And daddy's far, far away, pike-chewed, ice-clad, dissolved in the lake.*

Did she ever hear Jason's scream from that lake?

My sons! Give me back my sons!

Was she deaf to the fact that Jason had never died? Argo, brave Argo, faithful Argo, had never let the ghost depart from his mortal body. Had she heard those cries? Perhaps it had never occurred to her to listen.

Lazy!

She was just like me. Of course she was. We had grown up together, we had learned together, we were the lazy ones, she in her way, I in mine. I had loved her in another time; it was all I could do to keep the memory of that love at bay.

But it lay there, in my spirit-haunted head, like the most thrilling of memories, waiting to come back when the clouds dispersed and the sun came out.

I countered the feeling with the single thought: in all her life, no matter what forgotten life she had had with me, she had loved Jason more, and loved her sons more than Jason. She had left the Path for love; she had stayed away from the Path for hate.

And that was right. Whatever she had done, she had found a moment of true happiness. Whatever she had become, she was only living out the consequences of that moment of bliss.

A moment of bliss. In ten thousand years of living.

'Do you understand, then?' I heard her say, her voice a shock to me in the stillness of the grove. 'Do you understand at last? Did you never feel such a thing yourself? You must have done!'

She was standing behind me. When I turned, it was to take her in my arms, an action compelled by memories still hidden from me. But her body was like rock. There was no love left between us. Or if there was, she was not willing to let it be felt. I looked at her face, so beautiful despite the greed of Time, her hair still like polished copper; into her eyes, so lovely, so clever; her breath like summer fruit; our fingers intertwined briefly. A beauty that had not faded . . . lost in time . . . almost untouchable.

'Did you never stray?' Medea asked me, brushing my lips with hers.

'No. I left the Path. I found a few friendships. I watched the world from a distance. I never strayed in the way that you have strayed.'

'And *do* you remember how it was between us? Long ago, in the wildwood, in the bright clearings?'

She was strong. She would certainly know that I remembered a part of it. We were both awakening from a long sleep of years, discovering that we were not alone, that there were others like us in the world, and that we had shared life. But I said quite bluntly: 'No.'

She seemed almost saddened by that, but went on, 'I've let myself remember . . . just a little. It's there if you look. What a long life we've both had. We were together so briefly, Merlin. Oh yes, I know it's you, now. I didn't want to believe it, but I do believe it. But I cannot believe you never strayed from the Path.' She looked at me curiously. 'What a lonely man you must have been. You've lived so little. Some might call that: wasted. I feel sad for you.'

Like Niiv, Medea was scratching at my defences, though in more expert fashion than the Pohjolan waif, I sensed. But she knew what I knew, that neither of us could reveal ourselves when the contact was this close.

To detach myself from her powerful and fragrant charm, I thought of Jason.

'You've poisoned your son's mind against his father.'

'Of course! Both of them!' She laughed, looking at me as if I should have known better.

'Thesokorus hates Jason for no other reason than that *you* hate him. Is that how you use your charm? Your itching bones? By taking away the *lives* of your precious children?'

Grief flashed across her face, I swear it; a look of such pain, such anguish. And then she was hard again, bitter-eyed and watching me with that same angry intensity.

'Precious, Merlin? Yes. They are precious. And *why* are

they precious? Did you ever ask yourself that question? How many precious children do you think I've had? Do you think these were the only two?'

The world stopped still around me as I thought of Niiv, and her half-child—perhaps half imagined; and Meerga, her ancestor, and that wretched half-child that had been conceived and lived into old age, but always under the influence of the guardian spirit I had placed upon her senses. And of how I had always known that I could not risk again giving life to any child who would continue to live on in the ordinary world.

Medea had been bound by that same knowledge and she quickly saw that I understood. Were there tears in her eyes? She whispered, 'I lost count of the children that I had to send from my body. Can you imagine that? But I named each one before I let them go. I am haunted by them, Merlin!'

For the first time there was tenderness in the way she used my nickname.

'But I couldn't give them life; it would not have been fair to them. You *know* what I mean. You must do. Then again, perhaps you don't, lost in your own selfish world. Of all my children, only those two seemed to be of Jason and *only* Jason, when I looked at them, when they were inside me. I gave them birth. I was lucky with them. They are Jason's children. They have only a shadow of myself inside them. There is no danger in shadows. And I loved them. I sacrificed so much to be sure that we could have a normal life for as long as he and my children could *live* a normal life, in Iolkos! I expected to see them die, I always knew I would see them die. But that would not happen for years. I loved him as I had once loved you . . . all that time ago. We have forgotten so much, Merlin. But so rare, isn't it? So rare, to find such love . . .'

Yes, I said, giving in to her. Or did I only think the words? I can't remember. I was remembering too much of Medea before she had vanished from my world, lost in time.

'And he betrayed me,' she shouted, though more in pain than anger. 'He abandoned me for that other woman, Glauce.

He left me. And he *would* have taken the boys, my children. Tell me, Merlin: what was I supposed to do?'

She was pulling lightly at the fabric of her dress where it draped her breasts, a mime of the way she had rent her dress in the echoing corridors of her palace, distraught to the point of suicide on discovering that Jason had left her. In all the long years, still the manner of her losing Jason tormented her.

I had no answer to her question. I don't imagine she wanted an answer to that question. I simply said, 'But you took your children's lives away from them. What life have they had? You hid them from yourself as well as from their father. And after all that, they still don't see you. A pet gets more affection from its owner than Thesokorus ever receives from you.'

'Cruel words,' she said with a cold, pained look.

'True words.'

She shook her head. 'Not true at all. I'd lived without them for a long time. It's taken time to get used to them again. But I give them a mother's comfort in their sleep. When they were younger, I gave them each the comfort of the shadow of their brother. For company. When the time is right, I'll come into their waking lives and re-unite them. The time was almost right when *you* brought their *father* back.'

'And so you poisoned their minds. To suit your own end.'

She frowned and folded her arms across her chest, then looked down, as if contemplating a new reality. 'What's done is done,' she whispered.

'And you poisoned mine. I could have easily told Jason that you were here. But it seemed imperative that I shouldn't. That was not my reasoning at work.'

'Nor mine,' she said, looking up at me significantly, a half-smile on her face. 'You didn't tell Jason because you felt truer to me than to him. You still do, Merlin. You're just not letting yourself know it.'

I could neither move nor speak. Medea gazed at me sadly, then stepped forward and embraced me briefly. Her lips lingered on mine before she pulled away.

Her eyes shimmered. 'You have a long way to go to catch up with me, Merlin. But will you try? When Jason is gone, everything will be clear for us. He and his son are stalking each other even now, in the valley below us. When it's done, please try to find me. I shan't be far from you.'

Her pain and longing, and the sense of elusive love returning, had confused me, and I fell away from her even as she turned from me and also seemed to fall away, into the haze of heat over the grey rocks.

I literally fell from her, losing my footing and plunging down the steep slope, slipping and rolling through the bushes until I came to the bottom of the hill, to find crows feeding on human carrion, two naked Greeklanders, faces covered with helmets, bellies with blood.

Water rushed over rocks and I crawled, bruised and bewildered, to drench my face in the cool flow. Because of the dead men who were draped across the stream, I didn't drink, but my senses returned quickly. I rolled over and stared at the brilliance of the sky. And after a while, two dark figures peered down at me, one on each side of the bubbling river.

Their interest in me lasted for just a moment. Perhaps they thought I was dead. I'd certainly decided not to move. Besides, they had other things on their minds, and I peered briefly into one of them.

Emerging from the mountain into the sunlight, he had recognised the sanctuary at once, by the shape of the hills and by the high, white walls, near the river, that surrounded the False Oak, where untrue hearts were drawn. He looked up the hill to the tumble of craggy grey rocks, and the huge tree that grew there. Somewhere on its gnarled bark his sign, the young Jason's sign, had by now spread to a blur as the trunk had expanded with the generations.

He had run through the twisting passages for an age. He was exhausted. Sweat ran freely from below the leather rim of his iron helmet. But he had never been in any doubt that Dodona lay ahead of him: he could smell the honeyed air; he could hear the rustle of the summer oak.

Medea had vanished. He could not hear her or see her. She

had slipped into her own 'Ghostland', though Jason knew she would probably be watching.

Standing in the shadow of the cliff, he could see furtive movement in the distance. And three small, white horses, harnessing hanging loose, grazed nervously nearby. Otherwise, to his surprise, the whole area of the temple seemed deserted.

He approached one of the ponies, caught the reins, then led it down through the trees towards the water and the silent buildings of the shrine. Again, he caught sight of movement ahead of him, a man leading a horse among the rocks, crossing and re-crossing the small river, as if searching, Jason thought. It was hard to make out his features, but like Jason he was armoured in the short trousers and leather kilt and cuirass of the invader. His dark hair was cropped and spiky.

For a moment, Jason lost sight of the other man. Then, from back along the water, came the sound of a cry and tumbling stones. He left the horse and returned cautiously to the river, where it curved below the overshadowing oak of Dodona. He soon realised his quarry was also walking back, but on the opposite bank, keeping to the shadows, equally circumspect.

Jason heard him whisper, questioningly, 'Kinos? *Kinos?*' and knew at once that his search was ended.

A moment later they both came to my supine, soaking body, lying in the stream, helpless. For a moment Jason was startled as he looked down at me, then his gaze lifted to the young man across from him. Disappointment registered fleetingly on that young man's face, then suspicion. The two of them regarded each other in silence.

'I thought you might have been my brother,' Thesokorus said, as if an explanation was needed. 'I was told my brother was here. Are you with Brennos and the army?'

Jason continued to stare for a moment more, then sighed, with relief and delight. He shook his head, half smiling through his dishevelled beard. He took the rough helmet from his head and cast it aside.

'I thought I wouldn't know you,' he said softly, 'from just looking at you. I saw your ghost, at Delphi, but the face meant nothing. But I recognise every gleam and glimmer in the face I see now. I would have known you at once. This man, Merlin, this poor wretch at our feet, described you to me once—'

'Who are you?' Thesokorus interrupted in an angry whisper, his hand resting on the ivory hilt of his sword. He could hardly take his eyes from the old man who stood across the narrow water.

Jason kept his hands away from his body. His own sword was slung across his shoulders. 'He described you in the most flattering terms. He said: your son is young; eager; handsome! He added that there was something about you that "doesn't care". He said you looked nothing like me. But I don't know. I like your looks. I think this bastard was lying. I never bothered with mirrors. What do you think, little Bull Leaper? I can't call you "Orgetorix". Will you age to look like me?'

'Bull Leaper?'

Jason smiled carefully. The silence in the valley wrapped around the scene. The world was far away. 'You only did it once. You were four years old. But you were wonderful. In the bull-ring at Iolkos, do you remember? It was a small bull; you were a small boy; but you grabbed those ribboned horns and flung yourself over the head of the beast, dancing on its back with a triumphant laugh before running for safety. I was so proud of you!'

'No!' Thesokorus shouted. He stripped off the leather jerkin and threw it to the ground, then unbuckled his sword belt, holding it ready to draw the blade and discard the scabbard. 'I don't know you. I don't recognise you. This bastard has told you that story. He's a trickster. I should have known when I first met him. My father is long dead, long dead and grinning from a coward's grave.'

Jason's voice had an edge of unease in it. He was beginning to plead. This meeting was not going as he had expected; he had anticipated that persuasion would be the nature of the confrontation, not hostility. I had not forearmed him. 'But I'm not dead,' he stated carefully. 'Look at me. Very much alive. I searched for you through time and over half the world. Thesokorus—'

'No!'

Jason's words were enraging the younger man. Confusion boiled behind those dark, fierce eyes. *Through time? Through time?* I could hear him thinking, as if a part of him instinctively knew the truth. But the barrier of hate and emotional defence was too strong.

'Thesokorus . . .' Jason implored, almost angry himself, now, with his son's recalcitrance. 'We've been given a second chance. I *am* the man who caught you when you leapt from that bull. I know what your mother did to you. I know what I did to your mother. I was wrong. I was foolish. Do you have any idea how long I grieved for you and Kinos? I rode and sailed the world to bring you to the pyre! Year in, year out. I searched from Ithaca to Epidamnus; I sailed to every island. I crossed to Ilium and Ephesus. My search for your bodies was no less intense than if I'd thought I was searching for you both *alive*! I thought you were dead, Thesokorus. I saw your mother kill you. Don't you remember the trick?'

'*This* is the trick,' the young man spat. 'My mother hid me from my father because *he* would have killed me!'

'Not true. Not true,' Jason shouted. His voice was a cry of pain. Somewhere above us, I imagined I could hear Medea laughing. But it may have been the call of a ram, roaming wild in the thickets.

'Why did you ask about me at the oracle, at Arkamon?' Jason asked in a softer tone, a desperate attempt to get his son to relax his guard.

The question again startled Thesokorus. 'You know so much about me!'

'Of course I do . . .'

'But of course! This man here would have told you.'

The response was fury born of anguish. 'I'm Jason! I'm your father. I've waited a lifetime to find you. And now that I've found you, don't you see? We can share the rest of my poor, short life together. We can search for Kinos. I have the beginning of an idea where he is. On my shield, this is the truth.'

'Where do you imagine he is?' Thesokorus asked coldly.

'Between sea-swept walls,' his father answered. 'It's what the oracle told you. Isn't it?'

Thesokorus sneered. 'Oracles? A few days ago, on my way to Delphi, another oracle whispered to me that he was here. But all I found were these few men. Even the guards had deserted the place, though these fought well. It seems nothing is to be trusted.'

Jason raised his hands in a gesture of peace. 'Your mother shattered my world with two swift cuts. She stole my life. I can't deny I had stopped loving her, but I was in turmoil about you and Kinos. I couldn't think how to have you in my own life while leaving the two of you in hers. Thesokorus, I swear, again on my shield, that when I came to the palace that day, with the small band of men, it was to discuss arrangements with Medea that would have given you two boys the best of both worlds. But she thought differently and ran from me.'

'You pursued us, swords drawn!' Thesokorus snapped, outraged. 'Murder in mind. You had murder in mind.'

'She set her guards on us. She threw fire at us! She silenced our voices. I panicked. How could I have known that she'd planned to escape? Everything was ready for the act—knife, blood, chariot, ship. She had been waiting for me to come. She *must* have known I was coming in peace.'

'No!' Lies. More lies. I asked about you at Arkamon because I could never summon your name. But now I have it, and my hate for you is even greater. Yes, I see in your eyes that you *are* rottenbones! You are *Jason*! I'd thought you were long dead. But you haunted me, day and night. Now there is a chance to avenge my mother.'

'No!'

Jason's desperate cry went unheeded. I heard the rasp of iron on whetstone, a sword drawn swiftly from the scabbard.

'No! Not like this,' Jason begged again. 'I was in the underworld, neither alive nor dead. A ghost still living in the corpse. But Merlin saw you at Arkamon. He brought me back to the world to find you. I loved you. I despaired when I thought you were dead. Twenty years rotting on Argo, seven hundred years in hell. None of that matters. Now, nothing matters other than being in *your* world again. Time has been lost. We can't reclaim it. The time is *now*. And we have to *use* our lives. To find Kinos. To hunt, to harvest, to confront the unknown. To build!'

He fell silent, breathing hard, head shaking slightly as if suddenly exhausted.

But his son was not in control of his senses or his actions. Though he had listened to his father, he had not responded in any way. Now he whispered, 'This is the only life I have. This is the only world I know. Finding Kinos is the only thing that matters. Dead parents don't feature.'

Then only blood rage and grim vengeance were in his face. The muscles of his sword arm were flexed. The pulse at his neck was strong. His breathing was shallow.

Jason saw the warning signs and said quickly, 'Thesokorus . . . not like this!'

'Yes,' Thesokorus said quietly and with finality. 'Exactly like this.'

He stepped over my sprawled body. No magic of Medea's had paralysed me, nor silenced my voice. I had chosen this for myself. I had made myself vulnerable to Jason. By doing so, I had denied myself the chance to help him.

In a flash of bright iron, Thesokorus struck his father a cruel and vicious blow. Jason blocked the strike with his own sword, staggering back under its power, and for a few moments the air rang with the noise of iron on iron as Thesokorus tried to find the wrist and hack away his father's hand.

Thesokorus stumbled and Jason slashed at him, but it was a half-hearted strike, easily deflected. They closed together, crouched low in the Greeklander style, struggled in silence for a moment, then pulled apart. Jason's breathing was laboured. Thesokorus stood calmly, staring at his father, blade half raised.

Jason lowered his sword, defencelessly. He couldn't speak, but his eyes—narrowed, searching, sad—said it all. *An end to this.*

In that moment of lowered guard, King of Killers took two

quick steps and pushed his blade into his father's belly.

I saw the old man, my old friend, sink to his knees, then fall sideways, clutching at his flesh. The young Greeklander stood over him, the bloody blade shaking in his grasp. I waited for him to finish the other man, but he simply stood and stared.

How quick and brutal this had been, compared to the lengthy combat that had seen Urtha triumph over Cunomaglos.

Jason's gaze met mine.

'You betrayed me, Merlin. You let me think she was dead. You knew she was in the world. You could have told me. You could have prevented this.'

I willed strength back into my limbs and sat up, leaning on my left hand. 'I loved her long before you loved her, Jason. The pity of it is, I don't remember. I only feel. We were torn apart. We were made to forget each other.'

'You compound your betrayal,' Jason rasped. 'That lie compounds it all. You hollow man!'

Now Thesokorus was staring at me, a deep frown on his face. He came towards me and used the point of his gore-stained sword to raise my chin. The sweat ran from his torso on to my face.

'*Who* is in the world?' he asked quietly. The tone was strange. He half suspected.

'Your mother,' I told him. He searched my eyes, otherwise expressionless, listening. I said, 'She's up on the ridge there, near the oak. She's watching you even now. Jason is right: he has told you the truth. She has poisoned your mind against him. Your hate for your father is her hate, not your own. It's not too late to put things right.'

Though from the pallor on Jason's face, and the spread of blood on his belly, my words were probably optimistic.

Thesokorus, still standing menacingly above me, sword edge firmly held against my jaw, looked up at the hill for a long time. Was he hoping to see her? Or trying to decide whether to believe me?

Again his gaze questioned me. '*Is* she there?'

'I'm sure of it.'

He frowned. 'That can't be right. The oracle at Arkamon told me my mother was dead.'

'The oracle at Arkamon *was* your mother. It's where she went to hide after escaping from Iolkos. It's where she waited for the two of you to come back to her, you and Kinos.'

The point of the blade pricked my skin. I could smell sweat and the acrid scent of fear from Thesokorus, though to look at him you would have seen no sign of anything other than calm control.

'How do you know? How can you be sure?' he asked after a moment.

'I've scratched my bones a little,' I replied.

He shook his head, not understanding the reference, and for a moment I thought he would push the blade into my gullet. But he let the sword droop.

It occurred to me, then, that Medea—certainly watching—had taken her poison from the young man's mind. She had given Thesokorus back his freedom. Perhaps it had been intended as a gesture of remorse. But in doing so, she had dispatched him to the abyss.

'I came to this place to find a brother I'd believed to be alive,' he said wearily. 'Instead I find a father and a mother I'd thought dead. I kill the father. And the mother watches me from the trees, like a bird of prey. An anonymous man tells me that all I thought I knew is false. Even my actions.' He studied me for a moment. 'This is the sort of thing we Greeklanders write about in plays. But playing time is finished. This is all too much.'

He stepped away from his father, looked down, then cast the sword aside, staring at his hands as if they were filthy. 'Too much. Too much.'

'Thesokorus!' Jason cried weakly as his son picked up his cloak and jacket and strode away through the trees to where his horse was tethered.

Only a sudden gust of cold, sour wind greeted his call.

'It could have been different,' Jason murmured in agony. Gore was spreading further across his body, but he raised himself unsteadily, then seemed to find new strength.

His look at me was evil. His mouth was twisted in a grimace of pain and disgust. 'I won't forgive you, Merlin. Kill me now with that magic of yours, or hide from me. My son might almost have killed me, I don't know yet. He's certainly taken the wind out of me.'

I tried to summon the right words to persuade him to think again. But he groaned, gasped, then sat up straight.

'Stare at me all you wish,' he said with poison in his voice. 'Remember the gore. One day it will visit itself on your own guts!'

He heaved himself to his feet, shaking and unsteady. 'There is no Ullanna to take me home by cart, loving me. I have no bondsmen, riding in protection. Dogs? My dogs wait to chew my marrowbones . . .'

He staggered away from me. He found a broken spear and used it to lean on, his back to me as he cursed me in a final gasp of invective, adding, 'After I've found Little Dreamer, I'll find you again. Merlin! Dread the dawn when you wake to see me smiling down on you! Dread that dawn. Old man!'

He suddenly reached down, groaning with the effort, and picked up his son's wide-bladed sword where it had been discarded. He looked at it for a moment, at his own blood on the iron, then, with a roar, flung it at me. I moved just in time, and the bone grip struck against my shoulder.

Shaking his head, Jason limped away, towards the grove where his white horse was tethered by the stream. But he had not gone very far before he sank to his knees, head dropping, using his last strength, holding the shaft, to keep his body from keeling over.

I was running. I ran like a guilty child, up the hill to the ridge, to the oak of Dodona, which towered untouched, yet to be shaken by the approaching Celtic army.

There was no sign of Medea, but youthful Mielikki was waiting for me, tears in her eyes. She reached a hand for me. I started to weep, for the memory of childhood and the young woman who had become Medea, though not before we had shared love, a love I now longed to remember. And I wept for Jason, for the loss of a friend, that man, dying by the stream, crouching, clutching his side as he waited to see if his shade would rise and walk into Persephone's silent realm.

The Forest Lady embraced me gently. I leaned against her, helpless and in despair. If Niiv had stepped out of the shadow of the tree and tried to steal from me at that moment, she could have done so with ease.

'Nothing has turned out right,' I whispered, unashamedly sorry for myself. 'I don't know where to go next. I've lost the Path.'

'Fierce Eyes has softened towards you. That was unexpected.'

'Yes. But what have I lost? I've lost so much.'

'You can't know that. Not yet. Not until everything is finished.'

For a moment her words confused me. But I thought of Urtha, slowly returning to his own land, a country blighted by desertion and haunted by an army of angry dead. And of Kinos, hidden somewhere in that same land, perhaps searching for Thesokorus as the King of Killers had searched for him. And Medea would certainly fall back to protect her offspring from Jason, if the man recovered from his wound and journeyed again to the realm between the sea-swept walls.

Forest Lady was right. It was not yet finished.

She soothed me. The wind blew through the oak, and the scent of honey from the hives was sweet on the air. Somewhere, not too far away, the earth was shaking as horsemen cantered blindly towards us.

'It's time you went home for a while,' the Lady who held me whispered.

'Yes,' I said to her, clinging to that hope, that dream, with all my heart. 'Take me home.' I thought of Ghostland, and the memory was warm. 'Take me to Alba.'

She seemed surprised. 'To Urtha's land? To the wasteland?'

'*This* is wasteland,' I remember saying bitterly. 'Alba is as good a home as any.'

'Then that's where Argo will take you,' Mielikki whispered. 'We will both come with you. I can wait for the north. I don't mind waiting. Argo will take you home.'

She took my hand and led me back to the river. There was no sign of Jason. We sat on the rocks and waited for dusk. And with the passing of the light, the river began to deepen. The hills seemed to rise to enfold us until only a narrow band of stars could be seen above.

We stood and stepped into the water. And the small, beautiful ship drifted out of the darkness towards us, a spirit from Argo, pale by the starlight. She nudged me gently as she passed and I hauled myself aboard, settling down among the skins and blankets and untying the laces of my boots.

Free for a while, to breathe and dream.

Afterword

On this wistful note, the first extended narrative text of the Merlin Codex ends.

The continuation of the story deals with Merlin's return to Alba, hiding at the edge of 'Ghostland', haunted by Niiv's stolen vision of the future as well as the certainty that Jason, if he has survived the wound, will return to the island, to search for his second son, Kinos, Little Dreamer. As he tries to understand both the nature of the wasteland that has blighted Urtha's world, and the reason for the savage attack from the Land of the Shadows of Heroes, Merlin makes it clear quite quickly that he is in no doubt that Little Dreamer has much to do with the dark story unfolding between the 'sea-swept walls' of Alba.

He waits for Medea to emerge from the underworld again, and for the return of Argo, the Ship of Heroes; aware in both cases that circumstances have changed greatly.

R.H.
London, April 2000

Look for

IRON GRAIL

BOOK TWO OF THE MERLIN CODEX

by ROBERT HOLDSTOCK

Available in Hardcover
February 2004
from Tom Doherty Associates